A Crown in Shadows

Alecia B. Kirby

"To anyone who's ever been told they couldn't—yes, you can. Don't yield. It's not in your nature to break."

TRIGGER WARNINGS

The following triggers are found in this book and should be considered before reading:
Loss of a parent, death, blood, trauma, violence, discussion of sexual assault, profanity, alcohol consumption, and animal hunting.

CHAPTER 1

THE SUN HUNG low in the early morning sky, casting warm rays across the royal training field amid the clash of steel.

Anticipation filled the crisp fall air as I stood face-to-face with my trainer, Sir Topher—the most promising young knight in the King's Guard. Beneath the rising sun, his towering frame cast a shadow that felt as if it would swallow me whole.

Nervously, I shifted my weight, awaiting his next move.

An unwelcome crowd of fellow knights and servants gathered around us, their hushed murmurs of expectations filling my ears. Despite my years of training, no one had granted me a fighting chance on this field.

My throat tightened with suppressed anxiety, though Topher's equally anxious pacing offered *some* comfort. His muscular arms and broad shoulders seemed perfectly suited for battle, while onlookers might find my round, stubby figure laughable.

We circled each other, the gravel and mud blending beneath our boots. Even behind his helmet, I could sense his confident grin—likely relishing the prospect of an easy victory before breakfast. The observers held their breath, anticipating the commencement of our spar.

In the blink of an eye, we lunged. Our swords clashed, sparks flying with each strike. Time seemed to stretch as we danced around the field—unequal in skill but matched in determination. Something felt different this morning as we persisted. I felt *stronger*.

Dodging, parrying, and blocking with grace and precision, I managed to surprise everyone with how long I had already lasted.

Including myself.

Confidence surged with each strike, like a sudden charge fueling my body. Just as I felt the rhythm of the dance, my stomach growled—shattering my concentration in one single rumble.

Warriors shouldn't allow any distractions, including a hungry stomach.

Frowning, I mentally told it to *"shut the hell up"*. As I refocused, I had barely enough time to register the large arm aimed at me. Evading Topher's mighty swing, I dove into the dirt and landed flat on my now-silenced stomach.

"Come on, sweetheart," he teased, extending a gloved hand toward me. "Give the people what they want, and let's end this already. Just give up and yield!"

Scoffing, I dodged his assistance, sprung to my feet, and regained my sword.

Topher's cocky grin faded before he lunged forward. He wore his frustration on his sleeve as his increasingly forceful, and less calculated, series of blows grew sloppier. A small, uncontrollable smile formed on my lips as I took advantage of his carelessness.

Seizing my opportunity, I feinted left, sidestepping his oncoming strike.

Not allowing him the time to counteract, I pushed all my weight forward and connected my boot with his metal chest plate. Fumbling backwards, his large form struggled to find his footing, his sword and behind thudding to the ground in the process.

Gasps from the spectators filled the air as Topher's blue eyes widened in disbelief. After three years of training, he had underestimated me and now was paying for it.

What a sucker.

Panting but intoxicated by victory, I stood tall, the tip of my sword at his throat. "You were saying, '*sweetheart?*'" I cooed beneath my helmet.

Sitting up, he raised his hands in surrender. "I yield."

The small crowd erupted in tamed cheers and loud claps. A curse or two was exclaimed, followed by the clinking of coins. Bets must have been made and apparently lost.

Removing my helmet, relief washed over me as the cool morning air met my sweat-covered scalp. My long, curly copper hair tumbled free from the loose bun it had been tied in. The white hair that framed my face immediately clung to my sweaty forehead.

Removing my chest plate, I instantly felt the freedom to breathe.

As the cheers and banter subsided around the field, I took a moment to savor everything. It wasn't about winning the sparring match, even though that felt *fucking incredible.* No, it was about shattering the long-held expectations that loomed over my head.

Especially recently.

As the princess and sole heir to the Orphinian crown, I felt the need to prove myself. For years, every morning, I worked with Topher to train my muscles and confidence—recognizing there was more to this than just physical strength. One day, I would be queen, and to me, being queen meant more than sitting by my husband's side and nodding like a fool.

I wanted to show the kingdom I was just as strong and capable as any man.

Today marked that day.

Still catching his breath, Topher gazed up at me with a hint of pride and admiration. Alongside his role as my trainer, he had been a mentor, a protector, and, more importantly, a friend. Respect was always present between us, but today, it was on an entirely different level.

Removing his helmet, his blond locks clung to his sweaty neck. "Nicely done, Genevieve," he grumbled, voice still rough from the blow. "I would be lying if I said your skills were a surprise. I must admit, I had been waiting for you to kick my ass."

He could flatter me all he wanted, but I knew he was impressed with his own skills as a trainer—which, of course, I couldn't blame him for.

"Well, you did always say patience is a virtue, Sir." I said with a smirk. "It seems you've finally reaped the rewards of waiting."

He chuckled, a twinkle of amusement in his eyes. "Indeed. Your future husband should tread lightly if he finds himself on your bad side. I've seen firsthand what you're capable of today."

My smile quickly faded at the all-too-relevant meaning in his words. Before I knew it, I was lost in my thoughts. My upcoming arranged marriage, expectations held by my father's court, and the looming winter that threatened our kingdom every year all crashed into my mind like a wave on the shoreline.

For the past five generations, my kingdom had been entangled in a brutal and bitter war with Valoria, the homeland of the Faeries. Now, newly eighteen, I stood on the brink of a new chaptere—engaged to their crowned prince, Xander.

Despite the betrothal being announced and forged nearly a month ago, I hadn't met my future husband or anyone from his kingdom. Communication with the enemy across the border was strictly prohibited unless the king granted permission. The only thing I knew of their people was what was told to me. My father's stories of the horrors they had brought to the war front had done little to paint a favorable picture of my future family.

And it scared me shitless.

The concept of an arranged marriage wasn't *completely* foreign to me, but the prospect of marrying into an unknown world was admittedly unsettling.

The name Valoria might conjure images of an otherworldly realm any mortal would love to experience, but in my eyes, it brought a potential death sentence. Just northwest of our territory across a *very* large border, their land held many secrets.

Faeries, or *Fae*, possessed powers defying the natural order, making them formidable foes to anyone who dared cross them. The mere fact that we had endured this long was nothing short of a miracle.

My father, King Leonard, had often sat me down and regaled me with tales of past conflicts between kingdoms. The Fae Wars, as they were known throughout our history, left scars that ran deep. Stories of their magic, their beauty, and their thirst for vengeance had haunted my nights as a child.

As an adult, I had come to the unsettling conclusion that those nightmares were more reality than fiction.

As I continued to remove my armor, my mind was still far away from the field my physical body was in. Thoughts swirled about what sort of ruler the crowned prince of Valoria would be.

There were so many times I dared to defy the king and send a messenger raven across the border, but my nerves always got the best of me. Who knew if he would have even received them or written back?

Regardless, I doubted words on parchment would be able to convey the complexities of a person's character.

Maybe it was for the best.

Clearing my head, I let out a long breath, and turned my attention back to my trainer.

As I extended a hand to signify the end of our match, a smile returned. "Topher, as much as I enjoyed seeing that look of defeat on your face, I can't help but wonder what Father and Commander Robert might think. Their most promising knight beaten by their princess?" I tisked as my head shook. "Some may think you're becoming...sloppy."

Dropping his hand, I gave him a small wink, knowing how to get under his skin. Some court members would faint if they witnessed our exchanges, but this sort of banter was routine for us.

Since my first birthday, Topher, only five years my senior, had been my improvised sworn protector. Whether shielding me from the chaos of visiting royals in the castle or vanquishing imaginary monsters back to the deepest of shadows, he had always been my unwavering guardian.

It helped that his younger sister, Fiona, was my best friend and lady-in-waiting.

Fiona had stepped into the role once held by her mother, Lady Seraphina, who had been my mother, Queen Dawn's, lady-in-waiting. After my mother passed when I was eight, Fiona naturally transitioned into the role which allowed her mother to retire and return to their home village. The bond between us was unbreakable, and it seemed as if the transition had been written in the stars.

Despite the chaos in the world, the siblings were my sanctuary within the castle's suffocating confines, my refuge from the cold stone walls that surrounded me. Their unwavering presence was the comfort I needed when I felt most alone.

Which was more than I cared to admit.

After my mother's passing, I was consumed by darkness. Joy vanished from my life, and time crawled slower than a snail. It was Topher and Fiona who rescued me from that void. Topher's training sessions became my daily anchor—a means to channel my anger and find purpose. Fiona's nightly talks offered the companionship I had lost with my mother.

I knew I could never fully repay them, but their friendship had pulled me back from the pits of despair, and for that, I was eternally grateful.

Flashing me a warm smile, he ran a hand through his sweaty, dirty blond hair. Now fully on his feet, his arm draped around my shoulder as we began to stroll back towards the heart of Castle Quinn.

He playfully tugged at a strand of my hair, a mischievous glint shone in his eye, "Your father, dear Princess," he jokingly declared, "should name *me* High Commander in replacement of good ole Robert! Considering the daily bull shit I endure with you; I fully believe I've more than earned it."

Raising my brow, I opened my mouth to respond, but a strong voice boomed behind us before I had the chance.

"Is that so?"

Our steps abruptly halted, and I stifled a laugh, instantly recognizing the voice. Biting the inside of my cheek, I tried to maintain my composure.

"Nice one, *Commander!*" I whispered.

Topher swiftly withdrew his arm from my shoulders, executing a precise about-face to confront the approaching king.

I followed suit, not wanting to miss the show.

"Your G-Grace," he choked while dropping to one knee.

My father raised a bushy, gray brow, his face stern. "Is this how you talk to your future queen, Sir Topher?"

His blue eyes met my father's warm brown, a visible swallow tracing down his throat. "No! My words hold no disrespect, Your Grace, I can assure you."

Peering down at my kneeling trainer, I smirked before meeting my father's gaze. A wink was his only response before advancing toward Topher.

"Rise, Sir Topher," he commanded, and the knight complied.

Despite standing at least three inches taller than the king, Topher looked like a child in comparison, his chin raised high, anticipating a reprimand.

Like my mother and Seraphina, our fathers were the closest of friends. Sir Gabriel had served as the king's Sworn Shield. From the moment he took his oath until his final breath, he was the most feared protector in the realm.

The war with the Fae ultimately claimed his life, but from the stories I had heard, he didn't go down without a fight.

From a young age, Topher knew he would follow in his father's footsteps. Even with how far in ranks he had advanced, the pressure of living up to his father's name still lurked.

He knew it, I knew it, and it seemed like Father did as well.

A smile played beneath the king's thick beard. "Despite my daughter's *'bullshit,'* it takes one hell of a man to endure her every morning. Son, your father never held back when speaking his mind, and I don't expect you to either." He rested his tan hand on Topher's armored shoulder. "Just some advice from one man to the other: look around before opening your mouth. I cannot control what Commander Robert does to his men, and I would rather not have to fish you out of the moat."

Delivering a playful pat to Topher's back, I could see the tension escaping his shoulders. "My apologies, Your Grace. The blow from your daughter's foot this morning must have caused me to forget myself momentarily. It shall not happen again."

Father chuckled, "That's what I like to hear, son. Try not to let the embarrassment eat you up too much. After all, she gets her spunk from her ole dad over here."

He nodded in approval as Father made his way over to me. Although my giggling had subsided, I couldn't help but grin up at him, and an equally large smile adorned his aged face.

When I extended my arm, he gladly accepted it, and together, we walked back to the castle. Arm-in-arm, we moved to take the long way to enjoy each other's company. Topher seemed to have understood the unspoken message and quietly departed, granting us some much-needed father-daughter time.

The sun had barely made its way over the tips of the stone towers that covered much of the skyline, but I soaked in every second of it—feeling its warm embrace as much as I felt my father's arm entangled with mine.

The autumn leaves painted the path in shades of red and gold as we walked toward the castle. Although they would likely fall in the next few weeks, they were still enchanting. Ancient oaks stretched overhead, and birds sang from their branches, filling the air with melodies. An owl hooted in the distance, its white feather's moving from the corner of my eye into the clear sky.

"I watched you this morning," Father confessed, pulling me from my observations.

I looked at him in disbelief. He *never* came out to watch me, and of all days, I happened to win. I attempted to wipe the probably unmistakable shock off my face.

"*Really?*"

Despite his support for my training, his mornings were typically consumed by daily council meetings. While we occasionally met for breakfast, his mind often seemed preoccupied elsewhere, so conversation was sparse.

"Really, really," he replied, playfully bumping me as we walked. "I had some free time this morning and thought I'd see how you've progressed. I must say, I was not disappointed."

I glanced down at our synchronized footsteps and blushed. As much as I adored my father, our quality time together had become rare.

As I grew older, our once playful banter had evolved into formal meetings and grand banquets, where prying eyes deemed sticking one's tongue out at the king tasteless, even if it came from his daughter.

These moments of intimacy with him were cherished, and his praise made my heart soar.

It's not that I *needed* validation from my father, but any connection with him was...well, it was something I longed for. I didn't know the course of my future, and I didn't know how much longer I would have with him. Experiencing the loss of one parent was already an unbearable heartache, and I couldn't bear the thought of enduring it again anytime soon.

Time emerged as an unyielding opponent for my father, patiently awaiting the moment when it would inevitably take him away.

While he was no older than forty-eight, his face bore the resemblance of a man well into his later life. From the moment he could wield a sword, he took his place on the battlefield, fighting until he couldn't physically fight any longer. The horrors of his time at war had caused his hair to gray, his skin to wrinkle, and his tanned hands to callus.

As we strolled, the walls of Castle Quinn embraced us, their towering stones like silent sentinels, bearing witness to the passage of time. Beyond those walls lay a world I rarely ventured into, and my eyes couldn't help but wander over the landscape I could manage to see. Its exterior stood as a testament to generations of war, a protective cocoon of thick stone, once erected to repel the Fae.

Turrets rose high into the sky, each bearing a storied history of battles fought and victories won. Vines clung to the ancient stones, nature's attempt to reclaim what had been taken. Moss crept along the edges of the weathered stones, adding a soft green hue to the weathered gray of the walls that kept me from a land I would rule one day.

Lands I longed to explore.

Our strides halted as we approached the gates. The sun cast harsh shadows on my father's weathered face. A mask descended over his familiar features, revealing the king's countenance.

"I am aware these past few weeks have not been easy on you." His gaze became heavy. "I admire how strong you have been throughout all of this. From growing up in the middle of a war to losing your mother, and now the engagement...I did not mean to have so many hardships thrown your way. Regardless, your strength makes my job as a father and as a king a little easier. Tonight, well, tonight will be important for all of us, love. We will be hosting a dinner, where we will sign your betrothal agreement. Then, the engagement celebrations will start tomorrow."

My throat bobbed as I swallowed, the dread of the inevitable slowly sinking in. "If we're signing the agreement, that means the Fae royals will be here..."

"Tonight, yes," he confirmed. "Based on their communications, they will be arriving sometime after sunset. I need you to be ready and in your finest gown by no later than five o'clock. Best behavior tonight, do you understand? No pranks, no discussions of your training, and absolutely *no* cursing."

I loathed being serious, especially when the situation was serious enough on its own.

Attempting to lighten the mood, I managed a faint smile. "The cursing might be difficult, but I'll see what I can manage."

His stern expression remained unwavering. "Genevieve, please. For me. This alliance is crucial for the future of the kingdom and our crown. We cannot afford any...*incidents*."

My eyes studied him, finding nothing to save me from this

conversation. Sighing, I bowed my head in a faux curtsy, attempts at humor falling flat.

"No toads in their soup and no cursing. I understand, Father."

Offering me a faint smile, he turned back toward the castle and continued walking, not once looking back to see if I followed.

I blew a stray piece of white hair out of my face as my arms crossed over my chest.

"And apparently, no *fun*."

CHAPTER 2

MY FEET ACHED by the time I reached my bedchamber.

When I pushed the large wooden doors open, Fiona's anxious face was already rummaging through my wardrobe. Her wide blue eyes, strikingly similar to Topher's, sneered at my disheveled state.

"About time! It's nearly *noon*!"

She hurriedly ushered me towards the bathing chamber. The overwhelming scent of lavender filled the air from the warm bath prepared to wash away the morning's exertions. I knew I needed it, but I was *not* in the mood to be rushed.

"Fi, relax. I still have five hours to prepare for this stupid dinner. We have plenty of time."

Before presenting a counter argument, Fiona was already behind me, deftly removing my dirt-stained blouse and tossing it carelessly into the corner.

"Five hours is but a few moments when it comes to getting ready!" she exclaimed, taking a few sniffs in, "Especially when you smell like *that*!"

Rolling my eyes, I sat on the edge of the tub, working on the laces of one of my mud-covered boots. The corner of my lips quirked at her unusual sense of urgency. She was my emotional rock and took on the burden of always ensuring I met the kingdom's stringent expectations—especially during grand events like tonight's dinner.

Seeming to be in a manic state, Fiona bustled around, preparing various lotions and potions for a beauty routine I'm sure was going to last *hours*.

Her intensity made me laugh, "You act as if I'm meeting the entire Fae kingdom tonight!"

She shot me a playful glare before bending down to work on my other boot. "Whole kingdom or not, Liliana cornered me in the hall and threatened to beat me if I did not have you ready to go in time. Not that I wouldn't take a beating for you, but I do not particularly feel like enduring pain from your aunt this evening."

I chuckled at the thought of Fiona being cornered by my stern aunt, anger quickly rising at the idea of her laying a hand on my best friend.

My relationship with Liliana could be described as strained at best.

Aside from sporadic lessons on etiquette and the more than occasional dirty looks across the dinner table, Liliana was more of a stranger than a family member. She constantly had her nose up in the air, acting as if Castle Quinn wasn't good enough for her snooty life. I had never cared for her, but seeing the way she handled my mother's death was the last straw.

No emotions, no comforting words from her, *nothing*. I lost a mother that day, but Liliana lost her only sister and couldn't have cared less.

"Liliana can kiss my ass," I sighed, wiggling my freed toes. "Tonight will go how it's meant to. I have worried about this for far too long, there is no need to get all uptight about it. We'll meet, he'll probably flirt with me, I'll pretend to be flattered, our parents will talk of the agreement, we'll eat, I'll try to get drunk, and then I'll return here to scream into my pillow until I must do it all over again tomorrow."

Giving me a look that screamed *you're not fooling me, sister*, Fiona turned and checked the bath's temperature. "You say that now, but you're the princess and must make a good impression. Besides, you never know. Perhaps Prince Xander will be more interesting than you think."

I shook my head, *not* sharing her optimism. "I'll believe it when I see it." Sliding down my dirty pants, I finally entered the tub. "Shit, Fi! A little warning next time."

The water was far colder than expected, causing my nipples to harden immediately. As I sat on a stool behind the tub, the air around Fiona thickened and I sensed a lecture coming.

"You're starting to sound like my brother," she mumbled, pouring even *colder* water over my hair. "That mouth of yours isn't fit for a future queen."

Ah yes, there it was again—the lecture I'd endured countless times before. When not being dragged into council meetings or wishing for death during court sessions, I spend any free time with the knights. In their company, I was no longer their princess, but a warrior in training.

Their language choice was...*colorful* so naturally, I picked up a few words and phrases.

I leaned back into the refreshing bath, relaxing despite the chilly water. Fiona's fingers worked through my hair, massaging my scalp. Like similar times when I waited a little too long to get into the tub, the chilly water seemed to warm around me. Whether it was my imagination or my body getting used to the temperature, I'd never know, but I enjoyed it, nonetheless. My muscles eased at the sensation, almost as if the water worked magic on my tense body.

"You know," she continued, "it's not just about impressing Prince Xander. This engagement is all part of your father's vision. We're talking about the future of our kingdom, Evie! Well...*your* kingdom, really."

I sighed. "I understand, I do. But sometimes I wish I could be myself, not the *'Perfect Princess'* everyone expects."

Her fingers paused before she chuckled. "Well, that *'Perfect Princess'* is not the one I've known for years. I hate to break it to you, sister, but you've always been a bit of a rebel. But that's why I love you."

"I'm lovable, I know." She lightly smacked my head, causing me to laugh, "But I promise. I'll try to watch my language tonight."

Looking up at her from the tub, it was easy to admire my best friend. Her long, blonde hair was elegantly tied into a low bun, a few stray strands framing her delicate face. Although her skin was a touch paler from spending most of the day indoors, it still held a beautiful glow, much like her brother's. Despite their two-year age gap, they could easily pass for twins.

"No promises needed, Evie. Just be yourself. *That's* the princess we all admire—flaws and all." Taking a small bowl, she dipped it into the bath, filling it with water. "And trust me," she continued as she began to pour water over my hair, "as much as I know this marriage between kingdoms is needed, I would love to have you as my sister-in-law."

My mouth dropped open, causing a stream of water to rush directly into my mouth and down my throat.

"*What*?" I managed to sputter between coughs.

Fiona burst into laughter. "Oh, come on! You know Topher is head over heels for you."

I stared at her in disbelief, my eyes never leaving her as she moved from the tub to my vanity, grabbing my robe from the ottoman. A playful smirk had smothered her face by the time she returned. When she handed me the robe, I quickly rose from the tub and wrapped myself in it, attempting to speak but struggling to find words.

"Uh, no. Your brother loves only two things: multiple drinks after a day in the sun and admiring himself in his armor's reflection. I'm as much of a sister to him as you are!"

Returning to the bedchamber without looking back at me, she dismissively waved her hand. "Believe what you want, *Your Highness*. But trust me, he doesn't train you every morning out of the goodness of his heart. Men *never* do things out of charity."

My cheeks flushed past the point of no return.

It would be a lie if I said Topher was unattractive. I couldn't deny his handsomeness and to my own embarrassment, he was the owner of my first kiss. During my seventh Winter Solstice, I summoned enough courage to give him a small peck on the lips. I was mortified, of course, and made him swear never to speak of it.

We were children back then, but I had always hoped more would eventually happen as I grew older. It never did so naturally, I gave up.

Father told me to never chase after a man. If he wanted me,

he would have to show it. But since his interest in me was nothing more than platonic, I moved on.

With a deep breath, I stepped out of the bathing chamber and into my room. Fiona was already bustling around, laying out various gowns and accessories across the bed. Frustration surged through me, and I involuntarily collapsed on the bed, inadvertently squishing a few gowns as I let out a muffled scream into my pillow.

I heard her frustrated voice amid my exasperated cries. "Are you kidding me?"

"I propose a game." As I propped myself up on my elbow, my face felt flushed. "Let's find some pig's blood, dunk your hair in it until it's the *perfect* color, dress you up in my finest gown, and you can meet the prince tonight while I get drunk at a tavern."

Her eyes narrowed. "Pig's blood? Seriously?"

Yeah, as if *that* was the most shocking statement she'd heard from my mouth.

"As much as I know you'd love to see me in such a predica-ment," her voice was laced with sarcasm, "I think I'll pass on the pig's blood hair treatment, thank you very much."

Sighing dramatically, I rolled over onto my back. "Well, it was worth a shot, right?"

"I think *not*," a sharp voice cut through the room like a knife.

I raised my head toward the door, and a cool breeze swept through my robe. I shivered, my eyes landing on my aunt's slender figure in my now open doorway.

Liliana's icy eyes conveyed her disapproval of my grand scheme. "There will be none of *that*, young lady."

"Aunt Liliana," I managed through clenched teeth. Quickly

moving, I casually ignored the fact that my semi-wet body was most likely ruining numerous expensive gowns. "Thank you *ever so much* for knocking before you entered."

Ignoring me, she ventured deeper into my room, the door seeming to close behind her without being touched.

Liliana's long, ebony hair was partially pulled back behind her ears, the remainder cascading down to her waist. She was dressed *very* prematurely for the evening's events, a lovely, midnight-blue evening gown draped around her petite frame. Sticking out like a sore thumb against the fabric, her sharp, crimson-painted nails caused my skin to crawl.

Though equally beautiful as I remembered my late mother's, her face bore the subtle marks of time—delicate wrinkles framing her eyes and the center of her forehead.

Her deep brown eyes locked onto me with an intense hold, causing another shiver to trace down my spine. To describe the type of gaze my aunt possessed would be something only one who has experienced it could put into words. Cold and sharp, it felt like she was looking through your very soul, knowing all your deepest, darkest secrets.

Those eyes haunted my nightmares.

Ever since my mother passed, I had been plagued with countless, terrifying dreams featuring Liliana. For nearly a year straight, I had the same one every night until I thought I was going to go mad.

Mother would be seated at her vanity, her long, auburn hair cascading like a waterfall. From her reflection in the mirror, Liliana would approach silently behind her. Their eyes would meet, and the air would thicken with an unspoken tension between the sisters.

I would never be able to hear what they were discussing, but the vivid, haunting images were permanently burned into my memory.

Mother's pleasant profile would sour as Liliana's malevolent grin crept across her face. Vanishing as quickly as she appeared, Liliana faded into the darkness, leaving Mother alone. From the same darkness, glowing crimson eyes would manifest and with a flash of movement, Mother would release a bloodcurdling cry, then nothing.

She would just be *gone*, like the darkness consumed her. All I could do was watch it happen over and over again until I would awake drenched in tears and sweat.

Throughout my childhood, I couldn't shake the gut feeling that my aunt might have been the very same darkness that had swallowed Mother. But as I grew older, I had to convince myself they were simply childish fears. I was looking for someone to blame.

Beeling for my closet, the doors once more seemed to phantom open for her as Liliana reached in and retrieved a magnificent emerald gown from the depths of the wardrobe.

Fiona gasped; the gown somehow eluded her previous frantic searching. She rushed over, eager to take in the beauty radiating off the gown.

"Since your lady-in-waiting seems more preoccupied with senseless schemes than performing her duties," my aunt sneered before jerking the gown out of Fiona's reach, "I've taken it upon myself to have this gown commissioned for tonight, under direct orders from your father."

When she hung the gown on the outer side of the wardrobe doors, I wrapped my robe tighter around me and curiously crawled to the edge of the bed.

Even from afar, the breathtaking emerald gown was a

masterpiece. Its bodice was adorned with intricate silver thread-work that mimicked the moonlight dance on water. Even from a distance, I could make out tiny stars subtly woven into the fabric—a secret homage to my fascination with the night sky, no doubt.

The satin skirt cascaded in gentle waves, gold-threaded vines meandering through the verdant expanse—each adorned with delicate emerald leaves. The gown's train flowed behind like a river of emerald, and at the back, a corset was elegantly fastened with delicate silver buttons and laced with silver ribbon.

The gown had me entranced with its beauty.

It was like it had been woven from the night's dreams, a garment fit for a fairy tale. Despite the dread that came from the dinner, I couldn't deny I was excited at the thought of wearing the gown, even if I knew the true message it was meant to portray.

That I was the ultimate prize to be won.

Liliana began to retreat toward the bedchamber door, the brevity of her visit surprising neither of us. Her slender fingers extended toward the doorknob but paused just before making contact.

When she turned back to face me directly, her face was stone. "Tonight will not be pleasant for either of us. For the sake of this kingdom and the future of the crown," she turned the knob, the door swinging open. "do *not* mess this up."

Leaving only the echo of the door slamming behind her, Liliana vanished into the hall. The cold air seemed to follow her out, allowing the lit fire to warm the room.

"She makes my stomach hurt," Fiona sighed in relief, her attention drawn to the gown hanging before her. Tears welled in her eyes, and she seemed almost afraid to touch the exquisite creation. "This is the most beautiful gown I've ever seen! Evie, you're going to be an absolute *vision* in this!"

While my best friend marveled at the gown, I was slowly slipping into disassociation as the reality of the evening set in.

I couldn't shake the feeling that my very life might be coming to an end. Not in the sense of me dying, but the routine and comfort of my life. I thought of my training; would my husband disapprove of a woman fighting alongside men? It was highly inappropriate for a woman to fight, let alone the *princess*.

And what of my friendship with Fiona? Would this be one of the last nights I'd spend in my room, sharing laughter with her?

Anxiety filled my chest, and I squeezed my eyes shut, trying to control the rising panic attack before it consumed me. Fiona's gentle voice pierced through the turbulent whirlpool of my thoughts.

"Hey, are you alright?"

Swallowing down the rising fear, I threw on the mask of princess and mustered my best smile. Standing from my bed, I cautiously approached the dress and dared to touch the luxurious fabric. As I traced the subtle details woven into the fabric, a slight wave of calm washed over me.

Sighing, I sat at my vanity, knowing I could no longer delay what was to come.

"Alright, Fiona. Do your worst."

———+———

Evening arrived faster than desired as the sun teased its descent behind the stone walls that surrounded Castle Quinn.

The bright glow of my fireplace warmed my room, providing a calming ambiance as Fiona finished preparing me.

I couldn't tear my eyes away from the stranger reflected in the mirror. My tight curls, typically a chaotic mess, were elegantly gathered into a lovely bun, accentuating my round face. My distinct ghostly strands cascaded freely from the bun, delicately framing my cheeks.

Even my mother's golden tiara shimmered as it rested comfortably atop my head.

Its metaphorical weight outshone its physical, but I prayed it would somehow provide me the strength I needed to survive this evening.

Fiona was an artist at her own craft, expertly applying makeup to enhance my features without overpowering them, the glow of the light allowing my emerald eyes to sparkle. The black mascara coasting my lashes helped, of course. A soft, rosy blush gave color to my fair skin and the matching lip stain I was fighting not to lick away accentuated my pout.

Once on my body, the evening gown was truly a masterpiece. The stunning fabric draped over me flawlessly, perfectly hugging my curves while allowing me to breathe.

I felt transformed by its beauty.

The neckline dipped low to display the delicate curve of my collarbone, showcasing every freckle I had earned from genetics and time spent in the sun. Each tiny dot seemed to dance with the rhythm of my deep breaths.

I struggled to compose myself; not only did the image of the future queen look back at me, but so did my mother's reflection. I knew I resembled her, but if I didn't know any better, I could have easily mistaken the reflection for hers. My body trembled as a series of goosebumps etched across my skin, fully sensing her presence with me.

I swore, her ghost still haunted these halls.

Fiona approached from behind, her soft hands gently resting on my shoulders. "Like I said," smiling, she gently gave me a reassuring squeeze, "you're an absolute *vision*."

I gave her my best smile that didn't quite reach my eyes, the lingering sorrow on my face hard to ignore. Removing myself from her embrace, I plopped myself down into the fireside armchair that faced the window. The cool breeze was a welcome relief from the anxiety that continued to build in my chest.

Sitting at her normal spot on the edge of my bed, Fiona cautiously watched me attempt to steady my breathing.

"Fiona, I'm not sure I can do this."

Her eyes held warmth and understanding as she studied my face. "Evie," her tone was gentle, "I may not understand the depths of how you're feeling right now, but I know, despite the world feeling as if it's closing in around you, you're stronger than you believe. This is not the first challenge you must overcome, and I would be lying if I said it was your last. Regardless, you're not alone. You will *never* be."

I choked back a tear. "What if I don't even like him? What if he's nothing like me?"

"And what if he only has three toes and a lazy eye? Evie, you can't go into this with a *'what if'* mentality. No one, not even the gods themselves, know how this evening will turn out. I believe if you give him a chance, you might find something you admire—maybe even love one day."

Desperately trying not to ruin her work with my tears, I shook my head. "But what if he doesn't think I'm...acceptable?"

She furrowed her brow, obviously not understanding what I was failing at saying.

"All I mean is," I took another deep breath, "I've worked far too hard on loving the body the gods have given me. I'm just unsure he will reciprocate those feelings."

My body was not large, but I would not be described as slim either. The years of training had caused my arms and legs to fill out with muscle, but despite my efforts on the field, my stomach and curves never seemed to falter.

Father deemed me "healthy," stating a woman should have round hips. Liliana, however, would use words I could never imagine calling another woman.

Moving from the edge of the bed to kneel beside me, Fiona took my hands in hers and my heart rate immediately began to slow. "Then he truly would be blind. You are beautiful in every way imaginable—and I am not just saying that. Trust me," a wide grin formed on her lips, "I have seen you naked."

Laughing, I blinked back the tears before they fell. Per usual, her words soothed my frayed nerves.

"You know I hate it when you're right." My voice felt stronger as I playfully pushed her shoulder. "I can do this. But gods, why does it feel so overwhelming?"

Shrugging, she rose. "Because the unknown can be scary. Even a princess trained in combat can be frightened by something new and foreign. You cannot grow in comfort. Imagine how your mother must have felt. You're simply following in her footsteps; I'm certain she would be proud."

"Doesn't everyone seem just too relaxed about all this?"

She frowned. "What do you mean?"

I twiddled with my gown. "We've suffered from the Fae for over a hundred years, and then suddenly, I'm engaged to their prince, and we're supposed to forget it all? Act like our people haven't hated one another all these years?"

She hesitated. "I'm not sure we're *forgetting* by any means, and I know others have their hesitations. However, if it saves this kingdom at the end of the day, we can move past it. We must."

"Do you think it's seen as a betrayal to those we've lost?"

"I think it's a way to ensure they didn't die in vain."

"I suppose that's a good way to look at it." I bit my lip. "Thank you. I don't know what I'd do without you."

She chuckled softly. "You'd probably curse a lot more and forget to wear shoes."

A natural warmth spread through the room as our laughter bubbled. Interrupting our giggles, a light knock on the door signaled the night was about to begin.

Fiona made her way to the door while I fixated on the flickering embers of the fire. The door creaked open, a pause hanging in the air, followed by a soft snicker. I glanced over my shoulder at Fiona's head peeking out into the hallway, her movements playful as she closed the door.

"Girls only, loser," she teased the unknown visitor.

Smiling, I returned my attention back to the fire. I didn't need to see their face to know who she was talking to. A deep, annoyed sigh from the other side of the door confirmed it.

"I am Genevieve's escort tonight, *little sister*," Topher's impatient voice filtered through. "It's about a quarter till five, so let her know I'm ready when she is."

"I'm ready," I called out, rising from my chair.

Taking a step back, Fiona fully opened the door to her awaiting brother. Entering the room, he halted the moment our eyes met. His mouth hung slightly ajar as if he was about to speak, but no words emerged. I couldn't help but feel vulnerable, and I looked to the ground to avert his piercing gaze.

When I peeked back up under my lashes, Topher's armor gleamed in the soft candlelight of my bedchamber. Every piece seemed to have been buffed and cleaned for tonight's special occasion. The cape he wore highlighted his eyes—a royal blue that perfectly matched the Orphinian crest carved into his chest plate.

Topher, in every way, was the true vision of a chivalrous, handsome knight ready to escort me to destiny's doorstep.

Breaking the lingering silence, Fiona slapped Topher's armored shoulder, the sound of metal echoing. "Gods, big brother! If you hope to escort our princess tonight, you might want to close that gaping mouth of yours before you trip over it."

A faint blush colored his tan cheeks as he blinked a few times.

Offering me a sheepish smile, his armored hand reached the back of his hair and gave it a light scratch. "My apologies. It's just... *Wow*. You look nice tonight—like a girl!"

His failed attempt at a compliment only caused my face to flush further. Fiona peeked around her brother and offered me a raised brow accompanied by a sly grin.

Shaking my head, I narrowed my eyes before directing my attention to Topher. "Your words are too kind," I walked over to him, "but this *girl* can still kick your ass on that training field any day."

His head fell back in laughter, the sound causing me to smile.

"One single win and you're already too good for the rest of

us, huh?" Straightening his posture, he cleared his throat and offered me his arm. "Shall we, m'lady?"

Rolling my eyes, I performed my finest mock bow and gladly accepted his arm. Approaching the doors, I gave Fiona one final smile.

She threw me two thumbs up, her eyes already going misty.

I nodded back at her with a wink and a prayer, and then we took our first steps into the hall that led to my destiny.

Chapter 3

An awkward, thick silence enveloped us as we strolled through the castle's echoing halls.

Even in the isolation of just the two of us, it felt like a million eyes were on me. The paintings lining the dark walls felt alive and judgmental—as if the very figures were silently scrutinizing me. My attempts to ignore them did little for my anxiety, and Topher's occasional glances didn't help either.

"I can feel you staring, you know."

As I peered up to catch his startled expression, he quickly turned his head toward the corridor. Grinning, I playfully poked his fuzzy cheek.

Swatting my hand away, his voice was low. "I was just making sure you're alright."

Our nervous footsteps continued to echo. "I appreciate that. I'm just a bit nervous, that's all."

He offered me a reassuring smile. "I would be worried if you weren't nervous. But I've trained you to be tough, so you'll survive."

"Tough, huh? Is that your way of saying I'm stubborn?"

"Not exactly what I meant, but I have been taught to never disagree with a royal so..."

Reaching over, I lightly punched him on the arm, any blow protected by his armor. He chuckled as he rubbed the spot. "You know I mean it as a compliment."

I snorted. "A compliment to *yourself*, maybe."

Approaching the doors into the grand hall, Topher's demeanor shifted as a group of fellow knights gathered. Commander Robert spoke softly to his men, his eyes meeting ours long enough to send a disapproving sneer at our intertwined arms.

Dropping my embrace like a rag doll, Topher squared his shoulders. "Remember, I'll be right there with you. If you need an escape plan, give me a signal."

Rolling my eyes, I dismissed him. "I shall keep that in mind."

When he left me to join the other knights, my body paused at the threshold of the doors. A prickling sensation started to crawl up my neck, immediately quickening my heart rate.

Just beyond these doors was a future that would alter the course of my life, a future that was out of my control.

Inhaling deeply, I could smell the food being prepared in the kitchen and the scent slightly lightened my thoughts.

The tips of my fingers tingled as they toyed with the delicate fabric of my gown. In the soft, flickering light, the portraits of my ancestral queens watched me from the walls. I wondered if they ever felt the emotions I was currently enduring.

Had Mother felt this way when she was promised to Father?

The moment was suffocating, and it carried a weight both daunting and "honorable" for a woman in *my* position.

How *lucky* I was to be sold off like cattle for the slaughter.

Yeah, screw that.

I was venturing into uncharted territory where the course of my life would be forever out of my control. Panic fluttered back in my chest, threatening to pull me under.

All the weight from the expectations placed over my head suddenly hit me like a ton of bricks. I was expected to perform my duty not only for Father and for my kingdom, but also for Prince Xander.

My soon-to-be husband.

I was supposed to have a choice as heir to the throne when deciding my partner, but it had been ripped from me. Any action I took from here on out would be scrutinized by prying eyes. Political gain had taken over any hope of marrying for love.

I didn't want that.

Honestly, what woman in their right mind would want to be confined to a room for the rest of her life, only to emerge for appearances? Or worse, meeting my death on a birthing bed?

As cliché as it was, I wanted adventure, to see my kingdom and the rest of the world before I took over my father's duty. But I was out of time. This war was too big and had gone on far too long to let my selfish ideas take priority.

Feeling an approaching presence, I turned to face Topher, but instead was met with Commander Robert's bald head shining in the candlelight.

"Good evening, Princess," his rough voice greeted.

"Commander."

His hands were locked behind his back, his armor just as polished as the other knights'. "I wanted to speak with you briefly before you enter the hall, if you don't mind."

I looked up at the grandfather clock, the time roughly four fifty-three, seven minutes before I would be deemed late.

"I apologize, Commander, but I am to be expected—"

"By five on the dot," he interrupted. "I am aware. This shall only take a moment."

Concealing a frown, I nodded and followed him to a corner of the room.

If I had to guess, Commander Robert was closer to Father's age—most likely a few years older. His hazel eyes always hung low, as if he had never received the proper amount of sleep. Which, to his credit, he most likely never did due to the war efforts.

Though a few inches shorter than his men, he had a gaze that could strike fear into the heart of any creature. He was always kind to me, however, so I never feared him.

"I am sure you are aware of the importance of tonight."

Trying not to roll my eyes, I straightened my shoulders. "It's hard to forget when everyone seems to remind me of it on the hour."

His expression hardened. "Good. I am here to inform you that while tonight may be important, it is also dangerous. I would be a fool to think the Fae might not pull something tonight."

My stomach tightened. *I* must be a fool because that thought never crossed my mind.

"I'm sure you have trained your men well enough to be prepared for anything. I'm unafraid and unworried."

He sized me up. "Indeed. I am also aware of how well *you* have been trained."

To say I was stunned would be an understatement. When the topic of my training was first brought up, there were only two disagreeing opinions.

Aunt Liliana, naturally, and Commander Robert.

"With that being said, the king would kill me if he knew I was doing this, but–"

His torso shifted so he could reach for something in his baldric. My eyes grew as he pulled out a small dagger; the blade's tip was as dark as night, engraved red and gold vines crawling up the equally black handle. Never had I seen such an equally beautiful and terrifying weapon. It had to have been personally commissioned.

But why?

"This shall only be used for emergencies, do you understand?"

I didn't move. I *couldn't*.

His face fell in annoyance. Lightly grabbing my wrist, he moved to place the dagger in my hand, but I quickly pulled back.

"Commander—" I swallowed deeply. "I appreciate the concern and the attempts to help, but I will not go into this night expecting to use violence." The disappointment on his face was clear, but I refused to budge, "If it would make you feel better, I shall have a maid take it up to my room, where it will be safe."

"I never took you for a fool, Princess."

"And I never took you for a coward. Seems we're both surprised."

His cheeks flushed with rage as he gripped the dagger in his hands. Barely giving me a bow, Robert turned on his heels and returned toward the other knights.

Topher quickly rushed to fill his spot. "Do I want to know what that was about?"

I shook my head. "I'll tell you later."

He didn't press, but I knew he was curious. "The Fae

haven't arrived yet." His lips thinned. "Your father is inside with his court if you'd like to join him."

Not wanting to but knowing I had to, I took a deep breath and moved toward the doors. Topher pushed them open for me, and I stepped forward.

The grand hall was decorated so well, it almost took my breath away. The room was bathed in soft, flickering light from countless candles that adorned its grand tables and towering candelabras. The long, polished oak table stretched like a never-ending journey, laden with gleaming silverware, crystal glasses, and the finest porcelain dishes. It was all arranged with the precision befitting such a formal occasion.

My father sat at the head of the table, engrossed in conversation with several court members. Their voices hushed as I entered, and all eyes turned toward me. I could almost hear their thoughts, likely a mix of judgment and compliments. His court wasn't full of my biggest fans, often deeming me too reckless to be taken seriously.

Their criticisms never failed to reach my ears. However, after years of attending their meetings, I learned a thing or two about how to handle their thoughts and comments.

A lot of wine was usually mixed into that solution.

Not allowing my anxiety to show, I strutted forward, my emerald gown rustling softly behind me. Each member rose as I made my way to the table. My father, adorned in a deep navy outfit with a pure gold belt, nodded approvingly, his crown gleaming with sparkling jewelry as he moved.

The king's stern features softened into my father's warmth as I approached. "Princess Genevieve," he greeted, bowing slightly to me.

"Your Grace." I gave a small curtsy.

Formalities like these made me want to gag, but it was all a show for his court, just like everything else would be tonight—a *show*.

To my surprise, he engulfed me in a small hug, the hairs of his beard tickling the side of my cheek. "You look lovely tonight," he whispered.

Squeezing my shoulders, he pulled away to regain his stance at the head of the table. A squire moved swiftly to grab the back of my chair and pull it out. Taking my place next to my father, I smiled at the young boy, hoping my appreciation reached him.

Getting comfortable, I found Topher standing guard nearby. His gaze, a mixture of reassurance and silent encouragement, met mine. My heart fluttered, and I quickly returned my attention to the table before a blush could form on my cheeks.

"Please, my friends, be seated while we wait," the king commanded, and the court blindly obliged.

Chatter instantly returned and it was clear I had interrupted a rather heated debate. Liliana, sitting directly opposite, studied me with her typical, icy glare. Locking gazes, she gave a mild smirk of approval before turning her attention back to conversation.

Lord Harrington, a veteran of many battles from the Fae war and one of my father's most trusted advisors, was among the few who sat at the table with us.

"Your Grace," he was clearly frustrated, "as I was saying before, we have fought the Fae for generations. To ally with them now seems a tad too late to make the difference you strive for."

My father was far from amused as his face fell, fingers lightly massaging his temple. "Lord Harrington, I value your counsel and understand your concerns. However, the die is cast.

Genevieve will marry Prince Xander, and their engagement will be the cornerstone of a peace agreement. It is time to end the cycles of bloodshed that have plagued our realm for generations. This is the best choice for our kingdom and its future."

"*Whoring* ourselves out just to end bloodshed is far from noble, Your Grace," Lord Harrington spat.

Watching him take a long swig of his wine inspired me to ask for my own cup to be filled. If this was a preview of the night ahead, I would need a few drinks to make it through. Finding my little squire friend across the room, I lightly tapped the rim of my goblet, signaling my need. With a nod, he moved swiftly around the other servants, wine bottle in hand.

Liliana scoffed from her seat, her brown eyes squinting in the lord's direction. Even with the countless candles and roaring fireplace, the room still managed to feel cold in her presence.

"Lord Harrington, while I appreciate your *concerns*," she countered with a hint of sarcasm, "we must weigh the benefits of this alliance. But do tread carefully with your words." Her accusing finger pointed directly at him. "We all know you had once hoped to marry your eldest son to Genevieve. Some might suggest personal ambitions cloud your opinion."

The squire returned just in time, filling my cup with wine. Leaning in, I whispered for him to never allow my cup to be fully empty, and he offered me a faint smile before disappearing into the periphery. Raising the cup to my lips, I was fully locked into the conversation.

"Please, Liliana, spare me your accusations." He retracted from her pointed finger. "I am fully aware of the gravity of my words, which is why I've attempted to guide the king toward alternative resolutions for this war. Are we to believe the Fae will not manipulate the princess once she's in their grasp? Can we *truly* trust that their generations of pure bloodlines will cease with this union? A Human-Fae hybrid is, well, it's frankly unheard of. Who knows how it will sit with the god?!"

His eyes found mine and I forgot to swallow the wine in my mouth. I mean, he had a good point, and I certainly hadn't thought about what would happen when the prince and I inevitably had a child. Would it be mostly Fae? Or a sad little mix of both...

Father cleared his throat and Lord Harrington's gaze left mine. "Queen Adela and Prince Xander will be arriving shortly. This discussion ends *now*. Genevieve will marry, and that's final!"

Punctuating his statement by slamming his hands onto the table, Father rose from his seat and quietly excused himself. With a loud sigh, Liliana pushed back her chair and followed him out into the hall.

A thick, awkward silence overtook the room as I downed my first goblet of wine. Like a blessing, the young squire was already by my side, filling it for round two.

Not wasting time in my father's absence, Lord Harrington turned toward me. "And what are *your* thoughts on the matter, Princess?"

I raised an eyebrow. "Regarding what exactly, my lord?"

The old bastard's condescending eye roll didn't go unnoticed, and heat, whether from my growing anger or the wine, surged through me. "Apologizes for being *unclear*." His voice was sharp. "What are your thoughts on this union? Your *arranged marriage* to the Fae prince?"

The room held its breath as the lords and ladies of Father's court awaited their princesses' response.

I felt like a dog walking on its hindlegs.

Sitting tall, I cleared my throat. "The union, not only between Prince Xander and myself but also the union between kingdoms," my words felt slightly slurred from the wine I had just chugged on my empty stomach, "is one I am deeply honored to be a part of."

That sounded appropriate. Didn't it? Like something a committed princess ought to convey to her future courtiers?

A nasty laugh escaped him. "She's a damn child!" he said to the other members. "The future of this kingdom is *doomed*."

I wasn't sure if he was looking to provoke something from the remainder of the court or from me, but no one reacted to his comment. The tips of my fingers began to tingle as every candle in the room flickered, seeming to match my anger. I heard Topher take a cautionary step beside me, and Lord Harrington fell back at the sight of my knight.

If there were not nearly half a dozen other people in the room, I would have leaped at that piss-ant of a lord and shown him what this *"damn child"* could do.

Luckily for him, the dining room doors swung open, and my father, aunt, and Commander Robert rushed in. Father's eyes danced over me, seeming to take in every one of my features. I frowned, my anger shifting to concern.

Liliana followed closely behind. "Remember my words, child," she cautioned, her accusatory finger pointing at me this time. "Do *not* mess this up."

Approaching me, Father lowered his voice as his hands trembled. "Please, do not let their judgments sway you from your path."

His gaze darted back towards the doors, a hint of fear lurking in his eyes as if he feared prying ears.

My heart raced in response.

"I love you." He planted a swift kiss on my cheek and returned to the head of the table.

An indescribable, strange energy suddenly surged through the castle, and my heartbeat only intensified. Though it didn't make sense, it felt as if the very air changed.

The sensation, whatever the hell it was, was overwhelming. The tingling in my fingers grew until it felt like they were on fire. Desperately searching for some camaraderie of the feeling, everyone else remained passive, and only Liliana's eyes shot up to meet mine before quickly looking toward the closed doors.

I turned to Topher, "Do you feel that?"

"Feel what?"

Before I could even begin to explain, the doors swung open, and the royal steward cleared his throat.

"Queen Adela and Prince Xander, the true rulers of the Fae Kingdom, Valoria."

Stepping aside, the Fae royals entered, moving with an almost supernatural grace. They were accompanied by a retinue of half a dozen Fae soldiers, their presence as ancient as it was mesmerizing, demanding the immediate attention of everyone in the room.

Everything around me seemed to blur and fade as my gaze fixed upon my future husband for the first time.

As our eyes locked, it felt as if the royal executioner had called my name to die.

Chapter 4

BEING in the presence of the Fae was unlike anything I had ever experienced.

The moment they stepped through the doors, an overwhelming energy rushed through my body so violently, it left me gasping for air. I shook it off as adrenaline, my eyes dancing over the features of the foreign royals before me.

Although physically similar to us, other than their telltale pointed ears, the Fae queen and prince bled an aura that was otherworldly and rather...ancient. In simple terms, they were as beautiful and terrifying as any story portrayed them to be.

Rising from his seat, the king strutted toward the Fae royals. Each step exuded confidence, and I couldn't help but smile seeing him in his element. The rest of the court followed suit as we stood from our chairs.

"Queen Adela, Prince Xander." He bowed. "Welcome to our kingdom. I pray the journey from Castle Nola was not too arduous."

The queen's silver eyes sized up my father.

Her face, perhaps the most stunning I had ever seen on a woman, lacked any hint of emotion. She stood slightly taller than me, her head right at her son's shoulders. The black jeweled crown that adorned her long, white-blonde hair provided her with a few extra inches. The diadem reminded me of the rack of a prized stag, and it perfectly complemented her lavender gown.

Taking her hand in his, Father raised it to his lips and planted a light kiss. My head cocked to the side, wondering if her skin felt any different from my own.

Flesh on flesh, or flesh on...something else.

"Your Majesty." Her voice was velvet as she gracefully withdrew her hand. "Our journey was rather uneventful, thank you. Your Human realm holds little to admire, so we made it swift."

My lips thinned as I fought to maintain a neutral expression, her bluntness already irritating me. Prince Xander remained stationed at his mother's side, silent.

I could feel his stare on me like a brand. Silver eyes, ones that could rival moonbeams, locked onto me with an intensity that left me fidgeting. His expression was enigmatic, and as he was sizing me up, I was doing the same.

Hair nearly identical to his mother's, was neatly pulled back behind his sharp ears. It fell just past his shoulder blades, not one strand out of place. As if his pointed ears didn't already pull enough attention, they were lined and pierced with multiple, black diamonds. I had never met a man with pierced ears, let alone a *royal*, and dammit, it intrigued me.

I didn't fight my curiosity as I took in his slender frame.

The dark cloak draping along his body seemed filled with starlight, shimmering as if the moon perfectly illuminated it. Though thicker and more imposing, the crown atop his head mirrored his mother's. It fit so perfectly, it was almost like he had been born with it attached.

Perhaps he had.

Once we noticed each other's observations, neither one of us hesitated as we locked eyes. As he raised a single white-blond brow, the unspoken challenge rang loud and clear. This was no longer an observation of one's future spouse, but a silent battle for dominance.

And I had *no* intention of becoming the submissive party.

Whether I was being married off to this man or not, I would show I was not a woman to be walked over, not one to back down. The corner of his pale lips twitched, seeming to suppress a smile.

"And, of course, I would like to introduce you to my daughter, Genevieve."

Shit.

Reluctantly, I averted my gaze and our intense stare-down summarily ended. Setting down the wine I had forgotten in my hands, I gracefully bowed to my future mother-in-law.

"Queen Adela, Prince Xander. I extend my warmest welcome to you. I hope your stay in our kingdom proves to be enlightening and fruitful."

What complete bullshit.

Queen Adela's silver eyes met mine, and a small part of me knew she could tell my welcome was fake. Prince Xander's lips twitched again, and a spark of amusement danced in his lustrous eyes.

He gracefully bowed. "Princess Genevieve," his slick voice greeted. "A pleasure to meet you." His pearly pupils roamed my body, lingering on the bodice of my gown. "A pleasure *indeed*."

Heat rose to my cheeks, and Xander smiled in silent victory.

Bastard.

Clearing his throat, Father turned his attention to his surprisingly silent court. "Now that we are all assembled, I believe it would be best if we adjourned for a more private gathering. This is a significant moment for our families, and I would prefer it to be an intimate affair."

Confused murmurs filtered through his court at his decision, and Lord Harrington took a cautious step forward, shoulders slightly slumped. "If I may, Your Grace..."

His gesture made my blood *boil*.

Talking back to the king and doing it in front of the Fae was ridiculous, even for him. Before he could speak further, the king gave a regal wave of dismissal, signaling that their time to leave had arrived.

The grand hall, once buzzing with anticipation, now echoed with shuffling feet. As the doors closed behind them, Liliana's smirk was feral—as if she was *feeding* off their disappointment.

Turning his attention back to the remainder of the room, my father smiled and gestured to the now-empty seats. Father took his customary spot at the head of the table, while Liliana moved to my left. Now sitting directly across from the queen and prince, I was practically on display.

Knights from both kingdoms stood behind their respective houses, the air thickening with tension. It felt like a standoff, ready to erupt if anyone made the wrong move.

"It brings me such joy seeing our families together at last. I propose a toast," Father raised his goblet of wine, "to this momentous occasion and the union between our two great realms!"

We all raised our drinks and brought the rims to our lips.

Fidgeting in my seat, I couldn't shake the feeling it was now or never to make my mark on the evening.

Raising my goblet, I opened my mouth to speak, but Liliana's sharp voice cut through the air. "Genevieve!" she hissed. "Princesses are to be seen, *not* heard."

Her nails blended into the liquid as she forced my goblet back onto the table. My cheeks flushed with embarrassment as her thin lips smiled, satisfied with my defeat.

The room fell silent, but I wasn't about to let Liliana take over the evening. "And as the future *queen*," I said quickly, "I thought it would be appropriate for me to make a toast." Liliana choked slightly as I raised my goblet again. "To a future of unity, peace, and prosperity between our realms. May this union between our families be a blessing from the gods and bring an era of harmony."

Liliana's icy glare shot through me, but I kept my eyes forward. My fiancé raised his drink, giving me a look of respect.

Clearing his throat, Father regained everyone's attention. "Indeed, Genevieve. This union is a blessing bestowed by the gods themselves. My late wife and I had hoped to end this war without involving the children." His tone turned bleak. "But it seems the lines of peace have long been crossed."

Queen Adela's beautiful face never faltered. "The '*lines of peace,*' King Leonard, crumbled before the foundation was even built. It's rather difficult to end a war when certain parties don't admit fault in their mistakes."

Sighing heavily, he set his wine down. "Our past is riddled with mistakes, grave ones on both sides. I hope that with this union, we can heal old wounds and build a future where such conflicts need not arise."

A small burst of liquid courage overpowered me. "What are the true origins of the war?"

My question earned the shocked looks of practically everyone in the room. Sinking into my chair, I fiddled with my dress. "Not that I do not know them, of course. It's just that the royal scribes refuse to let others read their writings until the conflict is resolved. So, I have heard opposing stories depending on who I've asked."

Simultaneously, Liliana and Father opened their mouths to answer, but the Fae Queen raised a gentle hand, silencing them. Her silver eyes darkened with a hint of pain and sorrow. Despite showing no signs of aging, I'd bet she was a few hundred years old. She had witnessed the conflict since its inception—so who better than she to tell the tale?

"Allow me," she started, her voice calm. "It began with a mistake, a grave act that escalated beyond reason. Tell me, do you know how the Fae came to power?"

I shook my head.

"It was a blessing by the gods. You see, we Fae have been around for far longer than Humans. We learned the land and worshiped it with all our being. Our people did not enter this realm with our full magic. Well, at least not at first. We lived alongside the gods of the land and sea—doing their bidding and loving them as much as we loved our own. After a few loyal generations, the Goddess of the Sky, Aura, took a liking to us. She blessed us with some of the same magic she possessed, and the Fae and gods walked side by side for thousands of years—all until the first Human appeared."

I leaned in closer, captivated by her story.

"Small things, you Humans. Similar to us, yes, but so small. As Humans began to populate the world, we took on the roles the gods once held for us. We showed you the ways of the land, creating a delicate balance that intertwined our realms. But as time passed, your settlements expanded, and knowledge became power. A wedge formed between our worlds—a literal border between us. Humans became envious of our powers, and some made it their mission to gain some of that power, no matter the cost."

Her face fell, her words feeling like a warning. "Not all gods are as welcoming as Aura. She had many suitors, but none more persistent than the God of Mischief, Desdemona. For generations, he attempted to gain the love of the goddess, but her rejections drove him to a form of madness, one that outweighed any consequence his actions may cause."

My eyes darted to my father, his face pale. I had grown up with legends of the gods, but this was all new to me.

"To seek revenge for his rejections, Desdemona sought out the greediest of humans and bargained with them: their own powers in exchange for one of Aura's most valuable possessions."

Queen Adela's gaze met my father's. "It was *your* predecessor, King Leonard, who made the first grave error." Her voice grew sharper as she continued, "In their pursuit of power, they trespassed pnto our sacred groves, stole her relics, and imprisoned our kind to study how we harnessed our magic so they could control it once it was theirs. After they delivered to Desdemona, Aura fell into a deep depression—leaving us vulnerable and defenseless against the newly powerful humans. Their actions led to the loss of countless lives. From their hunger for power was born a new breed of evil, one that the world had never seen and was never prepared for."

I held my breath, waiting.

"*Witches*," she hissed, her nose flaring in disgust.

A beat passed as the room held its breath.

Or maybe that was just me.

"These *Witches*," she hissed once more, "were unlike anything the world had seen. Along with the careless wielding of magic, they also carried an insatiable hunger for power, one that was never truly satisfied. The harmony of the world we had built was shattered, and the gods vanished—fleeing from a world that no longer deserved them. They still sleep to this day, awaiting a safe world for them to return."

Her gaze shifted towards me briefly, the gravity of her story causing my chest to tighten, "Not only did they seek to master the very essence of our realm, they desired to bend it to their will. Their magic is purely dark, while ours comes from light. This darkness has corrupted the world's natural balance, giving rise to uncontrollable creatures of shadow and chaos."

"And that is why they are executed when discovered." I slightly jumped at my father's voice, "We understand our mistakes and try to fix them where we can."

"The key word in that statement, King Leonard, is '*try*'."

I felt like I was watching a sparring match, my attention bouncing back and forth.

"Witches can only be bred by Humans who were granted these powers," he continued, ignoring the Fae Queen's jab, "The longer the lineage, the more powerful they become. So yes. We *try*."

A shiver ran down my spine as their words painted a disturbing picture.

"A Human heart with the born ability of a god is a dangerous combination. These Witches forged pacts with malevolent entities from the darkest corners of existence, gaining abilities that defied the natural order. They reveled in chaos, sowed discord among our kind, and unleashed horrors. We attempted to ignore them, to allow the world's natural order to fix what was wrong...but they only continued to thrive. Their actions forced our hand," Queen Adela said, her voice softening with sorrow. "We had no choice but to defend our realm, to protect the fragile equilibrium that had existed for centuries. And thus, the war between our worlds began."

"But why?" I questioned. "If both Humans and Fae were targets of the Witches, why fight each other? Why not join and end their terror?"

This didn't make sense to me. The solution seemed simple yet was overlooked and ignored. Around the table, expressions were mixed. Liliana and Xander seemed bored, while my father and the queen wore expressions of heartache.

Adela's silver eyes bore into me. "Witches, cruel and clever, can hide in plain sight. When the power was first wielded and abused, any gender could summon it. As generations passed, only females were born with the power. Many Humans did not want to believe their families, loved ones, and neighbors were capable of such evil. An attempt was made to collect them and end their breeding, but innocent lives suffered when false accusations were made. It didn't take much for some fathers to go to war for their daughters."

A regretful smile crossed my face as I locked eyes with my father.

"Unless a Witch shows her power, they're almost impossible to point out in a crowd. Unlike us Fae, they hold no telltale signs of being different from the outside. I believe many of the diplomats on the Human side of the war didn't want to lose these powers, so they used their influence to persuade minds.

But with that growing power came their most sinister creation —the Shadow Walkers."

"Shadow Walkers?"

My heart raced, and I needed more wine.

Adela nodded solemnly. "Beings of darkness, twisted and corrupted by the Witches' dark arts. They move between our realms with ease, hiding in the shadows while striking terror into the hearts of both Fae, Humans, and anything else in their path. Countless lives have been lost to their malevolent whims."

"Can only Witches control them?"

Liliana scoffed and turned towards me, showing the most interest she had all night. "Shadow Walkers can only be *created* by a Witch, but anyone can use their powers...for a price."

Raising a brow, I waited for her to continue.

An eye roll and a cold shoulder were the only responses before she turned back towards the Fae. "Shadow Walkers can only be destroyed when the Witch who created them is dead. However, once they are released into the world, anyone can bargain with them to do their bidding. You must have something they want. Shadow Walkers have no true free will, but when they're not being used, they can run wild."

Adela nodded. "She's correct. And that is why there will never truly be peace until all Witches are exterminated. A greedy Human will always be looking to use their powers for their own gain. Once all the covens of Witches are erased from existence, we may find the peace we once had. With the two of you united," she said, looking between Xander and myself, "I pray to the old gods and the new that it shows the Witches they no longer hold power over us. May your marriage strike fear in their hearts."

The room fell silent as everyone absorbed the words. My

stomach churned with the weight of all the information I had failed to learn or be taught. Never once could I have imagined my people being so greedy and vile. The thought of Witches being able to use and abuse magic in such a way was a disgrace to the natural balance.

Just as Adela said.

My squire friend returned with a bottle to fill my cup, and I gladly drank the red liquid down.

The evening, thankfully, continued much smoother after our little history lesson.

Once the food arrived, stuffing our mouths provided a lovely distraction from the darkness. My drinking habit was quickly discovered by my father, who forbade my squire friend from bringing me any more refills other than water and perhaps some tea to sober me up.

Luckily, I was already feeling the blissful effects of the wine.

Surprisingly, Liliana and Adela engaged in conversation while Xander remained rather reserved, his eyes hardly leaving me. Father, bless his heart, tried to learn more about his future son-in-law, but his poor attempts were overshadowed by the prince's unwavering gaze.

The longer he stared, the more I felt like a caged animal on display. No matter how hard I pretended it didn't bother me, his watchful eyes felt suffocating.

Through my father's extensive questioning, I learned that Xander, despite looking only a few years older than me, was well into his fifties. Fae, blessed with the powers of the gods, were mostly immortal, never physically aging past their late twenties or early thirties. His father would have lived for over a thousand years if he hadn't met his end during the war.

Xander was only fifteen at the time.

I wondered what a life without fear of illness or dying in one's sleep must be like. Regrettably, I considered my future as a mortal with him, imagining getting sick and perishing while he watched, or worse—dying while having one of his children. The thought made my stomach turn, so I quickly pushed it away to avoid seeing my dinner a second time.

Xander played the role of a respectful prince well, responding when spoken to. Yet, I couldn't help but notice a small sliver of disdain in his voice, and I wondered if my father heard it, too.

Just as another question was about to be asked, Xander rose gracefully from his seat, brushing off any crumbs from dinner. The cloak he had worn earlier had been shed shortly after the food arrived, allowing me to observe his features more clearly.

Standing a little over six feet, he possessed long, slender arms and legs that gave him an almost spider-like grace. His jet-black, velvet coat and trousers accentuated his fit and lean physique, leaving no doubt about his handsomeness. His face bore the chiseled elegance of aristocracy, characterized by a strong, square jawline accentuating his masculine allure. High cheek-bones added regal charm while his smooth, porcelain skin exuded vitality.

He was the epitome of a Fae prince.

As if aware of my unspoken thoughts, Xander offered me a mischievous smile before returning his attention to the king. "Apologies. All this talk of war and proposals has made this room feel a bit stifling," he said, his composure unwavering. "I was wondering if it's acceptable to you, Your Majesty, if I could accompany Princess Genevieve for a walk in the gardens. We passed them while coming in, and I always adored the flowers of the human realm."

My face rose in surprise, my eyebrows practically touching the top of my hairline. I mean, he wasn't *completely* wrong—the room had begun to feel uncomfortably small, and the wine had heightened my body's temperature.

But my father would never approve of allowing me to leave unattended with the Fae prince, future husband or not.

Highly inappropriate. A scandal even.

"I think that's a marvelous idea!" Father boasted.

Or not.

"Wonderful!" Xander exclaimed. "I shall fetch her a cloak."

I opened my mouth to protest, but before I could utter a sound, Xander snapped his fingers, and a cloak as regal as my dress materialized around my shoulders. The weight of the fabric caught me off guard, and I couldn't suppress the gasp that escaped my lips.

Fae magic. I had never encountered it, but it felt oddly familiar.

Xander walked over and extended his arm toward me. Before I could accept, my father's hand rested on my newly cloaked shoulder. Looking down at me with paternal concern, he smiled softly.

"The gardens can be quite disorienting in the dark, even if you know them well," he cautioned. "Sir Topher will accompany you on your walk."

With a grateful nod to my father, I took Xander's arm, trying to ignore the lean muscles I felt underneath his garments.

Topher was behind us in no time, and I felt a wave of relief wash over me.

Future husband or not, this was still a stranger, and I had no doubt Topher would throw a much-deserved punch if needed.

As long as I didn't beat him to it.

CHAPTER 5

DESPITE WINTER'S IMPENDING ARRIVAL, the garden came alive under the moon's radiance.

A few resilient blooms adorned its well-maintained landscape, but the space's real beauty felt lacking. As Xander and I strolled together, our steps fell into a synchronized ballet, one step matching the other.

Topher maintained a respectable distance, allowing us some privacy without being too out of reach.

Clearing his throat, Xander broke the calming silence. "Thank you again for accompanying me. Talk of war and history bores me to the bone. I sensed your attention waning a bit after your wine was cut off, so what better way to catch a second wind than a stroll through the gardens? Could be a good opportunity for us to get to know one another."

It was refreshing to hear his honesty, although a bit surprising.

"In all fairness, I find this arrangement quite distasteful," he confessed. "No offense to you, of course, but why should we live with the burdens of our ancestors?"

Despite it being a *little* offensive, I sighed in relief. "It's such a breath of fresh air to hear you say that. This whole thing has taken at least a few years off my life. I will be glad when it's over by the week's end. No offense, of course."

In Orphinian culture, royal engagements normally lasted a week—two if the party was *really* going. However, with the severity of the outcome of this marriage, both parties agreed on a five-day engagement, with our wedding to end it all.

He nodded as a charming smile formed on his lips. "I'm glad to hear we're on the same page, Your Grace."

His gloved hand rested on the one I had laid across his arm. Despite being a nice gesture, I was unsure if it was to ensure I was steady on my feet after the not-too-subtle wine comment.

"Please," I offered him a warm smile, "I think being your fiancée has granted us the formality of calling each other by our names."

"As you wish, *Genevieve*."

Some small part of me was unsure about how I felt hearing my name on his lip, but I would eventually need to get used to it. Continuing our stroll, we soon reached the heart of the garden where a grand water fountain sat directly in the middle. Even in the cold, its waters seemed to flow endlessly.

Xander's strides ceased, halting our progress. Hu turned his pale face toward me, the only light from the half-moon above us. Even in my heels, I still needed to crane my neck to make eye contact with him.

Dropping my hand, his eyes roamed my features, and his penetrating gaze once more made me shift uneasily.

"I'm curious about something. I must admit, if I don't ask this, I may as well explode."

Wrapping myself tighter in my cloak, I shrugged. "I'm an open book."

To my surprise and *displeasure*, Xander reached out his long, glove-covered fingers and gently brushed them over the ghostly white hair that framed my face. I flinched, the sound of Topher unsheathing his sword reverberating through the tranquil garden.

A warning to the prince.

Xander quickly raised his hands in a placating gesture. As he turned his attention to Topher, his elegance never faltered.

"No disrespect, sir, I promise." Lowering his hands, he faced me. "I was merely curious about the white in your hair. For someone barely eighteen, it has puzzled me all night. Surely, our engagement has not caused you *that* much stress."

Looking back at Topher, I gave him a reassuring nod. Placing his sword back, I motioned towards one of the hedges—silently asking permission for more privacy.

Hesitantly, he moved out of sight.

I lowered my eyes away from the prince. "From what I was told growing up, my white hair," I gestured to the locks around my face, "is sort of a birthmark." Uncontrollably, my fingers brushed up against them. "I heard the tale many times from my mother. The night I was born, a thunderstorm raged throughout the kingdom. It was said a lightning bolt struck Castle Quinn at the very moment of my birth." I gazed up at the moonlit sky. "The midwives who assisted believed it was an omen—a sign of something extraordinary. Or terrible, depending on who you ask. My mother said it's what made me unique. No one truly knows the reason, but it's a part of me. No matter how short I cut it, the white grows back. So, I left it alone."

I looked back at Xander, his eyes curious at my tale.

"The storm that raged that night was rumored to be the worst Orphinian had ever witnessed. My birth, unsurprisingly, was also rumored to be one of the longest labors a queen had suffered in generations. My mother fought to deliver me with everything she had."

The idea of being in that position one day resurfaced, and I quickly swallowed down my fear.

"When I finally arrived, I didn't cry. Not even a squeak. The midwives and my parents, of course, were frantic with worry, but they all said I was as healthy as I could be. It's almost like my mother and the storm outside screamed so much in those long hours that I had no more left to give the gods."

Maintaining his steady gaze, he took a confident step closer. "Something tells me your mother was a powerful woman."

"She was, without a doubt."

"May I ask what happened to her?"

Any smile I had on my face disappeared.

"I don't mean to pry," he continued. "I just know what it's like to lose a parent."

Nervously, I played with the cloak's magical fabric. "I was young, so my memories are muddy. All I remember was she was fine one moment, and the next...she was just *gone*. It was as if the life had been sucked out of her."

"Were you with her when she passed?"

I nodded, not wanting to let the memories in. "She was getting me ready for bed. I had just pulled the covers over my head and had barely dozed off when I heard her body hit the floor. When I looked up, my room was blacker than I'd seen, but somehow... I saw her on the floor, and I just knew."

A hint of sadness lingered on his face, and I hated the thought of him pitying me. I didn't need it.

Time dragged by as we remained silent. The coldness of the night started to set in, and I shivered despite the magical cloak.

I was growing more uncomfortable by the minute and the lack of conversation after such a dark topic was not helping. Eventually, he stepped closer, and I lightly jumped at the sudden movement.

"You know, I had heard tales of your beauty," his voice lowered, "but listening to you speak with such passion...you're even more alluring. Life has a funny way of shaping us and I can tell you have grown stronger despite your trials. It's quite attractive for a future partner."

He took another step, and I instinctively retreated two, my movements slightly unsteady from the wine.

"May I ask *you* something?"

He smirked, halting his strides. "I'm an open book."

Though my fingers no longer felt on fire, I continued to fiddle with them. I suddenly became embarrassed, and my inner voice fought with my heart as I debated whether to ask the question. Was it the desire to connect or just my liquid courage pushing me? That, I didn't know.

But no day like today.

"Do you believe in what we're doing? That we can be...*good* for our kingdoms?"

His expression shifted, and he straightened his posture. "I believe we can achieve anything we desire if our determination is unwavering. The road ahead won't be easy, but giving in to resistance and resentment will only add to our burdens."

My cheeks flushed against the cold. Asking him such a question could have ended badly if he took offense to it. I looked at my feet in shame, and a flash of movement caught my eye. Xander extended his hand, holding an envelope so dark it blended in with the night.

My eyes shot up to meet his, and I frowned in confusion.

"I wrote you a letter once I learned of our engagement," he confessed. "I was going to wait until our wedding night, but now seems more appropriate."

Snatching it a bit too eagerly, I studied the intricate wrapping. Shining against an entirely black background, my name was elegantly scripted in gold ink. It seemed to gleam and cast a radiant glow that shone in the middle of the dark night.

Another small glimpse of Fae magic, no doubt.

"Genevieve..." He reached for my hand.

I withdrew, maintaining my composure despite the wine's influence on my steadiness. "Xander, I must apologize, but I fear I'm feeling lightheaded by the wine and the cold air. Would you mind if we returned?"

He managed a dry smile. "Of course. I wouldn't want my future bride to catch a cold."

Relief flooded my body, and I gave him a reassuring smile. Topher turned the corner, likely hearing every word of our conversation. As Xander held out his arm again, I took it, this time a little more hesitantly than before.

As we left the tranquil garden, only the sound of the restless crickets seemed to replace the rapid beating of my heart.

I couldn't reach my room fast enough.

After excusing myself and bidding everyone good night, Topher offered to escort me back to my bedchamber. Once I was out of sight of the grand hall, I slipped off my shoes and sprinted up the stairs—leaving him confused and alone without another word.

Pushing through the doors of my bedchamber, I found Fiona peacefully engrossed in a book by my fireplace. Seeing me enter, she snapped her book shut.

"Tell me, tell me, *tell me*!"

In a poor attempt to catch my breath, I stumbled onto my bed and flopped backward. Every muscle and bone in my body relaxed against the soft mattress. Jumping onto the bed beside me, Fiona crawled over until her blonde hair flooded my vision.

"Well, it was...something,"

"Details, Princess! I've been dying all night!"

Sighing, I rolled my eyes and pushed her face away so I could sit up. Instantly, Fiona transitioned into lady-in-waiting mode, moving to sit behind me and unlace my corset. Removing my mother's tiara, I twirled it in my hands as I recounted the night's events.

As my story continued, my shoulders seemed to lighten with every word. Fiona worked her magic, unfastening every inch of my dress before I even reached the part about the garden. Stepping up from my bed, I slid off the remainder of my gown and crawled under my blankets, relishing the cool sheets that soothed my overheated body.

"And the prince?"

"And the prince..." I hesitated. "Prince Xander... He's confident almost to the point of arrogance. It's like he's playing a game, but he's the only one who knows the rules. I felt like he was constantly measuring me, and his eyes..."

I couldn't help but shiver at the memory of his intense gaze.

She propped herself up on her elbows, eyes widening. Shaking my hair free of the endless pins that held it up, I tried to get the memories out of my head.

"I still don't know how I feel about all this. For some reason...I thought things would align once I met him and got through tonight, that I would be content with everything. But I'm scared now more than ever. Anything I felt with him this evening felt off. He's beyond handsome, as you'd imagine a Fae prince being...but I can *feel* it."

She frowned. "Feel what?"

"I can feel like something *bad* is going to happen. I don't know how or what, but I felt this way before mother passed..."

I dreaded saying it out loud—like voicing my concerns would somehow manifest them—but I couldn't shake the feeling. How he looked at me was *terrifying,* almost like he was sizing up a meal.

Fiona's expression shifted as she gently placed a hand on my shoulder. "Evie, I do not want to dismiss your feelings, but do you think this could be the nerves setting in more intensely? Seeing him makes it real now... Maybe your mind is just making things up that aren't there."

Lowering my eyes to the bed, I felt alone in Fiona's presence for the first time ever.

"However," she continued, "you can't ignore your instincts, and you can't let fear control your life."

I wanted the conversation to be over. I was overwhelmed, frustrated, and holding back tears. I loved Fiona with all my heart, possibly all my *soul*, but something felt off, like I was being shoved into darkness and locked away from the truth.

"If you continue to feel this way..." She sighed. "I would

confide in the king. He may have political gain in this union, but he is still your father. Be honest with him and see what he has to say."

I managed a smile. "You're right. Thank you for talking this through with me, like always."

She squeezed my shoulder warmly and leaned back. "Now, enough of these heavy thoughts for the night. You need rest, and tomorrow is a new day. Let's focus on that, alright?"

Leaping from my bed, Fiona began to smother the lit candles around my room. Sleep was a welcomed friend—although I knew it was less likely to come with how fast my mind was racing.

Tonight was an utter shit show.

Feeling anxious over things I couldn't control was a newer feeling, and I hated it. It was dark and overwhelming, and it suffocated me with no sign of letting me go.

Watching Fiona, she gracefully cleaned everything up and was headed to extinguish the roaring fire.

"Wait!" I rose from my pillows. "I think I want to keep it going tonight. I don't want the room to be completely dark. Please."

Giving me a nod, she removed herself from the fireplace. The soft crackling of the fire quickly soothed my thoughts.

"Can I get you anything else?"

"I'm good, Fi. Thank you again for everything."

She walked over to the side of my bed, and her arms embraced me in a comforting hug. As much as I wanted to be alone, feeling her embrace was a welcomed gesture. Pulling away, she smiled that lovely smile, closed the drapes of my canopy bed frame, and dismissed herself.

Alone in my room, sleep was *definitely* not a high probability, but I didn't mind. If tomorrow came slower, I was okay with that.

As soon as I heard Fiona's footsteps depart down the hall, my hands frantically rushed to grab the hidden black envelope Xander had given me. With shaky hands, I slowly ripped the paper until the outline of the letter showed. Pulling it out, I took a deep breath.

The fire's dim light allowed me to see the contents of the letter, and I immediately frowned. The letter wasn't a letter at all.

It was a *poem*.

In moonlit shadows, secrets weave, a dance of vows, our hearts believe. Two souls entwined, a mystic call, a realm where stars & spirits fall. A love like stars in midnight's sky, a bond in which we both comply. In cryptic verse, our hearts confide, two destinies forever tied.

-X.

Frustrated, I crumpled the paper and threw it into the fire.

What the hell did that mean?

I was beyond overwhelmed, and the mix of wine and anxiety was causing a nasty headache to form at my temples. Laying my head on the pillow, I looked up at the stars painted on the panel over my bed, wishing I could join them in the sky.

I'm not going to cry; I'm not going to cry.

I sighed into my pillow; no peptalk from my inner voice could prevent the first tear from falling.

And once it did, I didn't stop until sleep claimed me.

CHAPTER 6

THE SOFT MORNING light filtered through the curtains, gently stirring me awake.

Ignoring my small hangover, I was up as soon as the sun rose over the castle's walls. The night had been a restless one and I most likely only got three hours of sleep, but I was determined to engage in the one activity that could clear my mind and lift my spirits.

Training.

With a yawn, I pushed aside the covers and swung my legs over the edge of the bed. My feet met the cool wooden floor, grounding me in the reality of the day ahead. I quickly moved to my wardrobe and threw on my typical practice attire: trousers, a sturdy tunic, and freshly polished boots.

Seems like Fiona was bored enough to clean them.

Once I'd secured my hair into a loose braid, I was off.

When I reached the training field, the air was crisp with the scent of frost-kissed grass. Late autumn brought an indescribable feeling, and I let it ease my mind. A majority of the knights had already begun their stretching routines, smiling at me as I passed.

Reaching the armory, I was met by the familiar faces of Sir Tristan and Sir Aaron. Both men stood tall and ready, their training armor gleaming in the soft light of dawn.

"My Lady, you're *late*."

Exhaustion hid in his hazel eyes as Sir Tristan teased me.

Shooting him an un-amused look, I gathered my training armor. "Hardly, Sir Tristan. A princess is never late; everyone else is simply early."

He smiled wide under his long ginger beard.

Though not reaching Topher in height, Sir Tristian was a very *large* man—intimidating on the outside, yet a wholesome prankster at heart. Surprising no one, Fiona had fallen for his charms a few years back. He grew up alongside us, and they might have been married by now if it wasn't for the constant threat of him being called to the war's front lines.

Topher was over the moon, of course.

Tristan was loyal, kind, and could entertain anyone. He was more than happy to bless them when the secret affair was exposed and a selfish part of me couldn't wait until they had babies.

"Give her a break, mate," Sir Aaron said, meticulously sharpening his blade. "She had a big night last night; she *should* be sleeping."

Sir Aaron, one of the realm's most esteemed knights, often served as the king's spy. His compact, agile physique allowed him to blend into any crowd, while his wise countenance made him a trustworthy ally.

"Sleeping is for the weak, sir, but I appreciate your kindness."

The two knights exchanged knowing glances, a smirk playing at their lips. Rolling my eyes, I set down my armor and rested my hands on my hips.

"Out with it then."

Tristan's grin broadened to the point I could see every tooth. "We were just curious..." He began to circle me like a predator. "Did the Fae prince enchant you, or is there still some of our Genevieve left?"

"Oh, come now, boys," I laughed. "You know as well as I do that it's a political union—not a love match. Prince Xander and I barely exchanged more than a few words. Plus, our marriage would save your sorry asses from fighting for this kingdom. A *'thank you'* would be appreciated."

Sir Aaron, his face as smooth as a polished shield, raised a brow. "Ah, but those few words can hold the most power, my princess."

"Indeed. You know, they say the Fae are masters of enchantment. Perhaps he whispered sweet spells into your ear under that moonlit sky. Wouldn't surprise me from their kind," Tristan added.

I shook my head. "You two are incorrigible. There were no *'sweet spells'* or *'enchantments,'* I can assure you."

Stopping his rotation, Tristan grinned. "Well, just remember, if he ever tries to sweep you away to his enchanted kingdom before you're ready, you have two knights here who would gladly charge in to rescue you. We've dealt with the Fae for years, even their crowned prince won't hold us back!"

"All of this is to *end* the fighting, remember? Plus, I'm sure a certain knight would be the first to take charge if needed." My eyes searched for Topher. "Speaking of, where is he?"

Tristan exchanged a look with Aaron before shrugging. "Ah,

yes, our gallant Topher—the man of the hour. He mentioned something about an early morning task for the king before training, didn't he, Aaron?"

Aaron nodded, "Yes, yes. Said he had to attend to some important business. Very hush-hush. You know how those knights can be."

I frowned. "That's unusual. He's usually out here with us, rain or shine. Could Commander Robert not have performed this *task*?"

"King's order, my lady," Aaron responded. "Don't have much choice as a knight."

Knowing he was right, I let the subject go, but I had a sneaky suspicion there was more than what they were telling me.

Or *not* telling me.

Entering the field, I basked in the light that had started to bathe the grounds. The symphony of steel clashing began as barked commands filled the air and my heart swelled with an inexplicable joy.

This was my sanctuary—a place where I could lose myself in the rhythm of combat and forget the weight of my responsibilities.

Even if just for a while.

Looking around, I couldn't help but smile, but my heart yearned for one familiar face that was absent. As if summoned by my mind, a patch of familiar blond hair made its way through the crowd, and I was soon met with the blue eyes I would know anywhere.

"Well, look who finally showed up. Still embarrassed from your loss yesterday?"

The closer he approached, the more my smile faded. His expression wasn't the usual cheerful one I saw each morning.

"Genevieve." His tone felt uneasy as he stopped before me. "I apologize for being late."

"What's going on?"

His blue eyes moved over me with a mix of emotions—concern being the most prominent. "I am afraid your training sessions have been halted for the remainder of the week. I must apologize, Princess, but you can't be here right now."

Dread built as my stomach sank. "Princess? What's with the formalities? Stop messing around and grab your gear."

He didn't budge.

"Are you serious?"

"It's the king's orders. He believes you should stay away from the training field for a while. It's his way of...protecting you."

Frustration coursed through my veins as the tingling in my fingers from the night prior returned. "Protecting me from *what*, exactly? We've been training for years; I think I can handle myself by now."

He reached for my hand and lowered his voice. "You know damn well it has nothing to do with your skills, but there are...*appearances* that need to be upheld for the time being."

As I pulled my hand away, my body trembled uncontrollably. "Appearances for the Fae? They're probably still asleep!" I snapped. "I doubt they would even come out here looking for me! This doesn't seem like their scene."

"Look, I'm just as unhappy about this as you are, but when it comes to orders from the king, there's little room for negotiation. I couldn't refuse."

My frustration boiled over. "Did you even try?"

Turning his back to me, he didn't need to answer my question. He couldn't have talked back to the king and we both knew that. Emotions swirled within me like a tempest—anger, frustration, fear, all colliding to create a turbulent storm in my chest.

I had a burning desire to lash out, to scream at the unfairness of it all. But Topher wasn't the one responsible for this decision.

I took a deep breath, attempting to rein in my temper. "Can't you see? This isn't just about a week of training being put on hold. It's about the fact that they want to take this away from me. Permanently. I'll be the queen of *both* kingdoms, which means no more training, no more early mornings, no more...us."

Topher flinched at my words, obviously not realizing that this "appearance" I was meant to keep up would not stop as soon as I said my vows. I knew better, though. I knew this would never be allowed after the wedding. The world as I knew it would be gone.

Forever.

My frustration suddenly became swallowed by a new sense of determination. Wedding or no wedding, my father could use me as a bargaining chip to safeguard the kingdom, coerce me into a union I was far from prepared for, adorn me in extravagant garments, and suppress my natural inclinations. But the one thing he wouldn't take from me was a core part of my identity—the essence that had always rescued me.

The once-clear morning sky became shrouded in approaching rain clouds, accompanied by the distant rumble of thunder—rare this time of year but fitting for my mood. Raindrops began to fall onto the training field, and I pivoted on my heels away from Topher.

With resolute strides, I made my way directly back to the castle, ignoring every shout of my name from behind me.

I was on a mission, and gods spare anyone who got in my way.

CHAPTER 7

As I STOMPED through the corridors, the rain-soaked clothes clung to my frustrated body.

The unexpected storm outside mirrored my inner uproar as a small herd of servants rushed past me and out the doors to salvage whatever they could from the rain. I was shaking, my mind a whirlwind of anger and betrayal—emotions I couldn't hold back.

If I didn't confront Father, I would burst.

Reaching the heavy doors of his study, I didn't bother to knock before pushing them open. Sitting at his desk, Father wore his small reading glasses, engrossed in what I assumed were my engagement agreements.

As he heard me enter, his eyes widened as he took in my disheveled state—my soaking hair and clothes leaving puddles on his polished floor.

Dropping his papers, he rose, "Genevieve! What happened to you? Gods, did you fall into the moat?"

I couldn't hold back my anger. "What happened to *me*? I shall tell you what happened to me! *You* happened to me!"

His face turned cold. "Genevieve, please, sit by the fire. You're soaking wet."

Ignoring his suggestion, I began to pace. "You've halted my training? How the hell could you do that to me? And without even warning me before I heard it from Topher? Don't you think such information should come from your mouth? I believe I deserve at least that much respect."

He sighed heavily as his brows furrowed. "It's for your safety."

"My safety?" I scoffed. "I've been training for years, and now, suddenly, I'm 'not safe'? Try something new with me. I'm not buying that."

Taking his seat, he leaned forward. "This is not a matter of your skills, Genevieve. It's about appearances! With the Fae royals here, we must present an image of peace and cooperation, *not* violence and hatred!"

"Appearances?" I practically spat the word. "Gods, you must have coached Topher perfectly on what nonsense to spew to me. Is all of that more important to you than my identity? My training is a part of who I am, Father. You can't just take it away!"

"Is there an echo in here? Gods, Genevieve, please!"

"No, I can't accept this. You're taking away the one thing that has always been mine, and I will *not* let it happen."

"Enough with the theatrics!" His voice thundered so intensely I stopped my pacing. "Think about how it looks, love. A princess from a kingdom embroiled in a five-generation-long war, training to *fight* each morning? Regardless of your reasons, it does not present well."

"Then let me explain it to them!" I pleaded. "We'll explain how training every morning saved my life! Once they hear that, they'll know it has nothing to do with aggression towards the Fae."

Disappointment crossed his face. "It does not matter. My word is the law here, Genevieve Rose."

My middle name. Fuck. I was doomed.

Tears welled in my eyes, and I turned away, unable to bear the disappointment in his gaze. I couldn't stop my shaking and I questioned whether it was from my anger or how cold I was. He sighed, his chair scratching against the floor before the smell of his cologne reached my nose. Flinching away, I knew he was trying to rest his hand on my shoulder.

"You've gone too far this time." My voice quivered. "You're forcing me into a life I never wanted, a marriage that feels like a noose around my neck. I can accept that, but I can't accept you making me into some doll that can be traded."

I turned to face him, my wet hair clinging to my cheeks. His normally kind brown eyes were heavy, his lips pursed in a thin line.

"You knew what you were getting into," he stated blandly. "As future queen, it's not just about you or your wants anymore. It's about our kingdom's survival, about ensuring *peace*. I know it's a heavy burden, but it's one we must bear together."

I snorted. "I don't see *you* making any vows."

He reached for my shoulder, his grip firm but filled with a father's tenderness. "I know it's difficult, love, but sometimes, we must make sacrifices for the greater good. Trust me, I would never ask this of you if there was any other way."

Removing myself from his touch, I chuckled. "You just don't care, do you?"

His face flushed with anger. "Care about you? Of course, I

do. But do I prioritize the kingdom and its future over something as small as your training? Now, that's a question I won't answer." Walking to his desk, he returned to his seat. "Orphinian's future is intimately intertwined with your happiness and the safety of our people. It always has been. Someday, you'll come to realize that."

My gaze burned into him as the storm of emotions within me continued to build. There was no winning this argument, so why even waste my breath?

"Now, enough of this," he commanded. "Clean up and prepare for breakfast. We'll soon meet the Fae and commence with today's activities."

With a posed smile, I performed an exaggerated curtsy before the king. "As you wish, *Your Majesty.*"

Leaving his office, I stormed through the corridors, heart heavy with frustration. The echo of my boots whacking on the cold stone floors hardly drowned out the pounding of my heart. Everything around me was a blur of red as my thoughts became consumed by the clash between my dreams and my father's demands.

Lost in my bitterness, I turned a corner without looking and collided with something solid, sending us both stumbling. Instinctively, I reached out to steady myself, gripping the strong arms of the person I'd collided with.

Looking up into the silver eyes I desperately tried to erase from my memories, I was suddenly shaking for a new reason. His face was calm, and the corner of his lips rose as he gripped onto my arms tighter.

"Good morning," Xander purred.

His gaze left me speechless, and *not* in a good way.

Feeling his hands against my drenched arms, I became

acutely aware of how the rainstorm and the coldness of the castle were affecting my body, particularly my chest.

"Prince Xander," I stammered, stepping back from his grip. "I apologize; I was..."

"In a hurry?"

Crossing my arms over my *very* wet chest, I couldn't help but take in his attire. Xander wore a regal silver suit that perfectly matched the color of his eyes, causing them to sparkle.

"Distracted," I corrected.

He arched his brow. "Distraction's pull, a force unknown. In its grasp, our focus overthrown."

What the hell did that mean? Did this man constantly spew bad poetry?

"*Right*," I awkwardly agreed. "Well, if you'd excuse me, I need to freshen up for our breakfast."

"Of course, Genevieve. I look forward to it."

Giving a nod, I hurried down the corridor and up the stairs to my room.

This day had already been a series of unfortunate events, and it was barely eight in the morning!

Reaching my room, I lazily pushed open the doors. The last thing I wanted was to play dress up. Fiona awaited by my fire, book in hand. Looking up, she smiled warmly at me before frowning. Narrowing her eyes, she quickly jumped from her spot.

"Goodness, Genevieve! Are you trying to get yourself sick before your wedding?"

As she helped me out of my clothes, I detailed the events of my morning. I was already exhausted, feeling like I had lived a million lifetimes in the past twenty-four hours.

With every word I dumped onto Fiona, dread only

continued to consume me. I had a feeling deep in my gut that these whirlwind experiences would not be ending anytime soon.

To say I felt powerless would be an understatement.

I felt *doomed*.

The stranger looking back at me in the mirror was more authentic.

Fiona had worked her magic again—transforming me into the *"perfect princess"* everyone expected to see today. Gone were the layers of extravagant cosmetics and fancy hairstyles from last night. Instead, my face was graced with a lighter touch of makeup to enhance my eyes and bring out the natural color of my lips.

My hair, still slightly damp from the rain, hung loosely around my shoulders. Mother's tiara had been replaced with a simple, gold circlet. The gown chosen for today was also more casual. It was a light teal with gold details to match my head piece. The fabric, although not nearly as grand as the emerald gown, cascaded gracefully around me and enhanced my figure without the excessive layers.

I was more Genevieve today than the porcelain doll adorned for display. With a satisfied smile, Fiona admired her work.

"There. You're ready."

I returned her smile as a soft knock on my door instantly caused a knot to form in my stomach. Fiona opened the door and her brother hesitantly stepped inside. Although his attire wasn't as grand as the night before, he still looked equally handsome.

Rising from my vanity, I nodded a small "thanks" to Fiona and walked out my open door, not acknowledging Topher as I passed. In the hall, I caught a few muttered words from the siblings. A curse word was exchanged, and the sound of metal echoed before Topher joined me.

He shut the door behind him, and then we were alone.

He cleared his throat. "Genevieve, about this morning..."

I didn't want to dwell on it, so I raised my hand to stop him. "Look, I would rather not talk about it. My temper got the better of me, but what's done is done. It quite literally had nothing to do with you... I was just so angry."

"And you have every right to be. It's not like the Fae haven't ruined enough already," he spat. "I just wish there was more I could have done without being thrown in the dungeon for talking back to the king."

I snorted. "As fun as that would be to witness, I swear—you are not the one I am angry with. At all."

"Good. I wouldn't want you to be mad with your favorite training partner."

"Now, why would I be mad at Sir Tristan?"

His smile grew and he playfully draped his arm over my shoulder, pulling me into a side hug that could easily have slipped into a headlock. Laughing, I elbowed him in the gut, causing him to let me go.

"Friends?" he asked, holding out a hand.

"Best friends," I said, returning the grasp.

His grip lasted a moment longer than necessary. His touch had always been a comforting feeling—something I would be able to recognize in a crowd of thousands.

Pulling my hand away, I peered down the corridor. If we didn't start moving, I would be late and surely hear about it from Liliana. Feeling his eyes still on me, I turned back and met his gaze.

Like my father the night prior, it felt as if he was devoting every single one of my features to memory.

Leaning closer, his voice dropped to a whisper—as if worried the walls had ears. "Just between the two of us, I think you look *lovely* this morning. Maybe even more so than last night."

His lips lightly grazed my cheek before pulling away. The touch was so soft that if I hadn't felt the stubble of his beard, I might have mistaken the act. Blinking, I was fully taken back at both the compliment and gesture.

"Flattery two days in a row, Sir Topher?"

He grinned. "Only when it's sincere, my lady."

Offering his arm out to me, I gladly took it as we continued down the halls. Our steps fell into an easy rhythm, and for a moment, the weight of our world seemed a little lighter.

Perhaps a bit more bearable.

The remaining three days passed in a blur—each hour filled with a whirlwind of activities to prepare for my wedding.

Time sped by, every second consumed with choosing decorations, attending nightly dinners with the kingdom's nobility, and trying to navigate the world of my future court. If I wasn't being pulled in one direction by Liliana, I was being pulled in the opposite by Father.

Despite my reservations, I had hoped to spend *some* time with my future husband before we said "I do". His mother was a constant shadow, lurking behind him at every turn. Even if I wanted a moment alone with him, we were in the constant presence of one of our parents. I had never been courted before, but I was certain this was not how it normally went.

While my relationship with Father had somewhat improved, Liliana proved to be an absolute monster. Acting as if *she* was the one to be wed; her demands on having things her way or no way reminded me of a spoiled child. As hard as I tried to ignore her, she was always there.

Like a blemish that refused to heal.

Waking up the day before my wedding, I was exhausted. The final step before our big day was our engagement ball, and practically every noble in the kingdom would be in attendance.

Fae citizens, however, were *not* on the guest list.

The plan was to have a ceremony in Orphinian, where Xander and I would be legally married. Once completed, we would travel to Valoria for a traditional Fae ceremony.

The whole arrangement was laughable. Wasn't the entire point of our marriage to bring people together and *not* separate them?

Oh well. What did *I* know, anyways?

My final day as a single woman was nothing more than a continuous flow of meetings, last-minute fittings, and final discussions about what the hell would be prepared for dinner. If I was exhausted when I awoke, I was practically the walking dead by the time evening fell.

Fiona attended to me in her customary beauty routine, just as she had on that first night I met my future husband. Father had ordered another gown to be made in my honor, and I don't know how, but it made the emerald gown look like a frock.

It was...*breathtaking*.

Beyond breathtaking.

With its ethereal blend of white and silver, the gown left me wondering how my wedding dress would ever measure up. Intricate embroidery, reminiscent of vines, adorned the hemline and extended to my waist, stopping just before the bodice. A high, modest neckline left much to the imagination, its lacy collar connecting to a long, chiffon train that resembled a cape. My arms were exposed, showcasing the muscles I had built from my mornings on the training field.

I felt beautiful and confident, two feelings that were much needed after the exhaustion of the previous days.

Dark curls flowed gracefully down my back while my signature white hair seemed even more radiant against the backdrop of my white gown. Mother's tiara once more graced my head, its jewels catching the light ever so perfectly.

Nervously, I toyed with the gold engagement ring Xander had given me a day ago. Itt felt like the world's weight rested on my finger—the over-the-top diamond not doing much to help.

Once I was fully dolled up and ready to go, Topher awaited outside my door to continue his role as my loyal escort. Father must have felt a little guilty about my training being put on hold, so Topher had ushered me to whatever bullshit I needed to attend each day.

He was one thing I looked forward to seeing.

Attempting to hide the frown on his face, he plastered his

best smile. I felt grateful for my time with him, knowing it was about to end.

Taking my hand in his, he lifted it until his lips lightly planted a kiss on the top of it. "Ready for tonight?"

I took a deep breath, steeling myself.

"As ready as I'll ever be."

CHAPTER 8

APPROACHING the grand doors that lead to the ballroom, our steps slowed as my literal future awaited me.

Bathed in the soft, golden glow of rows of candles, Xander stood tall, his eyes already on me. An aura of confidence and charm radiated off him, making him truly seem like a god among men.

His white suit matched my dress, and it was far grander than any other garment he had worn since his arrival. In typical Xander fashion, his clothes fit his slender frame well.

Almost *too* well.

As he drank me in, I instinctively dropped Topher's arm. The smirk he wore was his classic, cocky grin. "My bride."

Still by my side, Topher sized up the Fae prince. Though a small height difference separated the two men, Xander's confidence made him practically tower over my knight.

While even the smallest act from Xander seemed to get under Topher's skin, my fiancé seemed indifferent.

Topher's jealousy grew with each passing day and, frankly, it was getting out of hand. His not-so-subtle acts of flirtation were draining me emotionally, and I was annoyed with his lack of consideration. But our time was limited, so I let it go.

Excusing himself, he departed through a side door leading into the ballroom. For the first time, I was alone with Xander. Since this ball was in our honor, we were expected to make a grand entrance as the engaged couple.

Wasting no time, Xander closed the distance between us and embraced me in a confident hold. There was a faint scent of alcohol on his breath as lowered his lips to my ear.

"You look *divine* tonight, love."

Who was I to judge someone partaking in some liquid courage? But gods, his breath *reeked* of a mix of wine and whiskey.

"As do you." I smiled kindly.

Soft strains of music drifted from the ballroom, signaling it was time to enter. My fiancé stood by my side, his confident smile somehow reassuring me. Staff members rushed into place before slowly pushing the doors open for us.

It took everything in me not to gape at the opulent ballroom that awaited us.

As our names were announced, the sight that met our eyes was nothing short of a fairytale. The ballroom was a true vision of elegance. Crystal chandeliers hung from the high ceiling, glowing warmly over the well-dressed guests. The normally bland stone walls were adorned with rich tapestries and intricate frescoes I always loved looking at as a child.

We stepped forward, and our presence immediately commanded the attention of the room. As we made our way through the parted crowd, the music swayed around us. Like a wave on the shore, each head bowed as we passed.

I observed the looks and gestures of every subject as we

made our way through. Many appeared pleased to see their princess and future king arm-in-arm, while others wore their disdain for the Fae proudly on their faces.

If Xander had noticed their sneers, he showed no signs of it. *At least some in Orphinian held the same hesitations I do.*

Seated at the back of the room, Father and Queen Adela occupied thrones that felt even more ancient than the Fae queen herself. Approaching our parents, Xander dropped my arm and bowed. Returning the same gesture, I gave a near-perfect curtsy to the two. After receiving nods of approval, we sat in our own designated thrones.

Liliana occupied her own chair, a small wooden seat that seemed to have been dragged out of a closet. Her cold eyes never left me as I moved. Her long, ebony hair was pulled into a low ponytail and the dress she wore matched her signature nails. Or maybe it was more like the color of wine? Maybe I was just looking forward to drinking some.

Standing, the king demanded everyone's attention with a clap of his hands. "Ladies and gentlemen, esteemed guests and honored dignitaries, I would like to thank you for joining us tonight to celebrate a momentous occasion." His gaze swept over the assembled crowd. "The joining of two great kingdoms, Valoria and Orphinian, through the union of Prince Xander and Princess Genevieve."

Polite applause and cheers filled the air, and he raised his hand for silence. "This alliance is not merely a bond of nobility but a pact for peace, prosperity, and cooperation between our lands," he continued. "It is a testament to the enduring strength of our kingdoms and our commitment to securing a brighter future for all our people. I thank Queen Adela and Prince Xander for joining us these past few days. Gathering after generations of turmoil has been a breath of fresh air, and I am forever thankful."

The Fae royals gave the crowd soft smiles that didn't reach their eyes. Father turned toward me, eyes misty before quickly blinking them away, the hint of emotion swallowed.

"To my daughter, our Princess Genevieve. I could not have asked the gods for a better heir. Your strength, determination, and love for this kingdom are the ultimate gifts in a future ruler —and I am beyond proud to be your father. With you in charge, I know this kingdom will prosper more than ever."

Tears grew in my eyes, and I swore Liliana scoffed.

"As we gather here tonight," his voice brimmed with pride, "let us celebrate not just the union of two individuals but the union of our kingdoms. Together, we shall write a new chapter in our shared history filled with hope, unity, and boundless possibilities."

As he raised a glass high in the air, the entire room followed suit.

The sounds of crystal clinking flowed through the ballroom as everyone participated in a collective toast for a brighter future. With another clap of his hands, the band again started, and couples flooded the dance floor.

Xander and I exchanged awkward glances, his lips semi-preoccupied on the rim of his very, *very* full goblet of wine. I assumed a first dance would be customary, but he didn't seem to be in a rush.

Which was fine with me.

Taking in the room, my eyes landed on Topher, who had already been looking at me. A reassuring smile radiated from him and just as I was to smile in return, a chilling presence crept behind me.

Without needing to turn, I knew Liliana stood by my throne. Just catching a glimpse of her from the corner of my eye sent tingles through my fingertips. Observing the crowd, she didn't even bother to look at me.

"Such a monumental night, isn't it, dear niece?"

"It is indeed."

"And to think," she mused, "you've gone the entire week without scaring the prince away. I would say I'm impressed, but it's hardly an accomplishment. Even for you, dear."

Suppressing the harsh words I wanted to spit at her, I decided she wasn't worth my time or energy. My lips curved into a smile that didn't reach my eyes as I looked up at her.

"How could I when you're already the most terrifying presence here? Fortunately for him, *you're* not the one he'll marry."

Liliana's laughter cut through the air like a blade. I followed her line of sight, her icy stare set on Topher. Uncomfortably, he turned away. A slim, frigid hand landed on my shoulder, and every hair on my arm stood as her long, red fingernails lightly dug into my skin.

Not enough to draw blood, but enough for me to feel the sting.

"What are you do—"

Her piercing brown eyes bore into mine as she knelt beside me. The grip tightened further, causing me to gasp. "Listen closely, you little *brat*," she spat. "You may think you've played your cards well so far, but remember, dear niece, the game isn't over yet. If you do anything, and I mean *anything*, to jeopardize this union, including your relationship with your *little knight*, you'll find that the consequences will be far more dire than you can fathom."

Ignoring the shiver that ran down my spine, I met her gaze

with defiance. I would *not* show weakness. The thousands of candles surrounding us seemed to flicker in response to the tension, and heat rushed to my cheeks.

"You can threaten me all you want, Liliana, but you won't control my life. Father does that enough for the both of you!"

"Oh, my dear niece, you vastly underestimate what I can do. This is your only warning." Releasing her grip, she stood and straightened her gown. "Now, enjoy the festivities. It's a night you won't soon forget."

Gliding down the steps that lead from the thrones to the floor, she quickly disappeared into the crowd. As I looked toward my father, he remained deeply engrossed in his conversations. Even Topher remained with his back toward me. It seemed no one else had witnessed my aunt's little show.

Lucky me.

Swallowing whatever sense of dread I felt, I rose from my throne and went over to my favorite squire, who blessed be him, already had a drink waiting for me.

The grand ballroom shimmered with the enchantment of thousands of twinkling lights.

Hours passed, yet the guests still mingled, sharing laughter and stories, offering congratulations on my "happy" union. I grew envious of how carefree everyone appeared. The laughter, dancing, and drinking were a wonderful sight after generations of war, but on the inside, I was *screaming*.

If this was a celebration, I was the only one *not* celebrating.

Even Xander seemed to be having a good time. He indulged in the wine more liberally than I had seen—his pale cheeks were flushed, and his laughter boomed across the ball room.

At least he was enjoying our party.

Each new song played by the orchestra left me dancing with a new face. My feet ached and the amount of hands that had graced my waist made me long for a bath. It seemed as if every male noble, both spoken for and single, wanted one last dance with the princess before she was shipped off to enemy territory.

Father and Queen Adela remained silent observers, watching closely from their thrones. Thankfully, Liliana never returned after our conversation, which was fine by me. She was unmissed in my eyes.

The clock on the wall's time was nearing a quarter till ten and I was ready to call it a night. As the orchestra's upbeat tango transitioned into a slow waltz, the lovely melody overtook me, causing me to sway with the enchanting sound. Couples from all corners of the room began converging towards the center—Xander among them.

I snapped out of it, the reality of what type of dance came with this music causing my heart to race. I had danced with everyone *except* my fiancé, and it appeared my luck had run dry. His steps were slightly unsteady, but his silver eyes locked in on me. He stepped to me with an outstretched hand, his confidence apparently unaffected by his drinking.

"My bride, may I have this dance?"

Swallowing my pride, I placed my hand in his. I let him pull me close, his grip firm as the other hand racked down my back before resting on my waist. I suppressed a shudder from the completely unwanted touch.

He moved us to the music, his proximity quickly unavoidable. "You look radiant tonight, love."

"So, you've told me." My smile was polite as I subtly leaned away to escape the lingering smell of alcohol. "But thank you. Have you enjoyed your time? The evening has been quite enchanting."

He leaned in closer. "Enchanting, indeed," he purred. "I can't help but imagine how enchanting our nights could be, just the two of us."

The music persisted, and his hands gradually descended lower on my waist. Despite my attempts to adjust, I couldn't create space between us.

"Although I adore this dress, my mind begins to wander, bride. To think," his silver eyes drank me in, "my Fae magic can do practically *anything* I want. With one snap of a finger, I could have you naked—right here in front of everyone."

Heat flushed my cheeks—not from his attempted charm but from the anger simmering within.

"*And to think*," I slightly mocked, "with one thrust of my fist, I could have you crying on the floor from a broken nose for everyone to watch. As a 'magical Fae prince,' I would assume that would be rather embarrassing for you."

Shit. Way to open your mouth, Genevieve.

I braced myself for the worst, but the sound of Xander's boisterous laughter took me aback. Guests turned their attention to us as he continued to laugh. After what felt like years, he wiped a single tear from his eye and struggled to regain his composure as our dance continued.

Flushed with amusement, his face softened. "There's that fire I knew you've been hiding all week! I was merely teasing, bride. Regardless, I must apologize. The wine has been a bit *too* generous with me tonight."

Though relieved, I was still on guard. "Our wine can be rather strong if you're not used to it."

"I suppose."

His gaze briefly roamed the room before returning to mine. We bowed to each other as our dance concluded, and I wasted no time in turning to return to my seat.

Before I could take a step, his hand gently grasped mine. "Meet me in the garden in five minutes," his warm breath whispered before pulling away.

As I opened my mouth to decline, he vanished into the bustling crowd, his presence still lingering in the air around me. Anticipation tingled through me, and my breath quickened as I contemplated his request.

We had walked in the garden together before; this should be no different. After all, he would be my *husband* in less than twenty-four hours...

Looking toward Father to find he was still deep in conversation with several court members, Queen Adela's silver eyes remained fixed on him. I found Topher once more. His expression had turned serious, and his usual cheerfulness vanished.

I wondered if he sensed what was unfolding. If he somehow knew of the rebellion I was about to undertake.

It would be highly inappropriate to be alone with a suitor, but what would it say about me if I declined his offer?

Would he think me weak? A coward?

Regardless, I was not going to find out.

With fear tightening my throat, I silently prayed to the gods that my courage wouldn't abandon me before I regained my senses.

The garden greeted me with a gentle, cool breeze and my heart raced as fear clawed its way up my throat.

Every instinct urged me to run—to seek refuge within the castle walls. I was unafraid of Xander...so why was everything in me screaming that this was wrong? Determination outweighed my unease, causing my feet to carry me further from the party behind me.

Reaching the fountain, my fiancé stood waiting for me in the distance. His slim figure leaned gracefully against a stone pillar entwined with ivy.

He turned to face me as I approached, his white attire shimmering under the moonlight. "Genevieve. I was hoping you'd join me."

"The ballroom was starting to feel overwhelming. The fresh air was a welcomed suggestion."

Taking a step back, his sterling orbs drank me in, a smirk curving his lips. I glanced around, uncomfortable under his gaze. The night was eerily quiet, save for the distant chirping of crickets and the soft rustling of leaves. This deep into the gardens, you could hardly hear the ballroom's music.

"I must admit," he said, breaking the silence, "you look even more captivating in the moonlight."

My head dipped down. "Quite the charmer tonight, aren't you? I should charge you for each compliment."

The crunch of fallen leaves under his feet signaled his

approach. Two cold, slender fingers gently lifted my chin, guiding my gaze to meet his.

"Tell me," his fingers dropped, "am I what you thought I would be?"

"My expectations weren't very high."

I hadn't meant it to come out so *cold*, but his face never faulted.

"And what did you expect, Genevieve?"

I paused, gathering my thoughts. "I had anticipated a more conventional royal demeanor. But you're...unpredictable. Unlike any prince I've encountered, if I'm honest. I suppose my expectations were colored by the stories I grew up with, leading me to assume the worst of you. I apologize for judging before I got to know you."

"Stereotypes often stem from hatred or rumors. We Fae have flaws, just like mortals. But when lives are at stake, things can get exaggerated. It makes me wonder if the things I've heard about your people are factual or not."

"I suppose we will have to find out. We have the time."

He rubbed his smooth chin. "I was indeed curious to see if the reports I had heard of the fiery mortal princess were true."

My eyebrow rose, "Reports?"

"Please." he chuckled. "Do you think Mother and I would agree to such a union without knowing what we would be getting ourselves into? I've had eyes on you for a while, bride. My favorite stories are of your training. My spies' recounts are rather...*intriguing*."

My annoyance flared, and I felt exposed. *Vulnerable*. The thought of him observing me, sizing up my kingdom for who knows how long, grated on my nerves. How did he even get someone beyond Castle Quinn's walls?

Or...was it even a person...

"I apologize if I didn't meet your expectations of the perfect bride," I managed through gritted teeth.

"No need to apologize. You merely piqued my curiosity even more. A woman with that type of spunk makes me wonder what you'll be like on our wedding night. Got me rather excited, really."

My mouth dropped open, my fists clenching at my sides. "I fail to see its relevance."

He started circling me, instantly putting me further on edge. He was drunk, and I needed to get the hell out of there.

"Oh, spare me," he chuckled, his words dripping with disdain. "You may play the innocent princess role to your father, but I see through you. I know your true desires, *bride*," he sneered. "A spirited soul like yours couldn't have possibly waited for the marital bed. Not that it bothers me, of course."

"You're a horrid drunk."

"And you're a tease."

My fists tightened until I feared I might draw blood. How dare he speak to me like this—drunk or not? All week, he had been courteous and kind. Was this the true nature of the man I was to marry?

"I must confess," he continued, "breeding with a Human is *far* from ideal. But after the time we've spent together this week, I can already tell you'll be a good fuck."

That was it. Instinctively, my hand shot up to strike him, but before I could land the blow, Xander's Fae reflexes intercepted—seizing my wrist before I saw him move an inch. He drew me closer, his warm breath grazing my ear. The sensation of his unwanted hold was suffocating.

"I can smell the desire radiating from your cunt," he whispered, his tongue sliding along my earlobe.

I stood paralyzed, save for the shiver running down my spine. My mind urged me to fight back, but my feet were stuck to the ground beneath me.

"Don't act all innocent. Despite how much you've averted his advances, I know you yearn for that want-to-be knight, and you must know he fantasizes about you, too. As do I."

Still grasping my hand, he slowly led it down until I was cupping him through his pants. He was already half hard, causing him to groan from the contact.

"Don't worry, bride. After you've produced me a few heirs, I'll be generous enough to share you with him. Maybe we'll even take turns making you *scream*."

That was enough for me to wake up.

A surge of energy flared in my fingertips, and I summoned all my strength to push him away. Surprise colored his face before fading into a sinister smirk. Closing his silver eyes, he leaned in for a kiss.

Seizing the moment, I lunged forward and drove my forehead into his nose. Our crowns clinked together, his falling off as he staggered backward. Thin hands flew to his face as he screamed in pain.

"You *whore*!" he spat, blood seeping between his fingers.

Footsteps approached from behind me, and I spun on my heels to the intruder. Topher emerged from one of the tell hedges, his eyes wide and face furious. Of course he had followed me out here, and thank the gods he did.

Because I was about to kill my fiancé.

Returning my attention to Xander, I raised my hand to

show him how much of a *whore* I could be, but before I could strike, Topher intercepted my wrist.

"Stand down!" he demanded, trying to maintain control. "Please, Evie."

But he was too late. Anger consumed me, my vision turning red, my body ablaze. Topher dropped my wrist and violently shook his hand as if sensing the heat radiating from me.

"Shit!" he hissed.

"Let me make this *perfectly clear*," I spat at Xander. "Everything I do and everything I will endure will be for my kingdom and my people! My duty is to them *alone*. My heart and body will *never* belong to you! I will not let you break me or use me for your pleasure. I will fulfill my role as your queen, but do not mistake that for affection. You may have my hand in marriage, but you will *never* have my heart! And if you ever, and I mean ever, try to take me like that again—I will fucking kill you, my *hus-band!*"

My rage surged like wildfire with every word, filling me with newfound strength as the night air seemed to charge. Xander removed his hand from his already-healed nose and straightened his disheveled attire.

For the first time in his presence, I felt tall.

"Humans are so sensitive." Shouldering past me, he made his way back toward the castle.

I could perfectly imagine an arrow slicing through that lovely, pale neck of his. With a flash of smoke, Xander disappeared into the night's air. I'm sure he was transporting himself back to *Mommy*.

Anger consumed me, and I dropped to my knees, no longer caring about the state of my white gown. Trembling, I found no solace in Topher's presence. Every emotion in me ran wild —*begging* to be released.

Closing my eyes, I attempted to calm myself by counting to ten.

One. Two. Three.

Every second added to my fire.

Four. Five. Six—fuck it.

Before Topher could bend down to comfort or help me up, my body was off the ground, and my feet were in motion. I could hear my name being called behind me, but it didn't matter.

Nothing mattered right now.

Rage had flooded my sight, and the moon's beams perfectly illuminated a path for me, guiding me back to the castle.

CHAPTER 9

By the time I returned to the castle, most of the guests had already started making their way out the doors.

Queen Adela and Xander were nowhere to be found—probably fleeing back to their rooms like cowards. Searching the still buzzing ballroom, I failed to find the one person I needed to talk to.

My *father*.

As I stormed through the halls, my anger barely allowed me to hear my own thoughts, let alone Topher's loud footsteps and desperate cries from behind me. Rushing to get ahead, his large frame blocked my path.

"Genevieve," he panted, trying to catch his breath. "You can't just run off like that!"

"Move!" I demanded, attempting to pass him.

"Talk to me!" he pleaded, his hand reaching for mine.

The feel of his calloused palm steadied me, but it didn't last long. When I locked my eyes onto him, his face dropped—reading my expression like the open book I claimed to be.

"*Please*," his voice so soft., "what happened back there?"

Withdrawing my hand from his, all I could do was shake my head before storming off again.

He didn't try to stop me a third time.

Reaching Father's study, I pushed open the doors and found him standing by his window. With a goblet of wine in his hands, he watched his departing guests.

He seemed so...peaceful.

"I'm not too sure what ancient herb you were on when you decided upon this union," I interrupted. "But whatever it was, it must have been *really good*."

He turned from the window, his expression stern and cold, far from peaceful. His eyes narrowed as they fell upon my dirtied gown.

Heavily exhaling, he settled into his seat behind the desk. "Would you care to explain to me why you laid hands on Prince Xander?"

My jaw practically hit the floor. That little snake had already run to my father with his version of events before I could speak to him myself!

"Laid hands on *him*?" I exclaimed. "It was the other way around, Father! *He* was the one who laid hands on *me*—all night! But naturally, you wouldn't have noticed that."

As he reclined in his chair, his expression was unreadable. "Xander informed me of the incident in the garden. While I appreciate the need to defend yourself, harming a visiting royal, especially one who will be your *husband* tomorrow, is unacceptable, Genevieve. Remember, this union serves a greater purpose for our kingdom—to end the war."

My breath caught in my throat, nails digging into my palms. "I understand the purpose," I spat, tears welling in my eyes.

"But I refuse to be treated like a common whore in my own home! We *both* know I'm meant for more than that!"

"Genevieve, you must try to see beyond your personal feelings in this matter. The peace between our realms hangs in the balance, and your role in this union is crucial."

His words only stoked the flames of my anger.

"Do you not care at all about what I feel? I am no longer a child and don't need to be talked down to by *any* man, nor be treated like an object to be bred!"

"You are my daughter, and I love you dearly, but you must understand the weight of the responsibility that rests upon your shoulders. Sacrifices must be made for the greater good. We have gone over this time and time again, and I'm growing tired of this dance."

"And what about my happiness? What about my feelings? My *dignity*?"

"Genevieve, that's enough! I thought we had moved past this. You will obey my commands. This union isn't about your happiness; it's about the survival of our kingdom. You will fulfill your duty as a princess—including producing an heir when the time is right."

Tears filled my eyes, but I remained tall. The fire in the room crackled and surged, seeming to breathe in my emotions as they peaked.

"First my training and now my respect? I know if Mother was still alive, she would—"

He slammed his hands down onto his desk. "I said enough!"

The room tensed as our eyes met—a silent battle of wills neither dared to surrender. The fire dwindled in the corner, and my breathing steadied.

"Leave my study, Genevieve. We will discuss this no further. You will marry Xander tomorrow afternoon, and you will be queen. It's about time you start acting like one."

No longer able to hold back my tears, they streamed down my face, ruining my makeup in the process. With my head held high, I left his study, paying no attention to the patiently waiting Topher.

I hope he enjoyed the *show*.

Each step felt like a struggle as I moped back to my room. My breaths came in ragged gasps as the sense of betrayal weighed heavily on my chest. It was consuming, and I no longer had the energy to fight it.

I stormed into my room, the weight of the confrontation with my father still heavy on my shoulders.

Fiona sat at the foot of my bed, a typical book in hand, waiting for me. Without a second thought, I removed my mother's tiara and flung it onto the bed—narrowly missing Fiona.

"Well, I guess your night went swimmingly."

Ignoring her, I stomped to the armchair by the fireplace and threw myself into it, kicking off my muddy heels. I stared into the dancing flames, not daring to look her way.

"You have *no* idea."

Abandoning her spot, Fiona stood before the warm flames and placed my shoes neatly aside. When I finally looked at her, her face immediately dropped as she read my emotions. The moment she took my hand, I began to weep.

"Oh, Genevieve!" she said, lightly squeezing my hand. "What happened?"

"It's...it's all falling apart," I managed between sobs.

Her eyes searched my face, begging for answers my voice wasn't offering. "Tell me everything."

I sniffled, "Honestly, it didn't start that bad..."

My words trailed off momentarily as I fought back tears, but I found the strength to continue. As I recounted the night's events, Fiona's eyes mirrored my growing anger and disgust.

"That Fae *prick*!" she spat. "There's no way your father would ever condone a marriage to someone like that, regardless of the war!"

"That's the worst part. After everything in the garden—I *tried* to tell him. It was like talking to a stone wall! Nothing I said got through to him, and he made it *painfully* clear that my sole purpose was to be a pawn, swallow my pride, and marry Xander."

On nights like these, I was thankful for the kinship I found in my best friend, but my heart still ached for my mother. I longed for her soothing words and the fierce protection I know she would have offered me in moments like these. I couldn't change the past, but some part of me felt like if she was still alive, this whole engagement would have never happened.

Fiona's face still frowned with worry, and I knew she was struggling to find the right words to comfort me. Although not her job, I appreciated her, nonetheless.

"You know," she began, "I would have paid good money to see you demonstrate one of your training lessons on that asshole."

I laughed for the first time since the ball started, the image of Xander's bloody nose coming to mind. I took pride in knowing I had done that to the Fae prince. "I would have paid even more for your brother to demonstrate a lesson or two. You should have seen how he came barging from those bushes."

"I told you!" she chuckled, throwing her hands up. "*Obsessed!*"

I lightly pushed her as we continued our laughing. My heart was lighter, but tomorrow's reality loomed over my head like a rain cloud, ready for a downpour.

Sniffling, I fiddled with my engagement ring. "I honestly don't know how I'll get through this. Especially tomorrow."

Her blue eyes bored into mine. "With the grace and strength you possess, no matter what life throws your way. And perhaps some wine."

"More like a lot of wine." I wiped away the last of my tears. "I don't know what I'd do without you."

Her warm smile radiated kindness and understanding. "You'll *never* have to find out. You're stuck with me! Even if that means I leave Tristan behind and follow you to Valoria."

Opening my mouth to respond, I stopped when a light knock echoed from my door before it slowly creaked open. Father's regretful face appeared in the doorway, his eyes finding mine. Clearing his throat awkwardly, he seemed to be struggling, a trait I rarely saw from him.

Recognizing the need for privacy, Fiona stood. "I'll leave you two. Ring if you need me, my lady."

Acknowledging her dismissal, I braced myself for the tongue-lashing I was more than likely about to receive. Giving the king a small curtsy as she passed, Fiona was out of my room, leaving just the two of us. Still seated in my armchair, I looked away from him, but his footsteps allowed me to track him as he moved.

My bed creaked under his weight and three solid pats on my mattress beckoned me to join. Peeking over my shoulder, I found his eyes were low and heavy as he sat at the edge of my bed. Once more, he patted the mattress.

Bracing myself, I slowly rose from my chair and joined him on the bed. I could have sworn I heard our hearts beating out of our chests.

He let out a large sigh, his shoulders slouched. "I couldn't allow myself to go to bed with how we left things this evening, and I think it's time I told you a story." His voice caught in his throat. "When I was a boy, my father told me horror stories of what the war with the Fae brought to the kingdom. It wasn't until I was older that I witnessed those horrors myself. Kings rarely fought in wars, everyone fearing the loss of the royal bloodline, but I couldn't stand by and watch good men die every day for what I claimed was mine."

My eyebrows scrunched together as I studied him. This level of vulnerability was new when it came to him.

"As soon as I was ready, I entered the battlefield with a hundred of the kingdom's best men. My father warned me that being a good king meant more than just being strong, but I hadn't believed him." His eyes shut as if trying to block off the painful memories. "I led those men straight into a massacre—more than half of them died almost immediately. The power of the Fae was more intense than I ever could have imagined. That battle lit a fire in me, and I didn't look back when it came to giving my life to the kingdom. I was barely sixteen, but I didn't care if I lived or died; nothing other than ending the war mattered to me."

Imagining my father, just a few years younger than me, marching off into battle made my stomach churn.

He opened his eyes and grabbed my hand in a soft embrace. "Nothing else mattered until *you* came into the world. I loved your mother with all my heart, but she knew what this war meant. She was strong and would have been fine without me if anything had happened. But with you, you were so small. When you didn't cry at your birth, my heart stopped. At that very moment, I would have traded my life for yours. When my last bit of hope faded, you opened those big emerald eyes and smiled at me. I knew nothing else mattered. I knew I had to keep *you* safe."

I gave him a soft smile as he lifted my hand to his lips, planting a loving kiss. "Seeing you tonight, how devastated you were from what happened with Xander, my heart broke and I grew angry at myself for allowing any of this to happen. This war is a terrible burden to both sides, and I pray you know how truthful I am when I say I tried everything to prevent you from being involved."

I gave his hand a light squeeze, feeling all the pain radiating from him. "I understand, Father, and I know how hard this war has been not only on the kingdom but for our family." I sighed. "But I can't excuse the fact that you would be willing to let me suffer without even searching for a solution. You're shipping me off to a foreign land to marry a foreign prince, and the moment I tell you something that could put me in danger, you dismiss me? How is that supposed to make me feel as your daughter?"

He gently withdrew his hand from mine, rose from the bed, and walked toward the window. "Genevieve, I can't express to you how sorry I am."

He couldn't mask the tears in his eyes as I joined him. Wrapping my arms around his broad frame, I embraced him as tight as I could. The smell of his cologne mixed with the ash from his fireplace brought me comfort. I doubted I could ever love two smells more.

Resting his chin atop my head, the hairs from his beard tickled.

Large hands gently rubbed my back, causing me to smile into his chest. The warmth of his love relaxed my shoulders and I completely forgot about the worries that awaited me in the morning.

"I'm calling it off."

I pulled back. "What?"

He smiled down at me, fully pulling away from our embrace and straightening his jacket. "You are the most important thing to me, and I refuse to subject you to a life of unhappiness, no matter the cost."

I was shocked and confused to say the least. He couldn't mean it...right? Even if he did, I couldn't allow my people to suffer any longer, but the last thing I wanted to do was marry Xander. My heart felt torn in two, completely conflicted with emotions.

"N-no," I stammered.

He raised a hand to quiet me. "I intend to speak with the queen in the morning. I've worked too hard to be the father you deserve, especially after we lost your mother. My love for you is unwavering, and I refuse to fail as a father while striving to be a good king." He clasped my hands in his. "Together, we'll find an alternative path to end this conflict. I promise."

My eyes welled with tears. Though I'd always felt close to him, this depth of love and understanding echoed my bond with my mother. Gripping his hands tightly, I hoped he could feel my appreciation. Deep down, I understood my duty to the crown and the kingdom as its future queen.

No matter how much I resented it.

Decades of war with the Fae had ravaged our lands, and a part of me believed I might hold the key to ending it all without further bloodshed—regardless of the personal sacrifices it entailed.

"I can't allow you to do this," I whispered. "As future queen, my allegiance lies with the crown. You taught me that, and now I understand. Xander may be despicable, but greater sacrifices have been made before. Witnessing this war's toll on our kingdom and you, Father—I can't bear it any longer. Soon, Topher, Tristan, Aaron, and all the other knights will be called to the front until there are none left. Fae magic has ravaged our land, and I may hold the key to preventing further devastation."

With a heavy heart, I released his hands and moved to the vanity. Sitting down, I carefully removed all my jewelry. His reflection smiled back at me from the mirror.

"My allegiance lies with the crown and my duty to the kingdom," I repeated softly. "I used to hope the war would resolve itself, but after hearing Adela's account the other night, I don't think there is much hope without me...and I'm okay with that. I've made my peace."

His face held a mix of emotions, mostly concern and pride. Approaching, he placed a comforting hand on my shoulder. "Genevieve, I—"

Like being thrown into an icebox, a sudden bitter grip seized the room, freezing his words. A sharp jolt shot down my spine, momentarily stealing my breath as if I had been stabbed. Energy flooded the room in a way I had never experienced before. Feeling pulled, I glanced at the corner of my room through the reflection, sensing a presence lurking there.

Somehow, Father felt it too, his head slowly turning over his shoulder. We both waited in silence and anticipation as a putrid stench filled the air, overwhelming and foreign to my nose.

A rumble, so deep and low that it shook the room, echoed from the dark corner. Out of thin air, crimson eyes manifested from the darkness. My heart raced as shapeless darkness gathered, coalescing into a humanoid figure—the void itself seemed to take form around those haunting eyes.

With unnatural speed, the shadowy intruder surged toward my father. In a swift, merciless strike, the creature plunged something into his back—causing him to gasp for air. Father's eyes widened in agony until I was certain they would pop out of his skull. As he reached and failed to grasp the object protruding from his back, a strangled cry escaped his lips.

Frozen in my seat, I could only watch in shock and disbelief as he crumpled to the floor, blood flooding his regal attire.

The shadowy assassin quickly dissolved back into the darkness. Despite its absence, its stench and malevolence lingered in my room. Snapping out of my daze, I hurried to my father's side, my hands shaking as I desperately tried to stop the flow of blood.

But it was *useless*.

His eyes had already glazed over, and his lips trembled—struggling to produce words that would never be spoken. Desperation and anguish welled up within me as I looked into his fading eyes, realizing that even if someone were to walk in right now, there would be no miraculous recovery, no last-minute rescue.

All I could do was watch and scream.

CHAPTER 10

THROUGHOUT MY LIFE, I could count on one hand the number of times sheer terror had frozen me in place, rendering me unable to move or even breathe:

1. The night Mother had passed away.
2. My first kiss with Topher during the Winter Solstice.
3. Experiencing my first menstruation.
4. Xander's drunken assault in the garden that evening.
5. Watching Father be brutally murdered by a faceless shadow.

I couldn't tell how long I'd been screaming or how tightly I'd clung to my father's lifeless body.

Time lost meaning the moment the light left his eyes. My once-white gown, tailored for me in his vision, was now soaked in his blood. My voice, hoarse from screams, barely produced a whisper as I prayed to the gods to bring him back.

But they never would.

Whatever that *thing* was...it was straight out of my nightmares. My encounters with magic had been limited to tricks by Xander and his mother, but I knew deep down that whatever had taken my father's life was indeed magic.

And it was *dark*.

I stared at his lifeless form, the assassin's blade still protruding from his back. Something overtook me and acting on instinct—or foolishness—I gripped the dagger and withdrew it, unaware of the amount of blood that would flow from the wound.

The moment the blade was out of his body, my vision was thrown into a storm of blinding white.

Visions, both clear and blurry, flashed before my eyes so quickly they made my stomach twist. Silhouetted hands against a dark background intertwined, as if sealing a deal. Crimson eyes appeared, followed by my father's face, alive and well at his desk.

Then everything vanished.

A tingling sensation spread from my fingers through my entire body, as if struck by lightning. Objects on my shelves and mantle shook violently until they smashed to the floor. It felt like an out-of-body experience but gradually, I was drawn back into my body and consciousness.

Being back, I felt like both a stranger and the rightful owner.

Still humming in my hand, the dagger's unique design caused me to gasp. Even in the dim light, its all-black blade and the red and gold vines on its hilt were unmistakable. It was the *same* dagger Commander Robert had tried to give me days ago.

Was it a coincidence? Or a setup?

Anxiety threated to consume me and each passing second only intensified it. I was gasping, unable to maintain a steady breathing pattern. I had never had a true panic attack, but I was pretty sure I was on the brink of one.

Distracted by my efforts not to faint, I failed to notice the approaching footsteps until it was too late. Behind me, a blood curdling scream shattered the air and echoed through the halls.

Turning toward the sound, Liliana stood frozen in the doorway, her legs trembling. Wide, brown eyes were locked in on my bloody hands still clutching the dagger. Realizing how damming the whole scene looked, I dropped it to the floor and lifted my trembling hands in surrender.

Everything was stained red with his blood. My hands, nails, and even my engagement ring dripped thick, crimson liquid. Closing my eyes, I tried to shut it out, but I was too late. I don't think I would ever be able to forget the look, smell, and feel of it.

Forcing myself to open them, Liliana sneered at me as if *I* was a *monster*. Given how bloody my hands were, I couldn't blame her. Nausea rose to my throat as I struggled to rise to my feet.

Liliana's eyes grew. "Don't you dare take another step, you little bitch!" she spat.

"*No!*" I pleaded. "Liliana, this isn't wha–"

"Guards! Someone! The king!" Her voice faded as she retreated from my door and bolted down the hallway. "The princess has *murdered* the king!"

Nausea continued to crawl up my throat until I was certain I would see my dinner again. I knew how bad it looked, but gods! In classic Liliana fashion, she didn't even allow me to explain. If I wasn't sick enough, the thought of my own flesh and blood thinking I was capable of such an act left me gutted.

It was *disgusting*.

She would have me arrested, if not *killed,* for this. No matter what defense I pleaded, the evidence was against me. The fight I had with my father earlier only made matters worse. His blood stained me, and no one would believe a "Shadow Walker" was responsible.

No, no one would unless I had *proof.*

Overtaken by panic and adrenaline, I rose to my trembling feet. It was now or never. I would either be wrongfully executed or die trying to prove my innocence.

I guess neither option looked the best.

Heart pounding, I seized the dagger and wiped it clean to prevent leaving a trail. Bolting from my room, my legs halted as I gave my father one last mournful look.

My whole world laid motionless on the floor, drowning in his own spilled blood. An afterlife seemed far-fetched to me, but if there was one, I prayed he had made it. He deserved peace. Despite how much I felt my body beginning to crumble, I needed to be strong for *him.*

Surveying the dim corridor, my options were limited. I had a fifty-fifty shot at choosing the opposite way Liliana had run, or I could run right into her. Suffocated by urgency and going off a gut feeling, I fled to my right. If I was limited to prayers to the gods, they were surely about to run out as I prayed for protection.

As I quietly made my way down the hall, the eyes of every portrait on the walls mocked me. No, they *screamed* at me.

"Murderer. Coward. Disappointment."

I swallowed their insults, the sound of rapid footsteps

drowning out their hateful voices, and I froze. If my heart didn't calm down, it would surely alert them of my presence.

Pressing my back against one of the mocking portraits, I held my breath and tried to remain as small and silent as possible. My body started to tremble—not from the growing fear of getting caught, but from the canvas shifting and rumbling behind me. Slowly, it moved until open, damp air hit my back.

As curious as I was, I wasn't about to be taken by a shadow monster, so I turned to flee. Gentle hands covered my mouth and wrapped around my waist, pulling me into the darkness before I could even take my first step away.

Even if I had a voice left to be heard, it was hopeless against the strong hold around me. I would rather lose my head than allow another creature to kill me like they had my father. Yet, no matter how hard I tried, no sound emerged from my throat.

As I was pulled further into the darkness, the hands that held me released their grip. Disoriented in the pure blackness, I heard a sound of something scraping against the floors until a heavy thump drowned out any squeaks.

Straining my eyes, I saw a faint light from a match grow into a small flame. Fiona's serene face appeared before me, holding a candle. Relief washed over me, and I could have collapsed into her arms. Taking my gaze from her, I cautiously surveyed our surroundings.

The stone-walled chamber was small, and I tried to ignore the countless cobwebs visible in the dim light. Beyond Fiona, a long, dark hallway stretched endlessly.

"What the hell is this place?"

Staying silent, she pressed her lips together in a thin line and turned on her heels, venturing down the hall. Not once did she look back to see if I would follow, but naturally, I did.

The height she had on me made me struggle to keep up. I had been so alert and on guard in my life. Every sense became heighted in the dimly lit corridor. The air was heavy with a musty, old scent. As we ventured further, the tunnel began to illuminate with flickering candles mounted on the stone walls, each shadow causing me to flinch.

If I didn't see those crimson eyes, I would be okay.

"These are the hidden servants' quarters," Fiona finally spoke, breath unwavering from her pace.

If our height difference didn't already make it hard for me to keep up, my bare feet on the uneven, dirty ground certainly did.

"They were used at the beginning of the war, specifically for hiding the most treasured jewels, books, paintings, and whatever else your great-great-grandsire deemed important."

Stopping abruptly, she contemplated the fork in the hallway ahead. Looking back at me, her eyes latched onto my blood stained dress.

Swallowing, she continued, "There are things about this kingdom, about your *people* that hold many secrets. Secrets you should have been told a long time ago."

"Fi, what the hell are you talking about?"

Her steps didn't falter as we approached an old spiral staircase. She descended without hesitation. "I don't mean to be so mysterious about this, but I *physically* can't tell you. I'm not only your lady-in-waiting." She sighed. "I was sworn to protect you, to watch over you. I took an oath when we were girls—a *blood oath* I cannot break."

Descending further down the staircase, I swore I was also descending further into madness. Each step only made me feel more off balance, and I struggled to find my footing. As we reached the bottom, tears uncontrollably streamed down my cheeks. My grasp of reality was slipping quickly through my fingers, and I despised the feeling.

"You're not making any sense! What blood oath? Who did you make it with? Why is this all happening?"

I desperately gasped for air, the walls closing in on me.

Fiona halted and turned to face me. "Whatever you take away from what I'm about to tell you, I pray you know that every single day of our friendship has been the best I will ever have." She closed her eyes, collecting herself. "There are things and forces in this world that have been hidden from you. Whatever you've been feeling this whole week...I've felt it, too. That sensation? It's been *overwhelming*. I was returning to check in on you and your father when I heard your scream and felt the castle move. I rushed to your door, but it was too late. That *thing* had taken your father, and Liliana was approaching. So, I hid behind one of the paintings and waited."

Her explanation hung in the air. It made no sense. "Blood oath"? What the hell did that even mean? I was getting more nauseous by the second. Reaching out, she gently took my trembling hand in hers. It was a lifeline in a world plummeting into darkness.

"You need to give me a little more detail," I pleaded. "These feelings... How did you know? Why did that *thing* take my father?"

"I wish I could give you all the answers, Evie," she whispered, "but I can only tell you this much. We're not like others in the kingdom, and this fucking oath won't let me explain it to you."

Hearing her curse caused a corner of my mouth to rise, but it didn't help the severity of the situation.

"Your mother..." She trailed off.

"My *mother*?"

Fiona nodded. "Your mother sh-she did *everything* in her power to protect you from this secret. But whatever happened tonight, it's a signal it can no longer be kept. You deserve better."

My mind raced as I tried to absorb everything. The tingling in my fingers, the vision...was I going mad, or was something bigger at play?

It was all too much.

She hesitated. "I will tell you this. That thing that killed your father tonight was composed of dark magic. The darkest anyone or anything can possess or wield."

"You know what it was?"

Nodding, her face paled. "It was a Shadow Walker summoned specifically for your father. You being with him wasn't an accident. I can feel it."

Shadow Walkers.

The very entities Queen Adela had cautioned about the other night at dinner. Some small part of me thought maybe she was pulling my leg or trying to scare me. But the fact that Shadow Walkers—creatures associated solely with Witches and their stolen powers—had infiltrated Castle Quinn on the eve of my wedding to the Fae prince was no accident.

It had to be connected or part of a larger scheme, perhaps even a warning. But was it a warning from the Fae themselves or from the hidden covens of Witches that lurked among us? Could my assault on Xander have driven them to seek the very thing they hated and summon one as revenge? Or was it a Witch who longed to see my family suffer? And why did it use the same dagger Commander Robert attempted to push onto me?

That, I had no clue, but I was going to find out.

Find it *all* out.

"I think I'm going to be sick..." I mumbled, trying to catch my balance on the stone walls. "Wh-what can be done? Liliana thinks it was *me*! Thinks I'm the one who..."

I couldn't bring myself to say it, to admit Father was *gone*.

Fiona stood tall, manifesting courage for both of us. "You need to find out who summoned that Shadow Walker. It's clear to me someone wanted to make it look like you were responsible."

As I shut my eyes, my mind desperately tried to take me back to that table to listen in on what Queen Adela had said about these creatures. The whole night flashed in my mind, but it was useless. The wine drowned my memory.

Opening my eyes, Fiona was frantically undressing. The beige frock she had donned for the evening was already in a pile on the floor at her feet, and she was working on the laces of her ankle-high boots. I watched her in a confused daze, the soft glow of the corridor accentuating the grace she moved with.

"We need to be quick. I don't know how much time you have!" she urged before quickly moving behind me.

I jerked back as her fingers tug at the laces of my gown. She moved at a pace that if it wasn't for all the confusion and shock, I would be impressed by.

"What are you doing?"

"Swapping clothes," she bluntly stated.

Unlacing the final string, Fiona gently pulled the gown down, leaving us both in our undergarments. Snatching her pile of clothes, she handed me different items.

"Topher's horse is in the stable. I need you to be as quick and silent as possible. I'll explain everything to him once things have calmed down," she instructed, throwing the garments over my head. "Take him to the neighboring village of Heim but avoid unnecessary interaction. There's a tavern called *Rose and Crown*; look for the symbol on the door," she instructed, focusing on adjusting the corset. "Tristan spoke of a man once who frequents there, distinguished by a scar over his right eye. He's a skilled huntsman, knowledgeable about tracking magical creatures. He may have information about the Shadow Walker or the coven behind it. Find him, show him the dagger, end who did this, and return home. We'll deal with the Fae later."

Stepping away from me, she admired her rushed handiwork. My hands trembled as I desperately tried to retain all her information.

Rose and Crown. Huntsman with a scar. Kill the Witch. Return home.

Looking at her, I swallowed the fear lodged in my throat. Her inspection continued until she landed at the top of my head. Frowning, she bent down and tore a long section of fabric from the bottom of the beige frock. Brushing my hair aside, she swiftly tied it around my hairline.

"Don't let anyone know who you are," she cautioned. "I can't begin to fathom the dangers that might lie ahead for you, and I refuse to contemplate them."

I tried to steady my breathing as I grabbed her boots and tied them as tightly as possible to compensate for the size difference. Once secure, we continued a little further down the hall until we approached a set of stairs leading to what looked like a cellar door.

Fiona reached into the corset she still wore and retrieved a small pouch. She threw it at me, the coins jingling as I caught it.

"Gold. You're going to need it to survive."

Toying with the coin purse, I noticed another missed detail: my engagement ring. Pulling it off, my fingers shook as I placed it in her palm. A small smile formed across her face as she embraced me tightly. I squeezed her, knowing that this might be the last time I ever saw her.

"Please don't die." Her eyes were misty as she pulled away.

Smiling, I gave her a confident nod. "Not today."

With Fiona's instructions firmly in mind, I slipped through the cellar doors and traversed the castle's courtyard with the stealth of a ghost—each step calculated and cautious.

The castle had grown quiet with the last guests' departure from the party. Despite the biting cold, I pressed forward. Reaching the royal stables, I mentally inventoried my supplies: a cloak, a sword, provisions, and whatever else I could carry without slowing me down.

Opening the doors, I sought out Topher's horse—Jupiter. Soft neighs echoed through the stables. His eager, brown eyes met mine, and his snow-white coat shone in the moonlight from the cracks in the walls.

Entering his space, I quickly stuffed a mouthful of hay in his mouth, trying to hush him. It seemed to do the trick, and I took advantage of his feast to grab his saddle. The soft jingling of the strap hitting his stomach along with his loud chomps filled my ears. Drowning in my own urgency, I didn't hear the approaching footsteps until they were practically on top of me.

"Genevieve?"

I twisted myself around, eyes focusing on Topher's tall frame coming from the shadows of the stalls. Looking surprised to see me, he took a few cautious steps forward—like a child with a wild animal.

"What are you doing out here?"

I could have asked him the same.

I knew he roamed the castle grounds on nights he couldn't sleep, but out of all places, he had to pick *here*? Now?

I wanted to explain all this to him, but I couldn't. Time was not on my side. As if proving my point, shouts from the castle reached our ears, commanding others to find the princess and seize her.

Commands to find *me*.

"Topher, I'm sorry but I can't talk right now. *Please*. I have to get out of here!"

He took a moment to look back towards the castle and his face became uneasy as he looked back at me. "Is this about Xander? Genevieve, running away isn't the solution. You know that!"

My heart sank. "No! It's not Xander. I don't have time for this!"

"We can go to your father! *Together*. I was there; I can vouch for you. But running awa—"

"My *father*?" I blurted in a hushed scream, tears welling in my eyes. "My father... He... I..."

I couldn't get the words out.

Finally recognizing my struggle, he rushed to my side like he always did—trusting me without getting any answers. His large blue eyes looked down on me, somehow still glowing even in the darkness of night as he helped me finish my task.

His silent understanding was my saving grace, and one day, I would repay him.

I swiftly secured the cloak and sword on my back, panic gripping the base of my chest. Topher remained in a confused and worried daze, watching me intently. Despite my strong urge to sit him down and explain everything, I couldn't delay any longer.

"There's no time to explain but I need your trust. Nothing is what it seems right now." Looking back at Castle Quinn, I could feel the tingling again in my fingers as the voices grew closer. "*Please*. Find Fiona! She knows everything and will explain—"

Before I could finish my plea, his strong, calloused hands caressed my cheeks, drawing my attention back as soft lips graced my own.

The stubble of his beard tickled my chin, and my eyes slowly fluttered closed in a moment of pure bliss. My arms distinctively draped around his tall frame and pulled him close.

In the chaos of the world around us, time seemed to slow as our kiss deepened. Topher's tongue traced my lips with a desperate invitation. Instinctively, I welcomed him, and his tongue slipped into my mouth. Our struggle for dominance made it a messy, emotional kiss—one that ended far too soon.

When we broke apart, our foreheads rested against each other's, our breathing fast and frantic. His eyes bore into mine, searching for anything that would help him understand. The intensity of the kiss lingered, but as the voices drew closer, the urgency of my situation overshadowed the moment.

Regretfully, I pulled back, not wanting the moment to end.

As I took Topher in one last time, he leaned down and with a final, lingering touch of our lips, he effortlessly helped me onto Jupiter.

Our eyes locked for one more heart-wrenching moment, one filled with affection, longing, and fear.

"Come back home to me," he said firmly.

Not a request, but a demand.

I nodded as I pulled the hood of my cloak over my curls. My focus landed on the path ahead to where the castle gates stood cracked open—my sole means of escape.

"Find Fiona," I urgently whispered, not daring to meet his eyes. "She'll explain everything. And tell my aunt—tell *Liliana* —that I'm sorry."

With one final, deep breath, I urged Jupiter away from the stables and into a gallop. I didn't look back, not at Topher, or my home, or even to check if the guards were closing in. My attention remained fixed ahead, and my heart raced faster the closer I came to freedom.

Approaching the looming gates, I could see them beginning to creak shut. By some miracle, the small drawbridge over the moat was still lowered—I had a fighting chance!

Refusing to let panic consume me, I urged Jupiter faster. The open land of my kingdom beckoned, but the window of freedom was closing rapidly. The moans of the gates creaking shut mocked me, fueling my determination. With one last push to my steed, the world blurred around us as we raced toward the narrowing gap of metal bars.

Time itself slowed and stretched into one final, heart-pounding moment.

Just as it seemed the gates would crush us, Jupiter's powerful muscles propelled us forward through the narrowing space. Just as we landed on the wooden bridge, the gates slammed shut behind us with a deafening thud, sealing our escape.

We did it! We fucking did it!

I took a moment to savor the victory, frantic voices of guards shouting from behind consuming us like a vice. They screamed to raise the drawbridge so I wouldn't escape.

But they were too late.

Not wasting another moment, we were off.

Their distant yells, filled with anger and frustration, faded as I escaped beyond their reach. The world outside the castle walls was already shrouded in darkness and uncertainty.

But I was ready.

And there was no turning back now.

CHAPTER 11

IT MUST HAVE BEEN WELL past midnight by the time I managed to elude the guards trailing me.

Venturing off the paved path that led from the castle grounds, I plunged deep into the forest until the voices of my once-friends faded into distant echoes. Now alone and disoriented, I faced the unsettling realization that I had no idea where the hell I was heading.

Fiona's instructions provided me with a *somewhat* detailed description of my destination. However, now that I was off any road, there was zero chance I would see a sign that would help point me in the right direction. It was too dangerous for me to be out in the open, so I was left with little to no guidance.

Relying on the constellations and protection from the gods, I looked up to find a clear sky, the North Star shining brightly.

Guess I'm heading north.

Momentarily out of immediate danger, the loneliness of the woods quickly took its toll. The night's events had left me utterly drained, both mentally and physically. No matter how hard I tried to focus on what was in front of me, my mind wandered. Gripping Jupiter's reins, my hands ached as much as my heart. I could no longer hold back the tears that blurred my vision.

Gods, I'm a mess.

Each heightened emotion fought for dominance in my mind. I was overwhelmed with fear, lost in an unfamiliar wood with no clear direction, with no home to return to—not unless I wanted to spend the rest of my days behind bars. I was also mourning my father, or at least trying to. It still didn't seem real that he was gone. Images of his lifeless body looped in my mind as anger threatened to consume me—anger at Xander and that...*thing*.

The Shadow Walker.

Not to mention, I was fucking confused by everything Fiona revealed. Could this huntsman really help me, or was I doomed to do this on my own? Maybe bringing Topher along would have helped me navigate this new world, but after that kiss... I knew it was better he hadn't joined.

That kiss was the last thing I expected, the last thing I *needed*. Even with the coldness of the night creeping around, the sensation of his lips against mine lingered, and I subconsciously reached my free hand up to touch them.

If I closed my eyes tightly enough, I could still see the way his calloused hands cradled my face—his touch both tender and possessive. The way he held me was a stark contrast to his roughness during training. It revealed a sort of vulnerability and dominance I didn't know he possessed. The warmth of his breath mingled with mine, the taste of him on my lips—it was everything I could have wanted from a kiss and more.

But I was angry.

Not *fully* at Topher—though I had my fair share of being

touched without permission for one evening—but mostly at myself. If he had truly felt this way all along, I could have chosen him as my suitor before Father chose for me. He could have been the one I was celebrating with this week.

If he had been mine, maybe Father would still be breathing.

But could his display of affection have been brought on by the fact that he could no longer have me? After all, his advances only started the moment Xander and I were introduced. Knowing I was someone else's bride could have pushed him over the edge.

But not just anyone's bride. I was about to be a *foreign enemy's bride*—the enemy he had trained his whole life to fight.

Was it love, or was it the fear of losing me?

Every thought, emotion, and memory flooded my head until I felt it would explode. Pushing them aside, the only thing that mattered now was finding who had done this to my father and proving my innocence.

Consumed by my internal battle, I hadn't realized how lost we were in the forest. When I looked around, it was clear we had ventured deeper than we should have, the path no longer in sight. With the moon hiding behind a few stray clouds, the night had become dark. Straining my eyes, I could only see a few feet in front of me.

Including the very *large* branch that hung directly on our path.

I didn't see it in enough time, and my chest collided with the unforgiving wood, sending shock waves of pain through my body as I was thrown off Jupiter and onto the cold, hard forest floor.

Clawing at my lungs, I fought to regain my breath. The moon seemed to laugh at my continued misfortune. Silently cursing it, I swallowed my pain and forced myself to sit up straight.

My heart sank as I watched Jupiter, startled by my fall, bolt from the grassy carpet now staining my cloak. Panic built in my chest as he darted further into the dark wood.

Fucking great.

Even an owl on a nearby branch hooted in laughter before flying off into the night. Slowly picking myself up off the ground, I felt around my back, double-checking that I still had the sword strapped there. Thank the gods, I did.

The strange dagger and the bag of coins were still strapped tightly at my hip. Unfortunately, the rest of my supplies were strapped to Jupiter. If I had any chance of surviving the night, I needed to find a place to rest, *fast*.

Alone and disoriented in the heart of an unfamiliar forest, all I could do was walk. Where exactly was I walking?

That, I had no fucking clue.

My feet stumbled as I fought to avoid the uneven terrain and tangled underbrush that clawed at my clothing.

Fiona's large boots did *nothing* to make the journey any easier.

Though it felt like half the night had passed since I fell, it was most likely only an hour or two. With sleep deprivation closing in, each step became more difficult.

Faint, strange whispers filled my ears the deeper into the woods I ventured. It could have been my imagination, or it could have been another creature of darkness coming to take me away. If I listened closely, I could swear the whispers were calling my name.

Ignore it, Genevieve. You're just scared and tired.

My steps became wobbly, and I feared passing out where I stood. But my mind urged me to keep going just a little further. Listening to my inner voice, I resisted my overwhelming desire to give up and sleep on the ground. I *had* to push through.

Something deep within me felt pulled toward something in the distance. When I tried to go another direction, the burning in my fingers ignited again, leaving me no choice but to follow where that strange pull led. The further I followed, the more my surroundings began to shift.

The dense, dark forest began to thin, allowing slivers of moonlight to pierce through the canopy. Even the air changed —the scent of damp soil giving way to the distant aroma of wood smoke and cooking fires. The magnetic pull was stronger than ever, and soon, I found myself stepping out of the forest's embrace, standing on the outskirts of a small village.

A weathered wooden sign welcomed travelers.

"Welcome All Who Enter Heim."

Well, at least I found the right village.

The village was picturesque, nestled in a clearing between the woods. In all my eighteen years, I had barely been able to leave the grounds of Castle Quinn, let alone travel to the surrounding continents—Father's order.

But this village seemed strangely familiar. Tiny cottages with thatched roofs were huddled together, aglow with warm candlelight. Winding cobblestone streets and vines adorned with vibrant buds spilled from window boxes, casting splashes of life onto the muted palette of night.

Distant voices, gentle laughter, and the strumming of a lute blended into a melodic symphony, guiding me to the village.

As I approached, the pull grew stronger—like an invisible hand guiding me. I suddenly felt awake with excitement. Finally, I'd found the source of the laughter and noise, and my heart raced as I stood in front of the doors leading to a small, old tavern.

The tips of my fingers began to tingle with anticipation as I fixated on the center of the tavern's door. Etched into the massive wooden barrier that separated me from my sanctuary, was a perfect rose and crown—precisely as Fiona had described.

This is the tavern I was supposed to find? Maybe I'll survive the night.

My breathing quickened as my fingers brushed the carving. The tavern's door bore a testament to skilled artisans, featuring a flawless rose illuminated by exterior torchlight. Delicate thorns adorned the lifelike stem, forming a captivating semi-circle. Atop the rose, a regal crown mirrored the one I had worn earlier that night.

Taking a deep breath to steady my racing heart, I raised the hood of my cloak and pushed the door open. As it swung inward, I was greeted by a wave of warmth and the familiar scents of wine and ale. I looked around to find the cozy interior featuring tapestries of scenes from old legends. Despite the late hour, the atmosphere was alive with an infectious spirit.

Patrons huddled at wooden tables and booths, clinking tankards together while a minstrel played a lively tune on a small corner stage, drawing laughter and applause from the audience.

Scanning the room for the man with the scar-covered eye, I saw nothing, but a large group of *very* drunk men huddled together at one of the larger tables. The moment they noticed me, their smiles and stares grew more intense. Swallowing, I pulled my hood tighter and continued into the tavern.

At the back, a small bar with a young barmaid chatting to a few patrons awaited. If anyone here knew of a huntsman, it would be her. Keeping my head high, I passed the table of men, avoiding eye contact. Their whistles and kissy noises sparked irritation in my gut, but I had bigger fish to fry than telling off a group of drunk pricks.

Taking an open stool, I double-checked to see if the fabric around my head was still in place before hesitantly pulling my hood down.

With glistening dark skin, pulled back curly black hair, and captivating hazel eyes, the barmaid turned towards me as I settled into my spot. I quickly lowered my fingers from my head and began to fiddle with them.

Seeming to notice my anxious fidgeting, she greeted me with a warm smile. "What can I get for ya, suga?" Her words danced in broken dialect.

Nervousness caused my throat to dry. "I just have a question for you."

Armed with a rag and an empty stein, she poisoned herself. "I'm all ears, lovely."

Leaning in, I lowered my voice, "I'm in search of a man who has been rumored to frequent here. He's um...a huntsman, but I don't know his name or what he looks like other than a scar over his right eye. Have you seen someone like him here?"

Her eyes darted around the tavern, and she seemed to tense up as she locked on a corner of the room before meeting my gaze again. After a tense pause, she leaned in closer. "Aye, a 'untsman comes evry' now an den for business. But folks 'round 'ere don talk too much 'bout 'em. Keeps to 'em self mostly—deals with tings folks in des parts like to forget."

"Do you know where I might begin to look for him? Even if it's just a starting point."

Before she could respond, a heavy arm draped over my shoulder, bringing with it the overwhelming stench of body odor and alcohol. Fighting the urge to recoil, I followed the arm until I was face-to-face with one of the inebriated men from the large table.

I had *severely* underestimated how intoxicated they truly were. He was a hulking figure, and the weight of his arm alone hinted at his massive build. Instinctively, I knew I didn't want any trouble.

"What's a little doe like you doing in a place like this?" he slurred, poking my nose with his stubby index finger. "I didn't plan on hunting, but it looks like I caught myself a prize."

A sloppy, lopsided grin spread across his face, revealing a set of uneven teeth through his thick, brown beard. Politely removing his arm from my shoulder, I tried to convey my complete lack of interest without seeming too rude.

"No thanks."

As I turned back to the barmaid, I felt his hand clamp roughly onto my shoulder, yanking me back so violently I nearly toppled off my stool.

The barmaid slammed her rag onto the counter with a whip. "Oi!" she hollered. "Devland, dats 'nough! Don makes me 'ave to kick ya out for da tird time dis week!"

She was apparently well-acquainted with this sort of trou-blemaker; her words dripped with irritation and authority.

Devland, as I now knew him, turned his drunken ire towards the bar. "And don't make me tell the owner what a *slut* his favorite wench is, Mags," he sneered. "Though I reckon he already knows."

She took a step back. Mag's eyes locked onto mine, a silent apology conveyed in the exchange.

My heart raced, and Devland's clammy hands seized my jaw, brutally turning my face towards his. "I've always heard a redhead is good in the sheets," he leered obscenely, tugging on one of my curls. "Care to prove 'em right?"

"Hasn't anyone ever told you that *'no.'* is a full sentence?" I managed through my gripped jaw.

His toothy grin widened. "No."

Flashes of Xander touching me against my will flooded my vision, bringing back all the anger I had felt. Using my rage to fuel me, I wretched my jaw free from his grasp and shot up from my stool, sending it clattering to the floor.

Catching him off guard, I didn't hesitate as I clenched my fist and delivered a solid blow to the corner of his mouth. The impact was direct and unforgiving—just as I had been taught.

Clutching his face, Devland's eyes widened in shock.

Shaking my hand to ease the pain, I stood my ground. His gaze darkened, and his breathing grew erratic as he removed his hand from his face.

"You'll pay for that, *red!*"

I stood firm, unwavering against his threats. After the horrors I witnessed that night, Devland was the least of my concerns. The dagger hummed at my hip, and I instinctively edged my hand closer to it—ready for the drunk bastard.

A large shadow moved behind him, and my breath caught at the thought of another creature of the night discovering me. Shifting my focus from the staggering drunk, I scanned for any trace of crimson eyes but found none.

A cloaked figure emerged from a dimly lit booth in the back of the tavern and strode purposefully in our direction. Without warning, the figure closed the distance with impressive speed. In a single fluid motion, he seized Devland by the shoulder, pulling him back with unexpected strength. Stumbling backward, Devland's eyes briefly flickered with fear before anger quickly overtook his features as he sized up the stranger.

"I thought we told you to stay out, *dog*!" he slurred.

Before Devland could make another move, the stranger's mighty fist connected with his jaw in precise strike—the impact followed by a loud thud as Devland's body crumpled to the floor.

The entire bar fell into stunned silence, and like a slap in the face, the confrontation was over.

Even the music stopped.

Finally realizing what had happened to their friend, the group of drunk men rose from their chairs. Taking a few sloppy steps forward, some reached for their swords strapped at their hips, their heavy eyes fixed on the cloaked man before me.

Turning his attention to the men, he lowered the hood of his cloak with his two large, tanned, tattooed hands. The sight of his face halted the oncoming men. Long, shaggy hair as black as night spilled out, but I strained to catch a glimpse of his other features.

A low, almost growl echoed from his chest, drawing collective gasps from the men. Exchanging uncertain glances, one by one, they sheathed their swords, backing down. Their eyes briefly flickered to Devland, unconscious on the sticky floor, before returning to their interrupted conversation.

Feeling the tensed air clear, I finally felt like I could breathe again. "Thank you," I whispered.

At the sound of my voice, his tense shoulders seemed to slightly relax. When he turned to face me, a small gasp escaped my lips as I fixed on three deep scars covering his right eye and much of his face. Our eyes locked, his widening before relaxing —a fleeting glimpse of emotion gone as quickly as it had appeared.

This the huntsman Fiona wanted me to find! And he just... protected me?

Locked in our stare-off, I was mesmerized by the scars adorning his face. They didn't mar his features. No, they seemed purposefully etched, as if crafted by the hands of gods themselves. The lines traced his olive skin from the tip of his widow's peak to the start of his thick beard.

One gold eye gleamed like warm honey, while the other icy blue eye, marked by scars, shimmered like the first frost of winter. They studied me just as intensely as I studied him. After a moment, he seemed to have seen enough and spun on his heels.

The patrons parted as if he was the plague and, with unearthly grace, he strode straight to the tavern's exit and out the door.

CHAPTER 12

COLLECTING MYSELF, I burst through the tavern door with the same urgency that had gripped the huntsman.

Despite my attempts to keep up, his large strides propelled him further into the darkness of the village.

"Hey!" My voice was swallowed by the cold air. "Please, wait up!"

He showed no signs of slowing. My stubbornness kicked in as I hiked up the hem of my dress and pushed forward into a light jog—determined not to let him get away so easily.

Though lacking grace, I rapidly closed the gap between us.

Looking over his shoulder, his gold eye gleamed with a hint of curiosity before he rolled them both and returned his attention forward.

I *refused* to give up.

"Just hear me out," I panted. "I need to ask yo—"

My voice broke as I tripped over the uneven cobblestone, collapsing to the ground. Bearing the brunt of the impact, my knees instantly welled with blood from the unforgiving pavement. Seating myself, I winced from the sting of my injured knees.

"Lovely," I muttered under my breath.

Loud footsteps approached, making me forget about my blood-stained knees. I raised my gaze to find the huntsman towering over me; disappointment etched on his beautiful face. His penetrating eyes scanned me, and although they were fascinating, I tried not to linger on the scars around his blue one.

"Do you enjoy getting yourself into trouble?" his voice rumbled, low and raspy as he reached out a hand, "or are you simply *that* unlucky?"

The sound of his voice quickened my heartbeat and tightened my throat. Hesitantly, I accepted his extended hand and as we touched, a surge of electricity shot through me, making me gasp. It felt like rubbing my feet on carpet and then touching metal.

Effortlessly lifting me to my feet, he scanned me once more with his mismatched eyes, seemingly unfazed by the spark. I withdrew my hand and tried to conceal the blush creeping onto my face.

Had he felt that too?

"Thank you...again," I managed, dusting off my dirtied dress.

With a nod and a grunt, he prepared to turn away. Quickly, I positioned myself in front of him.

"Unlucky *and* annoying," he stated bluntly.

Exhaustion and determination pulsed through my veins as I rolled my eyes and planted my hands on my hips. "Look. I'll make this as quick as possible since you seem to be in such a godsdamn hurry. I'm in search of a huntsman who frequents this village. He is supposed to have a scar over his eye," I pointed to my own eye to illustrate. "Before I waste any more of my time running after a random man, are you that huntsman or not?"

A hint of a smile tugged at the corners of the mysterious man's mouth, and my eyes narrowed in on the tip of a sharp canine escaping from his lips.

He crossed his arms, chuckling softly. "And what would a *little lass* like you need from a huntsman?" he challenged. "Lost your favorite dolly?"

Narrowing my eyes at the *"little lass"* comment, I ignored it. "Does it matter?"

His eyes seemed to glow in the dark, each color taking on a different intensity. "It does depending on what you need from me. I don't go on just any job that gets thrown my way. We both have precious time we can't waste. As you said, I'm in a hurry."

Reaching under my cloak, I grabbed the dagger from my belt and displayed it in my palms. His amusement instantly vanished as his face fell.

"My father was murdered with this dagger just hours ago," I confessed, my throat tightening as I voiced the painful truth for the first time. "A shadow figure appeared out of nowhere and stabbed him in the back. I have good reason to believe that it was a Shadow Walker summoned specifically to ensure *I* was framed for his death. I need to find out who and...and I need to kill them."

His face twisted in disgust. "I don't fuck with Shadow Walkers anymore," he stated plainly, attempting to sidestep me again.

As quickly as he moved, I moved with him, blocking his path once more. "*Please*," I begged. "I have no one else, and I can...I can pay you!" Remembering the sack of money Fiona had given me, I snatched it from the strap around my waist. "It's not much, but once we finish this, I can reward you more than you could ever need."

His face gave no indication of what he was thinking or feeling, he just kept his eyes on me, and I panicked. I tossed him the sack, and he caught it with lightning-flash reflexes.

Eyes still on me, he inspected the fabric and raised it to his scarred ear, the coins jingling together as he shook the pouch. He could have easily turned and run with it, but something told me I could trust him.

So, I did.

Still holding onto the coins, he crossed his arms. "You think I'd risk my life for some chump change?"

I blinked. "Isn't it enough?"

He let out a low, humorless chuckle. "If a small sack of gold was all it took, I would have died years ago from petty missions."

"I already told you I could pay you more when this was finished! I have nothing else to barter with you."

He took a step forward. "And I should believe you?"

I gritted my teeth. "You don't even know me."

"Exactly," he stated. "I have never seen you before and trust me, I see *everything*. So why me, huh? Why seek me out when you can hire any mercenary that crosses your path?"

"I don't need a mercenary. I need *you*."

He snorted, "You need a miracle, and I'm as sinful as it gets."

Heat crawled up my neck, but I shoved it down. "You don't understand—"

"No, you don't understand," he cut in. "Shadow Walkers aren't some back-alley thieves you can track down and arrest.

They are pure darkness and a vengeful Witch would be even worse."

I swallowed hard, my pulse roaring in my ears. "Then help me."

"No."

The word was so sharp, so final, it almost knocked the air from my lungs. But I squared my shoulders, refusing to back down. "People think I'm the one wh-who did it. I left to find *you,* and now I'm on my own. I even lost my fucking horse! Please, if I don't get help from you... I don't know what else to do."

The moon cast long shadows on the cobblestone beneath our feet as we stood locked in an unspoken standoff. My heart continued to race—every passing second felt like an eternity.

Finally, he let out a long breath. "I'm telling you; Shadow Walkers are not to be messed with. They destroy nearly everything in their path. There is no stopping them once they have been released."

My gaze remained fixed on him, my eyes uncontrollably tracing the moonlit contours that perfectly outlined every curve of his strong features.

"But it *can* be destroyed if the Witch who summoned it is dead, right? That's what I'm here to do: to kill the Witch behind this."

"That may be true, but Shadow Walkers are unlike other creatures that use regular magic," his voice carried the weight of experience. "They're bred in the deepest parts of hell, created by pure, *dark* magic by Witches who only seek destruction. When summoned, they're uncontrollable." He gestured toward the dagger still clutched against my chest. "That dagger you hold—I haven't seen something like that in years. Whoever you're dealing with is powerful, and the Shadow Walker they summoned is even worse."

I shook my head. "No, this dagger was gifted to me. The Shadow Walker must have seen it in my room and used it once it was summoned."

"Well, kid, maybe the person who gifted you that dagger is behind it. Thought of that?"

I kind of had, but Commander Robert had no gain in killing my father. "It wasn't him. I know it in my gut."

"Regardless," his brows furrowed, "it's still dangerous. More dangerous than you can handle on your own."

"Then help me! If someone is summoning Shadow Walkers for random attacks, it could be worse than anything we've faced with the Fae. I cannot let others suffer like my father did. I won't."

"I told you," he said, voice low and annoyed. "I don't fuck with Shadow Walkers anymore."

I clenched my fists. "And I told *you*—I have no one else."

The silence stretched between us, thick with something I couldn't name. He didn't speak, didn't move, just watched me. And the longer he did, the harder it was to breathe.

The seconds dragged, and just when I thought he might walk away, he exhaled sharply and ran a hand down his face. "This won't be easy, you know."

My head snapped up. "So you'll help me?"

"I have a feeling even if I kept saying no, you would follow me home until I said yes. So, to save us both a headache, yes. I'll help you."

I smiled. "You won't regret this! I promise. I think I've thanked you enough times for you to get the message, but—thank you."

"A part of me is already regretting it," he mumbled.

Taking a step forward, I reached for the sack of coins still in his hands. "Well, I suppose I could take this away if you're unsure..."

His gaze softened slightly as he withdrew his hand from my reach. "Very well," he agreed, "Give me the dagger, and I'll begin in the morning. I'll find you once it's complete."

My stomach dropped. "No."

A dark eyebrow rose. "No? Look, I need the dagger if I'm going to do this."

"No, I mean, I'm coming with you."

He barked a laugh. "Yeah, I don't think so. I work alone."

"Well, you'll need to get over it for this one. I'm coming with you, or I'll find someone else. I need to do this. I *need* to be the one who ends that Witch's life."

Gold and sapphire eyes stared at me before a smirk formed on his lips. "Annoying indeed. Fine. If you think you have it in you to take a life, who am I to stop you? We'll start at dawn. Until then, find a place to rest and gather your strength. I'll get you in the morning."

Gratitude welled up within me. "Do I get to know your name? Or shall I call you *'Huntsman'*?"

His lips curved. "Ryder."

"Ryder," I repeated, the name feeling comforting on my lips.

I stood there, like a *fool* just staring and smiling at him. He shifted uncomfortably. "You know, it's normally common practice to give a name once one is given to you."

My mind scattered as I tried to think of a name, *any name*, to give him. Obviously, he couldn't know my real one. Fiona made it clear I was not to let others know who I was, especially someone I was now *paying*.

I had to be someone new, someone unknown, someone without the weight of the kingdom's future on their shoulders.

The heat in my cheeks only grew as I spewed my first lie to the Huntsman. "Rose. My name is Rose."

Ryder cocked his head to the side, his eyebrows rising with curiosity.

Could he tell I was lying? I had been told before that I wasn't good at it...

"Goodnight, kid," he replied, turning away and disappearing into the shadows of the village.

Without another word, he was gone, and I was, once again, alone.

Any peaceful sleep I was getting was rudely interrupted by a wave of cold water soaking my face.

Jolting from my sleep and gasping for air, I nearly tumbled off my makeshift bed of hay barrels. As my eyes desperately tried to adjust to the morning sun, I was greeted with Ryder's smirking face and an empty pail of what I assumed was once water in his hands.

Leaning in closer, he inhaled deeply before nodding. "Yep. That should help with the smell."

Still partially reeling from the shock of the icy water, I raised my hands to my head to check to see if the headwrap had shifted from either my sleep or the unexpected shower. Thank the gods, it hadn't.

"What the hell is your issue?"

He placed the pail down. "I told you I would find you. All I had to do was follow the *smell*."

His large fingers pointed to the right of me. Following his gaze, my face dropped in shock as I realized I had chosen a *pig pen* to rest my head.

To say I was exhausted by the time he left me the previous night is an understatement. Not caring where I slept, I chose the first available spot I could find. Considering I gave Ryder all my money and Devland was most likely still knocked out on the tavern floor, I did my best.

Which obviously was *not* my best.

Rising from the ground, I immediately understood what Ryder had meant. The stench was *overwhelming*, and I could see bits of straw sticking out from my curls in my peripheral vision.

Gods, I must have looked like a mess.

Suppressing a cringe, I could practically hear my aunt's voice in my head, yelling at me for looking so un-princess-like. Unfortunately for her, it worked in my favor.

"Maybe you are unlucky." Ryder amused.

Removing the strands from my hair, I shot him a pointed look. "And maybe *you're* the annoying one," I retorted. "I didn't exactly have a luxurious, warm bed to sleep in last night. I did the best I could, okay?"

"And a pig pin was the best you could do?"

I scoffed. "Listen, *Mr. Huntsman.* Not all of us–"

I suddenly forgot how to breathe, the air hitching in my throat as my gaze met Ryder's. The previous night's darkness and his concealing cloak had left much to the imagination. However, in the clear morning light, Ryder stood before me, in all his glory.

And damn, was he glorious.

Gone was the black cloak, and I could easily understand why those men had cowered in fear. He towered over me; way taller than any other man I had met. I doubted if the top of my head even reached his chest. His height *alone* was intimidating.

Even with the thickness and wildness of his beard, he didn't appear unkept. The morning light kissed his skin, emphasizing the olive hue that spoke of his background and extensive time in the sun. His almond-shaped eyes followed my every move, and his wide nostrils subtly flared.

Ryder had rolled up the sleeves of his beige tunic to showcase his powerful, tattooed arms. The tunic's collar was slightly open, revealing a patch of black chest hair—just enough to say "hello."

I couldn't help but subconsciously bite my lip at the sight.

A perfectly fitted brown leather vest accentuated his body, seamlessly blending with the sword scabbard strapped to his back. His black trousers clung to his robust legs, highlighting their true size, while knee-high riding boots gleamed in the early morning light. A belt draped across his hips, adorned with various weapons.

Ryder's longer hair was half-pulled back, the remainder cascading gracefully over his shoulders. For such a feminine hairstyle, I had never seen something more manly.

When he cleared his throat, I was violently pulled out of my trance. Heat immediately rose to my cheeks, and I tried to avert my gaze, but it was hard to look away. Before I did, I could have sworn his cheeks held a faint flush as well.

Shifting his attention behind him, he reached for something out of my view. Before my curiosity could kick in, a pile of clothes came hurtling my way. Catching them before they met a piggy pin doom, I looked up in confusion.

"As much as I would love to smell you our whole trip," he stated sarcastically, "what you're wearing is impractical for anything other than tea-time with the queen."

"I wasn't aware you were in the fashion industry, Huntsman."

He grunted. "A dress won't help you if we have to hike or run, and those boots are too big. No wonder you tripped last night."

I somehow had forgotten the tumble.

Looking down, I found patches of dried blood that stained Fiona's frock, and I had to fight the flashbacks of my father's bloody body from probing my mind. I squeezed my eyes shut, trying to block them out before they became too overwhelming.

Swallowing my fear, I opened my eyes and nodded. As I turned toward the *Rose and Crown*, Ryder let out a loud click, stopping me before I ventured too far.

"Woah, woah! Where do you think you're going?"

"To change in the tavern?"

He shook his head. "It's six in the morning. Nothing is open, and I can promise you, you'll face more than that gaped-tooth drunk if you go banging on those doors at this hour."

Sighing, I placed an empty hand on my hip. "And where do you expect me to change?"

His long, knowing smile was the only answer I received before he turned and started walking towards the woods.

I couldn't tell if my shivering was the result of the early morning air or the fact that I was changing behind a oak tree in the middle of the woods!

Ryder's *brilliant idea* for a "discreet location" to change just happened to be outside the village's border amidst a cluster of trees and shrubbery.

And it was beyond *embarrassing*!

I was the princess and sole heir of this entire damn kingdom and here I was, naked as a newborn baby out in the open! Oh, if Fiona could see me now—she would have a damn field day.

Now matter how embarrassed I was or how much I didn't want to admit Ryder was right...my previous attire had been *highly* impractical. The more I changed into the clothes, the more at ease I felt. My fingers grazed the sleek black leather of the riding pants. They clung snugly to my legs, allowing for effortless movement without undue constriction.

A little long, but they would do.

I slipped the tunic over my head, the fabric soft and breathable, offering a comforting touch against my skin. The boots provided were sturdy and surprisingly comfortable, with just enough heel for riding but not so high as to hinder my walking.

And dammit—they were my perfect size.

Surprisingly, he also provided me with a belt to secure the dagger. For someone who just met me, he sure trusted me with the dagger we were using for this Witch hunt. Considering I knew just as much about him as he knew about me, I wouldn't complain.

I stepped out of the discarded pile of clothes, and my heart sank as I thought of Fiona. She had risked everything to smuggle me out of that castle, and I could only pray she was safe with Topher. My stomach twisted at the thought of her being in danger, but her brother would protect her.

I just *knew* it.

Holding her clothes in my arms, I brought the fabrics to my lips and gave them a parting farewell. Taking a deep breath, I flung the pile into a nearby stream and watched the colors sink and float along the water. Once gone, I returned to Ryder who awaited at the top of the hill.

"Any reason you threw that pile of clothes into the water?"

Feeling more comfortable, I adjusted my new attire. "It wasn't like I could use them anyway. Thought it was the most practical way of disposing them."

He scoffed. "Sure until they get caught around the neck of a swimming bear. And here I thought we would only kill a Witch on this journey."

My eyes narrowed. "I think the bear will live."

"Littering is a crime punishable by death, too."

No, it wasn't.

"I'm sure I'll be okay, just like the bear."

The corner of his mouth perked up. "You don't need to tell me I was right. I can already tell you feel better in those clothes."

"A million times," I admitted.

As much as I didn't want to give him the satisfaction, I couldn't deny how much better I felt. I looked over myself, and a strange realization hit me. I had just met this stranger less than six hours ago and one of the first things he did was give me a pile of clean clothes. Clean clothes…sized for a *woman*.

My stomach sank as I wondered if I was pulling him away from a wife and family. I subtly snuck a look at his left hand—he bore no wedding band on his finger, but that could signify very little in his line of work.

"What's that face for?"

Lost in thought, I must have showcased my guilt. "I, uh, was just wondering if the owner of these clothes might miss them out of her wardrobe."

Ryder looked me up and down and his face dropped.

A small growl escaped his throat before he looked away. "No, she won't. They're my sisters."

"Well, next time you see her, tell her I appreciate her taste in style."

His jaw tightened. "She passed away a while ago. I haven't had the heart to toss her stuff yet. So, it looks like you're in luck."

My face dropped, and I instantly regretted asking the question. However, a small part of me was relieved knowing I wasn't stealing his wife's clothes.

"I'm so sorry. I didn't mean to pry."

"It's fine," he stated. "You're not the only one who has lost people."

Turning away, he continued up the hill to where his horse waited at the wood's edge. The black steed was nearly the same shade as Ryder's hair, by far one of the most beautiful horses I had ever seen in my eighteen years. Even from a distance, I could tell how well it was cared for.

Ryder, a good distance ahead of me, called down from the top of the hill. "I think I found something of yours."

Climbing the hill, I could barely make out the glowing outline of Jupiter. His soft neighs reached my ears the closer I got, and excitement filled me. Sprinting up the remaining slope, I rushed to the horse's side.

"Jupiter!" I exclaimed. "Where the hell did you find him?"

"He was enjoying some of the food I left out last night," he explained, approaching the white steed and patting his mane. "I remembered you said you lost your horse, so I figured he could be yours." I opened my mouth, but he halted me with a raised hand. "Don't say 'thank you'—I get it."

Instead, I smiled and returned to petting Jupiter, pressing tiny kisses along his snout. Ryder turned to his own horse, checking all the reins and gear he had strapped to the beast.

"What's his name?"

"Reaper. And she's a girl."

"Spooky name for a horse..."

After confirming everything was to his satisfaction, Ryder effortlessly mounted Reaper. "We better get going. We have a few days' journey ahead before our first stop, and I don't want to face the first snow of the season."

"I doubt it'll snow this early," I said as I swiftly mounted Jupiter just as skillfully as the huntsman had his. "There hasn't been a ring around the moon. My mother used to tell me that once you can see a ring around the moon, a snowfall is to follow."

Turning, he gawked at me with a blank stare. "I'm telling you right now, I've spent a good majority of my life looking at the moon, and I have never seen a damn ring around it," he said blandly.

I shot him an annoyed glare, but a low rumble from my

stomach quickly distracted my attention. Ignoring the sound, Ryder cleared his throat, signaling it was time to get to business.

"Alright," he began, "a few ground rules for the road. First, always stay close to me. This isn't a leisurely stroll through the countryside. We're on a mission, and it could get dangerous. Second, don't draw attention to yourself. We're trying to move discreetly, so no shouting, big movements, and no starting any brawls."

"Fine, fine. I'll try not to engage in any tavern fights this time."

"Third, trust my judgment. I've been doing this for a long time and know what I'm doing. If I say to hide or stay put, you do it. Got it?"

I straightened my posture and gave my finest salute. "Aye-aye, Commander."

He scoffed. "Lastly, if we encounter any other type of creature, including Shadow Walkers, do *exactly* as I say. These woods are filled with creatures and magic I'm sure you haven't encountered in your day-to-day."

I suddenly became nervous, and my stomach dropped to my ass. "What you say goes. I got it."

With a nod, Ryder turned Reaper towards the open road and set the wheels of our "adventure" into motion.

Deep down, I wished I could wake up in my bed—that this was all just a bad dream.

CHAPTER 13

As we rode through the towering trees, the forest unfolded before us.

The morning sun and crisp air infused a sense of tranquility into the atmosphere, offering a delightful change of scenery despite everything. Even the birds serenaded us with their unique melodies as we passed.

Ryder remained silent, his gaze fixed straight ahead on the path. The further we went, the more my curiosity about him intensified. Like a phantom, he practically materialized out of thin air, and it was driving me *crazy*.

While I had encountered men from neighboring kingdoms and distant lands, Ryder was uniquely different. He couldn't have been much older than me, but his eyes carried a maturity that hinted at a past riddled with experiences and hidden secrets.

And my stubborn ass was going to uncover them.

"So," I dragged out the word, "care to tell me a little about yourself?"

"No."

I scoffed. "Well, aren't you just a delight? Come *on*. A little small talk never hurt anyone."

His grip on the reins tightened, but he didn't turn to look at me. "It's not like I'm courting you. We don't need to know more than the bare minimum."

I snorted. "Okay, for one, you *wish* you could court me. And another, you proved my point exactly. I don't even know your last name! *That* is the bare minimum."

"You're not used to someone saying '*no*' to you, are you? What was that phrase you used last night?" He held his finger up to his chin in fake thought. "'No is a full sentence'?"

Silence.

He sighed. "It's Hemming."

Honestly, asking his last name was not the most important question on my list, and I had no clue why I even asked. As a princess, I didn't have a last name—just a first, middle, and title.

Princess Genevieve Rose, heir to the Oprhinian Crown.

Gag. Maybe some small part of me envied that missing piece of my life. The formalities of it all seemed silly outside the grounds of Castle Quinn. Having a last name seemed so... casual, like something a *real* person would have.

"And what brought you to the tavern last night? Do you frequent there often?"

The question hung in the air.

"Business."

"A man of many words, I see."

"Less words, more action. You'll thank me for that one day."

My nose scrunched. "And what kind of *business* was that?"

Ryder's jaw clenched. "I'm a huntsman. I track things, people, creatures, whatever I need to for those who can afford to pay, like little red-headed kids who ask a million questions when they should focus on the road before they lose their horse again."

"This *'little kid'* trope of yours is already getting old." My eyes narrowed, "I'm eighteen, thank you very much."

A loud laugh escaped his throat. "Exactly—a *child*. Anyone who told you otherwise is either a liar or an ass-kisser."

"Like you're much older?"

"Older than *you*."

"By what, a few years? That means *nothing*. Age is but a number. It's about maturity, skills, life experiences—"

"Which you have had at the young age of eighteen? I would *love* to hear those tales. Take your time, I'll wait."

I squared my shoulders, refusing to let his attitude get under my skin. "Well, maybe I have more life experience than you think. For instance, I'm currently dealing with an insufferable huntsman who refuses to share anything about himself!"

"Your determination to dig into my life is a little unsettling. What do you hope to find?"

"A human being," I retorted. "Someone with thoughts, feelings—a past. I refuse to travel with an emotionless mute."

Glancing at me, his gold eye betrayed a hint of amusement. "Is that what you want? A glimpse into my soul? A sob story to bond over?"

"Well, if you have one."

Shrugging, he turned back to the road.

I crossed my arms. "Oh, my gods, there must be more to it than that! What about your childhood? Any family? Friends?"

"Don't have a family and friends are overrated."

"Everyone has a past," I insisted, "something that shaped them. Don't be so cryptic, share a little. Please?"

He groaned, eyes never leaving the path. "Alright, *gods*, if it'll get you to shut up. Since you're so insistent on knowing, I grew up in a small community I'm sure you have never heard of. I learned to survive and fight, and now here I am. Satisfied?"

I frowned. "Hardly. Nothing more exciting to share? No grand adventures, tragic losses, or forbidden romances?"

Or how you got that scar.

A dry, unamused sound escaped his throat. "I have all of that, but it's not as grand as you make it seem. Life on the road isn't a fairytale. It's about survival. No time for romanticizing."

"You're telling me your life is dull?"

His gaze met mine, and for a moment, something unreadable flickered in his eyes. "Far from it. But excitement isn't always a good thing."

"Well, at least tell me about your sister. You said you haven't thrown her stuff out yet. Do you live in that village, or is there a whole wardrobe waiting for me in one of Reaper's satchels? What's her name?"

The loud sigh from him filled the tranquil forest. "Amarisa had an apartment there. I stay there when I'm in town."

Amarisa—a lovely name compared to "*Ryder.*"

My shoulders tightened. "So, you let me change in the middle of a fucking forest instead of taking me back to your sister's flat for some privacy? Honorable of you, truly."

He mockingly laughed. "Is that what you expected from me? To invite you into my dead sister's place when I don't know shit about you? Sorry to disappoint, but I didn't invite you to her apartment because—despite how I may look—I don't like to take advantage of women who need a place to stay or change. Plus, I saw you give that prick your right hook. I knew you'd be okay if any woodland creatures looked your way."

I couldn't help but smirk, taking his comment as a potential complement. "No," I confessed, "I didn't expect that. I was mostly giving you a hard time, so I apologize. But speaking of my right hook," I continued, undeterred, "why did you even help me in the first place? No one else seemed to give a damn in that tavern about me or what could have happened."

The forest held its breath as my question hung in the air. Even the crickets ceased their chirping in anticipation of Ryder's response. Without a word, he gently pulled the reins, bringing Reaper to a halt. I followed suit, our steeds standing still amid the unfamiliar forest.

The silence was *killing* me.

"What? Can a man not help a damsel in distress nowadays? I don't always need to be paid to help others."

I scoffed. "A damsel in distress? Is that what it looked like to you when I punched that creep in the face?"

He shrugged. "Okay, maybe *'damsel in distress'* is a bit of a stretch. Regardless, I've met men like him, and no matter how well you hold your own, I can promise you wouldn't have liked that outcome."

I raised a brow. "Huntsman turned hero. Maybe you're not as heartless as you try to appear."

"I don't *try* to appear any type of way," he confessed. "People will always judge me before they get to know me. It comes with the territory."

"Well maybe if you weren't so hard-headed when others asked about you, people would give you a chance."

He snorted. "Doubtful."

Leaning slightly forward, I met his gaze. "Why? I'm giving you a chance right now."

"You're *paying* me," he stated flatly. "You're giving me a chance because you have to."

"True. I am paying you." I moved Jupiter further up until our horses stood side by side. Reaching over, I placed my hand on his arm and felt that same rush of heat I felt the night prior. "But I'm also choosing to get to know you. I could remain silent and not give a damn, but I'm treating you like I would any other person I'm seeking to know."

"You're persistent, I'll give you that."

"I prefer determined," I countered. "And I'm not easily deterred."

Ryder chuckled. "Clearly."

I moved my hand and lightly poked his cheek, which he didn't appreciate. Swatting my hand away, I giggled. "Thanks for showing me you're not made of stone. Maybe we'll get through this thing without killing each other after all."

Rubbing the spot where I had poked him, he shot me a sidelong glance. "Now why would I do that when I'm enjoying your company *so* much?"

Sarcastic bastard.

"You're impossible, you know that?"

"Guilty as charged. Now, enough questions and eyes forward."

Slapping Reaper's reins, he continued forward, and I followed his lead. The forest came back alive, and I drank in every bit of its beauty. We had only been riding for probably a few hours at most, and Ryder refused to tell me where we were going.

"For your safety"—or something like that.

But it didn't matter; it wasn't like I would know if he told me.

I was a foreigner in my own land, getting to experience more of the kingdom outside the castle walls for the first time. I took note of *everything*. Shafts of light pierced through the leaves of the trees above, illuminating patches of wildflowers and ferns. I marveled at the sheer diversity of life that thrived in this lush wilderness.

The forest was a tapestry of yellow, orange, and red—each shade more vivid and enchanting than the last. Occasionally, I'd catch glimpses of elusive woodland creatures; a squirrel darting up a tree trunk, a fox disappearing into the underbrush, the distant call of an owl hidden among the leaves.

The sense of freedom I felt despite the uncertainty of our destination and the danger looming ahead was one I had never felt before. It was as if the forest had opened its arms to welcome me home, offering a glimpse of a world I had only dreamed of.

For the first time ever, I wasn't a princess on a pedestal; I was a traveler in a land of wonder.

Venturing deeper, a raspy voice echoed in my mind. "Rose?"

Startled, I snapped out of my trance as Ryder's call cut through my thoughts. "Rose!" he repeated, pulling Reaper to a stop and turning to face me. I hadn't realized I'd been riding ahead, lost in my own world. "Are you with me?"

I blinked, shaking off the haze. "Oh, I'm sorry. I got lost in all...*this*." I gestured to the surrounding forest.

His lips curved into a small, understanding smile. "It's easy to do."

I nodded. "What did you say?"

He maneuvered Reaper, so we were riding side by side, a

gesture that sent an unexpected flutter through my stomach. "I asked if you have any siblings."

Ah. So he is curious about little old me.

"Oh, uh...nope." I shrugged. "I'm an only child."

"Ah. That explains why you're so annoying."

Scoffing, I tightened Jupiter's reins to guide his rear until it bumped with the back of Reaper's.

The huntsman chuckled. "Mom and Dad saw one look at you and retired, huh?"

"You can't beat perfection."

Another wide grin crossed his lips. I wondered how much conversation he usually engaged in. With how everyone in the tavern reacted to him, it seemed like he wasn't the most *liked* person in the village. Or perhaps he was just the most feared— or least understood.

Life on the road must be lonely, and a part of me regretted saying his life was dull. But maybe he enjoyed it like that —*alone*, just him and his horse against the world.

And now...me too.

"From what I've been told, my birth wasn't exactly easy on my mother." I confessed.

"Doesn't she worry about you being out on this hunt for your father's murderer?"

My expression fell. "Would be rather hard to worry from the grave. She passed away about ten years ago."

Ryder's gaze softened. "I'm sorry to hear that."

I shrugged, trying to shake off the heaviness. "It's been a while. I miss her, of course, but life goes on, right?"

"It has to." His tone was as soft as his gaze. "If we got consumed by our losses, we would never grow, never get away from our day-to-day lives. We would simply—"

"Exist?"

His scarred brow rose in surprise. "Exactly."

For some reason, it was easy to smile around him. "And you? How do your parents feel about your life choices? I'm sure they worry about their son being a huntsman."

Silence passed between us. "My ma and pa don't really talk to me anymore, so I couldn't tell you. After Amarisa...our family kind of fell apart. No one's to blame; it just happened."

"I bet they miss you, though. Losing one child is enough of a burden on the heart."

His throat bobbed as he swallowed. "You have no idea."

Offering me a small smile that didn't reach his mismatched eyes, he returned his attention to the road and dropped the conversation. I knew better than to pry, and I was thankful he opened up as much as he did.

Despite such a dark conversation, I felt pure contentment as we continued. It was strange in an unfamiliar way, but I didn't mind it. As the hours passed, the sun continued to grow warmer.

Ahead of us, there seemed to be no end in sight to the miles and miles of picturesque trees. The landscape was filled with the warm colors of fall, and even though I had no clue what was waiting ahead of us, I wasn't worried about the uncertainty.

I was *excited* to unveil it.

CHAPTER 14

I THINK if my stomach growled one more time, Ryder was going to jump his horse and kill me.

Whenever it made a noise in pure desperation, his entire body would tense. His occasional dirty looks were even more proof of how annoyed he *really* was with my growing hunger. Another growl was building from the depths of my stomach, and I wrapped my arm around it in hopes of muffling some of the sound.

It didn't help.

Throwing his hands over his ears, Ryder let out a loud, frustrated groan. "That's it!" he annoyingly spat. "I can't hear a damn thing—let alone myself *think*—with that monster of a stomach growling every two minutes!"

I crossed my arms over my chest, my annoyance quickly matching his. If I was reading the sun correctly, it was well past noon.

"Let's not be *dramatic*," I retorted. "I'm not used to waiting this long to eat. I can't help that you're starving me."

"Ever heard of fasting? Gods, imagine if we were being followed! They'd catch your loud ass in a heartbeat."

Bringing Reaper to a halt, he jumped off with ease that was more than impressive. Opening the satchel on her hip, he pulled out a bow and a quiver that held about half a dozen pitch-black arrows.

I sarcastically raised my hands in pretend surrender. "Woah, now! We can talk this through."

His face fell. "*Ha. Ha*. I wasn't aware a *jester* was in my presence."

I couldn't help but smirk. Approaching, he offered his hand to help me off Jupiter. I dismounted gracefully, my hand tingling in Ryder's grasp. Quickly withdrawing it, I subtly wiped my palm down my leather pant leg, hoping to ease the tingle.

Why the hell does that keep happening?

"If we're going to continue at a steady pace, there will be minimal time to stop in passing towns to gather supplies," he said dryly. "I'm going to teach you how to hunt. You okay with that?"

I crossed my arms. "And who says I don't already know how to hunt?"

A dark eyebrow rose. "Do you?"

"Well...no," I admitted, dropping my arms. "But I know how to shoot. I just have never used it to *kill* anything before."

"Well, today's the day. If you're going to kill a Witch, a rabbit should be easy for you." Moving to tie the horses to a tree, he was back by my side in a heartbeat. "First, we'll need to find a good spot to hide. Small game spooks easily, so we'll need to stay concealed."

Rolling my eyes, I took the bow. "I know the concept of what I need to do."

I found a concealed spot near a thicket where the rustle of leaves and chirping birds would mask any noises. Crouching down, I readied the bow, my eyes scanning the surroundings for any sign of movement.

I looked back over my shoulder, finding Ryder by the horses, ankles crossed over one another as he leaned against Reaper. He silently observed me, an obvious look of amusement plastered on his smug face.

Smug, handsome face.

After what felt like an eternity, a small rabbit hopped out from the underbrush. Steading my breathing, I silently knocked my arrow, squinting my eyes as I started to aim. Just as I moved my fingers to release, Ryder's warmth enveloped me from behind and caught me off guard.

My shot went wide, missing the rabbit *completely*.

The small creature looked in our direction before taking off back into the brush. My stomach sadly rumbled in disappointment.

"You know, if you were aiming for that ant hill, I think you were spot on."

I whipped my head around to face the huntsman, the arrogance radiating from him filling my nostrils. My cheeks burned with a mixture of frustration and embarrassment.

"You *deliberately* startled me! How am I supposed to concentrate when you sneak up like that?"

He chuckled, unapologetic. "In the wild, you won't get a warning when danger approaches. Consider it a lesson in staying alert."

I scoffed. "And consider this a threat. Back. The hell. Off."

He took a bold step toward me, and I had to crane my neck to meet his gaze. "Or else, what, killer? You going to knock an arrow in my direction and miss?"

"Fuck you."

His smirk only grew. "For such a lady, your mouth is as dirty as it gets. Where did you say you were from again?"

Pursing my lips together, I blanked on a single location to give him. "Just around," I lied through my teeth.

Rolling his eyes, he took another step closer, moving his hands under my arms to raise them. I jerked them away before the heat could set in.

"Can you *not* touch me right now?"

"Relax," he said calmly. "I'm trying to show you something. Get in a position like you were about to draw."

I stood in my taught stance, and his body moved closer to mine. Ryder's fingers lightly brushed my arm, hesitating before correcting my posture. "Is this okay?"

Despite my annoyance, I appreciated him asking for permission. "It's fine."

"Hold the bow steady. You need to find your focus."

Yeah—like I'm going to be able to focus with how close you are.

An electrifying tension crackled between us as he continued to correct me. Ignoring his warmth, I lowered my bow momentarily and rolled out my shoulders with a light crack.

Taking a deep breath, I raised the bow again.

"Good girl," he whispered. "Now, pull back on the string, but not too hard. You want a steady draw."

"I know how to pull back the bow!" I whispered back, trying to ignore how his praise made my stomach flip.

"Yes, you do, but you're too stiff. You'll burn out if you remain that unforgiving."

Taking a deep breath, I adjusted my pull, and a small grunt of approval from Ryder encouraged me to continue. I could faintly hear him inhaling and exhaling deeply behind me, the sound slightly covered by the leaves rustling in the wind.

"Get ready," he cautioned.

The small rabbit returned to the opening. I tried not to let his presence behind me throw me off, but gods, he smelt really *fucking* good.

"Steady," he whispered, his warm breath caressing my cheek. "Focus on your target. Feel the bow, feel the pull of the string. Hunting is an art. You need to be connected to your weapon to use it properly."

Trying to regain my composure, I took another deep breath as I drew back the string. Taking a moment to get the aim right, I hesitated and released. The arrow sailed through the air and hit its mark with astonishing accuracy. The rabbit let out a brief squeak before slumping to the ground—*lifeless*.

I looked over my shoulder, Ryder's eyes wide in surprise as we lowered the bow. His touch, still on my arm, felt *electrifying*.

"Well, I'll be damned," he admired. "Not bad, Wiyahna."

A surge of pride welled inside me as I left his touch and moved to where the rabbit lay in the grass. As I hunched over my prize, a small pool of blood formed around the tiny thing, and the sight sent me right back into my room.

The image of my father flashed where the rabbit once was, and the once-alive forest transformed into cold, lifeless stonewalls that towered above me like a prison. The calming scent of pine and damp earth was gone, replaced by the metallic tang of blood in the air.

I couldn't move.

Couldn't breathe.

Couldn't *think*.

The bow I once held was replaced with the bloody dagger, and my fingers trembled as I stared down at the crimson staining my skin, spreading like ink across a page. Slowly, I could feel my chest rising and falling as I started hyperventilating.

A sharp inhale shuddered through me. Then another. My breaths came too fast, too shallow. A ringing noise filled my ears. I wanted to let go of the dagger, to wipe my hands clean, but I couldn't move.

Then, warmth—solid, steady—pressed against my shoulder.

"Rose?"

Ryder's tone held a hint of concern, and it slowly pulled me back. Blinking, I tried to focus back on the rabbit but the image of a man still remained.

He knelt beside me. "Everything alright?"

I swallowed, but my throat was dry and tight. My fingers curled into fists, nails digging into my palms. I didn't trust my voice, so I gave the smallest shake of my head.

He didn't press me. Instead, he shifted closer and gently reached for the bow. "Give it here," he said quietly.

My fingers twitched as he took it, but I let him. Putting it on the ground behind his back, only then did he meet my gaze again.

"Breathe," he murmured.

I exhaled shakily.

"In through your nose," he guided, "out through your mouth."

I followed his lead and slowly, the image of my father started to disappear.

Seconds passed. Maybe minutes.

Finally, my chest no longer ached from the force of my breaths. My hands stopped trembling. The ringing in my ears faded.

Ryder nodded. "Better?"

I licked my lips. "Yeah."

"The first kill is always the hardest and you actually did really well."

He was right and I knew it. No matter how much the blood bothered me, this was a necessary part of survival, and I had to confront it. If I struggled killing a rabbit, how would I ever kill a Witch?

It was okay to have killed it. It died so I wouldn't. It's okay.

Taking another deep breath, I picked up the rabbit. "I did it." My voice was weak. "I caught lunch."

Ryder offered me an encouraging smile. "You *hunted* lunch," he corrected. "And you'll get better with practice. Hunting takes time to master. Fun, isn't it?"

"Not too sure *'fun'* is the proper word, but..."

A small flash of orange darting from the underbrush drew my attention. My head instinctively followed the movement, and I spotted a group of animals ahead, their orange fur nearly blending in with the fallen leaves on the ground.

"Foxes!"

I was eager to approach and forget about what I had just done, but Ryder gripped my arm to stop me. He shook his head as his mismatched eyes remained on the animals. "No," he whispered. "They may look like them, but those aren't foxes."

"Then...what are they?"

My enthusiasm faded as I studied the creatures. Upon closer inspection, they moved in a strange, almost unnatural way.

Their forms seemed to shimmer and shift as if they were made of liquid rather than flesh and fur. Their eyes locked onto mine with an unsettling intelligence.

"Shifters," he murmured. "They can take the form of any animal. Most of them do a damn good job of acting like them too. But if you look close enough, you can see through their illusions."

Stepping forward, Ryder's imposing figure dwarfed the creatures. I watched curiously as he approached the pack. The largest of the foxes shifted its gaze from me to the huntsman.

Looking up, the fox...*smiled*.

"Huntsman," its cunning voice hissed from its mouth.

My eyes widened so much I feared they might pop out. The fox had just spoken, uttering *actual* words! Maybe the hunger was getting to me because...what the hell? The other foxes slowly backed down and away, leaving the huntsman in a standoff with their leader.

Ryder showed no surprise. "Vixin."

"Such a delight to see you here. What has brought me such honor?" Vixin's accent was foreign to my ears, the words flowing like a melodic dance.

He smirked. "Coincidence, mostly. But stop playing fox, and maybe you'll find out."

Vixin sighed, "Never just a friendly '*Hello*' from you, aye?"

Before I could process what was happening, the small fox transformed into a stunning woman, and I was left even more speechless. Vixin's long blonde hair reminded me of her fox tail, the stunning locks pulled back to frame her beautiful face. Her golden eyes were as piercing as Ryder's.

Oh, and she was also *completely naked*.

She went right back to staring at me, and I felt uneasy under her piercing gaze. I couldn't help but shift my weight from one foot to the other.

I had heard legends about shifters from the knights, usually when they were drunk around a campfire. They loved telling stories about creatures we all thought were myths. Now, standing face-to-face with one, I started questioning everything.

"Can you not *smell* her?" Vixin asked, her nose flaring.

Ryder stepped in, blocking me from her gaze. "My nose is too occupied with how badly your pack smells to be bothered with her."

I turned my head and took a deep sniff of my armpit. Did I smell great? No, I smelled like sweat and the outdoors. But thinking I smelled *so* bad that a woman thirty feet away noticed? That was just ridiculous.

Maybe I still smelt like the pigs.

Vixin's gaze locked onto Ryder like a predator sizing up its prey, and her full lips curled into a sly smile. "And what can I do for you, Ryder-Roo?" she purred, her voice velvety and seductive.

The way she looked at him stirred something deep inside me. My chest tightened, and I felt a weird heat rising to my cheeks. It was like a thorn had lodged itself in my side—sharp and unrelenting.

Get it together, Genevieve Rose!

"We're not children anymore, Vixin. I was hoping to run into you eventually. I believe you have something I need. Some information."

"Ah, yes." She began to circle him, her fingers lightly tracing his broad shoulders. "If I recall correctly, I have *many* things you need."

Ryder quickly grasped her wrist, firmly removing her hand

from his shoulder. His expression stayed relaxed, denying Vixin any satisfaction. "You can recall what you want, but you were Amarisa's plaything, not mine," he declared, flicking her wrist away.

With folded arms, Vixin challenged him with defiant eyes. She brushed a stray strand of hair from her face. "You utter her name as if a curse. She was a *blessing* to us all."

"Vixin," he cautioned, his authority echoing through the forest, sending a shiver down my spine.

She cowered slightly. "Always so rude."

"The old Vale of the Sprites. Does it still lie at the end of the Black Wood?"

Vixin's smile returned, her interest renewed. "The Vale of the Sprites?" She smacked her lips. "We both know their Vale fell long ago during the war. Humans—" she spat in my direction, "thought Sprites were the easiest prey, a way to hurt the Fae even more. So, they hunted them down. Little did the humans know, the Fae had used the Sprites as slaves for generations, so no one cared enough to rescue them." She turned her focus to me, scrutinizing every inch of my being. "Have you ever encountered a Sprite, girl?"

I shook my head, trying to stand tall under her judgmental scrutiny.

"Sprites were vastly different from the Fae your kind went to war with. They were innocent and pure; they didn't deserve punishment and genocide!" Her temper flared. "If you'd ever been blessed by one, even touched by their tiny hands, you would never harm them—let alone *slaughter* them!"

Ryder pinched the bridge of his nose. "She was not the sole reason for the Sprite's genocide, and I didn't ask for a history lesson. Is The Vale still there? Yes, or no?"

Vixin responded with another sly smile. "Perhaps. Rumors speak of a twinkling light near The Vale if you catch the sun just right during golden hour, but don't expect to find anything. Although...we're *both* aware their melody still haunts the grounds."

Ryder nodded, satisfied with the information. Turning to join me, Vixin let out a small chuckle that stopped him in his movements.

"Whatever you're seeking there," she said, addressing neither of us in particular, "just remember, all magic comes with a price."

Shifting back into a fox, she rejoined her pack and disappeared into the underbrush. I let out a sigh of relief, glad the awkward and intense encounter was over. Ryder walked over to me with a confident stride, looking completely unbothered by what had just happened.

"Ex-girlfriend?" I asked, attempting to lighten the awkwardness.

"Not one of mine," he stated flatly. "As much as I loved my sister, she was...complicated. And had many complicated friends."

Another wave of relief hit me, and I was *immediately* annoyed.

"Let's head back," he suggested. "I'll show you how to clean and prepare the rabbit for cooking. The faster we finish, the faster we can get moving."

Nodding, I trailed behind him, my hands still clutching the lifeless legs of the rabbit.

Vixin's words kept replaying in my head. *The Vale of the Sprites...* I had never heard of it, nor did I know about how my people had slaughtered them in revenge against the Fae. I always thought the Fae were the true villains in our stories, but could we have been just as bad?

Her story flipped everything I thought I knew upside down.

The brutality against innocent lives, magical or not, was unacceptable. But the idea of enslavement didn't sit well with me either.

Was there any true goodness left in this world?

I wished I could ask Father and get his side of things. But since that wasn't an option, I guess I was going to figure it out on my own.

"After lunch, we head to The Vale?"

Ryder turned to look at me, his eyes calm. "To The Vale."

CHAPTER 15

WE CONTINUED RIDING with minimal conversation until the sun dipped below the horizon.

The forest became shrouded in darkness, and with Winter Solstice approaching, the days would only get shorter. We rode until we found a clearing to Ryder's liking. He insisted The Vale was still over half a day's ride, so continuing in the dark was pointless.

Dismounting, we divided the tasks of clearing twigs and debris from the chosen spot for our camp. I noticed no camping gear on Reaper's hips, so I mentally prepared myself for another night sleeping under the stars.

At least there were no pigs this time.

Finishing, I wiped my hands on my pants to rid them of any dirt or bugs. Ryder wandered over to one of the satchels on Reaper's hips and opened it, pulling out two small vials, each containing a piece of cloth. He casually tossed them onto the ground, and to my amazement, they instantly sprang to life. Before my eyes, two fully set-up tents materialized.

My mouth hung open in awe.

Noticing my fascination, Ryder offered a faint smile. "Elven craftsmanship," he explained, as if it was the most *ordinary* thing in the world. "I traded for these a few years back when I ventured into the Elven territories. They're pretty handy, especially when you're on the road as much as I am."

"Seems convenient."

Unfurling one of the tent flaps, he revealed the comfortable interior, complete with a sleeping cot already neatly arranged. "Convenient and enchanted so they'll keep ya warm on the cold nights and cool in the dead of summer. Elves are annoying as shit, but skilled in the art of magical crafting. So, once you have something worth trading for, they're not so bad."

I cautiously stepped inside one of the tents, still amazed by how it had sprung out of nowhere. The inside was warm and much roomier than I had expected. My fingers danced over the cot, marveling at the fine workmanship.

"I don't think I'll ever get used to this," I admired softly.

He studied me. "No magic back home?"

I settled onto the cot and ran my hands over the soft blanket. My body instantly relaxed. "No. I grew up with stories and legends of it...but my father never allowed it into our territory. Some mystic healers would enter to tend to the wounded, but that was it. Elven territories? Shifters and Sprites? All I knew was of the Fae and their border."

"Magic can be beautiful, but dangerous as hell if abused," he mused. "I don't blame your father for hiding you from it."

"But I feel so *childish*," I confessed. "I've been in this world for eighteen years and just now learning. I'm truly seeing things for what they are, not what I've been told."

He smirked. "Well, good news for you is that there is a big

world out there to explore and a lot of life left to live. Don't be so hard on yourself for things you can't control."

I returned his smile, and he left the comfort of my tent. Feeling pulled, I followed him out and found him monitoring the darkening sky.

"You know how to start a fire?"

"Actually, yes."

Even though it wasn't exactly proper of me, I often found myself tending to the fire in my room on my sleepless nights. Pulling up a chair, I would poke and revive the flames until the soothing crackles eased me to sleep. There were many mornings I would awake to my faces covered in ashes and cinder.

"Good." He nodded. "Start the fire, and I'll be back soon."

"And where do you think you're going?"

Ryder moved his gaze from the sky to me. "I don't think a rabbit will keep your *demanding* stomach silent for long. I'm going to go hunting for something else."

I frowned in disappointment, not liking the thought of being alone in the dark.

Patting my shoulder, he chuckled. "Don't give me that look. I'll be back before you can even warm up." He looked down at the dagger sheathed at my hip before nodding towards it. "In less than a day, I've seen you throw a solid punch, use a bow like a pro, and mount a horse twice your size without breaking a sweat. I have a strong feeling you'd handle that thing well if you needed to use it."

I mean, he wasn't *wrong*.

My training focused on swords, but we had to learn daggers too. Did I ever actually use those skills outside of practice? Absolutely not. Still, I felt confident in handling them.

The dagger on my hip had been the one to take my father's

life, and part of me worried it was tainted by the darkness and magic of the Shadow Walker. My fingers no longer tingled around it, and that vision thing only happened once...so maybe it was a one-time occurrence. Maybe once it took a life, the magic was gone.

I didn't really know, and honestly, I didn't want to find out.

With one final glance in my direction, he retrieved the bow and quiver and disappeared into the deepening shadows of the forest.

By the time darkness had fully enveloped the campsite, I had anxiously chewed away the remnants of my once-pristine manicure.

Time crawled by, each minute stretching longer than the last. I tried to keep my attention on the crackling flames and ignore the pitch-black unknown that surrounded me on all sides. The fire blazed for what seemed like hours, but Ryder was still gone.

Logic cautioned me to not venture from the safety of the camp to look for him. It would be a reckless move. I could risk getting lost, hurt, or even worse—jeopardizing the already fragile trust he placed in me. So, despite my nerves, I stayed put and on guard.

Shadows from the flickering flames danced around me —*taunting* me. I couldn't help but clench my fists at every sign of movement, nails digging into my palms as I struggled to stay calm.

Trying to ignore the looming shadows, I turned my attention toward the sky and hoped the familiar constellations would offer me some solace. Since I was a girl, they had been a source of comfort. The night was clear, and without the lights from the castle or a village, the stars twinkled brighter than ever. Never had I seen such a night. Taking a deep breath, I closed my eyes and allowed the cool air to soothe my nerves.

Ryder said he would be back with dinner, and I need to trust him.

The longer I sat, the more an unsettling sensation stirred in the pit of my stomach. It didn't feel like dread, but it was enough to keep me alert. Opening my eyes, I scanned the campsite. I think for the rest of my life, I would always search for the eyes that took my father and pray to never see them again. Finding nothing, I swallowed the feeling, just brushing it off as my anxiety.

Preparing to close my eyes again, a rumble emerged from the darkness. It was different from the Shadow Walker's—more animalistic. Regardless, the sound caused every hair on my neck to stand in attention. Even the sounds of nature paused, waiting along with me.

From behind me, a haunting howl pierced the still air and echoed through the silent night. I immediately jumped to my feet and unsheathed the dagger. Body trembling, I desperately looked around.

That howl was primal and *close*.

It had to have been only a few feet away from me, hidden in the dark of the night. Every sense in me heightened, and a pull, the same one I felt the night prior, urged me to look behind me. Resisting, I told it to *"fuck right off"*, but it persisted, demanding my attention.

I didn't want to, but I gave in.

Slowly turning my head, I confronted the abyss of pure blackness, the fire's glow failing to illuminate the source of the howl. Fear gripped me as my imagination conjured unsettling scenarios.

Is it a lone wolf or a pack? Did the scent of Ryder's hunt pull them in? Or am I as unlucky as he said?

I was shorter than most of the other women in the castle. Never meeting Liliana's "ideal form," I had an unsettling feeling that my plump frame could be seen as a tempting meal for wolves. I could try to outrun them, but they would have the advantage no matter what.

Fuck, why didn't I do more cardio?

Another howl pierced the darkness, closer and louder than before. Panic set in as I gripped the dagger tighter. It may have taken my father's life, but it was the only chance to save mine.

Surveying the darkness for any sign of movement, my gaze locked onto a pair of harsh, glowing eyes. I gasped and fumbled with my dagger, nearly dropping it in pure terror. The eyes, unlike those of the Shadow Walker, were fiery gold, positioned unnaturally high in the air. Judging by their height, they had to be at least six or seven feet off the ground.

They *towered* over me.

A growl emerged from the eyes, and bile rose in my throat. They watched me as intensely as I watched them. Unlike the Shadow Walkers, they held no malevolence, no hint of harm. But I knew better than to judge what I didn't know.

I gripped the dagger tighter, my knuckles turning white. Knowing my chances of survival were slim, a silent prayer slipped from my lips—a plea for guidance or perhaps a small miracle from whoever might be listening.

Calming my fast-beating heart, I stood firm, feet planted and ready. When I blinked to refocus, the eyes were gone, vanishing just as quickly as they had appeared. Like I had imagined them, there were no signs of the creature. Relief washed over me, but I remained on edge. There was no way a creature that big could just disappear.

Minutes lingered, and I stood there, vigilantly scanning the surroundings in every direction. Hearing a noise behind me, I whipped my head around as Ryder emerged from the shadows. A small fawn was slung over his back as if it weighed nothing. His movements exuded the fluidity of a predator in perfect harmony with the forest.

He was a huntsman through and through.

"Sorry for taking so long," he called out. "But my ma always says good things come to those who wait."

Stepping further into the light of the fire, he effortlessly laid the fawn down, not a bead of sweat on his brow. When his eyes met mine, he frowned. "What's wrong?"

My throat was suddenly dry as I sheathed the dagger. Looking to the forest, I was anticipating the eyes looking back. "Didn't you hear it?"

His brow furrowed. "Hear what?"

"The howls," I said, pointing to the darkness. "They were so loud! Practically on top of the camp."

"Rose, we're in the middle of the woods, in a million different creatures' territory," he said dismissively. "No need to get worked up because you might have heard a wolf."

"I'm *not* getting worked up over the possibility of a wolf," I clarified. "I'm concerned because of how large it was. I *saw* it. It had to have been, gods, at least the height of a horse. And its eyes glowed, just like the Shadow Walkers, but...warmer."

He looked behind me and with a sigh, he retrieved a long knife and wiped it on the hem of his tunic. "Well, we're together now. If it comes back, we'll deal with it then. Got it?"

I bit my lip, suddenly feeling silly with how dismissive he was. I know what I saw and what I heard, but he was the seasoned hunter out of the two of us... Maybe he knew best.

Focusing back on the fawn by the fire, his well-practiced motions made it look effortless. The gleaming blade he wielded for skinning hinted at years of seasoned expertise. The fawn was barely visible in the dim light, and I was thankful. After recent encounters with blood, I had no desire to witness more.

Ryder's gaze briefly met mine, capturing the firelight in a way that made my heart race. Mismatched eyes shimmered in the flickering flames, their colors shifting and blending, casting enchanting reflections within their depths.

"Watching me won't make me work any faster."

His sarcasm was like a blade.

"I can imagine you've done this a time or two."

"Take random maidens on a voyage into the woods for an entity that could kill us both?" He smirked. "Can't say I have. You're my first."

I rolled my eyes, unable to contain my smile. "I meant skin an animal, you ass."

He grinned widely, briefly removing the blade from the deer to switch its position in his hands, offering me the handle. "Care to give it a go?"

Yeah, no thank you.

"How about I clean up instead?"

"Deal."

Kneeling beside him, I gladly watched as he worked—casually noting to myself that Ryder smelled *remarkably* good after a hunt.

Throwing me an extra shirt, we prepared to turn in for the night.

Amidst his packing, he forgot to provide me with anything else to wear, let alone something to sleep in. Not that I minded —I was quite content sleeping in the nude. But given the circumstances of being alone with a stranger, it probably wasn't the smartest choice.

I was becoming giddy at the thought of sleeping on the cot, but I wasn't quite ready to turn in. Sitting around the campfire and eating, Ryder slowly started sharing bits of his mind. He spun captivating takes of this magical land I found myself in.

His stories had me hooked and I was envious of the life he'd led in such a short time. The way he described things, with such vivid detail, made it sound like he'd lived a hundred lifetimes.

Making our way to separate tents, we exchanged awkward, sleepy glances as the silence of the night crept in.

Giving me a lazy smile, Ryder stretched his arms over his head. "Well, goodnight. If you need anything, don't wake me up."

I rolled my eyes. "I'll keep that in mind, *old man.*"

His laughter followed him as he disappeared into his tent. Tying mine closed, I wasted no time changing and diving right into bed. Moving the sheets to the side, I slid into my cot, the fabric offering little comfort compared to the luxurious chambers of Castle Quinn I once had called home.

But it didn't matter—it was a bed, and I was thankful.

CHAPTER 16

I AWOKE ABRUPTLY, feeling disoriented and entangled in my sheets.

Attempting to adjust to the morning light, my heart quickened as I realized I was back in my bed at Castle Quinn. The lavender and gold damask wallpaper that adorned the four walls was a welcomed sight. Even from the mesh cream-colored canopy that hung over my bed frame, I could tell it was early.

Was everything just a nightmare? Did I make up everything in some drunken stupor? Gods, I needed to cut back on the wine.

I pushed the fabric aside and, stepping out of bed, the ground beneath my feet felt unusually cold. Wrapping myself in a robe, I cautiously opened my door and searched for confirmation of my fears. The halls were quiet...almost too quiet, given the hour. An unnatural stillness pervaded the corridors.

More people should be awake by now. Maybe they're still all recovering from my engagement ball.

Suddenly remembering what had happened to Father, I rushed to his study. My stomach twisted with knots as I approached. The doors stood slightly ajar, and I hesitated before entering. The room was dimly lit by flickering candlelight, not nearly enough light for me to see without entering. As I stepped inside, my heart pounded in my chest as I saw my father seated at his desk, his back to me.

Relief washed over me as I audibly sighed.

It was just a bad dream. He was *alive.*

"Father?"

No response.

Taking a cautious step closer, my unease grew. The room's atmosphere turned colder, and shadows danced menacingly around the edges of my vision. Reaching out to touch his shoulder, my hand recoiled as he crumbled into a pile of lifeless ashes, the particles scattering around me.

The room suddenly warped and shifted, the walls closing in fast.

Panicking, I turned to run, but the door had vanished.

I was trapped, surrounded by walls that seemed to be getting closer and closer, the air thinned around me. Desperation clawed at my chest, but my attempts to scream were futile. The room twisted and threatened to crush me against its four walls. I covered my ears and shut my eyes, trying to block out the horror that awaited me.

Wake up! Wake up! Wake up!

A cold hand encircled my neck, and my eyes shot open to find Xander before me. His once-charming features were now contorted into a grotesque mask of fury. His hand, now with elongated talons, lightly dug into my flesh. He leaned in, his lips inches from mine, silver eyes seeming to burn a hole through my soul as his hot breath enveloped me.

"You belong to me," he hissed.

Removing the hand that constricted my throat, he roughly

gripped onto my left hand, raising it to his lips. My engagement ring burned into my flesh, the pressure intensifying until it felt like it grazed my bone.

He pulled me closer, and his lips met mine, sucking the air from my lungs. Paralyzed, I wanted to scream, to *move*, but I was trapped in the nightmare's grip. Relinquishing his hold on my lips, his mouth slithered to my ear, his tongue tracing it, just as he had done in the garden.

"Till death do us part, my bride," he whispered before sinking his teeth into my neck.

With a jolt, I woke up drenched in a cold sweat and screaming.

My fingers clawed at my neck, still feeling the pressure from where his hands had been. Looking around, I was back in my tent, the glow from the filling moon filtering through the canvas walls. My heart was racing, and even though I knew I was safe, the remnants of the nightmare clung to me like a leech.

I gasped for breath, my pounding heart slowly beginning to calm, and the sounds of the forest pulled me back to life.

This is real. I'm okay. I'm safe.

Just as I started to breathe normally, my tent's entrance flung open. Bursting through, Ryder stood there with eyes wide, his hair disheveled from sleep.

He held his hunting knife in his hand, his chest heaving. "Rose? Are you alright?"

I rubbed my eyes, my thoughts still foggy. "R-Ryder," my voice shook, "I'm fine. Just...just a nightmare."

He let out a sigh of relief, his shoulders relaxing. "Gods, you nearly gave me a heart attack! I heard you screaming, and I thought—"

Seeing him genuinely concerned caused my cheeks to flush. "I'm sorry," I mumbled.

He took a step closer. "Do you, uh, do you want to talk about it?"

"It was..."

My voice caught as I became all too aware that he was *shirtless*.

My gaze followed the lines of his silhouette. Even in the darkness, his tan, muscular chest was undeniable. It wasn't that I hadn't seen bare-chested men before; I had observed many knights training shirtless, including Topher.

However, Ryder's physique was...*captivating*.

The small patch of hair I had noticed earlier, peeking out from his tunic, turned out to be more like a dense forest, covering most of his chest and gradually thinning as it descended to his...

I shook my head, trying to clear the unholy thoughts flooding my mind. His abdomen was as chiseled as I would have imagined, and the tattoos on his arms extended down to his stomach. There were more than I had thought, and each design was unique and mesmerizing.

"...it was nothing," I finally finished.

He hesitated before nodding. "Get some rest. Tomorrow is a new day, and we have a long journey ahead. I don't need you falling asleep on your horse from exhaustion."

I remained silent as he turned to leave. Reaching for the flaps, he paused and looked over his shoulder with sleepy eyes. "And Rose?" he said, turning to face me. "Nightmares can be a bitch to handle, especially after what you've experienced. If you ever need to talk about it, or if you're scared, don't hesitate to wake me up. I can be a good listener when I need to be."

I snorted. "Oh? And here I thought I wasn't supposed to *bother you* if I needed anything."

His eyes softened. "Well, I've changed my mind. Bother me anytime you want."

Turning again, he left.

I watched him leave, and a whirlwind of emotions swept through me. Despite his tough exterior, it was becoming clear he was more than meets the eye. His words were sincere, and damn him, they made my heart flutter.

Stupid Huntsman.

Though the nightmare lingered, I found comfort in knowing I had Ryder to talk to if needed.

Pulling myself back under the covers, I eventually drifted back to sleep, leaving behind the haunting corridors of Castle Quinn to instead envision a beautiful, scarred face.

Ryder was awake before me—no surprise there.

By the time I was dressed, he had already cleaned up his tent and had the horses ready to go, which was more of a surprise. Returning my tent, he double-checked that everything was packed and good to go. Satisfied, he jumped up on Reaper, and I followed on Jupiter.

With the first rays of dawn breaking, we were off. The rhythmic sound of our horses' hooves on the forest floor echoed through the trees, creating a calming cadence. As we rode, Ryder would occasionally point out various plants and wildlife.

Listening to him talk about the forest was mesmerizing.

The way he described the natural world showed his deep admiration and love for it. His words painted such clear pictures in my mind, and I could tell his connection to the land ran deep.

"And that there" he pointed to a winding path of delicate, luminescent flowers, "are known as '*Feyblooms*.'"

"Feyblooms?" I repeated.

He nodded. "They're rare and magical. That's why they look like that."

Following his direction, I admired their beauty. Each blossom radiated with a unique, inner light that created an almost otherworldly glow. Their petals were a captivating mix of blues, purples, and silvers, standing out against the fallen leaves covering the land.

"Legend has it that feyblooms hold a unique connection with Sprites. Where a Sprite has touched or blessed, a feybloom is rumored to grow."

Before us, the path stretched like a radiant ribbon, seemingly extending for miles. Outshining any flowers in my garden or those presented to me from neighboring lands, these feyblooms were the most exquisite blossoms I had ever seen.

"Wait...did you say that feyblooms can only grow where a Sprite has touched?"

His smile beamed as he nodded. "I did."

"But Vixin said all the Sprites had been slaughtered early during the war. How can they possibly grow decades later?"

"She did say that, didn't she?"

I stared at him, trying to read his expression. If The Vale was attacked and all the Sprites were slaughtered, the feyblooms couldn't be thriving as they were in front of us. Unless...

"So, the Sprites..."

"Are *alive*," he affirmed. "Well done! I guess there's a brain in that head after all."

Disregarding his insult, I watched Ryder guide Reaper toward the blossoms. Keeping Jupiter stationed, I gazed at the trail ahead. After a moment, I attempted to catch up with Ryder.

I had a nagging feeling of unease.

"And if we follow the trail," he continued, seeing me catch up, "it'll lead us right to The Vale."

"That doesn't seem like the wisest thing for them."

His face shifted. "Why do you say that?"

I swallowed. "It's just... If Humans purposefully sought to wipe out all the Sprites and they still live, wouldn't they fear we would return to kill them again? I mean, why have the feyblooms thrive so obviously in nature? Why have them lead straight to where they find sanctuary?"

Ryder slowed Reaper to match our pace. "Good question, but the answer is...complicated. Long story short, when everyone thought the Sprites had been wiped out, a handful managed to hide. They had to start from scratch—living off the land and tapping into the magic all around them. Could you imagine?" He laughed lightly. "Everything you knew and loved, just poof, gone?"

Yes. Yes, I could.

"Anyway," he went on, "over time, they figured out that staying hidden gave them a shot at surviving. But about twenty-five years ago, when King Leonard took charge, he saw the pointlessness in hunting them."

My heart raced at the mentioned of my father's name. I could feel my cheeks flush as I tried to steady my trembling hands on the reins. All these years, Father never said a word

197

about any of this. Honestly, he hardly talked about anything except the Fae.

He *must* have known something if he stopped that hunt. But why would he keep this from me?

"He was too late by that point. The war had already taken so many lives, both magical and regular." His gaze darkened. "So much of the land was ruined. I was just a kid, but even I knew he was sick of the bloodshed. We all were. So, he finally did what any other of those damn kinds failed to do and called off the hunt. Hell of a bold move, but one that gave me respect for him. Slowly, the Sprites started to come out and rebuild. Not everyone knows about them, but those who do keep it close. Like they should."

"People like *you*?"

"People like me, and now, like you," his face became serious. "Don't give me a reason to regret sharing this knowledge with you. Got it?"

My heart sank and I frowned. I knew very little of the lands I would rule one day and having this much darkness and magic hidden from me made me feel like a fool.

Straightening my shoulders, I corrected the slouch that had crept in and crossed an *X* with my pointer finger over my heart. "You have my word."

Quietly, he kept going, following the trail of blossoms. My mind was racing, and I couldn't help but blurt out yet another question. "What are we looking for at The Vale?"

Ryder paused, his eyes focused on the trail. After a moment, his gaze shifted back to mine, and a hint of tension crept into his expression, making his scars appear a shade darker.

"Answers."

CHAPTER 17

THE FEYBLOOMS' trail continued seemingly without end, though we had been tracking it for probably an hour.

Anticipation grew as we rode, and my eyes scanned in every direction, hoping for a glimpse of a Sprite. I had no clue what I was looking for, but a part of me knew I would know one when I saw one. As we progressed, the once brilliant blooms began to fade. The colors dulled and the petals wilted. Eventually, the trail led us to the edge of a large patch of weeds.

I was...confused, to say the least. Unable to conceal my disappointment, I felt a frown form on my face.

"Well, welcome to The Vale!" Ryder hopped off Reaper and walked over to me while I sat on Jupiter.

He looked oddly blissful, totally at peace in the middle of this dead garden we'd stumbled upon.

My nose wrinkled. "This...? Ryder, this is just a weed patch."

He stroked Jupiter's jaw, and his amusement faded. "No. *This* is The Vale. What did Vixin say?"

Shit. What had she said?

I was too preoccupied with her intense gaze and naked body to absorb every word she was spitting towards me. "She said something about a rumor with twinkling lights where The Vale used to be?"

"And what time is it?"

I tilted my head back to check the sky. The canopy of trees provided some shade despite the falling leaves, but with the sunlight filtering through, I got a good idea of the time.

"About four in the afternoon?"

He nodded again. "Probably four-thirty but close enough. When did she say we would see the twinkling light?"

Groaning, I swung my leg over Jupiter and hopped down. "I'm sorry; I didn't realize I needed to *take notes*. She said it would be around golden hour. I get it now—we must wait."

Towering over me, he leaned down and until his face was inches from mine. My heart immediately began to race as I sensed the warmth of his breath against my skin. Intense golden and blue eyes stared deeply into mine, sending shivers down my spine. I couldn't help noticing the freckles scattered across his face. His scars, more prominent up close, hinted at a lifetime of battles.

I quickly looked away, resisting the urge to keep staring.

"So, we wait. Thanks for paying attention; makes my job easier."

Leaning away from me, he turned and began unpacking. His sass was *not* needed and an extended middle finger from my right hand directed straight to his back slightly eased my mood.

Even though it felt like we hadn't done much on this trip so far, I was glad for the chance to rest. Riding hadn't been overly strenuous, but my unaccustomed thighs and tailbone were grateful for the break. I could only imagine how the horses felt carrying all our shit.

Walking over, I helped unpacking. "You know things would probably go more smoothly for us if you weren't so damn mysterious."

"I'm not being mysterious. Some things are better left unsaid, while others deserve to be heard."

"Like how you know all of this in the first place?"

"Exactly."

I nudged him playfully with my elbow. "Come on, you can't just dangle all this intrigue in front of me and expect me not to want to know more. How did you learn about The Vale, the Sprites, all of *this*?"

He chuckled and rubbed the spot where my elbow had jabbed him, like I'd *really* done damage. "You're a stubborn little thing, aren't you? The woods that make up the kingdom, Rose, they're the best damn tutor you'll ever find. I mean, think about it. Even the gods found refuge here once. The trees surrounding us have seen everything since the dawn of time, and the magic you've been hidden from? It's all around us, raw and waiting. If you listen close enough, it'll teach you. You just gotta open your heart."

The way he spoke, the depth of his words had this way of reeling me in. His deep love for nature was admirable to say the least. Despite his youth, which I guessed to be his mid to late twenties, he spoke as if he had been around since the gods walked with us.

The more he opened, the more I could see him visibly softening.

"My folks weren't around much," he confessed as he started a small fire. "It was mostly just me and Amarisa. We spent a lot of time together, filling our days with nature and getting lost in its secrets. My people have always had a sort of connection with these lands, but I swear, Rose, it's like it opened its arms to me. I bonded with the creatures, learning their stories and legends. But as I got older, my eyes were opened to the darkness behind the beauty to the dangers that lurk when you're not looking."

His demeanor changed, mismatched eyes growing darker. I could feel the sadness radiating from him, and I didn't know how to react. Satisfied with the small flame he had produced, he began rubbing the tattoos on his arms, fingers tracing the intricate ink covering his olive skin.

"There's a saying that all magic comes with a price, and I've seen it for myself, trust me. Believe it or not, I didn't grow up wishing to be a huntsman." He chuckled. "But when it found me, I was consumed. I had always been good at tracking and hunting, but when more than food needed to be put on the table, I knew it wasn't enough. Eventually, I got damn good at extracting information. Some information I've heard over the years should never be shared, so I got good at keeping secrets too."

He paused, swallowing hard. "I had stumbled onto The Vale during a mission. Sure, there had been rumors about it existing, but I never cared to find out for myself. Anyways, I got hurt and I was bleeding pretty badly. I was barely holding on by the time I managed to crawl into that lake over there."

Nodding behind us, I hadn't even noticed the lake's existence when we first arrived. The water shimmered with the sinking sun, seeming to invite me in as well.

"I passed out at some point and when I woke up, I was lying on a bed of feyblooms surrounded by these tiny blue creatures who risked everything to save a total stranger."

Feeling like I'd seen it all myself, my heart swelled. "They must have seen something in you that day. Revealing themselves like that? That's special, Ryder."

He nodded, a soft smile gracing his lips. "My grandpa used to call me '*Lakotawe*,' which means 'The Lucky One'. So, yeah. I owe them everything. I pledged myself to them that night, to protect them anyway I could. Even when the war was worsening, I was going to help them relocate to a more hidden spot of the kingdom, but they wanted to stay here. But it's been years since I last visited. That's why I asked Vixin if The Vale still stood. This '*weed patch*' is all that remains of those who dared exploit what once thrived."

The beauty and brutality of the world shimmered in his eyes. My heart ached at the depth of his connection to everything around us.

"It's a fine line," he said, kneeling to add more branches to the fire. "These Sprites—they're tough as shit. No matter how much the world has screwed them over, you'll never meet a nicer creature. The world gave up on them, but they stood their ground. It just shows no matter how small you are, you can always be stronger than those trying to take you down. I guess it speaks to me. It shows me that in a world as dark and messed up as ours, there's always a glimmer of hope."

"So why now? Why let *me* in on all of this? If you've been guarding their secret for so long, why expose it to me?"

Illuminated by the dancing fire across his face, his golden eyes gleamed. "Because even for someone as annoying as you, I can see you have a good heart. I think they saw I had a good heart when they saved me, so just like them, I'm taking a chance on you."

If my heart was as good as you thought, I wouldn't need to lie to you.

Guilt crawled up my throat. He saw good in me...yet I had barely said any truthful things about myself. I had never doubted I was a good person; I knew that to be true. But if I was one, why were such bad things happening to me? Happening to those I love?

"So, do I get to know why we're here?"

Dragging over a nearby log, he sat and rested his arms on his knees. I joined, sitting close but not too close, still feeling the heat radiating off him.

He looked at me,."I think they'll be able to tell us where that dagger came from."

Well, that wasn't what I was expecting to hear.

"Wait...*what*? What do you mean?"

Leaning back, he took a deep breath, like he needed all the oxygen in the world to tell me. "Their connection to the natural and magical world runs deeper than any other creature we could run into. If that dagger was forged with magic, which I'd bet money on, they can sniff it out for us."

I shook my head. "Regardless of whether the dagger itself is magic or not, we know the creature who used it *was*. Why do we need to know the origins of the dagger?"

"I told you already, this isn't an ordinary dagger. Regardless of your theories on how the Shadow Walker got its hands on it, it's a piece to the puzzle. And, before you ask, just because Shadow Walkers come from a Witch's magic doesn't mean the dagger did."

His explanation did nothing to make this feel any less like a riddle that was impossible to solve. I felt dizzy, my mind racing in a poor attempt to absorb everything. I had a feeling the dagger was the source of darkness. Why else would I have had such a reaction when I touched it?

"And what if they can't?"

"Then we track down the Witch behind it. Summoning a Shadow Walker isn't some simple spell; it costs the Witch a piece of their soul. When something that dark is called, the whole coven is affected. Even if they weren't aware their sister was doing this, whatever coven she's attached to would know now."

"All magic comes with a price" is a phrase I've heard more in the past week than I had my entire lifetime. My aunt, Queen Adela, and now Ryder had all mentioned using such powers would come with a price, but I never could have imagined it would be a piece of their very *souls*!

Why would Witches want to risk that? Was revenge worth it?

"You know quite a bit about Witches. Have you ever met one?"

His eyes scanned me up and down, stopping at the red hair braided down my chest. "Once or twice."

The world of magic overwhelmed me.

Each day away from home revealed how much had been hidden from me; myths and stories—every one of them true. Deep down, I understood that if I had remained sheltered, I would have *never* discovered any of this.

Resentment grew with every passing moment.

To be the future queen yet remain so ignorant of my kingdom felt *embarrassing*. I grew up privileged, and I knew it. I acknowledged that my upbringing was far easier than most in my kingdom. Yet, encountering someone like Ryder and hearing about the world he grew up in left me feeling like I had lived in the poorest part of the land.

Any envy I felt was being swallowed by unease. The dagger hummed at my hip, like it knew it was consuming my thoughts. Could an object be evil? That had to be the only explanation for the reaction I had. I could blame it on going into shock after seeing my father murdered, but I would just be lying to myself. I was practically thrown into another world the moment my skin touched the cool metal.

And Father... He must have known the dangers magic brought. The walls he built, both figurative and literal, kept the world out and *me* in. Marrying me off to Xander would have opened a whole new world. He must have known that. So why keep it from me?

In a world as large as ours, all magic couldn't be evil... Right?

But *Witches*.

They were as evil as the Fae, if not worse.

The war started with a simple mistake, a misunderstanding that should have been easy to fix. But no one wanted to own up to it, so lives were lost. My people, so *many* of them, died! It was all because of some greedy humans hungry for power! The suffering that came from this war was endless and I had a feeling no amount of rain could wash away the blood covering my family's hands.

Was there any good left in this world?

My body moved before my mind caught up. Ryder's eyes followed me, but he remained quiet and still. Another unseen pull was drawing me to the very lake he had almost died in. I looked into the gently rippling water, and my reflection stared back—a far cry from the polished image of a princess.

Frizzy hair framed my face, and the band around my unruly strands felt like a mask, concealing my identity. Fatigue weighed down my eyelids, making me look anything *but* regal.

Feeling the weight of everything pressing down on me, I sighed and knelt beside the lake. Dipping my hands into the cool water, I fought off a shiver as I cupped a handful and splashed my face.

I needed to wake up from this dream I found myself in.

The sun was slowly sinking behind me, causing the water to grow darker along with it. Wiping my eyes clear, I nearly stumbled back when I saw a reflection that wasn't mine staring back at me from the water.

Yellow eyes, like the sun itself, stared back at me where my emerald gaze had been just moments before. I scrambled away from the shore as a blast of blue light shot out from the lake, heading straight for me. With arms raised in defense and eyes squeezed shut, I held my breath, bracing for impact.

But it never came.

Instead, a soft, melodic sound like tinkling bells wrapped around my soul, instantly calming me. Opening my eyes, my heart skipped a beat as I watched a small, radiant blue being flutter right in front of my face.

Its translucent wings flickered like a miniature sapphire beacon as it hovered before me, no bigger than my hand. The creature's skin resembled water, all glistening and fluid, with tiny fingers ending in delicate webbed digits. Its hair flowed like a waterfall, the color of a pristine ocean, following its every movement.

Overwhelmed yet full of wonder, I hesitantly reached my trembling hand towards the creature; fingers outstretched to dare and touch it. Slowly, it drifted closer, letting me feel its skin's gentle, cool texture. Up close, I could see the necklace around its neck, tiny luminescent crystals highlighting its collarbone.

Its cheeks flushed, turning the little blue face a simple shade of violet, like a ripe blueberry. I smiled. The creature's small, magenta lips mirrored my own, revealing tiny dimples no bigger than the head of a pin. Its pointed ears twitched, and, suddenly, it all made sense.

I was face to face with a *Sprite*!

Ryder approached from behind as I continued to observe every inch of the Sprite. Two warm hands lightly rested on my shoulders, filling me with a scent that was purely...*forest*.

As he knelt, his warmth enveloped me. "Well, hello Iris."

The little Sprite's eyes left mine and focused on Ryder—her little cheeks seeming to blush further in his presence.

"Iris, this is Rose, and she's a friend. If you don't mind, we're here to learn some things from you."

The Spite, Iris, raised her little brow in my direction. Ryder chuckled softly, his laughter mingling with the warmth of his hands still resting on my shoulders. "I know, I know. But trust me, okay?"

Iris responded with a series of delicate, high-pitched musical notes that seemed to dance in the air. I couldn't understand her, but Ryder somehow could.

A Huntsman full of surprises.

As she continued, Ryder nodded in agreement at whatever she was saying. "You know I wouldn't have risked coming here if it wasn't important, no matter how much I missed you."

Her blush deepened, and I smirked, *very* aware of how effortlessly the huntsman could turn my cheeks pink too.

The gentle, pulsating glows from her necklace seemed to

answer for her, prompting Ryder to withdraw his hands from my shoulders and stand. "She says she can help, but we'll need to follow her."

Iris buzzed until she was inches away from my face. "It's a pleasure to meet you, Iris, and I appreciate your eagerness to help me."

Ryder reached a hand and effortlessly pulled me from the ground. Straightening my clothes, the sinking sun cast a golden light that shimmered perfectly against his dark hair, and I had to glance away before getting too lost in it.

Iris fluttered her way up to my cheek, tapping it lightly with her little fingers.

I nodded. "Lead the way!"

CHAPTER 18

GUIDED BY IRIS, we re-entered the heart of The Vale.

The sinking sun had to have been playing tricks on my eyes because the deeper we ventured, the more the humble weed patch transformed into an otherworldly garden. The flowers dazzled like feyblooms, their colors ranging from gentle pastels to intense, vibrant hues. Nature's artistry wove a captivating tapestry across the landscape. As the flowers opened and bloomed, countless tiny blue Sprites fluttered from the petals.

Stretching their arms and wings, their eyes tracked our movements—hesitant yet curious as I passed. Hovering in the air, their wings cast a soft, iridescent glow, adding to the enchantment.

So that's what Vixin meant about the "twinkling lights" during golden hour.

It wasn't stars or mystical artifacts; it was the reflections of the setting sun on the Sprites' wings. Bathed in the sun's warm, golden glow, their wings sparkled like the most exquisite jewels, casting a magical radiance throughout The Vale.

I couldn't help but smile wide, utterly filled with wonder and awe.

Iris led us to a magnificent oak tree that towered above the others. Its sprawling roots twisted through the soil like giant serpents, each one thicker and longer than the last. The other Sprites followed behind us silently, their bright eyes curiously watching our every move. Iris hurried to the center of the majestic oak and lightly tapped her tiny knuckles on its ancient bark.

Ryder took a cautious step, moving beside me. His mismatched eyes stayed fixed on the oak, and I could feel the tension in his shoulders without even looking at him. As I started to move towards it, Ryder's firm grip on my shoulders stopped me.

When I glared back at him, his face was stern. He gently pulled me back, bringing me to his side. "Give it some space."

Without questioning him, I stood and waited. The silence of The Vale broke as the leaves rustled in the trees. The Sprites began to hum, as if beckoning to the oak. Just as I thought about taking another step forward to investigate, the ground beneath us began to tremble. Tiny pebbles shifted around us, a low hum resonating, matching the Sprites' song. They moved slowly towards the tree, the vibrations growing louder by the second.

Suddenly, the massive oak split open down the middle with such force, it nearly knocked me off my feet. Ryder's strong arms caught me just in time, saving me from falling face-first into the dirt. A brilliant blue light burst forth, causing me to shield my eyes. When I dared to look again, the radiance had faded, revealing a single Sprite nestled within the heart of the tree.

Her hair was long and gray, eyes almost as ancient as the oak she emerged from. Unlike the others, she bore the marks of time. Gnarled lines decorated her face and wings. Despite her probable age, her beauty shone. I felt mesmerized just as I had been with Iris—if not more.

Flowing through the air like a breeze, the elder Sprite approached us, her gaze set on me. Ryder removed his hold and gracefully knelt. I hardly registered the small tug on my arm until it became more forceful the second time. Ryder shot me a look that screamed for me to follow his lead.

Falling to my knee, I bowed my head—heart pounding audibly in my chest as the sound of fluttering wings grew near. A small, raspy melody emerged from the Sprite's lips and after a moment or two, Ryder shifted his weight from his bent knee and confidently stood. Unable to hold my curiosity, I tracked his movements.

The elder Sprite continued to advance until she was only a foot away from his face. She spoke again to the huntsman, and I strained my ears to try and catch anything I could potentially understand. Still, it remained foreign.

Ryder nodded along as the elder Sprite kept talking. His gaze briefly met mine, and then he motioned for me to stand. I must have been holding my breath because I felt lightheaded as I rose. Trying to steady myself, I studied his face, hoping to catch any hint of emotion about what they were discussing.

When the bells finally ceased, Ryder slowly turned his face towards me, his throat bobbing. "This is Elder Madrona," he introduced. "She is one of the survivors of the genocide. It was her and a handful of others who rebuilt everything you see."

Briefly looking over his shoulders, I was met with

Madrona's yellow eyes on me, *studying* me. Her tiny face remained unreadable.

"She welcomes you to The Vale. As a friend of mine, you are considered a friend to her and the rest of the Blessing,"

A group of Sprites is called a "Blessing." Noted.

"She also understands why we've come and requests to see the dagger."

Shit. I forgot the whole reason we were here.

Fumbling like a child, I reached for the weapon, and my hands trembled as I presented it. Madrona's yellow eyes locked onto the dagger, her ancient gaze unwavering. With a delicate hand, she reached out her tiny, webbed fingers and hesitated before touching the blade's hilt. A low, resonant hum filled the air as her touch met the dagger's blade.

Her lips formed a long, knowing smile, and her eyes took on a ghostly white hue. I was growing more anxious by the minute, and my stomach felt like I was doing cartwheels. Madrona's aged features remained stoic. Her fingers traced the intricate engravings on the dagger's hilt. As her eyes returned to their normal yellow hue, her melody once again filled the forest.

"The blade is dark," Ryder translated. "Made only from the deepest evils that roam under the ground beneath us, one only a few can access without giving their lives to the King of the Below."

Well shit.

"The Below" is a place you wouldn't want to end up after death. Its where damned souls linger in eternal darkness. Unlike the ancient gods who once roamed alongside the Fae, the King of the Below is a...newer addition. Legends say he emerged from the essence of darkness itself, much like the Shadow Walkers.

The realm stayed unclaimed by any deity for centuries until he took it as his own.

Madrona's lips moved in a series of delicate, high-pitched notes as she continued. Ryder listened intently. "She's explaining that the magic it holds predates even the Fae. It's older...*shit*...older than the realm itself. When it was forged, it was made with the power of the gods. But over time, it turned *dark*—turned dark when our world did."

My stomach twisted. "Okay... So we know where it came from. But that doesn't explain why it was gifted to me and then used against my father."

Her melody echoed through the forest, as if understanding me despite my language barrier. Ryder furrowed his brow as he listened, his expression darkening.

He nodded once, his jaw clenched. When he turned toward me, the intensity in his gaze sent my heart racing. "The dagger has been lost for generations. It was forgotten among humanity, turned into a legend," he explained. "It's not just a weapon; it's a key to forbidden realms and a harbinger of shadows. The engravings on its hilt are a binding spell, connecting it to forces that seek to exploit its power."

I was going to throw up.

"The Witch or Witches who summoned the Shadow Walker did it on purpose, specifically to make it come out of *that* blade. Rose, I know you don't want to believe it, but it wasn't an accident that it was gifted to you. They knew what would happen when the time came."

I gulped. "And what of it now? Is it even safe to have with us? Could...could another come?"

Madrona's hum took on a mournful tone. "She believes it's fine now. Once its purpose was fulfilled, it was no longer a gateway. A Witch would need it in her possession again to harness its magic. We should be safe."

Should. We *should* be safe.

For what felt like the millionth time in the past several days, my stomach churned with anxiety.

I think I had frozen up or forgotten to breathe. Whichever one, I was brought back when Ryder spoke my name.

Refocusing, Elder Madrona's piercing yellow eyes felt like icy shards that penetrated my core. If I wasn't feeling uncomfortable enough, her gaze didn't help. Warmth filled my side as Ryder also studied me with a different type of intensity—one of worry and care. I looked towards him, his lips pressed into a thin line almost hidden beneath his thick beard.

No amount of combat training or education could have prepared me for this. I was scared shitless. I knew this journey wouldn't be easy, but realizing that the dagger—the one gifted to me, always on my hip—was a harbinger of shadows and death?

Scared shitless doesn't even cover it.

I was overwhelmed with questions and emotions. All I wanted was one of those heart-to-heart conversations with Fiona. If I squeezed my eyes, I could almost see her perched at the edge of my bed, eager to hear every detail of my day. She was always ready to share laughter, tears, or deliver the reality check I so often needed.

She was *always* there.

Always ready to take some of my emotional baggage.

Castle Quinn, a place of comfort and familiarity, felt a million miles away. A small part of me missed the routine I had there and the companionship. Father and I butted heads more than once, but he was an extraordinary and caring man. As king, his duty was to preserve the kingdom's legacy, and as his sole heir, I was ready to sacrifice everything to ensure its prosperity.

This included sacrificing my very soul to find out who killed him.

My purpose as heir was to rule my kingdom and restore peace. I thought that meant marrying Xander, but maybe there was more to my destiny than that. Maybe I could restore peace in a *different* way. Maybe this dagger was the key to something completely new. If it had been lost all this time, maybe its resurfacing wasn't a coincidence.

Guilt crept up my throat at the thought.

Without the tragedy of my father's murder, would I have ever encountered any of this? Would this dagger have resurfaced regardless? I swallowed the guilt before it consumed me. Despite everything, I was more determined than ever. Even if I died trying, I would find who murdered my father and bring them to justice.

Even if that meant I would had to burn every Witch until I found the one responsible. They deserved it anyway. Once they were out of the way and I claimed the throne, I would reunite the realms and usher in a new era marked by goodness and unity.

I felt it in my bones.

Facing Elder Madrona, the gravity of my destiny weighed heavily on my shoulders. For the first time since encountering the wolf the previous night, my fingers began to tingle. Madrona's unwavering gaze shifted long enough to look at my hands.

Could she sense the change too?

"Elder Madrona said we could camp here for the night. Mind setting up while I walk her back?" Ryder's voice broke through my thoughts, and I realized that not only the elder's eyes were still on me.

I nodded and cautiously secured the dagger at my side, though it still trembled a bit. The Sprites around us murmured and returned to various parts of The Vale while Ryder walked Elder Madrona to her tree. Her melody lingered in the air as Ryder glanced back at me.

Moving away from where my footsteps had left a shallow trench, I returned to the horses. Jupiter's brown eyes followed the Sprites flitting around him, and I smiled at his amusement.

Grabbing the vials that constrained out tents, I shook off the lingering unease and began setting up our camp. The rhythm of building helped ease my kind for a little. Small flashes of blue danced before me as I added more wood to the fire.

After a few minutes, Ryder returned. His eyes met mine in the pulsing campfire glow, and the look of worry on his face didn't go unnoticed.

"Rose," he said gently, "you doing okay?"

"Oh, yeah! I set up the tents just like you showed me and kindled the fire. Do you think their flowers will be fine?"

His concern lingered, but his warm, reassuring smile returned. Settling in beside me, he took over whatever small task I was messing with. "I was more checking if you were okay with what Madrona said, not about the camp. It was heavy for someone who just lost their father."

"Oh," I laughed awkwardly. "Heavy is an understatement. But I...don't know. Can I get a rain check on that one?"

He smirked. "Of course."

Watching him work, a new wave of guilt settled in my gut. If all of this scared me, how the hell did it make him feel? I dragged practically a stranger into this mess and was asking him not only to help me uncover my father's murderer but also to risk his own life.

We both knew the dangers involved, but it didn't ease the unease clawing at me.

No matter his profession, he didn't know *me*, didn't know who I *really* was. He only knew me as "Rose"—the clumsy stranger who had begged for his help in that village.

I was Princess Genevieve, the heir to the Orphinian throne, and my father's murder likely marked me a traitor.

If we were caught, Ryder would be seen as my accomplice.

Ryder would be seen as my accomplice. Shit!

If I was found and arrested, they'd take Ryder, probably subjecting him to torture for answers. It was a terrifying thought, one I hadn't considered until now, and it sent chills down my spine. There was no way I could reveal my identity to him now; it was too risky.

Maybe that was a stroke of luck.

At least he could honestly say he didn't know who I really was.

If something happened, I'd protect him. Even if it meant never finding the answers I desperately sought, I'd sacrifice myself for him. It was the only option. Danger was everywhere, whether from the Shadow Walker or anyone else.

"You know, it's never too late to back out of this."

He went rigid. "Come again?"

"I just mean...with everything getting so *dark*, I'd understand if you would rather not continue with me. Just because you're a huntsman doesn't mean you need to put your life in danger for me."

As he faced me, his expression turned cold, almost angry—almost as if I had offended him deeply. Instantly, I regretted my words.

"Rose," he sighed heavily. "When I agreed to this, it wasn't because I liked your eyes or the way your nose crinkles when you're upset. I agreed because it's my *job*. But now that we're here, I'm in too deep. Sorry, but you're stuck with me."

I crossed my arms over my chest, trying to forget the nose-crinkling comment, "You're never in too deep until you're *dead*—and that's what I'm trying to prevent."

A muscle in his jaw clicked. "Stop trying to control the world around you and accept the help that's given, okay?" He took a deep breath. "Look, all of this is bigger than just your father. Bigger than *us*. I can feel it."

Our gazes locked, and a tightness gripped my chest. I'd known Ryder for only a few days, yet I felt a closeness to him that stirred my soul.

"So," he continued, "regardless of what you think is best for *me*, I'm staying. I *want* to stay. Like it or not."

My heart fluttered. As much as I wished he would just walk away and forget all this, forget *me*, I was relieved he chose to stay. Making him stay would have been one thing, but knowing he did it of his own accord made me feel a little better.

Stubborn Huntsman.

Standing, he wiped his hands on his trousers and walked away. My feet instinctively moved, following his lead as if I had a rope attached to my waist. "I didn't mean to upset you," I whispered, struggling to keep up.

He stopped.

"Nor offend you if I did. I just...I don't want another life lost because of me."

He turned to me, his face soft—his mismatched eyes heavy as he looked down at me. "Whether I live or die, your father's death was *not* because of you."

Lowering my gaze, I felt the sting of tears forming in my eyes. Warm fingers lightly engulfed my chin, gently pulling my head up until I couldn't look away.

When he dropped his fingers, I instantly missed the contact. "And, despite how annoyed you get with me and wish for my death—I will *not* die."

Heat rose to my cheeks. "I would never want you de—"

"Let me finish, please," he said, interrupting me. "I might not be able to promise a smooth journey or that you'll be back in your own bed by week's end, but here's what I *can* promise." He gently took my hands and knelt. "I'll see this journey through to the end, and I'll be your shield when you need it. Whether it's for you, your father's memory, or the sake of the realm—I'm with you."

Emotions swelled in my heart. The man kneeling in front of me was so different from the one I'd hired to help me. The warmth of his palms in mine, the intensity in his eyes—it all added to the storm inside me. I bit my lip, hoping I wouldn't blurt out something foolish and spoil the moment.

Grateful as I was, I couldn't help but feel confused.

What had Elder Madrona said to him on their walk? Had it influenced his gesture? A part of me didn't want to know, while another said to accept his allegiance and let it be.

At least for now.

I rolled my eyes and casually withdrew my hands from his, playfully giving him a shove. "Don't get all sappy on me!" I joked, putting on a show to hide my emotions. "If you're going to be my shield, I'll need my big, scary huntsman."

Our gazes locked, and his sincerity was undeniable. Those mismatched eyes held such a depth that it drew me in. By his side, I felt a surge of confidence like never before.

He nodded with a faint smile then turned to the Sprites encircling us. Their forms glimmered in the growing darkness, their voices humming and singing, casting a comforting aura over us.

When he turned back to me, Ryder's lips curved into a smile.

"Ready to party?"

CHAPTER 19

IN MY EIGHTEEN YEARS, I had attended numerous parties, balls, banquets, and other events that bored me to the bone.

But this was...*unique*.

The sun had sunk by the time we had finished setting up the camp and as soon as darkness consumed the grounds, the Sprites sprang into action. Music began to play almost immediately throughout The Vale, and dozens of little Sprites emerged around us. Their music, made up of their voices and strange little instruments, felt like a symphony of enchanted patterns and melodies.

Each note felt as if it carried a piece of the forest's magic.

I couldn't help but sway to the otherworldly rhythm. All the guilt, fear, and dread that weighed on me earlier seemed to vanish. Ryder and I kept warm by the fire, watching as Sprites of all ages and genders danced and sang around us. It was an enchanting spectacle, a welcome distraction from the darkness of our earlier conversation.

Amid the festivities, a few Sprites approached and offered us their best harvest. Plump fruits, vibrant vegetables, and other exotic foods glowed with an inner radiance. The flavors were unlike anything I'd ever tasted, each dish a blend of sweet and savory that left me craving more.

Watching Ryder savor each bite, his eyes briefly closed as pure bliss overtook him, I mirrored his gratitude and fully let the generous hospitality of our diminutive hosts consume me.

The Vale was alive with magic and life—a scent I never expected to encounter but instantly recognized. As I watched the joyful creatures, another sinking feeling gripped my gut. The Sprites' melodies and harmonies grew stronger with each new song. Some even drummed rhythmic beats on nearby tree stumps, adding to the cacophony.

Leaning forward towards Ryder, I attempted to raise my voice over the sounds. "Is it safe for them to be so...loud? Won't it draw unwanted attention, especially if someone comes across The Vale?"

"Don't worry," he said with a mouthful of fruit. "The Vale has a natural barrier. It conceals sounds and movements from outsiders unless a Sprite invites them in. We could be throwing a whole festival, and nobody outside would have a clue."

Magic was new to me. Obviously.

But it still didn't feel safe. The tingling in my fingers only reinforced that feeling. But Ryder's confidence told a different story, so I pushed the unease aside, not wanting to spoil the moment.

The little blue Sprites, survivors of a past genocide that turned their whole existence upside down, seemed okay with their celebration. So why should I question it?

Nervously, I re-braided my hair, the cool air grazing the nape of my neck as I shifted the autumn braid past my shoulders.

Iris danced around me, and her melody rang louder than all the others. Though I couldn't understand her words or song, I didn't need to. Her small presence felt familiar and comforting, easing me a little. When we locked eyes, her yellow hues sparkled with mischief. Grabbing the end of my braid, she gently tugged until I was forced to stand.

Caught up in the whimsical enthusiasm of the night, I gladly rose to my feet. Ryder, too, was being pulled up by a group of larger male Sprites, each as mischievous as Iris. They playfully nudged him backward until our bodies collided with a light thud, throwing me off balance. In a swift move, he turned, and his strong arms caught me before I could stumble further.

A flicker of surprise, or perhaps embarrassment, crossed his face as his eyes warmly met mine. Stepping away, I casually fiddled with my braid, trying to play it cool. Iris fluttered around him; her melody so rapid I doubted even Ryder understood. He rolled his eyes playfully and gently shooed her away.

As he turned, his smiling face toward me, my whole chest warmed. "They want us to join the dance," he shouted above the music.

My mouth dropped open at the thought of Ryder, the scary huntsman dancing with a bunch of tiny creatures in the middle of the woods. A burst of laughter bubbled within me, and I quickly covered my mouth to prevent it from escaping.

A large, warm hand enveloped the base of my back, pulling me close and silencing the giggles. I gasped at the unexpected touch, my cheeks flushed as Ryder's mismatched eyes lazily drank me in. His throat bobbed as he swallowed, nostrils flaring.

Though I'd danced with countless men over the years, his touch was unlike any other I'd felt.

Including Topher's.

His eyes held such a *fire*, one I didn't dare extinguish. I didn't want to. It was like he could see straight through me, sensing the effect his touch had on me.

I would gladly give up all the money in the world to keep him looking at me like that.

My pulse quickened, drawn in by the magnetic pull of his gaze. In one smooth move, he lifted my arm to rest on his shoulder, our fingers intertwining effortlessly in the other. The size difference between us was...laughable, but the comfort it provided was welcomed. Despite my upbringing, I felt stiff and awkward, far from the polished dancer I was supposed to be.

Seeing my hesitation, Ryder's lips curled into a knowing smirk.

Confidence radiated from him like a wildfire as he leaned closer, his voice low by my ear. "It would be a little rude of us to decline, and we wouldn't want to offend our gracious hosts." Pulling back, he towered over me. "Would we?"

I shook my head, still speechless. His face lit up with a wide, beaming smile, canines sparkling in the firelight. Without another word, he swept me into the lively dance, his strength and grace taking me by surprise. The Sprites' melody enveloped us, and soon we were spinning and laughing, our movements perfectly synchronized.

With each wild spin and messy dip, laughter bubbled from within me at the sheer absurdity of the situation. I could have easily gotten lost in his arms. His smile was the most genuine I'd seen, and it made my heart soar.

Amid the joy and festivities, I felt an undeniable thrill. The lively music and Ryder's infectious laughter created an atmosphere in which I felt free and alive.

I didn't know how badly I needed it.

As our chaotic dance continued, Ryder closed the gap between us, bringing our bodies intimately close and we moved as if we were one, not even an inch of air between our stomachs. The warmth of his body against mine was intoxicating.

I think even in the hottest desert, I would still crave his warmth.

Golden and sapphire eyes, so unique and inviting, lingered on me. They seemed to trace every curve of my form, as if he was truly seeing me for the first time. It thrilled me to my core.

I'd never been looked at like that before, not even by Topher.

Topher. Shit!

That was the second time his face had intruded into my thoughts. I was instantly confused all over again about what the hell that kiss meant between us. Yes, I was technically engaged to another, but my damn emotions still felt tied to Topher. Being this close to another man... Why was it so overwhelming? Topher had always made me feel secure., but with Ryder...I felt *alive*. I felt like I could be myself, not what others constantly expected from me.

He held no expectations over my head. I wasn't a princess to him, I was...*me*.

And here he was, wearing a gorgeous, encouraging smile, leading me in a joyful dance. The pull I felt towards him, regardless of the amount of time we spent together, was undeniable.

It was too much. Everything was *too* much!

Anxiety clutched at my throat, and I reluctantly pulled away from Ryder's strong arms. The look of disappointment on his face hit me like a slap to the cheek. My eyes darted around The Vale, desperately trying to find a way out.

I needed to *breathe*.

"I'm s-sorry," I stammered. "I just... I need some air."

Watching me closely, he didn't press.

Honestly, if he had said something, I wouldn't have heard him. My mind was far gone as I stepped away from the heart of The Vale and made my way into the dark forest.

Every step I took led me further and further away from the music and light of the fire. I steadied my breath and urged my feet to move faster, quickening my pace. Stepping through a thick force, I pressed past the barrier of The Vale—the music and light being lost behind me. The transition was startling, like moving from one world to another.

But I needed the silence, needed the *space*.

Compared to the music, the overwhelming hush of the forest was night and day—but I welcomed it. Gazing around at the absolute nothingness that surrounded me, my emotions peaked to the point I could no longer contain them.

Everything came crashing down like a wave breaking onto the shore. The sheer weight of solitude bore down on my shoulders, and the familiar lump in my throat returned. For the first time since the chaos engulfed my life, I allowed myself to release every emotion.

And I cried. *Hard*.

Tears streamed down my face, their warmth cutting through the chill of the forest. I tried to muffle my sobs with the sleeves of my tunic, but the release of my grief was unstoppable.

I leaned against a gnarled tree, my body trembling with each heaving breath. The overwhelming sadness and loss I had endured crushed me, and I felt smaller and more vulnerable than ever.

What the fuck am I doing?

Bending down, I let my head sink between my knees, my body convulsing with intense sobs. Grief, confusion, and a jumble of other emotions streamed out, every tear and every sob a relief. I felt the emotional burden lifting from my shoulders as I released it all.

My defenses had collapsed, and that inner voice returned, loud and unwavering.

Get it together and stand up!

I didn't. I couldn't. I *needed* to let this out. I *needed* to release everything and clear my head before I returned to The Vale.

The tingling sensation coursed through my fingers, intensifying as I raised my head from my knees. A twig snapping behind me spun my head around, but I remained seated. The forest's darkness loomed impenetrable; I couldn't see beyond a few feet in front of me.

Another branch snapped, this time from the opposite direction. I jumped to my feet, wiping my tear-stained eyes dry with the back of my left hand while my right inched toward the dagger on my hip. I fought to control my breathing, making each breath as silent as possible.

Run back to Ryder. Now!

Finally listening, I forced myself away from the tree and took my first step. Before I could move, I sensed a presence behind me—an unseen watcher.

And from the darkness, it spoke.

"Princess?"

CHAPTER 20

I GASPED as the figure emerged from behind a tree, a small oil lamp in their hands helped cast light upon their face.

I recognized them instantly.

"Sir Doyle?" I was dumbfounded. "What are you doing here?"

Although we had never challenged one another directly, Sir Doyle had spent many mornings sparring and training in the yard beside me. His distressed armor was barely visible in the dim light, but the Orphinian crest on the middle of his chest was clear.

Exhaustion coated his face, as if he hadn't slept in days. His brown eyes were wide, equally as surprised to see me as I was to see him. Sweat coated his brow and his brown hair clung to it despite the coolness of the night.

He took a step closer, and I instinctively took two steps back. "Princess Genevieve," he practically hissed. "Pardon my lack of formalities, but it's been a long forty-eight hours, and I'm tired."

The hint of disdain in his voice sent a sinking feeling to my stomach. His tone was unexpectedly cold and fierce. My hand, still resting on the dagger's hilt, twitched as I contemplated drawing it. A low humming reverberated through it, and I couldn't tell whether it emanated from the object itself or the trembling of my fingers.

Hesitantly, I looked past him. I had no fucking clue which direction I had come from. In the dark of the night, everything looked the same and that damn barrier prevented me from finding an easy escape route back to The Vale.

I would be a fool to think running into him was a coincidence. I knew why he was here—he was here for *me*. And where one knight treads, more are surely to follow.

Once again, I put on my mask of nonchalance. "I can see you're fatigued. Perhaps you should return to Castle Quinn." I tried to prevent my fear from showing. "You are rather far from the barracks, and I'm sure Commander Robert is wondering where one of his men ran off to."

He let out a light laugh. "And who do you think commanded me out here? Surely you don't think I traveled so far on holiday." He smacked his lips. "You haven't been a good princess, my lady, and it's time you return home for your crimes."

I had retreated so far backward, my back ran into the bark of the tree. I was *trapped*. Sir Doyle wasn't a big man, but he was quite large compared to me. His days on the training field had toned his muscles, but his nights in the tavern left his belly large. I knew I could hold my own in a fight, but not if he had others with him.

Summoning my best smile, I lifted a foot to lean casually

against the tree. It was a poor attempt to hide how trapped and scared I felt, but it was all I had. "I must apologize for the *inconvenience* of your travels, but I will not be accompanying you tonight. You may return to your men, and I shall return when I'm ready."

Even in the forest's darkness, I could see his features sinking. Maybe it wasn't my best idea to provoke him like this while I was alone, but I was also trying to give myself some time, praying Ryder would decide to look for me.

When he didn't move, I straightened my shoulders. "That's an order."

He threw his head back, releasing a spine-chilling laugh that sent shivers through my body. Disgust crept over me, my nose wrinkling at the sound.

When he found his composure, his eyes met mine. "You're in no position to give me orders, Princess. I have been tracking you since the moment you left the castle grounds. You did a good job throwing us off when you ran into the woods but were sloppy when you entered that village. Once the citizens found out the *princess* was missing, they sang like a morning dove. Although I see you covered the white; your hair is quite memorable. Not too many see hair like that nowadays."

He retreated a few paces, gaze sweeping over my features until finally settling on the handle of the dagger I clutched tightly—knuckles likely whitened from the grip.

His eyebrow twitched. "Did you know that red hair used to be an omen for a bloodline descended from Witches?"

I physically flinched. No, I'd never heard that before. My autumn-colored hair came from my mother, a trait I grew to appreciate despite hating it as a child.

"*Dirty blood*," he spat. "*They* tried to warn your father of it when he announced his engagement to your mother. *They* said the marriage would only cause the kingdom more suffering. More *death*. He didn't believe them, obviously. Now look where the old bastard is. Dead. Dead by...well, by your hands, Princess."

His words filled me with rage, and my hands tightened harder around the dagger. Pushing myself away from the tree, I took a step forward, completely unafraid of him.

"You know *nothing* of my father's death!" I spat through clenched teeth. "You also know nothing of my mother or our blood. So, as I said before, I suggest you shut your mouth and return home before you really piss me off."

"Oh, I plan on returning home, Princess," he took a wobbly step forward, "but I don't plan on returning empty-handed."

Moving quickly, Sir Doyle reached for my wrist. Before I could react, he pulled me towards him, twisting my arm behind my back. I yelped at the sudden pain—the smell of whiskey invading my nostrils as he lowered his face towards mine.

Why the hell would he be drinking during a hunt?

He pulled me closer until my back rested against his chest. "Do you want to know why I'm alone?"

"Because you couldn't stand the thought of fighting for my attention?" I sarcastically spat.

He showed no amusement. "I started with three other men —the best in the kingdom at tracking and hunting *criminals* like yourself. After speaking with a few locals in Heim and finding a dirty royal maid's frock in the river, we knew you weren't far."

Fiona's dress. Dammit! I had unknowingly left them a bread-crumb.

"We tracked you from the village to the woods last night. Even with another set of impressions next to yours, Jupiter leaves a distinct set of tracks. Did you know his horseshoes have our crest engraved on the bottom? His are rather worn, but we knew what to look for." He let out a small laugh, and I held back a gag from the smell of his breath. "Night came quickly, and I knew we were close. I could *sense* it. As we closed in, w-we were *attacked*! It came out of nowhere—a flash of black fur in the darkness of the night. It happened all so quickly! Before we could react, it had one of my men in its jaws. In a blink, his neck was broken, practically sliced in two from its canines. The beast moved on, taking each man down one by one until its eyes bore into mine."

He remained very still behind me, and I used it to my advantage, shifting my feet to improve my stance.

"The devil, I saw." His voice was a whisper. "Its eyes were like fire and ice all at the same time, and its teeth...like *daggers*. So sharp, so thirsty for blood. Never had I seen a wolf so large."

I stopped shifting my feet.

A wolf? I knew I had heard howling!

I thought the wolf in the shadows had come for *me*, but it...protected me? Or did those men just fall victim to it before I even had a chance to be eaten?

"All I remember is pain and red flooding my vision. When I awoke, my men were all dead, and my leg was soaked."

Looking down at his legs, I could barely make out the large gash in his left calf, but it was there. It started at the base of his ankle and up to his knee. Though the fabric of his pant legs partially covered it, I knew it was deep and raw.

And most likely infected.

I now understood why he needed to drink the whiskey.

He was in *pain*.

"I was able to escape the massacre and continued to track you. All the horses ran off during the attack, so I had to continue on foot. You'd be surprised how much pain a bottle or two of whiskey takes away. The gods put me through a trial and rewarded me with you falling into my hands. What a *sweet* reward it is, too."

He moved his face so our cheeks touched. The grip on my wrists tightened, and I could faintly feel his lips move into a grin.

"So, what now?" I tried to move my face away from his breath. "How do you expect to drag me back to Castle Quinn with a bum leg and no horse?"

"Dear Princess," he chuckled. "I sent a messenger raven back to the palace as soon as possible. Once we make our way back to a main road, it should take no time at all for more of my men to find us. Then, you'll get your judgment day. I pray the gods don't have as much mercy on you as they did on me."

He twirled me around so I was now facing him, my wrists still clenched in his hands. Pulling me closer, our faces were mere inches apart. "A shame, too." His heavy eyes lowered to my lips. "We all had such hopes for you. It's a pity you won't be much good to us without a head."

"Like *hell*!"

I exploded.

My skin felt warm again, and I moved fast, sending the tip of my boot into his exposed wound. It didn't take long for him to let go of my wrist, all his attention falling to his leg. He collapsed on the cold forest ground, hands grabbing at his leg to minimize the pain.

Through gritted teeth, he let out another chilling laugh. "Now, now, Princess. Is that any way to treat an old friend?"

"An old friend wouldn't be personally escorting me back to my death sentence, regardless of the crime you *believe* I've committed."

I moved to step past him, wasting no time in my escape. Just as I was about to break into a sprint back to The Vale—back to *Ryder*—Sir Doyle's strong hand clamped around my ankle. I stumbled to the ground, my cry of surprise echoing through the forest.

Struggling to catch my breath from the impact, my body shifted as he dragged me closer to him. My chin caught on fallen branches, sending waves of pain through my body. Using all my strength, I maneuvered my body until I forced myself to flip onto my back. Caught off guard, Sir Doyle's grip momentarily loosened, and I was able to kick free, one blow satisfyingly landing square across his jaw.

He gripped his face, and I knew I had broken his nose. A small smile crept on my face as I sprung to my feet, dagger now fully unsheathed in my hands. If I ran in the direction I thought I came from, I could possibly lead him straight to The Vale. But the elements could take us both out if I ran in the opposite direction.

I had to end this. Right here, right *now*.

The dagger hummed in my grasp. I felt it calling to me —*begging* me to use it to end his life. Sizing him up, I knew that even despite his injury, I couldn't underestimate his skill. His experience showed, no matter how much his leg and face hurt him.

Slowly rising to his feet, he wiped the blood from his nose

and smiled. "That'll be the last blow you land on me tonight, Princess."

"Doubtful."

He launched himself at me, unsheathing his blade as he moved. I only caught a flash of light from the moon's reflection before he aimed it for my throat. I swiftly deflected the strike, our blades clashing with a metallic ring that reverberated through the silent woods.

We circled each other, tension so thick in the cool air, you could have choked. Deciding to wait him out, I knew it would only be a matter of time before I used enough of his energy to tire him out. Either exhaustion or the crippling pain would cause him to pass out, and I was ready to wait it out.

Finally, he lunged at me, using up a good portion of his strength to send a series of rapid punches in my direction. How he moved reminded me of a cornered animal—nervous and guarded. I evaded most of his strikes, but his right hook grazed my cheek. The impact stun, a small gash instantly forming. He smiled, and my fury rose.

That was *enough*.

Channeling my heightened anger, I launched a powerful kick straight at his injured leg. The impact landed, and the cry he uttered as he stumbled back was music to my ears. His face twisted in agony, and I made my move.

Seizing the moment, I swept him off his feet and sent him stumbling. He staggered backward, desperately trying to catch his footing before he hit the ground. Not allowing him the opportunity, I jumped, and he crashed with a thud. I saw red; my fists flew in a flurry of punches that relentlessly drove him further into the forest floor. Though he tried to parry my strikes, his face twisted in agony with each movement.

Adrenaline overtook me and I never felt stronger. My heart pounded like a drum to keep me pushing. The voice inside only encouraging me further.

He's weak! Use it to your advantage!

Being the stubborn old bastard he was, Sir Doyle was not about to give up. In a move I didn't see coming, he closed the gap between us and grabbed me, his hands like vices on my wrists. Shifting his weight, he rolled us over until I was certain his body would crush me. My back hit the ground so violently I saw stars.

The blood dripping from his broken nose dripped onto my cheek and I channeled all my energy into moving my hand from his wrist to end the job, the dagger still humming in my hand.

Skillfully, he moved to disarm me and used pressure points on my wrists until I was forced to release the dagger. I gasped from the pain, my muscles went limp untilI was left helpless beneath him.

The forest floor hummed where the dagger lay, and I aimed my full attention at it—silently begging for it to somehow return to my grasp. Whether it was the adrenaline pumping through my veins or an illusion caused by the night, I wasn't sure...but I could have *sworn* the dagger twitched an inch towards me.

The stare Sir Doyle held as he straddled my waist was firm. Refusing to show weakness, I met his gaze. A victorious glint shone in his eyes as an evil grin showed the true depths of darkness in his soul.

Breathing heavily, his voice was barely a whisper, "It didn't have to be like this, Princess."

I spat in his face, a mix of liquids forming on his cheek. His smile never faltered, and the smell of alcohol returned to my nostrils. Fear fluttered through my chest, and I desperately ran through multiple scenarios on how the hell I would get out of this.

None of them looked good.

His hands released my wrists, but I still couldn't move them. I was frozen in place. Whether it was from fear or the pressure points, I didn't know. He leaned in closer, his hands moving towards my throat—his fingers tightening as a sinister smirk curled on his lips.

I gasped for air as my mind fought against his deadly grip, but my body refused to move. I could feel the darkness creeping in, threatening to consume me.

"Long live Queen Liliana!" he said, gripping tighter until I thought my throat may burst.

W-what? L-Liliana was...Queen?

Fight, damn you! Fight!

My inner voice was screaming at me, but I couldn't. My body couldn't fight. Sir Doyle was sent to find me, to return me to face my *"sins"*. Dead or alive, if I had to assume.

Looks like *Option A.* was the winner of the evening.

Despite the numbness in my limbs, I could still feel my fingers on fire. It was the same intense sensation I had felt with Xander in the garden. The trees around us began to shake, showering us with countless leaves. The harder he squeezed, the more it felt like something inside me was screaming—no —*begging* to be let out.

But I was too weak.

My body felt like it was both dying and electric at the same time. A surge of energy rushed through me, but it didn't help the numbness in my arms. As Sir Doyle removed his hands from my neck, a flash of light crossed his face. He stared at me in shock, as if *I* was the source of the light.

Where did it come from?

Regaining his resolve, he was quickly back at it—squeezing my neck until there would be nothing left of me but a corpse.

Ryder's face flashed in my mind as my vision dimmed. I knew he'd come looking eventually, but by then, it might be too late. I'd either be lying dead on the ground, branded as a murderer, or vanished without a trace after being dragged back by Sir Doyle.

The thought of hurting him, leaving him *alone*, stirred something inside me, but it wasn't enough against the hands around my throat.

Ryder didn't deserve to find me like that, bruised and gone. Though death wasn't a stranger in his profession, he deserved *love*. Someone who could match his strength and wit. Someone to be there since his family wasn't.

For a moment, as we danced under the stars, I dared to believe *I* could be that person for him. Even if it was just as a friend, I *wanted* to be that.

I could be, if he allowed me.

But not if I was dead.

As my eyes began to shut from the loss of air, a low growl pierced the stillness of the night, causing me to force them open. Sir Doyle's head shot up, his grip faulting around my neck.

His eyes grew as he whispered, "*Psychopomp*," before crawling away from in pure terror.

Gasping for air, I regained my vision as quickly as I could. Weakly raising my head, I could barely make out the origin of the horror until it was *all* I could see.

The wolf with the same fearsome eyes I had seen at camp stood merely a few feet away. The creature's massive lips curled around its teeth, and drool puddled around its paws. Its eyes were locked on the now trembling knight. For someone who had almost taken a life, I had never seen such a scared man.

In an instant, the wolf lunged towards him with a blood-curdling snarl. All I could do was watch as the creature collided with Sir Doyle, its powerful jaws clamping down on his arm. His scream spread throughout the woods as he flailed and fought desperately against the relentless assault. Blood splattered across the ground, leaves, and trees, leaving the once peaceful forest now a crime scene.

Finding my strength, I crawled backward, coughing and gasping for air as I clutched my sore throat—dagger somehow back in my palm. The forest's silence had transformed into chaos, a gruesome dance of life and death unfolding before me.

Seeing the wolf fully for the first time, I was awestruck. My initial guess had been spot on; it stood as tall as a horse and had the breadth of a bear. Its fur, a midnight tapestry, absorbed the slivers of moonlight as it prowled. Those warm eyes that had watched me in the camp's darkness last night now gleamed with primal focus as they locked onto their prey.

Keeping silent despite my raspy breaths, I remained still. As terrifying as it was, it was also...gorgeous. The large wolf looked as if it was taken straight out of one of the paintings in the Grand Hall. It moved fluidly, as if this was its sole purpose in life.

To *kill*.

With a low growl, the beast let go of Sir Doyle's leg. It was like watching a deadly game of cat and mouse, and the bleeding knight was the smallest mouse around. He tried to crawl away, but before a heartbeat passed, the wolf bit down on Sir Doyle's neck. The crunch sent ripples of nausea through me. With a final, savage shake of its head, the wolf dropped the knight's lifeless body to the forest floor with a heavy thud.

For the first time in what felt like hours, the forest was silent.

Panting heavily, the wolf slowly raised its head from the lifeless body and met my stare. Its eyes were stunning and the gaze they held was almost...understanding, like it knew I was no threat to it and it had done me a huge favor. The way it looked at me, the warmth of its gaze, felt almost familiar.

It immediately sent shivers down my spine.

Like a fluid dance, it effortlessly shifted its massive body in my direction, approaching slowly. My heart pounded so hard I thought it might jump out of my chest.

The closer the black wolf came, the more its size became apparent. Its paws, each the size of a dinner plate, moved gently toward me. I sat frozen, watching intently. The massive head lowered until we were eye-to-eye, a perfect representation of fire and ice in its gaze.

Just as Sir Doyle had described.

Lowering its head even more, the wolf nudged my hand with its blood-soaked snout. My eyes widened, heart racing. Unsure of what to do, I hesitated, watching the creature closely. After another nudge of my hand, I cautiously placed it on top of its head.

Its glowing eyes softened as it leaned into my touch. Surprisingly, its fur was soft, and the warmth radiating from the creature began to soothe my racing heart.

"T-Thank you," I whispered.

As if it understood me, its large eyes blinked before gracefully stepping away. Slowly, my breathing started to steady. Like a ghost, the wolf moved deeper into the shadows, giving me one last glance before nodding its head and disappearing into the night.

The forest grew almost too silent as the minutes stretched on. I sat in the darkness, my gaze locked on the direction the wolf had gone. Finally deciding to test my strength, I wobbly attempted to stand.

A voice frantic with worry, pierced through the distance. It was Ryder, calling out for *me*.

"Rose!"

I could hardly see him as he emerged from the darkness. I opened my mouth to respond to his call, but my voice failed as my legs gave out from under me. I crumpled to the ground, any adrenaline the gods had blessed me with leaving my body in an exhausting rush.

Everything went hazy, my vision darkening as I struggled to stay conscious. I knew I was going to pass out.

Would I wake up? Would I die in his arms?

Coming into view between my heavy eyelids, Ryder's face matched his tone as he hovered over me. Without a second thought, he gathered my limp body into his arms, pulling me close.

"Rose? *Rose!* Stay with me," he urged. "You're okay. You'll be okay."

His eyes bore into me, and warmth rushed through my chest. The worry etched on his face was enchanting, like he genuinely cared. Though barely visible, I knew his brows were furrowed. His calloused hands brushed over my hair, damp with my blood. I stared at his face, his eyes seeming to glow in the darkness of the night.

"Fire and ice," was all I could manage to croak before slipping away further.

His hands brushed frantically over my face and side, searching for injuries. "Don't you pass out on me, okay? Not yet! I'm sorry I didn't get here sooner! I'm so fucking sorry."

I tried to respond, to tell him about the wolf and Sir Doyle, but darkness claimed me before I could say a word. The last thing I remembered was the sound of his voice calling my name.

Begging me to stay.

CHAPTER 21

I GRADUALLY AWOKE in my softly illuminated tent.

My head was aching worse than ever, even worse than a morning after sneaking wine with Fiona and the knights. My body felt like an anchor, pinning me to the cot. No part of me wanted to move, but for the sake of knowing how bad the damage was, I slowly forced my body to rise.

As I stirred, I struggled against the blanket I was deeply tucked into. In the corner of the tent, a small, flickering lantern cast gentle shadows across canvas borders. Looking around, Ryder sat nearby, his eyes glowing with relief as he noticed me stirring awake.

He moved quickly to be by my side, hands gently resting beside mine on the cot. "Hey, Wiyahna, you're awake," he whispered. "How are you feeling?"

I groaned softly and attempted to sit up, my arms straining as I propped myself on my elbows. "Like I've been run over by a carriage," I rasped. "What happened?"

Shifting his weight, he held his leather canteen of water towards me. I gratefully accepted and took a small sip.

"You tell me." His tone was more serious. "One minute, you're taking a walk, and the next, I find you on the brink of passing out with a dead knight next to you!"

As I took another sip, vivid memories of Sir Doyle and the wolf resurfaced. My fingers instinctively touched the scabbing wound on my chin and the other on my cheek.

I managed a small smile. "Sounds like you missed one hell of a party."

His face fell. "Stop it. Seriously, what the hell happened out there? After you didn't come back, I got worried and went looking for you. And I guess I was right to be... You looked like *hell* when I found you."

My eyes narrowed. "Worried *and* complementary? You flatter me."

He smirked, though the seriousness of the situation was evident. His tattooed arms crossed as he watched, waiting for me to spill the truth. Summoning my strength to sit up, I positioned myself straight and tried to ignore the ache in my ribs that felt worse with each breath.

"If I said he didn't like how I looked, would you buy it?"

His face remained unmoving.

"Yeah, I didn't think so." I took a deep breath, hands rushing to grip my side. "Damn, fine. I might not have been *completely* honest with you when we first agreed to this...arrangement."

I didn't dare look at him, but I could feel his eyes on me—waiting for me to continue. "What I shared about my father is the truth. He was murdered in front of me by a Shadow Walker, and I'm being accused of it. But my father held a...*somewhat* significant position within the royal court. So, his death caused a sort of chain reaction. When I was found next to him holding the bloody dagger, my aunt freaked and publicly declared me the murderer. So... I'm being pursued. Hunted, if you will."

His face twisted in a mix of confusion and anger as I continued. "I was overwhelmed, so I went on a walk thinking some fresh air away from the noise would make me feel better. But I went too far, and I lost sight of The Vale. He...he came out of *nowhere*, like the night gave birth to him. One minute, I was alone, and the next, he was there, and I was cornered." I swallowed, trying to piece the memories together. "He was a knight from the Royal Guard—sent to bring me back to face my '*sins.*'"

"Have you met him before?"

I nodded slowly. "His name is—*was*—Sir Doyle. I suppose he knew my father well enough to be sent after me." A small lie. "He was drunk and said his troops had been tailing us since we left the village, but they were attacked last night by some sort of...creature. He ended up being the only survivor and drank his way through the pain. When I refused to give in and go back with him...that's when he...when he..."

I trailed off, unable to put the horrific details into words. Shutting my eyes, all I could see was Sir Doyle's drunk face smiling down at me. Even the smell of his breath lingered in my memory.

Ryder hesitated but eventually rested his hand on mine, giving it a small squeeze. "Take your time."

I struggled to swallow, but eventually, I found my courage. "I always thought I could hold my own," I rasped. "I had been trained to defend myself. But he got the upper hand, and I'm pissed at how easily I was overpowered. The way he gripped my neck... Ryder, I thought I was going to *die*. All I could think about was you finding my dead body out there, bloody and blue. Just as I was passing out, that bastard got attacked by the same creature he had spoken of. Only, it wasn't a creature—it was a wolf! A huge, *gorgeous* wolf! It *saved* me! I still don't understand why it didn't attack me, but if it wasn't for its timing, I wouldn't be here."

His eyes darkened, gaze fixed on my neck. I knew what he was looking at. There was no way my throat wasn't bruised with how badly it was aching. Hesitantly, he removed his hand and gently brushed the tips of his fingers against the tender area.

I didn't flinch from his touch—not even an inch. The warmth that radiated off him as our skin touched was enough to cause a million butterflies to rush through my stomach.

A growl of anger built in his throat as he pulled away. "I should have killed that bastard," he muttered through clenched teeth. "Does it hurt when you swallow or talk?"

"A little, but I've endured worse."

"I doubt that." He scoffed.

We both sat in silence. I could see the anger in Ryder's mismatched eyes, making me feel guilty. I didn't know what to say, and honestly, given the state of my throat, I didn't mind the silence.

Walking away last night, I started thinking maybe, just maybe, I was better off on my own, that being away could save him. But...I *did* need him. Maybe the time away from training had made me...weak. *Vulnerable*. Vulnerable enough to *kill*.

Or maybe, I was never as strong as I thought I was...

"Why didn't you tell me?"

"How could I?" It was an honest question. "I had just lost my father and was afraid, on my own for the first time. I didn't know you, and you *definitely* didn't know me. You could have turned away in a heartbeat and would have never known the difference. But once you agreed, I didn't want to scare you off. You didn't sign up for this part of the job. You were helping me, and I didn't want to burden you with the truth. I didn't want you to feel responsible for the problems I created for myself."

His expression slowly softened. "Let me get this straight. You were worried I wouldn't help you not because of the danger from the Shadow Walkers...but because of the danger from the people pursuing you?"

Gods, hearing him say it made it sound so stupid!

"It made sense in my head. The threat of the Shadow Walker wasn't guaranteed, but I knew I would be followed no matter what. I tried to throw them off the best I could, so I thought maybe we were in the clear. But I was wrong, and it was unfair for me to keep it from you. That's why I gave you an out...I didn't want you to get hurt because of me."

He exhaled deeply, his shoulders relaxing a bit. "Rose, I'm not thrilled you kept such a huge detail from me. Whatever danger we might have faced, it would have been a hell of a lot easier knowing upfront so I could watch your back. But I get it and you're right. We didn't know each other and it's not like I run background checks on folks who pay me. But with you, it's different. Understand?"

Why was it so easy for him to accept and forgive my sack of bull shit lies?

"But why? What makes it different? Why go and pledge yourself to protect a total stranger? An *annoying* one, might I add."

His expression lifted, like he had just pieced together a puzzle. "Is that why you left me?"

I could feel my cheeks warming despite the coolness of the

air. Embarrassed, I turned away from him, fixating on the small glow from the lamp.

"I've tried to work it out in my head, to make sense of how my mind and gut work when it comes to you, but I can't. I can't explain it other than I feel like something has been pulling me for a while now. Like the other night in the *Rose and Crown*? All day, I just couldn't shake the feeling I was supposed to be there...and then I met you. Look, no matter how much of a pain in the ass you are or the risk of everything, I can't walk away. I won't."

He paused, his thumb gently tracing a pattern on the blanket. "I've spent my whole life wandering, helping folks who can't help themselves. Nothing ever felt like it was the right thing to do. *This* does. I know you paid me, but you're just not another client. Some feral part of me feels protective over you. So, I'm not walking away, not if I can keep you safe."

My nostrils flared as I fought back tears.

"So, long story short," he continued, "it's different because *you're* different. Take that for what it is, okay?"

If I didn't die from this mission, the overwhelming guilt surely would eat me alive. "Please don't throw your life away based on a feeling," I begged. "I am *not* worth it. I am not *worthy*."

He scoffed. "Says who? You? Sorry to break it to you, but you don't get to decide what others think—no matter how privileged and proper you grew up."

Flustered, I felt the ache in my throat finally win, causing me to sputter and stumble over my words.

"It might be better if you saved your voice," he said after a moment or two of me attempting to speak.

He was right.

My voice was raspy, barely a whisper, and drinking the water he gave me hardly helped. Slouching into my cot in defeat, I could see him out of the corner of my eye, his attention on the lantern's feeble light.

"We've got a few more hours until sunrise. You should get some rest. If you need anything, I'm just in the next tent over."

Nodding, I found some of my voice, "Thank you."

His lips peeled back in a kind smile. "Stop thanking me; I get it by now."

Rising from his spot on the ground, he moved towards the tent's flap. Stopping before pulling back the fabric, he looked me over again as if we hadn't spent the last ten minutes staring at each other.

"By the way, minus all the twigs and leaves, you should wear your hair like that more often. The color makes your eyes pop. Like the first bit of grass emerging after a snowstorm."

Without another word, he exited my tent, and I was alone again.

My hair? What the hell was he talking about?

Reaching towards my head, my fingers danced over the messy braid up to...fuck! My hair wrap was gone, and my white hair was on full display!

Had it been off this whole time?

Panic fluttered in my aching chest. Frantically, I looked around, hoping it had fallen while I was asleep. Finding nothing, that meant it was lying in the dirt somewhere, probably surrounded by Sir Doyle's blood.

I stared at the flaps of my tent as my fingers brushed the white locks. It was common knowledge that the princess had white in her hair. Hell, it's been the talk of the kingdom since my birth! But did that mean Ryder put two and two together?

Surely, there must be another eighteen-year-old out there with auburn and white hair...right?

Damn it.

This whole night was one disaster after another. I was a coward who ran away straight into danger. Not only that, but I could have *died*! I was anxious, annoyed, and in way more pain than I would admit to Ryder. And damn it, he was honest and open with me—something I had been begging from him.

So why did it make me feel so much worse?

Knowing I lied to him and that this whole time, he could have known who I was based on my hair made my stomach cramp.

"It's different because you're different."

Stupid Huntsman.

I settled into my cot, every joint and muscle aching. I tried to quiet my racing thoughts and sink to sleep while I could, but the image of the wolf lingered in my mind like a haunting melody.

Its glowing eyes watched me behind my closed lids. Ryder ignoring the part about the wolf didn't go unnoticed, but he was a huntsman after all. Wolves must have seemed like child's play when compared to things like Shadow Walkers and drunk, murderous knights, even if the wolf was the size of a horse.

The warmth of the tent and the soft rustling of the wind through the trees should have been comforting enough for me to eventually nod off, but the tension within me persisted. Despite the discomfort, my eyelids gradually grew heavy as my mind calmed.

Just as my eyes were fluttering shut, a small blue glow from the corner of my tent illuminated my vision. As I watched the light pulse, a lovely, calming melody resonated from its small form. I watched in awe, the luminescence guiding my tired eyes. Without needing to investigate, I snuggled deeper into my cot, smiling at the fact that Iris felt the need to watch over me while I slept.

With my eyes finally shut, the gentle glow of the Sprite's light wrapped around me like a comforting blanket.

Finally, my mind and body relaxed, and I drifted into the welcoming arms of sleep.

Iris had disappeared by the time I awoke.

Slowly opening to the gentle sunlight of a new day, my eyelids felt like boulders. I adjusted slowly, knowing I was going to be sore. Even if it took me an hour to move, I wanted to get up before Ryder so I could see if it was even possible for me to move without his help.

Taking a deep breath, I pushed the blanket off my stiff body and made my first attempt at getting up. A squeak of pain escaped my lips as my muscles experimented with moving, but I pushed through. Every little movement, even too deep of a breath, was a struggle.

Maybe I had been hit by a carriage.

Hobbling over to the tent's flap, I pushed it open and nearly stepped right onto Ryder. He was bundled up in a cocoon of blankets, sleeping deeply by the dying fire. Guilt hit me as I watched his chest rise and fall in the comfort of his spot on the cold ground.

Did he sleep out here to watch over me?

Seeing him sleeping with his eyes gently closed and his face relaxed made my heart flutter. The fact that he slept outside my tent in case I needed anything made it race even more. I wanted to wake him, to tell him it was okay to get an hour of rest in his own tent, but he looked so peaceful. He seemed to belong in the open air, nestled beneath the stars.

Glancing around at our camp, I noticed the beautiful flowers from last night were once again gone. The Vale was nothing more than the plain weed patch it had been when we arrived. Careful not to step on Ryder, I crept away from our camp and approached Reaper. Opening one of her satchels, I grabbed a towel and slowly hobbled to the lake.

I hadn't "bathed" since Ryder *graciously* showered me with a pail of water, and it was starting to show. The pain that clung to my body took my breath away, but I couldn't ignore the need for cleanliness. The amount of blood and dirt that soaked my clothes and hair made me feel soiled.

Dirty, as my blood apparently was.

Plus, the cool water could help aid in soothing my aching muscles.

I reached the shore, the dark lake glistening. After a quick look around to make sure I was alone, I slowly undressed, wincing as I stretched my sore limbs. I dipped a toe in to check the water and immediately pulled it back. It was *freezing*, and I second-guessed my idea of bathing.

Taking my time and trying to ignore the temperature, I slowly got used to the frigid water one step at a time. Unbraiding my hair, I finally stepped all the way in. The cold water wrapped around me, stealing my breath, but I knew I needed it. Trying to relax, I let out a sigh of relief as I submerged myself. Moving my aching arms, I washed away the grime and tension, the water barely above the peaks of my breasts.

The longer I stayed submerged, the warmer the water felt. It was like a warm hug, easing my muscles even more. Maybe I was going into shock from the temperature, but honestly, I didn't care. I could see why Ryder chose to lay here when he was injured.

If I thought I was about to die, I think I'd pick here too.

Smiling softly, I let the water fully envelop me as I tilted my head back into the lake. My neck relaxed as my unraveled curls were drenched. Taking a deep breath, I lowered myself completely under the surface until I was fully submerged.

Under the lake's embrace, I felt lighter than air. Little fish swam around me, curious about the stranger in their home. Letting my mind relax, I let go of everything from the past few days. The world above felt muffled and distant, and for a moment, I found a sense of calm.

The trials, dangers, and secrets all seemed to recede into the depths of the water. My lungs started to protest, reminding me I couldn't stay under any longer. As much as I wanted to stay, I had no choice but to resurface.

Breaking free from the water, I gasped for air, the sweet smells of The Vale filling my lungs. Wiping my eyes, I opened them to find a large, tan figure watching me from the shore.

Ryder stood on the edge of the lake, arms crossed and a lazy smirk on his face. Crossing my arms over my bare chest, I was filled with embarrassment and panic, knowing he could have seen...well, *everything*.

Despite the cold, my cheeks instantly flushed, and my teeth chattered. "R-Ryder?"

"Well, good morning, killer!" he called out. "I wasn't sure if you were swimming or drowning. Maybe both, knowing you."

"I w-was bathing! H-haven't you ever h-heard of p-privacy?"

He chuckled, his eyes reflecting the morning light as he drank me in. "Relax. I can't see anything past your shoulders."

"T-that still d-doesn't give you the right to s-sneak up on me!" My eyes narrowed, and I removed one of my hands from around my chest to flip him off. "L-learn to a-announce your-self, p-please."

Running a hand through his hair, which was *annoyingly perfect* despite him just waking up, he shook his head. "Well, since you said '*P-please*,' I'll leave you to freeze in peace."

My middle finger quickly became a thumbs-up. Looking down at my chest, I breathed a sigh of relief, realizing he was right. The lake's inky hue concealed any *revealing* details.

"Take your time but once you're done, we need to move out. Please for the love of the gods be careful when you come to shore; the stones can be slippery, and I think you're already injured enough for a lifetime or two."

With a laugh, he turned and headed back to camp, giving me the privacy I needed. I ran my hands over my limbs to make sure all the blood and dirt were gone before wading toward the shore. Taking my time, I carefully avoided slipping on any rocks and wrapped myself in a towel. Shivering, I hurried to dry off and get dressed.

Every movement still brought shooting pains and discom-fort, but I pressed on. Throwing my tunic on, I looked down in disgust at the dried blood splattered across the front. Whether it was mine or Sir Doyle's, I didn't dwell on it. My mind was already burdened with enough dark thoughts.

I quickly tied my hair into a messy, damp bun and returned to camp. To my surprise, everything was packed and ready to go. Ryder stood by the horses, patiently waiting for me. He wore his classic black tunic tucked into his pants, his dark cloak draped gracefully over his shoulders and down his back.

My gaze momentarily traced the tracks of scars on his face, looking away as his eyes met mine. Approaching, he raised a brow. "How are you feeling?"

I managed a weak smile. "Well, I didn't drown. But I've had better mornings."

His gaze fixed on my exposed neck, and the pupils of his eyes dilated the longer he stared. He flared his nostrils, disgust echoing across his features. After what felt like minutes, he hesitated before shaking his head free of the trance my bruise held on him.

"Can I touch it?"

Not trusting my voice, I nodded.

When his warm fingers grazed my skin, a cascade of shivers coursed down my spine, leaving me even more breathless than the cold water had. His touch held a gentleness that, despite the pain, was strangely comforting.

"It'll continue to bruise," he growled, "but thankfully, he didn't crush a windpipe. As long as you're still talking, I'm happy."

I let out a raspy laugh. "That's a shock."

Pulling his hand away from my skin, I almost missed the contact. Turning toward our horses, he retrieved my cloak and gently swung it around my body, fastening it around my neck— being careful not to put weight on the bruise. His gentleness left me in awe, my mouth falling slightly open as I watched him take care of me.

Cold, damp curls were already slipping out from my loose bun and onto my face. Before I could adjust them, Ryder softly brushed his fingers across my cheek, tucking the strands behind my ear. His eyes held mine before he withdrew his hand and stepped back. From his pocket, he retrieved a small vial filled with a greenish liquid.

My nose scrunched. "What the hell is that?"

"Elder Madrona gave me this after I brought you back. It'll help you heal. The taste is a bitch for sure, but you'll be feeling better before you know it."

I hesitated, looking at the vial in his outstretched hand then back to him. Crossing my arms over my chest, I shook my head. "I am *not* putting that into my mouth. It looks like *sludge*."

Effortlessly unfolding my arms, he urged the vial into my clenched hands. "Just trust me, you don't want to be feeling like this while we ride."

He was right. Again.

With a regretful nod, I removed the cork from the vial's rim, and I downed the liquid in one gulp, desperately trying not to throw it up immediately. The taste was a mix of sour milk and sweat, the formula burning my throat on its way down.

Coughing slightly, I suddenly felt warm—almost immediately feeling its effects. A tingle coursed through my chin and cheek, my hand moving to the scratch and wounds no longer there.

Sprite magic, no doubt.

My skin felt tight and fresh, almost like the marks had never been there. The ache in my neck was still there, but it was slightly easier to swallow. I was positive that no matter what, the bruise would remain for a few days.

"See? I knew you'd feel better."

Smirking, he turned towards the horses and began checking their saddles. Following him, I snatched the canteen of water and washed down away the stale aftertaste lingering in my mouth. Completing his preparations, he turned toward me and reached under his cloak.

"Here. I held onto this while you were asleep."

The dagger gleamed in the early morning sun, its dark blade absorbing the light, making the red vines almost glow. I felt a tingle in my fingers, anticipation building as I took it from his grasp. The hum returned; it didn't urge me to use it this time, almost as if it was pleased to be back in my presence.

"I hope you at least got a good stab or two in with that thing before that fucker died."

I shook my head, trying to recall the night. "I can't remember. It happened all so fast."

Ryder's face fell. "Not to assume anything, but do you know how to use that? I mean, I've seen you throw a punch and use a bow, but a dagger like that could be useful if you know how to use it right."

"I do." I confessed, "But I might be a little rusty. I used to train every morning, but it's been...*gods*, almost two weeks. Maybe my muscles are forgetting the rhythm."

He stepped forward, the heat radiating off his body hitting me like a stone wall. "Muscle memory is a beautiful thing, but it's not always going to help you. You gotta be prepared for anything."

Nodding, I understood that knowing how to use something and being proficient were two different skills.

Reaching up to fix my fallen bun, I winced as my arms strained to reach over my shoulders. Ryder's hands gently caught my wrist, halting my attempt.

Smirking at my raised brow, he took a step closer. "Turn around for me."

Mouth suddenly dry, I did as he said and moved until my back was to him. Releasing my wrist, a shiver ran down my spine as his fingers carefully unraveled the damp strands of my bun.

"What are you—"

"Shh," he murmured softly, his touch gentle against the nape of my neck.

Before I could protest further, he gently pulled my wet hair into his warm palms. The more his fingers and hands worked, the more I understood what he was doing.

"Are you...are you *braiding* my hair?"

He chuckled. "I grew up with a sister, remember?"

How could I forget? I'm wearing her clothes.

As his fingers continued to weave through my hair, a wave of pure tranquility washed over me. Each gentle tug and twist brought comfort and a sense of security I hadn't realized I'd been craving. As his hands traced further down my back, I found myself never wanting him to stop.

Gods, his hands are like magic.

Finishing all too soon, he released my hair and reached into his pocket. Before I could spin around to see what it was, he was back, fingers deftly securing my forgotten piece of fabric around my hairline. After tying it in place, I turned to face the huntsman who continued to impress me.

"As much as I love your white hair, I figured you were hiding it for a reason," he explained. "Thought you might want this back."

Love.

"Where, uh, where did you find it?"

He offered me a gentle smile, reaching out as he moved to help me get onto Jupiter. I accepted, trying not to wince as I swung my leg over the saddle.

"I went back to give that knight a proper burial and found it in some nearby bushes."

Any joy I was feeling was quickly replaced by a small surge of anger. It pulsed through my veins as I struggled to understand why the *hell* he would do that.

Seated securely, I watched as Ryder mounted his horse. Feeling my eyes on him, he met my gaze and read the concern written all over my face.

Releasing a defeated sigh, he lowered his eyes. "Look, I know what he did to you. I will *never* forget how you looked when I found you like that. But every soul deserves to be properly at rest. Nature's balance depends on it."

Sir Doyle, despite everything from the night prior, was an honorable man. Until his last breath, he protected and served the crown, even if the person he was serving was wrong. He followed his duty and expressed his unwavering support for my aunt, who somehow had become queen in my disappearance.

I still had no clue how that would have happened in less than two days, but it wasn't my problem right now. I would deal with that when I returned.

"I understand. But you didn't have to do that."

"I know," he said, meeting my gaze again, "Trust me, I would have gladly left that bastard to rot if I didn't have my morals."

A little bit of joy returned to my soul. "I admire your morals."

If I didn't know any better, I would have sworn a light blush crept onto the huntsman's cheeks. Fighting back a smile and clearing his throat, he straightened his shoulders and urged Reaper forward.

"Let's get going."

"Do I get to know where we're heading?"

"Next village we pass, we're getting you a change of clothes," he called back. "Can't have you running around in those blood-stained rags."

"What? Blood and dirt aren't in style nowadays?"

Ignoring me, he continued, "Once you don't look like a crime scene, we'll push forward until you're back to normal. Then, you and I are going to do some training."

I raised a brow. "Why are we going to train?"

"Do you even listen to me when I talk? I just told you. You're strong—but I need you *stronger*, Wiyahna. No one will ever, and I mean *ever*, touch you the way that bastard did again. If I can't be by your side, I need to know you'll be okay."

There was that word again. Wiyahna.

"I've trained with some of the best knights in the kingdom," I rebutted, hating how quickly I gave up a little more information about myself. "What makes you think anything you teach me will be different from what they taught me?"

He snorted. "Knights are too stiff. All they know is how to play with a sword and march off into battle. I can teach you how to be one with nature, how to fight like your life depends on it. And, most importantly, I can teach you how to fight like *me*."

CHAPTER 22

THANK the gods I had Ryder with me, because I had no idea where the hell we were or what direction to go to even get close to a village.

He said the nearest one that would have the most supplies, called Sambor, was about a three day's journey if we were swift. The nasty liquid medicine from Madrona had worked like magic, easing the worst aches. Riding, however, still proved to be rather uncomfortable.

We trekked in silence, Ryder on high alert to every rustling of trees or small animal that ran by. Not only did I fear finding the crimson eyes of a Shadow Walker hiding in the shadows, but I also now feared seeing a familiar face.

Sir Doyle had made sure of that.

"I sent a messenger raven back to the palace as soon as possible. Once we make our way back to a main road, it should take no time at all for more of my men to find us. Then, you'll be due for your judgment day."

My "judgment day." A reckoning for "sins" I didn't

commit. Returning to a palace now ruled by a queen who hated me.

Fuck that.

In just two days, so much had already unfolded, and Liliana's ascension had taken me completely by surprise. In most cases, a kingdom without a clear heir is a kingdom in peril. Instead of appointing one of my father's trusted advisors as a temporary ruler until a proper decision could be reached, they had hastily crowned Liliana—someone who lacked a direct bloodline to the throne.

It was an unprecedented choice that left a bitter taste in my mouth, and I could envision her smug grin alongside Sir Doyle's every time I closed my eyes.

While practicing the whole "honesty" thing, I informed Ryder of Sir Doyle's warning that more men would follow our scent. He assured me we would be fine, that we could handle it even if we came across more knights. We. Not him—*we*. The belief he held in me was a welcome surprise and I didn't take it lightly.

Regardless of the reputation that came with a title like his, Ryder was a mountain of a man. Just his size made people think twice about messing with him, and the scars on his face didn't help either. I saw that firsthand the night we met.

But I saw beyond that.

I saw the man who asked about my nightmares and braided my hair when I was too weak to. The man I had gotten to know over the last couple of days made me feel safe and secure. Did he tease me? Yes, of course. Would I ever admit that I liked that? No, no, I would not.

A low rumble emerged from the depths of my stomach, and I nervously glanced at Ryder to see if he had heard. With his attention still fixed on the road, either he didn't hear, or he just didn't care.

To prevent another rumble and a lecture on eating, I quickly opened one of Jupiter's satchels for some jerky. I reached down, my fingers grazing something very small and very much *alive*.

Yelping, I pulled my hand back, thinking a mouse had found its way into the pack. Ryder, hearing my cry, pulled Reaper to a halt, eyes wide with worry. Before either of us could check, a little blue blob darted out and fluttered in front of my face. I flinched, but a sweet humming and singing filled my ears, relaxing me.

I laughed. "Well, it looks like we have a stowaway!"

Iris danced in the air, her delicate form glowing with an otherworldly light that made my heart leap with joy. Ryder was off Reaper and by my side in a heartbeat, his brows practically touching his hairline.

"Nope!" He shook his head. "No, no, no! Absolutely not!"

Iris continued her musical explanation, speaking in a language I couldn't understand.

Ryder's lack of amusement never faltered. "Don't care, Iris. You need to return home to The Vale. *Now.*"

As Iris continued her serenade, her sparkling eyes flitted between us. "Oh, don't be such a grump. Let her come! It's not like we need another horse to carry her."

He scoffed. "That's not even close to the point. We have enough shit going on right now without a little blue Sprite following us around and drawing even *more* attention."

Iris's melody seemed to sadden, her head bowing, and her fluttering slowed in pace. Her song rang through Ryder— almost as if I could see the music wrapping around him as she sang. His expression softened slightly, though you would miss it if you weren't watching.

"Really? Elder Madrona said *that*?" Sighing, he pinched the bridge of his nose. "You've got to be shitting me... Fuck it, fine. If she's determined, I guess I don't have much of a choice."

Iris's sassy, confident song told me everything I needed to know. She had just won the argument.

Smirking, he turned to me. "Be careful what you wish for. Congratulations, Rose; you've just been promoted to be her glorified babysitter."

Iris responded with a melodious laugh, her sparkling eyes reflecting the dappled sunlight filtering through the forest canopy.

"Does she have any rules like I do?"

"As much as I would like to say '*No*' to mess with you, yes—she needs to stay hidden when we're around anyone else, and don't let her eat all the food. I can't stand the sound of your stomach rumbling all day."

Returning with a piece of meat in almost perfect timing, Iris dropped the jerky in my lap. "Do Sprites even eat meat? They don't scream 'hunters' to me," I called out, throwing the jerky into my mouth.

"They will eat *anything*," he warned, "And they don't know when to stop, so keep your eye out for how full our stash is and how big her stomach is getting. Don't be afraid to give her a good flick either."

Rolling my eyes, I turned to my little blue adventure buddy. "I will *not* be flicking you, don't worry," I whispered. "And don't let him fool you—we're delighted to have you with us. The same goes for you too, you know. Give *him* a good flick when he deserves it."

Iris's eyes glistened and her laughter seemed to weave through the wind. She fluttered closer to my face, perching on my right shoulder, and her tiny face nuzzled my cheek. As we continued down the path, Iris began to hum a sweet, melodic tune.

Despite not knowing what she was saying, the music offered me a warm embrace. I didn't need to know what she was saying to see the kindness and happiness radiating off her. It was almost contagious, and I could see how it already had affected Ryder. Even though his attention remained fixed on the road, his shoulders visibly relaxed.

Eventually, the rhythm of her song began to slow, and her movements grew more languid. Iris's tiny body settled against my cheek, and her humming gradually faded into the gentle lull of sleep. I continued to ride alongside Ryder, one hand holding the reins and the other gently removing her from my face, resting her in my lap.

Hearing the silence, Ryder's gaze finally shifted toward us and he lightly laughed at the sleeping Sprite.

"What's so funny?"

"I just seem to have a knack for attracting stubborn women."

"A woman? I thought I was a 'kid' to you, Huntsman."

"I called you 'kid' maybe three times at most. Get over it. After getting past your temper, you're actually pretty..." his eyes briefly flicked to my chest before he cleared his throat. "...mature."

I playfully gagged. "Sure. I won't forget the 'little girl' or 'dolly' comments you made either."

"Well, compared to me you are rather little."

"We can't all be as tall as our egos, now can we?"

He let out another laugh and I swore it shook the forest. Iris stirred a little, her wings twinkling in the sun.

"While she's asleep," I said, changing the subject, "what was with the hesitation? For someone *so* against her tagging along, you gave in rather quickly. Is it because it's dangerous for her to be seen, or are you worried she could be a distraction?"

He shrugged. "Both. Sprites thrive on family bonds and connections. It's rare for one to be away from the Blessing, and I'm worried she doesn't fully understand what she's getting into. I just don't have the time to babysit her."

My thumb unconsciously traced gentle circles across her back, eliciting a soft flutter of her wings. "You won't need to babysit her. You already do that for me. And wasn't I just promoted?" I heard him snort. "But if what you say is true, why would Elder Madrona allow it? Wouldn't she advise against it to protect the Blessing and Iris?"

"Elder Madrona has a reason for everything she does," he mused, a hint of uncertainty in his voice. "But this one...I'm not sure. Maybe we'll find out. Or maybe she's just messing with us. Has to get boring living in a tree for several decades."

The laugh that escaped my throat caused Iris to stir in her sleep again before a small hum filled my ears and she peacefully resumed her snoring.

"What did she say that got to you?"

Ryder's attention stayed fixed on the road, his eyes alert to every movement and sound. "Something about Iris' destiny, that this was a path she had to take. I may be hardheaded, but who am I to interfere with destiny?"

"How can you understand them?"

His posture subtly tensed. "I don't know; I just can."

"I'm calling bullshit on that one," I stated dryly. "There is no way the gods just graced you with the ability to understand the language of a civilization the world thought to be dead."

"Except that's exactly what happened," he snapped.

His tone had suddenly shifted, and I involuntarily flinched. The ensuing silence only made the moment more intense. After a while, he glanced back at me, annoyance melting into regret. I knew he sensed how his words had hit me. Avoiding his gaze, I felt the weight of his stare piercing into me, tightening the knot in my stomach.

The air around us felt like the aftermath of a storm, unsettlingly calm yet crackling with awkward tension.

"I didn't mean to snap at you like that, I just... You don't think I haven't questioned the same? When I passed out in that lake, I didn't think I would ever wake up. But when I finally did, they were there, and I could understand them like it was my first language. Whether I was born with the curse or if it was given to me, I don't know. But trust me, it has bothered the hell out of me for years."

My eyebrow raised. "Curse? Understanding their language seems far from a curse."

Ryder let out a dry chuckle, his eyes drifting to the road ahead. "Not all knowledge is a blessing. Sometimes, it's a burden."

I couldn't wrap my head around it—how knowledge could be a curse. You'd think knowing everything would only benefit you in life. But his words lingered, sparking a deeper curiosity about the man before me. His depth surprised me, far greater than I had imagined. It was baffling.

The more I learned about him, the more it became clear: Ryder wasn't just a huntsman. He was a man who possessed a wealth of experiences and understanding of the world that surpassed anything I could hope to gain. When the world turned its back on him, he found his home in nature and embraced it.

In many ways, he was extraordinary.

"For example," he continued, "not that I mind it, but it would be easier if I didn't have to translate everything Iris says to you."

I snorted. "Oh, I didn't realize it was such a *burden* on you."

"Stop it. You know what I mean. It's not your fault. I was just giving you an example. Plus, I know you're *dying* to know what she's saying." He paused, glancing back at us. "On second thought, maybe it's a good thing you two can't communicate. You would gang up on me in a heartbeat."

I turned my attention to the slumbering Sprite nestled on my lap. "I doubt that. I think she likes you a little too much for her own good."

Even the thickness of his beard couldn't hide the large grin he wore. "Well, yeah. Can you blame her?"

I playfully glared at him, eliciting a hearty laugh from deep within his chest. "I can see the allure."

"You know, Iris healed me that day. Her healing? It's a natural talent. Elder Madrona says it was a blessing after everything they had to go through. Iris was the first mystic healer since before the genocide."

"They'll miss her, that's for sure," I whispered as I admired the blue blob.

"Yeah, but she seems content with you. She wouldn't leave you last night. She even bit my finger," he said, showing a small, red bite that marked his tan finger as proof.

Seeing his minor injury warmed my heart, both for the little

Sprite and the big huntsman. Even though they hadn't known me for more than a few days, they showed the kind of caring I had longed for. Their protectiveness didn't worry me—it brought me comfort.

Because I felt the same way about them.

The thought of Iris biting Ryder was something I wished I'd seen firsthand. I couldn't help but laugh, and for a moment, Ryder looked away from potential dangers of the road and joined in my laughter.

The days progressed calmly as we kept riding through the forest, enjoying the peaceful silence.

Steady hoofbeats and the gentle rustle of fallen leaves in the breeze were the only sounds. Even though I knew I was in good hands, every random noise still made me jump. Other than that, the forest felt easy.

The distinct noises began to blur together, and the further we rode, the less the forest sounded like itself and the more it felt like someone was whispering in my ear. Time dragged on, and that familiar pit returned to my stomach.

My fingers started to tingle, the sensation crawling up my arm like a phantom hand. Anxiety crept back, and I struggled to keep my breathing steady. As I tried to control the sensation, the world around me became blurred and muted.

Get it together, Genevieve! Push it down.

But I couldn't. Not even deep breaths were helping.

Sensing the same shift in the air that had caused my fidgeting, Ryder stopped Reaper. His eyes scanned the forest with the intensity of a predator. I was about to ask what was wrong, but he raised his hand, signaling me to stay quiet.

He took a deep breath, his nostrils flaring. A low growl emerged from his chest. "We're not alone," he whispered, voice barely audible above the rustling leaves.

"How do yo—"

Cutting me off, Ryder steered Reaper to the side of the trail and motioned for me to follow. Once I got my breathing under control, we guided our horses into a dense thicket. Ryder effortlessly jumped off Reaper and was by my side before I could blink. I scooped Iris up and he firmly gripped my waist, helping me down from Jupiter.

Leading me deep into the thicket, we huddled together to conceal ourselves as the thunderous sound of hoofbeats echoed through the forest.

Or was that my heart beating against my rib cage?

The closer it got, the more the pebbles beneath our feet quivered with each vibration. Iris woke with a flurry of high-pitched notes, and Ryder quickly hushed her before her song could grow too loud. As her tiny form settled into my hands, Ryder's arm slipped around my waist, pulling me close and keeping us low.

In a less alarming situation, I might have blushed at the contact.

Hell, I probably still was blushing.

As I took another deep breath to get my hormones under control, horror gripped my chest as a contingent of knights emerged from the forest path—their armor gleaming in the dappled sunlight and their banners unfurling in the breeze.

Sir Doyle fulfilled his promise.

I saw familiar faces of men I trained with every morning flooding my vision—Sir Aaron and Sir Tristan among them. The more who passed by, the more anxious I became. Among the flood of faces, one was missing.

Topher.

Commander Robert knew the trio of Aaron, Tristan, and Topher was golden in any situation. Why wouldn't he include him in the cavalry? Topher would have known how to find me better than any of them. Unless...unless *he* was one of the men with Sir Doyle that night...

No! It's not possible. I know it.

Just the thought made my stomach turn, and Ryder's grip tightened around my waist as I wayed backward. Sir Doyle was an ass of a man, and his manipulative words had been playing on repeat in my mind since last night. I knew deep down he would have exploited Topher's death for all it was worth. Everyone in the knightly circles knew how close Topher and I were. Using our friendship to lure me back to Castle Quinn would have been a cunning move.

So maybe I was wrong, but something deep in my gut told me he was alive. I had to trust it. For now.

Thank the gods, they passed quickly, completely oblivious to us hiding in the bushes. Once the coast seemed clear, Ryder's hand left my waist as he maneuvered to get a better view through the thicket. The way he moved reminded me of a wild animal, both predatory and beautiful, each step calculated.

As he moved further away to scout, I grew more anxious about him being spotted, but he remained unconcerned. Meanwhile, Iris cautiously fluttered out of my hands and returned to her perch on my shoulder, quiet as a mouse despite her barely audible breaths.

Ryder returned before my anxiety peaked. "They went the opposite direction of Sambor," he said softly. "Looks like the gods are favoring us today."

Despite the tingling in my fingers, relief washed over me. I nodded, and Iris snuggled closer to my cheek.

Springing to his feet, Ryder extended a hand towards me, and I gratefully took it. "Let's give them some time to put distance between us before we head out."

Pulling me up, I failed to notice a root jutting from the forest floor a few feet ahead. I moved too quickly, my toe catching on it, sending me stumbling before I even fully rose. The forest floor rushed up to meet me, and my sore muscles delayed my reflexes, but Ryder's were quick.

His strong arms encircled my waist, saving me from a face full of dirt. Finding my balance, I looked up to meet the huntsman's wide eyes, and for a moment, time seemed to stand still. Concern furrowed his brow as he held me, his mismatched eyes studying me intently, lips slightly parted enough for me to see a glimpse of his tongue tracing the inside of his teeth.

Gods. Has he always been this handsome?

I could feel my cheeks flush as we stood there, locked in each other's embrace. Ryder's tan face seemed to warm with a slight blush. His eyes widened a fraction, his throat bobbing as he swallowed. He tightened his grip around my waist, and I felt my heart race against my ribcage. Mismatched eyes traced down to my chest, and the warmth in his expression deepened.

Could he hear my heart?

Iris' melody fluttered between us, breaking our trance. Ryder cleared his throat as we slowly pulled away, and his face paled. My hands instinctively went to the braid he had given me hours earlier, trying to regain my composure.

The little Sprite's song intensified as she approached Ryder's face. He gently shooed her away with a small grin and she zoomed up to my face, cheeks purple and bright. It was clear our flushed faces weren't the only ones affected by the unexpected moment.

"There's no need to be jealous," I whispered. "I'm just clumsy."

Iris turned her little face toward him, her tiny hands on her hips. His grin broadened. "It's true. Clumsy, annoying, unlucky... Should I keep going?"

"Sure, if you want a rock thrown at your big head!"

Sending me a wink, he puffed out his chest and took a deep breath, as if smelling the air. Glancing over his shoulder, he scanned the road ahead.

After a moment, he nodded to himself. "I think we're clear for now. But let's keep our guard up, just in case another troop decides to follow."

I nodded, brushing off any lingering traces of the forest floor from my clothes and climbed back onto Jupiter. We fell back into our usual formation, cautiously continuing our journey. Despite the unlikelihood of another troop following so closely, dread lingered.

Even the joy of being in Ryder's arms couldn't shake it off.

CHAPTER 23

REACHING Sambor after our little run-in didn't take long at all.

After spending the past several days in the middle of the woods, the thought of civilization was a welcomed relief. So why was I so anxious? We secured our horses at a tree on the edge of the village, and Iris crossed her little heart in promise to keep hidden while we were gone.

No matter how much I tried to calm it, my heart raced faster than ever as I nervously bit the stubs of my nails. Shifting back and forth on my heels, I waited for Ryder to finish his tasks. I could feel his presence approaching me from behind, his natural warmth enveloping every one of my senses.

One of his large, tattooed hands reached over my shoulder, gently lifting the hood of my cloak over my head. I turned to face him.

"It might help ease your nerves if your hair wasn't so visible. Even without the white showing, I can tell you try and hide it as much as possible."

I bit my lip. "Is that why you braided it for me?"

His eyes tracked every movement. "That poor excuse for a bun wouldn't have lasted an hour's ride," he laughed. "At least you can hide the braid under the hood without worrying if it'll fall."

The act was simple, but the reassurance it gave me drew me closer to the huntsman. He draped the soft fabric over my hair, shielding me from prying eyes.

As a princess, I'd been taught that my hair was one of my greatest sources of pride. Hiding it now felt wrong, but I knew it was like a beacon that could attract unwanted attention, even without my white hair showing.

"Dirty blood." Sir Doyle's stupid words echoed in my mind.

"Thanks," I murmured, offering him a small smile. "Can I ask you something?"

"Even if I say no, you'll ask anyway."

Despite the unease, a smile tugged at my lip. "Sir Doyle... Before we fought, he said something about my hair. Have you ever heard that people with red hair are descendants of Witches?"

His face, so tan and handsome, remained unfazed. "I have, but it's just an old wives' tale, something folks made up at the start of the war to make finding the enemy easier. As far as I know, there's no proof to back up that bullshit."

"He said my mother and I had dirty blood... That *we* were the reason for my father's death. A curse or a bad omen, or some bullshit." I started pacing. "I can't stop thinking about it, like there's something *wrong* with me, or I pissed someone off enough to have all this happen."

His face fell. "I'm sure you *did* piss someone off, knowing you. But I doubt that's the reason for all of this. Your blood is *not* dirty. There is no such fucking thing. If there were, my family would have been screwed a long time ago."

I shrugged. "He seemed convinced enough by it to choke me out."

He took a step closer, his eyes intense as he grabbed my shoulders to stop my pacing. "Rose, people say a lot of crap, especially when they're trying to hurt you. But none of that defines who you are or your worth. Your hair, your blood— who cares? All that matters is how you come out after a bad hand has been delt."

Dammit. He was right—like normal.

Sir Doyle's words hadn't made sense, and I was pretty sure it wasn't just the booze. Why even bring up my hair if he wasn't looking to quickly blame me for my father's death? Out of everything, my hair was the last thing I thought he'd blame. My engagement with Xander? Sure, but my hair?

Regardless, it still made me feel dirty. Damaged—damned. Like I was this plague that reaped the land the moment I was born.

"And for the record," he took a step closer, "I think your hair is beautiful. *You're* beautiful, Rose. Dirty blood or not."

My breathing hitched and I desperately tried to find its normal rhythm.

He's just distracting me, trying to make me feel better, nothing more.

"I just want to forget that night," I mumbled, looking away.

Reaching out, he gently adjusted my hood. "Sometimes the toughest battles we face are the ones in our heads. Not everything people say is true, especially when it's driven by hate or ignorance."

One of my eyebrows rose. "When did you become such a scholar?"

"There are plenty of sides you haven't seen of me yet," he said with a wink. "If you're lucky, maybe you'll see a few more before our time together ends."

Turning, he led the way toward Sambor. Entering the small community was a slap in the face compared to the vibrant atmosphere of Heim. The moment we stepped foot across its border, something felt...wrong, almost sad, and I hated it.

Even the sun hid behind clouds.

The energy around us was unsettling. The worn-down buildings, the cracked roads, and the expressionless faces of the villagers only added to the unease.

"What's wrong with this place?"

Ryder's shoulders tensed. "We're not too far from the Fae border. With the battlefront nearby, it seems this place has taken a hit or two over the years."

I unconsciously tugged my hood tighter. "Surely, King Leonard knew about the state of this village. He must have sent some aid over the years."

There's no way my father would have let this village remain like this if he had known. Even on the opposite side of the kingdom, these were still his people. *Our* people.

"The royal family hasn't cared about this side of Orphinian in years," Ryder scoffed. "Unless it's to keep his precious daughter safe or to send more troops to the front, the king couldn't care less about the people in his kingdom."

Just yesterday, Ryder had praised my father so warmly, it felt like I was rediscovering him all over again. But now, hearing this perspective, it made my stomach churn. I couldn't believe it— couldn't accept it. Yet, standing in this village and seeing its despair firsthand, how could I deny the abandonment by my own family?

"I don't know if I believe that," I rebutted. "The king has always seemed to care about his people."

Ryder shook his head. "Not everyone is how they appear. We all wear masks."

When we reached the market square, it felt almost deserted. Only the stall owners were out, their sales more out of necessity than enthusiasm. We passed a forlorn fruit stand covered in small gnats, and the vendor's eyes locked with mine. I tried not to let his stare unsettle me, but my skin prickled, nonetheless.

He seemed afraid—of me, perhaps, or of my bodyguard. His defeated expression mirrored the mood of the entire village, and I couldn't help but feel pity for him.

Ryder's firm grip on my arm gently pulled me from the stranger's gaze. Even a few steps apart, I still felt the weight of his stare lingering on us as we moved.

"My gut is telling me to get what we need and leave this shithole as quickly as possible," he warned. "If I give you some money, can I trust you find practical clothes without getting into any trouble?"

Almost too afraid to speak, I nodded. He pulled out the sack of gold I had given him, withdrawing a few coins. My hand trembled as he placed them in my palm, fingers still tingling.

"Only get what you need and meet back here in fifteen. Can you do that for me?"

"I'll be careful," I assured him. "I promise."

Giving my shoulder a reassuring pat, he headed off in the opposite direction. Watching him go, I envied his confidence as he delved deeper into the market. People turned to look as he passed, fear evident on their faces.

Taking a deep breath, I unfroze. My footsteps echoed on the uneven cobblestones as I foolishly prayed to the gods this would be the easiest part of my day.

The gods seemed to have made it their goal to prove me wrong.

Despite my mounting anxiety, I pushed ahead in a desperate search for a vendor or shop selling clothes. Every turn, every face I passed added to the sensory overload. The merchants' voices grew louder, each one clamoring for a sale. Avoiding eye contact, I quickened my pace, trying to blend in.

As I passed each muted face, my posture slouched further. The deeper into the market square I ventured, the smaller I felt, and I hated it. It didn't help that the tingling in my fingers grew into an overwhelming burn. My inner voice was screaming at me to remain cautious, and I was trying my best to listen.

Everything felt off, dark.

And then I heard *it*.

At first, it was as faint as a whisper, and I wondered if it was just the wind. But as I ventured deeper into the market, it grew louder. Déjà vu washed over me, and suddenly, I was back in my bedchamber the night before my wedding. The whispers, initially soft and vague, intensified until it felt like I'd been struck by lightning.

They were whispering my *name*.

Tripping over my feet, I spun around so fast I almost lost my balance. I searched the crowd desperately, hoping to spot a familiar face. All I saw were the curious gazes of strangers. I quickly looked away, silently grateful my face remained concealed; otherwise, my embarrassment would have been written all over it.

You're just paranoid, Genevieve Rose.

I could have convinced myself that, but then I heard it again. And again. And *again,* until the noises surrounding me became so muted I was forced to focus on the sinister whispers.

"Genevieve. Genevieve. Genevieve."

It was overwhelming, like a summer storm persisting outside my window. The voices were too strong—*too loud.* It felt like my very sanity was being clawed at. I couldn't prevent the panic as it gripped my chest. I clamped my hands over my ears, but the ghostly calls only seemed to grow.

"Genevieve. Genevieve. Genevieve."

The cobblestone beneath me hit my knees as I sank. The ground hit my trembling body hard as my head swam in a maelstrom of confusion and fear. My breaths shuttered in uneven gasps as I tried to shut out the relentless choir of voices. Everything around me spun out of control and I was soon spiraling with it.

The corners of the marketplace collapsed onto me—suffocating me. Through my blurry vision, I caught a hold of something moving toward me.

Something almost fluid.

Something *dark.*

Despite the voices seeming to surround me, that corner of darkness seemed to be the main cause. Just as I thought I might be seeing things, a familiar black figure emerged from its depths, *smiling* at me.

"Genevieve. Genevieve. Genevieve."

Slowly, almost painfully so, it inched toward me like a feline on a hunt. Its black mass shifted and those crimson eyes that haunted my nights emerged from the void. A Shadow Walker, perhaps the same one that killed my father, had found me.

This is it. This is where I die.

Fading fast, I knew if I didn't get my breathing under control, I was going to pass out.

"Genevieve. Genevieve. Genevieve."

I couldn't calm my breathing, and the black mass seemed to sense my panic, its phantom smile widening. Just as darkness threatened to consume me, another voice pierced the air. The Shadow Walker halted in its tracks, its dark form recoiling and retreating back into the corner from which it had emerged. Struggling to stay conscious, I strained to focus on the sound.

The voice was a faint chant, too soft and indistinct for me to decipher the words. It was lighter, more feminine.

"Su fo enon mrah dna emoh ruoy ot kcab taeter, soahc dna noitcurtsed kees ohw snomed."

The Shadow Walker continued to sink back into the darkness as the chanting grew louder. Each repeat of the foreign phrase felt stronger than the last.

"Su fo enon mrah dna emoh ruoy ot kcab taeter, soahc dna noitcurtsed kees ohw snomed."

A guttural shriek escaped from the creature's mouth as it retreated fully back into the shadows, fading away like a wisp of smoke. As quickly as it began, it stopped.

The silence that followed was deafening. Fear still gripped me as I struggled to control my breathing. I didn't dare look around or even open my eyes. It wasn't until I felt a hand on my hunched back that I dared to open them—my head spinning to find the owner of that palm.

I met the gaze of an older woman, her wrinkled hand

pulling away as I moved. Her gray hair was tied up in a tight bun, and her apron, splattered with paint, covered most of her dress. As she crouched beside me, every line on her face seemed to tell a story.

"Child? Are you well?"

Still trembling, I hesitated before letting her guide me back to my feet. My breathing slowly steadied as I regained some of my composure. I quickly attempted to mask my terror, my face growing as calm as I could manage.

"Yes, I am. I'm so sorry; I think I just got a little...overwhelmed."

Her eyes crinkled as she smiled. "It's easy to become overwhelmed in a village such as this, especially for newcomers who aren't used to the effects of the war. Many voices flit around you, don't they?"

My eyes widened. "I'm sorry?"

I surely didn't hear her right.

She extended her hand and gently took mine. "What do you seek?"

I swallowed hard, the sound of the Shadow Walker still fresh in my mind. "I just need a new tunic."

She let go of my hand and gracefully turned, walking deeper into the heart of the marketplace. She cast a look over her shoulder, her hazel eyes sparkling as they met mine.

"Follow me. I can lead you to what you desire."

CHAPTER 24

Following the strange, elderly woman, I kept my head down.

As she led us closer to wherever the hell we were going, the streets began to give way to a more secluded part of the village. Despite her age, she moved *fast*.

Approaching a small shop, she swiftly unlocked the door and motioned for me to enter. From the outside looking in, this would be just a simple shop, but the inside was a whole other story.

Exotic herbs dangled from the ceiling while strange crystals glittered in the dim light. What looked like tattered scrolls and thick books were scattered across the worn wooden tables. Her shop walls were lined with rows of shelves—all holding items that seemed as unique as the woman.

"What type of shop did you say this was?"

Her feet shuffled as I observed every little thing I could. Nothing made sense in their order—no sort of organization to be found.

Everything was just...*there*.

"I didn't," she said nonchalantly.

Taking my eyes off the shelves, I found her in the shop. Her smile was warm, eyes devoid of the village's usual sadness. Ryder would have a fit if he knew I followed a stranger into a random shop, but something about her felt familiar. It felt safe.

"When I'm not searching for crystals or growing herbs, I tend to collect things in my old age." She shuffled to a small dresser in the corner of the shop. "Some would call me a hoarder; I prefer the term 'collector.' It helps pass the time. I don't have a family anymore, and this war has done enough damage to this village alone to make me not want to waste a day of my life. Things hadn't always been so dark...but we do what we can to get through each day."

I understood that. Hell, I'd been experiencing that.

Ever since I became engaged to Xander, each day felt like a test to measure my strength, to see if I had what it took to make it to the next day.

With this village being so close to the battlefronts, I couldn't even imagine the horrors they had seen.

She opened the drawer, a small cloud of dust escaped as she began rummaging through. After several moments of searching, she turned towards me, a small pile of clothes in her frail arms.

"The things I collect, well, sometimes, they seem to find me at my lowest. Somehow, I still believe they are little reminders from the universe that there is always a brighter tomorrow. A beacon of hope, if you will." Her tiny feet shuffled back to me. "Other times if I come across something that calls to me, I tend to bring it here. Very much like you, my child. I heard your call loud and clear."

Standing in front of me, she raised her arms and handed me the clothes. Without looking through them, I could tell they were for women. A fresh tunic lay on top of the pile.

My brows furrowed. "No disrespect, but you must be mistaken. I didn't call you. I don't even *know* you"

"Not all calls are from the mouth. But you know all about that, don't you? If I can read your aura correctly, many things have called to you over the last few days, haven't they, Genevieve?"

The sound of my name on her tongue caused me to freeze. The world around me once again began to blur, and I thought I might faint.

This *stranger* spoke to me as if I had known her all my life.

Dropping the pile of clothes from my hands, I struggled to find my balance, grabbing onto the nearby desk for strength.

Who the hell am I with right now?

Scoffing, she rushed to retrieve the pile from the floor. "Now you don't have to go throwing things!" Her voice was more annoyed than angry. "Those were very much clean and ready for you."

Anxiety fluttered through my chest as I struggled for air. This should have been enough of a red flag for me to get the hell out of there, but the tingling in my fingers was nowhere to be found.

Attempting to regain control, I took a deep breath. "Okay, hold on. I think I missed something."

Her hazel eyes shot up at me, lips thin. She moved to place the clothes on the desk I was using for support.

"No, I don't believe you have. You're just not looking correctly, my princess."

Reclaiming her seat, she studied me. Pushing forward off the desk, I threw another mask on and stood straight.

"Who *are* you?"

"I've worn many names in my lifetime, some nicer than others. But for our time together, you may call me Shamira."

Shamira. Why did that sound so familiar?

"And how do you seem to know so much about me, Shamira?"

Leaning forward, she chuckled. "Full of questions. Good. That means you still care." Shaking her head, she clicked her tongue. "The eyes that watch you are not always malevolent. Believe what you want, but you have been observed and guarded more closely than you may have thought outside the castle walls. But something tells me you already knew that; you have felt both the dark and light eyes on you."

My stomach dropped. "Yes. Every day."

"As you might for the remainder of your life. Those voices, child—the worst they can do is what you allow. If you pay them no mind and give them no power, they will not have a hold on you. The deadliest beast is the one inside your head, not the one that accompanies you. Learn to block it out, or you will end up like your father."

The color drained from my face as a chill swept through me. "What the fuck do you know of my father?"

Rising from the chair, she moved back toward the desk. "I heard you had a mouth on you." She laughed. "To explain all those things, I'm afraid, will take longer than you're meant to be here, child."

The room fell silent as she cleared her desk of clutter and picked up one of the old scrolls. Spreading it out on the desk, she locked eyes with me from across the wood.

"Come."

Obeying, I stood next to her, focusing on the old parchment. The scroll was covered in black scribbles, and as it unfolded, it revealed a complex pattern that made my head spin.

Shamira pointed to the scroll. "These markings," she whispered, "tell a story, one woven into the very fabric of your existence, though you may not realize it. They reveal the truth of a power older and more profound than anything you've known —a connection between you and your lineage that is far more intricate than you could imagine."

A shiver ran down my spine. Even though the tingling in my fingers had faded, her words now sparked a new sense of awareness in me.

She traced the symbols with her finger. "Your mother is not the only one in your family with a unique gift. Her power courses through your veins, and you may find it manifest within you in times of great need."

Oh. She's senile.

"Listen, lady," I nervously laughed, "I think you've got your redheads crossed. My mother was the daughter of a nobleman who died too soon. She didn't have powers and neither do I."

Narrowing her eyes, she shot me a look of disappointment. "Are you not Princess Genevieve, heir to the Orphinian Throne? Daughter of King Leonard and Queen Dawn?"

My face paled as I remained silent.

She snorted. "I thought so. Now, this isn't your first time hearing these words, child. It's time you start learning to believe the ones you trust most and disregard what you grew up learning."

I couldn't stop my mind from doing somersaults every time she spoke. As wild as it sounded, she made sense. That night I escaped, Fiona said something similar. But what did it all mean? *Powers*? The idea alone was so far-fetched I'd never even thought about it. Even with the tingling in my fingers, it couldn't be real.

She continued, sounding annoyed. "As I was saying—it is a legacy passed down through generations, a force that has protected your family for as long as this power has existed. And now, it has chosen you."

I couldn't breathe. Her words stirred up more questions. As she spoke, the shop around us faded away. My life's direction had always been uncertain, even before my father passed. It wasn't until I became engaged to Xander that I thought everything was falling into place. I thought my purpose was ending the war through marriage—but maybe it was something else entirely.

Maybe *I'm* something else entirely.

"So, what now? If you believe I have these *powers*...where do I even start?"

She met my gaze with a knowing smile as if she had anticipated my question. "What you do next, dear child, is take what I give you, find your companion, and embrace your heritage. Unlock the secrets hidden within these markings. This scroll will guide you in understanding not only who you are but the force that brought tragedy to your family."

Her finger ran over the scroll. "Follow the path these markings illuminate. Discover the source of your strength, and you will find the answers you seek. But be forewarned, Genevieve—this journey will be dangerous. The forces that took your father are not to be underestimated, and they will stop at nothing to prevent you from discovering the truth."

Nothing was adding up.

The longer I stayed away from Castle Quinn, the less I felt I knew who I was. Had my entire childhood, my entire *life*, been a lie?

Did I truly know my mother before she passed?

Did...did I even know *myself*?

So many mixed emotions swirled inside me.

It was like being in a fever dream, tossed in circles and through hoops just to make it through the night. I wanted to ask her more questions, to delve into what she knew about my family and my future path.

But her attention had already turned back to the closed door of her shop. About to speak, I was cut off by her raised finger.

When she turned back to me, an excited smirk lit her lips. "We've got a visitor!"

I looked at the front door just in time to see it burst open. Ryder stormed in, his dark eyes blazing with urgency as he scanned the shop. Relief washed over his face the moment he spotted me.

"What. The. *Hell*?" he managed as he rushed toward me. "Do you know how long I've been searching for you? Gods, I thought the worst!"

After he scanned me quickly for signs of injury, his warm hands reached for my arms. His eyes looked even darker than I first thought, the black circles of his dilated pupils masking the gold and sapphire hues I had come to adore.

Brushing him off, I reached for his scarred face. "Relax, I'm fine," I reassured him. "How did you even find me?"

Briefly leaning into my touch, he pulled away once he noticed we weren't alone. His gaze locked onto Shamira beside me, glaring down at her. Despite their significant height difference, she stood tall, completely unfazed.

Stepping away, he straightened his shoulders and cleared his throat. "I followed your scent."

My irritation flared. "You followed my *scent*? What's happening that makes you think I have such a potent smell? I *don't* smell!"

"I never said you smelled—"

"That's not true!" I interjected. "You said I smelled and doused me with a bucket of water a few days ago! I understand bathing in a river isn't the epitome of personal hygiene, but it's certainly better than some of the things I've witnessed *you* do recently!"

He pinched the bridge of his nose. "Oh, my gods. Listen, Ge—"

Shamira cleared her throat, cutting Ryder off before he could say whatever he had in mind. "It's so lovely to have you join us, Huntsman. Don't fret; we were just about to say our goodbyes."

Ryder glanced at me, then shifted his attention back to Shamira. Giving her a quick nod, he lightly brushed my lower back. "Do I even want to know who this is?"

"You're a big boy." My eyes rolled. "You can make that decision for yourself."

Before he could reply, Shamira quickly gathered the scroll and the pile of clothes, handing them back to me.

"Child, keep hold of these," she said urgently. "The clothes should fit you. They belonged to my daughter long ago and will serve you better than they would me. Remember, the road ahead is full of mystery and danger. Trust in your legacy and your inner strength."

With the possessions in my hand, she promptly signaled for us to leave her shop, the door swinging open seemingly on its own. Ryder's hand remained on my back as we approached the exit.

"It's better if you don't linger in the village longer than necessary," she advised. "The forces you seek are not confined to this place; your journey awaits beyond these borders. Go, and may the universe be kind to you both."

With one final thin smile, she stepped back from the door. My eyes searched hers desperately, unwilling to let our conversation end so abruptly.

As the door closed behind her, I clutched the pile of clothes, the scroll hidden within the fabric.

My chest rose and fell as I tried to steady my breathing.

Feeling Ryder's glare, I turned slowly to face him. His pupils remained dilated; his jaw clenched tight. I knew he was mad. Hell, I knew it before he even burst through her shop.

"Should we talk about 'stranger danger'? Seems like your tutors skipped that lesson as a child."

"Imagine what they would say if they saw me here with *you*."

"I thought we agreed to gather what we needed and regroup at the horses. When I couldn't find you in the market, I panicked."

"Worried about little old me? And here I thought you didn't care."

He blinked a few times. "I'm pretty sure I said the exact *opposite* just a few hours ago if you don't remember. Maybe you are suffering from some head damage."

He lightly flicked my forehead.

My smile widened as I pushed his hand away. "Well, you

found me, and all is well in the world. There's no need to get all worked up."

A hint of a smile played on his lips before quickly fading.

He gritted his teeth slightly, attitude changing. "We'll discuss who the hell that woman was and why you have a whole wardrobe with you when we get back to the horses, but right now, we need to get out of here—and fast, preferably as *silently* as possible."

I furrowed my brow. "Why? What's going on?"

Ryder reached into his back pocket and retrieved a rolled-up piece of paper. As he unfolded it, my eyes widened, and my heart sank.

It was a wanted poster, and the face on it was *mine*.

WANTED ALIVE:
Princess Genevieve, former heir to the Orphinian Throne.
MURDER
TREASON
CONSPIRACY
A hefty bounty will be offered to any person, creature, or being who can either provide information of their whereabouts or returns the outlaw to Castle Quinn.

I forced a swallow, a wave of cold chills sweeping over my skin.

Pure, unabashed terror gripped every fiber of my being.

I stared at the poster in disbelief, seeing my own face staring back at me. Every part of me wanted to run away, to hope Ryder wouldn't chase after me. The poster looked exactly like me, and even if I tried to lie, chances were slim it would work.

When I finally looked up from the paper, Ryder's expression was grim. "Because you're wanted, *Princess*."

Summoning my courage, I stood straight. "How pissed are you?"

His eyes were back to their full golden and sapphire hues. "Not enough to stand here and talk about it before getting to the horses. Be swift and keep that *fucking* hood up."

He grabbed the clothes from me, and we rushed through the village as fast and quietly as we could. My cloak's hood hid my face, but I still felt uneasy. As we neared the village's edge, my anxiety grew, as if everyone in the marketplace was staring at the *Wanted Princess* from the posters.

Ryder moved smoothly through the crowd, a skill I wished I had. I made sure to stay close. His long legs moved fast, and I kept pace with him, feeling my heart race as the forest came into sight.

The sun was still high enough for us to cover some ground before nightfall, but I couldn't shake the feeling that those posters would keep following me.

Leaving Sambor was uneventful, thank the gods.

Relief flooded through me as we reached our tethered horses. Iris perched on Jupiter's head, wide, yellow eyes betraying her caution. She fluttered over to me, her urgent melody echoing our own feelings as we hurried.

Quickly untying Jupiter's reins, I finally felt a semblance of safety. Ryder did the same with Reaper, stashing my clothes and the scroll into his satchel.

Just as I was about to explain myself, he cut me off. "This isn't the place for *that* conversation." His tone was firm. "Mount your horse. We need to put some distance between us and this place."

I nodded, knowing it wasn't the time or place for an argument. Iris fluttered over to Ryder as he mounted Reaper, her song taking on an urgent tone.

Settling onto Jupiter, Iris gracefully returned to her spot on my shoulder, by my cheek. I could sense Iris picking up on the unspoken tension between Ryder and me as we urged our horses forward.

I was just glad to leave that village behind.

CHAPTER 25

FOR NEARLY AN HOUR, we rode in complete, *agonizing* silence.

The battle between my impatience and frustration grew with each passing minute. Iris, most likely uncomfortable by my tense shoulders, eventually retreated to my lap. Her small form quickly found sleep, and a part of me envied her ability to escape while the huntsman and I suffered silently.

I kept glancing over at Ryder hoping I could catch his eye, but he was focused on the road. I knew in my gut I had disappointed him. How could I not have? The thought of it killed me.

Why is it killing me?

Just yesterday, he had asked *one* simple thing of me—to be open and honest. *"Just from now on, try not to keep anything too big from me, okay?"*

He had asked a simple favor, and I betrayed him within a day. With each mile we traveled, the burden grew heavier. Unanswered questions lingered between us, and I knew I had made things even more complicated. As Iris slept soundly in my lap, unaware of my inner turmoil, I promised myself I'd become someone Ryder could trust. I'd share my fears, secrets, and true self with him.

Whether he accepted that side of me or not.

In the quiet of our ride, I silently vowed to be honest—no matter how difficult or dangerous the truth.

Because he *deserved* the truth.

The sun sank behind us as we rode on, and I knew we'd need to make camp soon. Ryder slowed, letting me catch up until we were side by side.

Finally, he glanced back at me. "Since we spent more time in that village than I had wanted, we'll have to ride past dark. Can you handle that?"

The tension in my body had eased a bit, but Sir Doyle's hits still lingered. Despite the discomfort, I didn't want to show weakness to Ryder, especially after already letting him down.

I nodded silently.

His posture sagged slightly—as if he knew I was lying. "Let's just make a quick stop for you to change and eat, okay?"

Iris perked up at the sound of Ryder's voice. Fluttering away from my lap, she made a beeline for the forest ahead of us.

"Stay close and be back in fifteen minutes!" he called after the Sprite, her fading melody the only response.

Dismounting, he walked over. Despite the tension, there was a comforting kindness in his eyes. Pressing his lips into a thin line, he extended his hand to help me down. I hesitated for a moment before taking it, and he gently guided me to the ground.

Our eyes met, and for a second, it felt like the world faded away, leaving just the two of us. He searched my face; finding nothing, he turned back to Reaper and rummaged through the satchels.

Damn trying to be patient. I needed to explain myself. If I let this tension continue, I would go insane before morning.

"Ryder..." My voice slightly trembled. "I-I don't even know where to start or what to say."

A dry sensation gripped my throat, prompting my fingers to reach instinctively for the bruise on my neck. His gaze tracked my movements as my fingertips lightly brushed the injured skin.

"I can understand if you hate me or no longer wish to continue helping me," I squeaked out. "I made a promise to you, and I broke it. I fucking *broke* it. I know in my soul I should have told you by now. I just...I enjoyed not being the princess. As selfish as that sounds, I wasn't ready to be Genevieve again. Just not yet."

Ryder walked to me and gently wrapped his fingers around my hand, stopping me from touching the bruise on my neck. The warmth of his hand against mine sent a series of goosebumps up my arms.

I somehow always forget how truly warm he is.

He clasped my hand securely, his eyes meeting mine while his thumb traced lazy circles on my palm. After a moment of silence, he sighed. "I had my suspicions, but I wasn't sure."

It felt like a slap of surprise. "I'm sorry, what? How could you possibly have been suspicious of me being the princess and not said anything?"

"My job is to gather information and find answers based on what I uncover, remember?" He shrugged. "You always struck me as proper, despite all the cursing. But it all made sense when you opened up a bit the other night. And seeing your hair just confirmed it...*Princess Genevieve.*"

His mouth formed a subtle smirk at the use of my full title, and *damn,* did it sound good on his lips.

"Plus, Madrona hinted toward you being more than what you seemed. I thought maybe she had meant...something else, but I understand now."

"So, you're not mad?"

Dropping my hand, he crossed his arms behind his neck, lightly stretching as if we were engaged in the most *casual conversation* in history.

"Mad? Oh yeah. At you? Nah. I'm pissed about those wanted posters, though. We were already in enough danger, but now it's open season on you, and people will be hunting for both your blood and the reward."

His choice of words was not the most ideal and I frowned at the thought. Ryder went back to Reaper and picked out a blouse from the pile Shamira had given me. In the process, the scroll slipped and fell to the ground. He quickly picked it up and casually put it back into the satchel, not giving it a second thought.

"You going to tell me who that woman was and why she gave you all this shit?" he asked, tossing the blouse towards me.

Snatching it mid-air, I fidgeted with the fabric. I knew that whatever I was about to share wouldn't sound remotely close to sane, but I vowed to be truthful.

Taking a deep breath, I recounted my day in Sambor. I told him about the encounter with the Shadow Walker and how Shamira seemed to know everything about my father and me. Ryder listened intently, his expressions changing as I spoke.

When I finished, I felt a weight lift from my shoulders. Ryder took a deep breath, absentmindedly running his fingers through his beard before picking up the scroll. I watched his chest rise and fall rhythmically as he unrolled it.

He cursed as his eyes quickly scanned the contents.

Joining him, I finally got a good look at the scroll. Even as daylight faded, I squinted at the line, trying to decipher its cryptic information. Meanwhile, Ryder stayed fixated on the scroll, his brow furrowed in concentration.

My patience was wearing thin. "What does it say?"

He finally looked away, his face grim. "That little old lady said this would help you unlock your family's history? That it would lead you to discover who was behind your father's murder?"

I crossed my arms over my chest and nodded slowly, the tingling in my fingers returning as a subtle hum. "Well, her name is Shamira, for starters, and yes—she said something along those lines. Why?"

Ryder ran his hand through his hair and a whooshing breath. He rolled up the scroll with a small, somewhat sarcastic laugh and carefully returned it to the satchel.

"Because, Princess, this is a map—and an *old* one at that. It'll lead us straight to The Hallows."

My heart sank at that name.

"By the look on your face," he lightly chuckled, "I'm guessing you've heard of it?"

I had heard some stories, but not much. Like most of the stories I grew up hearing, I had just assumed it was a myth.

The Hallows, a cursed piece of land, was said to be avoided by humans, Fae, and everything in between. Rumor had it, it served as a sanctuary for powerful Witches escaping execution. Despite the chilling tales, no one dared venture across its borders to verify the truth.

Or if they had...they never returned to tell the tale.

"Damn," he said, shaking his head. "I should have known. I should have *fucking* known. Where else would a Shadow Walker with a dagger like that come from?"

"I mean, sure, but why would a map of The Hallows help me unlock family histories?"

"Doesn't it make sense? Your whole lineage is tied to the war. Your great-great-great grandsire was the king, and now, the king is dead after promising his only child to the Fae prince? It could be revenge."

His words left me momentarily frozen.

"Either that or you could be a Witch..." he mumbled, his eyes locked on me.

I stared at him in shock, my heart racing. There was no way in hell those words just came out of his mouth. Then, everything hit. With how intense his eyes were tracking my features from head to toe, I doubted he was even close to joking.

But it wasn't possible. I didn't want to believe it was.

Shamira was convinced my mother and I had some sort of powers, that Sir Doyle's remarks about my hair all tied back to the possibility of his words being true.

So maybe it *did* make sense.

But if I did have some sort of power, it was from a race of beings who started this war. Their selfishness and greed caused thousands of innocent lives to suffer for over one hundred years. If I truly was a Witch, that meant I was a part of that in some way or another.

The thought made me sick to my stomach.

From the moment my father died, I resented Witches. I would have burned every single one if that meant I would find his killer. How could I be one of them? I wasn't perfect, but I always believed I was a good person. Could my heart be as dark as theirs?

After a brief stare-down, Ryder shook his head and turned away, pacing and muttering to himself. My anxiety spiked as I strained to catch fragments of his words, which were barely audible.

"Okay," he finally said. "This complicates things. I had plans to head closer to the border to gather information on potential coven hideouts, but it looks like The Hallows is in the opposite direction. *Shit*. I'm sorry we wasted some time, but I think we're on the right track."

Great.

"How many days?"

"A few," he admitted. "It looks like Claremont Harbor is the closest landmark before it gets fuzzy. But on the bright side, I know a place along the route where we can stay."

I was hopeful about the idea of sleeping in a real bed instead of the wilderness, but I was still hesitant. "Do you think The Hallows is a real place?"

"I know it is. Have I ever been? Hell no, but I've been around enough to know it's real."

"And you think it could hold the answers? That I'm a...a Witch?"

His face fell. "I think it's our best option right now. Witch or not, you deserve some answers."

"But," I couldn't stop talking, "do *you* think I'm a Witch?"

"I think you don't know who you are, and that's not a bad

thing. Right now, we need to focus on getting to where we need to go to find out for ourselves."

Not finished with my questions, I was interrupted by Iris's melody. I turned toward the sound, my stomach sinking as she zoomed toward us with such speed, her glow was all I could see. Any fear quickly turned to amusement as she approached, carrying something heavy and beautiful in her tiny hands.

A smile lit up my face as she buzzed up to me, her cheeks flushed. She held a flower crown, nearly twice her size. Where she got such blooms this time of year, I'd never know.

With a gentle touch, she pulled back my hood and placed the crown on my head. Warmth flooded me, instantly banishing the dark thoughts from my mind.

Her melody enveloped me, and even though I couldn't grasp her words, something inside me resonated. As her song crescendoed, she leaned in and planted the softest kiss on my already flushed cheek.

Turning back to Ryder, I found him wide-eyed and slightly open-mouthed, witnessing it all.

"What's wrong?"

His gaze never faltered as he approached, his hand gently untying the cloth covering my white hair. I was so mesmerized by his actions that having my hair exposed didn't worry me.

"*Beautiful,*" he muttered, stepping back. "When a Sprite offers someone a flower crown, it's an invitation into the Blessing. She sees you as an equal—as her family."

"Me? What did I do?"

"Do you ever not ask the most obvious questions? It's pretty simple, so stick with me if you can." His wink sent my heart racing. "Just look at yourself. For a runaway princess, you're unexpectedly resilient, and your heart is way too big for your own good. The moment your father died, you could have claimed the throne and ruled with an iron grip. But instead, you're here—putting your life in danger every day to avenge him. That alone says a lot about who *you* are."

I snorted. "Sounds like a lot of bull shit to me."

"Genevieve," he stressed my name, as if he was savoring it, "I want you to understand, I'm not sticking around just because you're paying me. I'm here because you've become more than just another assignment. You've become...a friend. She sees it, too. We both see the worth in you, no matter how unworthy you think you are."

A friend. Of course, he only sees me like that.

"A friend, huh? Careful, Ryder. You're risking your notorious huntsman reputation by getting all mushy on me."

"Don't get too excited, Princess. I could take you down in a heartbeat, flower crown and all."

With a smirk on his face, he flicked my crown, and I quickly shooed his hand away. "Well, you did just call me resilient. What makes you think I couldn't stand a chance against you?"

Taking a step closer, a hint of mischief was written all over his face. "Just because you're resilient doesn't mean you know everything. Don't forget: I'm the *master*."

"Master of being a smart ass."

Another laugh of his echoed through me as he moved swiftly. He stepped closer, his gaze playful and his grin, along with his captivating eyes, mesmerizing me.

Getting a bit too close, he suddenly lunged forward.

Before I could react, he had pinned me to the ground, his knee on my stomach and his arm extended, holding my wrist down in the dirt above my head. The impact knocked the breath out of me, but the warm hand cradling the back of my head left me even more speechless.

He leaned closer, his voice turned teasingly low as his warm breath tickled my ear. "Like I was saying...*master*."

I laughed at his ridiculousness, rolling my eyes as I playfully tried to shove him off me. "I'll remember that for next time."

Moving his hand from behind my head, he grabbed my other wrist, pinning it beside the first as his mismatched gaze swept over me. "You know, I think I like the look of you under me—face flushed and eyes wide."

Oh, two can play this game.

"Yeah?" I said, turning on my charm. "Imagine how good I would look on top."

His eyes doubled in size, clearly taken by surprise at my response. His grip relaxed slightly, and I wasted no time in slipping my wrists from his grasp and seizing his shoulders.

Rolling us over, I reached for the dagger sheathed at my hip and effortlessly drew it. Straddling his broad waist, I couldn't help but smirk as I held the dagger lightly against his throat.

Leaning in closer, I pressed the blade gently against his skin. "So what were you saying, '*master*'?"

Even more surprise and a hint of admiration crossed his face. As we lay together, our chests rising and falling, a smile spread across the huntsman's lips.

Laughter filled the clearing as Ryder lay pinned beneath me, his mismatched eyes sparkling with amusement.

When he looked up at me, his grin sent butterflies fluttering in my stomach. "Definitely better." He winked. "And I think I like you calling me '*master*' even more, *Princess*."

Trying to ignore the warmth pooling in my stomach, I let

out a triumphant laugh and stood, extending a hand to help him back to his feet.

"You truly are impossible," I teased. "But please, for the love of the gods, don't call me 'Princess.'"

He accepted my hand and stood, brushing dirt off his clothes while maintaining his grin. "But why would I stop when it's so much fun?"

"Kicking you in the shin also seems like a good bit of fun. Shall we test it?"

"I think I understand now," he chuckled, "why you chose the name 'Rose' as a cover."

I arched an eyebrow, intrigued. "Oh? Do tell."

"Just like a rose, you're beautiful—truly stunning. But roses have thorns, and your bite, sweetheart, is definitely not to be underestimated."

A flush crept to my cheeks. "Actually, Rose is my middle name. But thanks for the compliment, Huntsman."

His own face flushed as Iris flew back to us, holding my forgotten flower crown delicately in her tiny hands. A wide smile spread across my face as I accepted the bundle from her, carefully setting it back atop my head.

"Thank you, Iris," I whispered. "I didn't say it before, but I'm truly honored and grateful for your kindness."

Ryder cleared his throat as he rummaged through Reaper's satchel. Finding a piece of jerky, he handed it to me. "Here, have a snack and change your top. We need to hit the road again. We won't reach the main resting place tonight, but we can stop again in a few hours."

Nodding, I took the jerky and chewed on it while removing my cloak and flower crown. Placing them on Jupiter's back, I moved around a large oak and swiftly changed into a simple, dark green tunic.

Stepping back into view, Ryder gave me an approving nod. Reaching into his pocket, he pulled out a small, copper piece of fabric.

"One more thing." He reached for my hand, "I picked this up for you. The color isn't exactly the same as your hair, but it'll blend in better than that dirty thing."

Iris danced around us, her joyful melody seeming to express exactly how grateful I felt for his act of kindness.

"Thank you, Ryder."

Instead of telling me not to thank him like I expected, he looked me over and smiled.

A pure, soft, genuine smile.

"You're welcome."

Gracefully mounting Reaper, he gently caressed her mane. "Flower crown can stay on if you want, but I will not stop if it falls off. Got it? And Iris," she shimmered in response, "out of sight, out of mind. Understand?"

Her melody was subdued but equally enchanting as she acknowledged his instructions. Tying the new fabric around my white hair, I placed the flower crown proudly on my head. Clasping the cloak around my healing neck, I mounted Jupiter and prepared myself.

Iris took her usual place on my lap and swiftly folded her wings over her form to conceal herself. With one last glance in my direction, Ryder and Reaper took the lead. The sun had already begun its descent, and a chill settled over me after the excitement of our earlier sparring. I raised my hood, grateful for the warmth it provided my ears.

With another step forward, the thought of sleep seemed more and more exciting.

I'm wasn't sure how long we'd been riding or how often I caught myself drifting to sleep, but the way my neck kept snapping up told me I wouldn't last much longer.

We spent some time chatting, sharing laughs and stories about learning to fight. I opened up to Ryder about my father's support in my training, recalling the memory of my first victory against Topher on my last day. I told him all about Topher and Fiona—how they were my saving grace after my mother passed away, how Topher dedicated his mornings to working and training me.

Our conversations felt effortless, like we were old friends catching up after years apart.

Ryder's words tapered off as the moon climbed higher, casting a serene glow across our path. Fatigue settled in, weighing heavy on my eyelids. Iris, awakening with the moon's ascent from her many naps, was now fully alert. Ryder explained Sprites rested in their flowers during the day, only venturing out under the cover of night.

She flitted between us, curious about our surroundings. Her gentle melodies helped keep me awake, though sleep still threatened to overcome me.

It's no wonder that just before I closed my eyes, my mother's face would often appear. We talked about her a lot; naturally, she was on my mind. Her comforting presence made it feel like she was right beside me. I could almost feel the soft touch of her lips on my forehead, a loving gesture just like when I was a child drifting off to sleep. Her emerald eyes, just like mine, seemed to glow in the back of my mind, as if she was still watching over me.

Despite the decade since her death, I still heard her laughter echoing vividly in my memory. As sleep beckoned, she would reach out to me, drawing me into her warm embrace. Just as I was about to reach her, I would snap awake, eyes wide open in the dark forest.

The rhythmic gallop of Jupiter carried me onward, fatigue gently wrapping around my mind. The night's darkness was both comforting and haunting, lulling me toward slumber. There was no use trying to fight it. As I drifted once more, my world dissolved, and my mother's loving face materialized before me.

She was so pale, her emerald eyes meeting mine with a mix of warmth and urgency. *"Genevieve, my love, you must..."*

Her words trailed off like a whispered secret, and I strained to catch her message. Panic gripped me as I watched her lips move in silence, my heart racing in the effort to understand. Still, her words remained just out of reach.

A sickling stillness enveloped us, and my mother's gaze shifted behind me, eyes widening in fear. I tried to turn to see what had frightened her, but I was frozen, unable to move. She mouthed words I still couldn't hear, her expression pleading. Darkness began to swallow her, consuming her until only emptiness remained.

Her voice emerged from the darkness. *"Do not trust him!"*

Who? Who should I not trust?

I reached out, but my feet were rooted in place. The darkness around her shifted, and a sudden, sharp pain pierced my chest, leaving me gasping for air. Despite the pain, I couldn't look away.

A low, menacing growl echoed from the shadows, triggering my fight-or-flight response. A wide, pale smile flashed in the darkness, taunting me. In an instant, it vanished, and the cold, relentless blackness closed in around me, like a predator pouncing on its prey.

My scream pierced the still night air as I violently jerked awake. Clutching Jupiter's reins tightly, I barely stopped myself from falling off his back and hitting the forest floor. Gasping for air, my heart pounded in my chest as I tried to convince myself it was all a dream.

Ryder was off Reaper and by my side in an instant.

How the hell does he move so fast?

His warm hands steadied me, keeping me from falling. "Woah, what happened?"

Even in the darkness of the night, the worry on his face was obvious. "I-I had a dream," I stammered. "My mother, s-she was trying to tell me something, but I couldn't hear her. She was so pale...so scared. It *ate* her... The *darkness* ate her."

"Shit. You fell asleep? Genevieve...that's not safe."

"It's not like I did it on purpose, Ryder!" I sleepily snapped.

Steadying me, he offered a reassuring grip on my knee that had way more of an effect on me than it should have. "I know, I know. It was just a dream," he said softly. "I'm here. You're safe. Try and take a few deep breaths for me, okay?"

I nodded, feeling my racing heart gradually slow down. Ryder's hand rubbed my knee soothingly, a calming gesture I only fully noticed once his touch was gone. As I watched him, his gaze shifted toward the night sky, a subtle tension set in his posture. Rolling up his sleeves, his tan skin pebbled under the silvery light of the full moon.

When he moved his neck to the side, a small series of cracks echoed in the quiet night. "We've been riding long enough. How about we rest here for the remainder of the night? I can't handle you falling off your horse...*again*."

I gave him a sleepy thumbs-up, lacking the energy and desire for banter. He helped me down from Jupiter, delicately taking the forgotten flower crown from my head and setting it into a satchel. Moving to help the unpacking process, Ryder raised his hand, signaling for me to stop.

"I've got this," he said softly, his eyes reflecting the moon's glow. "You've had a rough few nights; take a moment to rest. Can you do that for me?"

Reluctantly, I nodded and sat on the forest floor, my back leaning against a tree. The heaviness of my eyes grew with each passing moment, but every time they fluttered shut, my mother's pale face stared back at me.

Her voice echoed in my mind. *"Do not trust him!"*

But who? Did she mean Ryder? Or...someone else? Someone I maybe hadn't even met yet...

Shaking my head, I attempted to dispel her voice from my thoughts and wake myself up. Looking for a distraction, I shifted my attention to Ryder efficiently setting up the camp—a vision of grace and strength in the moon's soft glow.

He looked strong and undeniably handsome. The moonlight accentuated the shimmer of his black hair, as if he belonged under the celestial glow. Even beneath his thick tunic, I could see his muscles flexing as he worked, a small canine hanging from his mouth as he concentrated.

That stupid beard really hides how full his lips are.

Ryder turned toward me, his gaze resting on my tired form leaning against the tree. There was a hint of wildness in his eyes, and it only drove my imagination further. The way he looked on top of me today was enough to make me question any morals I had. Even though Topher often made his way into my mind, he never made me feel the way Ryder did daily.

Looking me up and down, it felt like he was reading my very thoughts. The crooked grin on his lips only further made me feel he could.

Thank the gods he can't, because he would never let me hear the end of it.

As he inhaled deeply, his nostrils flared. Shaking off a shiver, he sent me one final look before he resumed his work. Soon, our tents were up, and a crackling fire lit up the woods.

Feeling satisfied with his progress, I decided it was time to rest. As I approached my tent, Ryder watched me closely, the flickering campfire casting a mesmerizing glow in his already mesmerizing eyes.

"You alright?" I asked, noticing his stare.

His expression remained neutral, but a hint of mischief danced in his eyes. "Just relieved you didn't take another tumble from your horse...*Princess.*"

Rolling my eyes, I went to push open the tent entrance. "Goodnight, *master.*"

A warm hand caught my wrist, stopping me. Looking back, Ryder's face was inches from mine, eyes even more wild than I realized.

"Genevieve..." His throat bobbed as he swallowed. "I, uh—"

For once, my huntsman was at a loss for words. Tracing every contour, every line, and every scar on his face, I waited for him to speak. How long did we stay like that, locked in each other's gazes?

I could stay here all night.

He cleared his throat, eyes flickering to my lips. "Just, uh, goodnight."

Swallowing back any sleepy, false hopes, I slipped out of his grasp and into my tent. Exhaustion weighed heavily on me, and I could barely muster the energy to remove my cloak and pants, let alone make sense of what just happened.

All I could hope for was Ryder's warm eyes to find me in my sleep instead of the coldness of my mother's.

CHAPTER 26

THE SNAPPING of branches and crunching leaves outside my tent was enough to wake me from a rather *inappropriate* dream about Ryder.

I blame the way he looked at me all day. His stupid warmth and stupid mismatched eyes followed me even in my deepest of sleeps.

Stupid Huntsman.

My face felt warm as I glanced around. It was still dark outside, so I was unsure how much time had passed. Judging by the small puddle of drool on my pillow, it had probably been at least a few hours.

Trying to calm my racing heart after the dream, I lay there, listening for any sounds. The rustling grew closer, but the tent's thick fabric blocked my view. With only the faint silver glow of the full moon visible, I was left blind to the outside threat.

Hearing heavy footsteps, I knew it had to be a larger creature. When I realized a rabbit hadn't come to pay me a visit, a sinking feeling settled into the pit of my stomach as the sounds grew closer. Though I hadn't had much experience with wolves,

I had a feeling it wasn't one outside. The movements were too calculated, less wild than I would assume a predator would be.

But I'm pretty sure it wasn't human either. Heart pounding out of my chest, I reached for the dagger hidden beneath my pillow.

I was *not* going to be caught off guard for a third night in a row.

Straining my ears, I desperately tried to figure out what the hell it could be. Panic set in as I realized Iris was gone from my tent.

Shit. Had she even joined me to begin with?

My mind raced, wondering if this was just another nightmare. Maybe the dream I'd just had had twisted into something more sinister. I took a few deep breaths, trying to convince myself to wake up.

Dread washed over me as a nearby howl pierced the night. Realizing I was awake, and the wolf had returned did nothing to calm my nerves.

Was it *my* wolf? Or a hungry pack?

Adrenaline surged through my veins, making me feel dizzy. Silently, I climbed out of my cot and pulled on my pants. Gripping the dagger tightly, I mentally braced myself for whatever was out there in the moonlit forest.

A shadow approached the tent, its outline distorted. My senses sharpened, and every hair on my body stood on end. The silhouette reached my tent's entrance, and I tightened my grip on the dagger.

Filled with adrenaline—or maybe just stupidity—I charged forward, ready to defend myself against the perceived threat. But as soon as the entrance opened, I stopped dead in my tracks, feeling the hit of reality like running into a stone wall.

In the dim moonlight, Ryder stood before me, eyes wide and wild. He was shirtless, his chest covered in black ink and what looked like dirt. As I looked him over, it was clear he'd either been sleeping on the ground or had fallen.

My fists unclenched, and my body gradually relaxed as I worked to calm my racing heart. With a sense of relief, I tossed the dagger aside, no longer in need of it.

Relieved, I let out a long breath. "Ryder, it's you."

I sat back on my cot, thankful it wasn't a hungry animal. He stayed quiet, just watching me. The more I looked at his toned body, his chest rising and falling with heavy breaths, the more I noticed how tense his muscles were. When I finally looked at his scarred face, I saw a look of primal fear.

Was it fear...or something else?

"Ryder? What's the matter?"

He stood unmoving, like a rock—firm, almost predatory as his eyes locked onto mine. Even in the dim tent, I could make out their near-blackness, hints of gold and sapphire barely visible. His breaths continued to be heavy and quick, making his chest rise and fall in a way that made me nervous.

"Uh, hello? Ryd—"

Before I could finish speaking his name for the third time, he pounced.

Strong hands pushed me onto the cot, pinning me just like he had earlier that day. His intense gaze sent shivers down my spine, and his warmth felt almost overwhelming. Try as I might to push him away, his strength was impossible to resist.

"What's wrong with you?"

With his face close to mine, I could see the true depth of darkness in his eyes. He smelled of the forest, as he always did, but there was something...*different* about his scent.

It was alluring, and I found myself taking deep breaths to both steady my composure and savor his aroma.

Even with the dropping temperature outside, he was sweating more than usual. I tried to move my hand to feel his forehead for a fever, but he held onto me firmly. His grip was strong, yet surprisingly gentle.

Dark eyes stayed fixed on my lips, and the feel of his firm body pushing down against mine elicited a soft moan of surprise. Almost instinctively, I responded, mirroring his movements, lifting my hips to meet his.

His eyes widened, and a darkness flickered in them as my lips trembled. "W-what's happening?" I whispered.

When he swallowed deeply, his intense gaze left my lips and locked onto my eyes. His mouth hung slightly open, his warm breath caressing my face as he spoke. "I could *smell* you," he uttered in a voice so deep and raspy it was almost unrecognizable.

A sharp laugh escaped my mouth. "If all you're here to do is tell me I *smell*, you can get off now, asshole." Now annoyed, I tried to nudge him away, but he remained firmly in place, his proximity overwhelming. "Come on, Ryder. This isn't funny. Get. *Off*."

But he didn't move. Those nearly black eyes locked onto mine with an intensity that stole my breath.

"Not bad," he growled before leaning into my hair and inhaling deeply. "Never bad. Fucking...*intoxicating*."

Without giving me a chance to react, he moved fast—his lips attacking the side of my bruised neck. Gasping, I quickly melted into his touch. The sensation of his lips on my neck was unlike anything I had ever experienced. Any sound once surrounding my tent was soon overpowered by the rhythmic sucking and kissing noises escaping his lips.

A small nip from his canines grazing my skin caused me to jump. He didn't bite me hard, but I knew it was a warning of what he could do if he wanted.

If *I* wanted.

As he licked the pain away, his lips were back to marking my skin as his own. My eyes fluttered shut, and I allowed myself to become fully vulnerable under him—no longer caring about the wolf or other creature that may or may not be outside our camp.

One of his hands reached the center of my stomach, lightly tracing his large fingers further up under my tunic. His movements were slow and calculated, extremely different from his earlier wildness. The feel of his fingers touching the bottom of my breast was enough to push me over the edge, moaning in response.

The sound that escaped from my lips was foreign on my tongue, but Ryder let out a low growl—his hard body pushing deeper into mine. I practically whimpered as his lips left my neck, dark eyes once again met mine. Smiling, the canines were on full display.

Have they always been that long?

"Is this okay?" he asked, voice still low.

I couldn't speak, so I let my body do it for me. As I moved my hips in response, he frowned, the smirk leaving his face. Pinning my hips down with his hand, he looked far from amused.

"I need to *hear* it."

My mind was a jumbled mess of hormones and feelings as I fought to find words. My eyes locking on his hungry eyes, my lips quivered as I produced what he needed to hear, what I wanted to say.

"Y-yes."

The smirk returned. "That's my good girl."

Warm lips returned to my neck. If the bruises left by Sir Doyle were fading, Ryder was quickly taking their place. His once-firm grip vanished, and my hands instinctively moved to his long hair, urging him to continue.

At this point, I had no idea what the hell was happening, but every ounce of my being longed for it to continue. The feel of his body over mine was the definition of euphoria—as if a missing piece of my life's puzzle had finally been returned. Our bodies moved in a captivating duet, fitting and molding perfectly together. His lips trailed a burning path from my neck to my collarbone, my nails digging into his scalp with each touch.

Moans of pleasure escaped my lips and filled the tent. It was a seductive melody I was unaware I could produce. Ryder's low growls echoed in response.

Making his way to the collar of my tunic, he wasted no time untying the laces that held the neckline in place. With more and more skin exposed, the more and more I never wanted him to stop.

His lips brushed the top of my breast as his fingers remained just below them. I encouraged him to continue, my back arching to the point I was practically levitating off the cot.

Feeling a cool breeze on my chest, I looked down to see my now fully exposed breast—nipple hard from the chill of the air. Ryder licked his lips, and in a blink of an eye, he attached to my nipple, and I immediately saw stars. Using his hand that remained under my breast, he gently squeezed and lifted it higher, giving him room to take more of me in his mouth.

A man's touch wasn't *completely* foreign to me.

I lost my virginity on my sixteenth birthday with some visiting royal from a neighboring continent whose name I would never remember. Liliana had pulled me aside during the celebration, letting me know I was officially a woman in the kingdom's eyes and that my one true purpose as the future queen was to produce heirs for my future husband—that being "*pure*" and "*obedient*" were the only reasons for me to exist.

Fuck. That.

Rage filled me that night, and I stormed through the Great Hall, tasting my first drink of wine until I was drunk enough to make my first move. He was decently attractive, skinny, and awkward—like most young men at that age. We met in a closet after Father had retired to bed. The boy lasted less than five minutes, but the damage was done, and Liliana could kiss my non-virgin ass.

But this... *This* was different, better than I ever imagined a man's touch could be—and he had barely begun.

Topher's departing kiss was new and exciting, but this was beyond words. The pleasure I felt from Ryder was intense, damn near magical. The way his hands and tongue worked was wicked and wonderful, skilled and warm.

Gods.

Had I been so deprived of touch that this affected me so much? Or was it Ryder? Was he the sole reason behind such an immense amount of pleasure? I'll admit, my attraction to him had grown since we first met. I just hadn't realized how much I'd been suppressing it.

Not until now.

My hands left his scalp and made their way to his exposed back—nails digging further and further into his tattooed skin. I was gasping at this point, feeling feral in the best of ways. The tingling in my fingers had stopped but seemed to travel through my body until it stopped right between my legs.

And I only ever wanted to feel *that*.

Wrapping my legs around his wide torso, I could feel how much he wanted this too. And it drove me even *more* insane.

"P-please don't—"

I didn't want him to stop. But between gasps and moans, I couldn't fully form the plea.

All pleasure stopped almost too abruptly when Ryder's mouth left my nipple, and it took everything in me not to force his head back to the swollen bud. Opening my eyes, his golden and sapphire pools looked back at me. My once-dizzy vision returned, and I could easily see how pale he had become.

Any lust or desire in his eyes was gone, causing my stomach to drop. "Ryder?"

He was off me before I could register it and I quickly pulled the blanket back over myself, covering my exposed breast. My cheeks were burning with embarrassment, and I could have screamed. He appeared flustered and nervous, chest heavily rising and falling.

His now fully colored eyes avoided mine as he ran a hand through his tangled hair. "I'm so sorry, Genevieve," he stammered, "I didn't mean to... I shouldn't have..."

I reached for him, but he recoiled from my touch. Actually *recoiled*.

Without allowing me to respond, he busted out of my tent, only leaving a brisk breeze in his wake. Sitting there, I was stunned.

What the fuck just happened?

Shaky hands nudged me to the edge of my cot, and I quickly sealed the tent flaps to keep out the cold air. Flopping back, I finally regained some composure. My teeth found my lower lip as I tried to make sense of everything.

His lips, the look in his eyes, the way he felt against me... *Shit*. But then he just...left. Gone as if nothing had happened, like he had *wished* nothing had happened.

A fever could have caused him to hallucinate. Like he was having some sort of wild dream his body was acting out without his brain's consent.

But he asked for *mine*. And I gave it.

Groaning, I rolled over and buried my face in my pillow. My mind raced with emotions and thoughts, leaving me completely overwhelmed. This whole thing was already complicated enough; I didn't need to add confusing feelings to the mix.

But would it be the end of the world if it happened again?

Based on his reaction, I doubted he would want that anyway.

Was it me? Did I say something that made him realize this was all a big mistake? Or did he just not find me attractive? He called me beautiful earlier, but being beautiful doesn't mean someone finds you attractive.

Damn it!

Flipping onto my side, a soft blue light seeped through the tent flaps. A smile spread across my lips as Iris fluttered closer. The look on her little face told me whatever had happened between Ryder and me was *not* a secret to her.

"Sorry if you overheard. Have any idea what the hell that was?"

Not that I was expecting a response, but she answered with

her usual cheerful melody, though her tiny shoulders seemed to shrug in response.

"Yeah, me neither."

Pulling my blanket tighter around me, I fought off a shiver tracing its way down my spine. The feeling of the unknown was something I had been dealing with for weeks at this point, but not knowing what awaited me in the morning when I woke with Ryder was killing me.

Iris nestled on my chest, forming a compact blue ball of gentle hums as her melody comforted me. Despite my lingering thoughts, my mind wandered, and fatigue set in as my eyes grew heavier and heavier.

The final sound I registered was a faint, animal-like whimper echoing in the distance.

The sun had been in the sky for about an hour, yet I remained cuddled in my cot.

No part of me wanted to get up and face Ryder, but it would have to come sooner or later. Considering I hadn't heard him moving around the camp, I would bet he felt the same.

At some point during my endless tossing and turning, Iris had shifted from my chest to the side of my pillow. Not wanting to wake her, I quietly pushed the blanket off and rose to stretch.

The lingering ache in my body had mostly faded. I reached up to my neck, flashbacks of the night before hitting me, bringing the wonderful tingling sensation with it. I quickly shook my head to push away the memories before they took over. Not feeling any soreness or tenderness where the bruise had been, I gave my neck a quick stretch and moved on to the next spot.

Gentle rustling outside my tent signaled Ryder had awakened, and my heart instantly skipped a beat. My old friend Dread washed over me like a looming storm, but I knew I couldn't avoid this confrontation.

Taking a deep breath, I stepped out of my tent and found Ryder tending the fire. He gave me a lazy, half-smile, his face calm like nothing had happened.

The mask of a huntsman.

"You're up," he remarked. "I thought you might sleep in this morning."

I crossed my arms over my cold chest, realizing I'd forgotten my cloak. "I was pretty restless," I confessed. "I also kept hearing noises throughout the night."

He let out a light, awkward chuckle as he re-focused on the fire. "Any nightmares?"

Gods, this small talk was brutal.

"Uh, nope. Not after I nearly fell off Jupiter."

"Good, good."

A heavy, uneasy silence fell over us, the forest eerily quiet. With a deep sigh, I settled down next to him by the fire. "So...do you want to talk about it?"

He released the long stick he'd been using to tend the fire and turned his focus to me. The color had returned to his cheeks, and his eyes no longer held that wild look.

"Not really."

Rolling my eyes, I gave him a playful shove. "You don't leave me much choice, Huntsman. If you don't want to start, I will."

His smirk disappeared as he paused "It's a funny story,

really. You'll probably laugh," he began, avoiding eye contact as he stared at the fire. "Yesterday was a long day, and I crashed pretty hard once you went to bed. Sometimes, when I'm that tired, I sleepwalk. Been doing it since I was a kid, so you can imagine how embarrassing it was for me to wake up on top of you and realize I had done it again. Honest mistake."

When he finally looked at me, his expression was a mix of embarrassment and a strained attempt at sincerity. I blinked a few times, trying to process his words.

"So you...sleep walked into my tent?"

He nodded, his face flushed. "Yeah, it's usually not that...*intense*."

"You sleep walked and...*kissed* my neck?"

He shrugged, his broad shoulders giving off an air of nonchalance. "I don't know what to tell you, Genevieve. You asked if I wanted to talk about it, and that's all I have to say."

I paused, my lips twitching into a hesitant smile before I burst into laughter. The sound echoed through the peaceful forest, the sheer absurdity of the situation easing the tension. As I caught my breath and turned to Ryder, his expression remained unamused.

"Sorry," I said, my laughter fading. "It's just... I don't know, Ryder. I can't believe you'd sleepwalk into my tent and, well, *you know*." I moved my hands to point at my neck. "You looked more possessed than asleep."

"Sleepwalking is like possession. I had no control of my body."

"Oh, I could tell. But that doesn't mean it was an accident."

A muscle in his jaw twitched before the corners of his lips turned up. "Believe what you want. Next time we get to a library, you can research it."

I smiled. "I'll make it a top priority."

No matter how much we could pretend nothing happened, the tension lingered. I wanted to laugh and move on, but any hint of a smile faded as the awkwardness set in. I knew last night's events weren't caused by sleepwalking, but I chose to let it slide.

With a weary sigh, Ryder's shoulders sagged under an invisible burden. "Regardless, I'm sorry. I once told you I wasn't a man who took advantage of women, and that's exactly what I did last night. It was wrong and I can promise you it won't happen again."

I tried to hide my disappointment and softened my expression. Maybe it *was* for the best. Summoning a smile, I reached out and touched his knee. It was almost comical to me, because despite how much he "regretted" the night prior, he had no issue leaning into it now.

"I'm not upset with you. You may not remember, but I told you it was okay at that moment," I reassured him. "But can we please retire the *'you smell'* commentary?"

"I never said you smelled," he chuckled. "I said I *could* smell you. There's a difference."

Oh. So, he remembered that part.

His eyes searched for any sign of forgiveness. "Are we okay?"

"We're fine. Call it even for me hiding that I was the princess."

Giving me a satisfied nod, he reached over and pulled one of the satchels resting on Reaper onto his lap. Opening the flap, he rummaged through it, as if looking for something specific.

"Care for a cup of coffee?"

"A cup of what?"

"Coffee," he repeated, glancing up at me. "I picked up some

grinds at the market, but with everything that's been happening, I forgot all about them. Never had coffee before?"

I shook my head. "No, never. What is it?"

His eyes seemed to sparkle in excitement. I watched with fascination as he explained and worked with the grinds. The process was interesting but not too different from brewing a kettle of tea. The way he spoke, even about a drink, had me locked in.

The camp soon filled with a strange, rich smell.

After a short process, he poured the coffee into two small, steel mugs. "Here," he offered with a grin. "Give it a try."

He handed it to me, the warmth that seeped through the mug onto my hands a welcomed relief from the cold morning. I took a cautious sip and was immediately met with the bold, slightly bitter flavor. It was unlike anything I'd ever tasted, and I enjoyed the warmth that spread through me.

"Thoughts?" he asked while blowing on his mug.

I took another sip, ensuring I got a full and fair taste, "It's bitter. It's not like tea, and," I coughed, "it's *strong*."

"Most folks add milk and sugar to mellow out the bitterness. I'm surprised you never had it at the palace."

I shook my head, cradling the warm mug in my hands. "Father was quite particular about what was allowed within the castle walls. With the ongoing war, he insisted on using only what could be produced within the kingdom's borders. Quite cheaper too. I assume coffee isn't grown in Orphinian?"

"You'd be correct. The beans thrive in consistently warm climates, unlike the changing seasons in Orphinian lands. They mostly grow them down south in Arable, then ship them up to Meridian Harbor for trade."

"Arable," I echoed. "I remember them from my mother's

funeral. Their customs were strange, but this coffee? Damn! No wonder they stayed out of the war. I wouldn't want to risk losing this either." Savoring another sip, I appreciated everything around me. It felt like a bit of magic in a world I thought magic was rare. "How did you learn all this?"

He leaned back to relax. "Years of traveling, Genevieve. I've been everywhere in Orphinian, from the coast of the Kai Sea to Claremont Harbor. I doubt there's a piece of land I haven't passed through. Being a huntsman has no boundaries. Where a job sent me, I went."

A shadow passed over his face, and he looked away to fixate on his mug. The sadness written on his beautifully scared features revealed the weight of everything he must have endured while out on the road.

"Never ventured across the sea? Explored other kingdoms and continents like Arable?"

"Sailed the ocean?" He barked a laugh. "Fuck no. Large bodies of water and me don't mix. I'll stay land locked until the day I die."

I took another satisfying sip before asking another question, and Iris fluttered her way over to us.

Ryder's head snapped up. "Absolutely do *not* let her near that! She'll bounce off the trees for days if she has a single sip."

Iris buzzed around the warm mug, and I quickly covered it with my hand to stop her from sneaking a sip. Her melody was low and mournful, like a funeral progression.

"You'll survive," he reassured the little Sprite.

"So, what's the plan for today?"

"We still got a few days' worth of riding away, but the cabin we're staying in tonight is closer. Unless we run into some issues getting through Forest Sylvie, we'll make it there before tomorrow's sundown."

"Forest Sylvie? I've never heard of such a territory."

I earned another smirk from the huntsman. "Not many have unless you've lived near or in it. But that's all you'll be getting, Princess. You'll see it when we get there."

Disregarding the *"Princess"* remark and its effect on my body, I nodded, satisfied with our plan for the day.

"May I finish up before we leave?"

Agreeing, he leaned back, muscles visibly easing. We savored our cups of coffee by the crackling fire, the surrounding forest gradually stirring to life with the arrival of a new day.

After cleaning up, we were off.

Iris was not happy I chose to opt out of wearing her flower crown. Although I tried to explain to her it was out of safety and not disrespect, her melody was harsh and short throughout the morning. Instead of perching on Jupiter with me, she fluttered around, occasionally emitting sharp, minor notes.

I knew it was her way of cursing me out. Ryder's occasional smirk after an *extra* sharp note was even more proof. Eventually, her little wings gave out, and she settled in my lap, emitting a short, sweet tune.

"Still mad at me?" I whispered to her.

Fatigue showed in her yellow eyes as she looked up. I reached into my pouch and pulled out a piece of jerky. Her eyes grew with delight as she eagerly took the treat.

Holding back a giggle, I observed her devour the jerky—her cheeks puffing up like a chipmunk's. "Now do you forgive me?"

"I saw that," Ryder's voice called out from over his shoulder.

In a surprising turn of events, the rest of the two days flowed rather smoothly. We made good progress, only stopping briefly to stretch or attend to our basic needs. During the day, the awkwardness from the night before seemed to have vanished, but at night I still secretly hoped he would enter my tent again.

On the second day, the sun dipped below the Dalia Mountains earlier than the night prior.

Approaching a dense wood, Ryder turned to me, his expression serious. "Stay sharp and alert," he cautioned.

We ventured into the heart of the forest; our horses' hooves barely audible on the thick carpet of grass. A dense fog enveloped us, obscuring our vision of what surrounded us. I had seen fog before, but this was unlike any I had encountered. It seemed almost alive, slithering through the air like a garden snake, cold and deliberate.

Ryder's voice cut through the swirling haze, "Don't get off Jupiter until we are out of this. It's safer on the horses."

My nose crinkled. "Why? What's wrong with it?"

His eyes stayed fixed ahead, as if he could see through the fog itself. "It's the forest's trick to throw off outsiders. It confuses them, obscuring their sense of direction and conjuring images to lead them away. Only those the forest trusts can find their way through. So...stick close to me, alright?"

Confidence radiated from him with every step, his posture tall and assured on top of Reaper. We pressed on, the world around us transforming into a maze. The fog twisted and shifted with an eerie presence, making navigation nearly impossible. Despite the thick, damp air, Ryder moved through it effortlessly, as if it was nothing more than a light mist.

"Can I ask a question?" I called out from behind him.

His laughter echoed. "You'll ask it anyway."

"Hypothetically, what would happen if I was walking instead of riding? Like...if my whole body was in the fog, would it eat me?"

His laugh only grew. "No, it wouldn't *eat* you, but it could consume your mind."

"Ew. *What*?"

"Not in how you're thinking. It might lead you back out of the woods to where you first started. Or worse—it could lead you towards the edge of a cliff. The fog manipulates what you see, and outsiders tend to fall for its tricks easier than you'd think."

I was about to ask another question about the fog's origin, but before I could, he jumped in as if he could read my mind. "And before you ask—which I know you will—yes, the fog is magical."

"Magical like The Hallows?"

"That's a question I don't have an answer for," he confessed. "Long ago, these lands were home to a tribe called the Waya. When war broke out, the elders feared for their homes, their families. They turned to Calantha, goddess of nature, offering her a place of rest in exchange for protection. The fog we're in, it's her gift. It's said she sleeps here still, watching over these woods, waiting for a time when the world might be ready for her to wake again."

"You said 'were home.' Is the tribe no longer around?"

He shook his head. "Not like they once were. Some of their descendants are still around, but the tribe died off long ago."

"Descendants like *you*?"

Even though I couldn't see him smiling, I knew he was. I could *feel* it. He turned his head to glance at me. "You know, for someone who grew up so sheltered, you're pretty smart."

A warm smile played on my lips, and my cheeks flushed. "The best education tax money could provide."

He chuckled before turning his gaze to the mist. "My great-grandpa was the last chief the tribe ever had. When the war broke out, he sent most of the men to fight, hoping to protect our land. You can imagine how that turned out." There was a hint of sadness in his voice. "We used to spend our summers here. My pa taught Amarisa and me the ways of the Waya—hunting, tracking, listening to nature. We learned it all." He sighed softly. "I haven't been back here since...well, since Amarisa. It felt like there was no reason to return after she was gone."

I empathized with him, understanding his emotions all too well. Entering my mother's room was one of the most heart-wrenching experiences after her passing. The haunting presence lingered in the halls, as if I could feel her ghost with me.

Glimpses of her reflection greeted me in the mirror.

No matter my age.

"I'm sorry for bringing you back here."

"Don't be. If anyone was going to make me return to this place, I'm glad it's you."

"You know, I'm here whenever you want to talk about what happened to her. To Amarisa. No pressure, of course."

"I know. And that day will come, Princess. I promise."

We continued in silence, the thickening fog enveloping us as we delved deeper into the woods. The usual sounds of birds chirping, and animals rustling were absent, replaced by a profound quietness.

Just when it seemed the fog couldn't get any thicker, it began to dissipate.

As my eyes adjusted to the emerging landscape, I spotted the faint outline of a quaint cabin. With each step forward, more details emerged—the weathered wooden walls, the thatched roof showing signs of age and wear.

Pulling Reaper to a halt, Ryder's eyes locked onto the cabin. "Well, this is it. Home sweet temporary home, Princess."

Chapter 27

My nose crinkled at the cabin before us.

Not that I was expecting much from a cabin in the woods surrounded by a magic fog that could or could not eat people... but this was *something*.

Watching Ryder, a range of emotions crossed his face like ripples on water. He dismounted from Reaper and approached the wooden structure with cautious steps. The imposing huntsman I had grown to know transformed into a small boy, reminiscent of one eagerly seeking approval to enter his summer home.

A smile spread across my lips as I watched him move. He turned back to me, his expression illuminated despite the approaching sunset.

Suppressing my emotions, I delicately lifted the sleeping Iris from my lap. "We're here. You can go explore now," I whispered.

Her yellow eyes slowly opened, still heavy from the deep sleep she had been in. As she took in the surroundings, a soft hum escaped her lips, and she hesitantly buzzed above my hands. Fixing her gaze on the cabin, she zipped through the air and pushed the crooked door wide open. Her blue light vanished into the darkness inside, the curious melody fading with it.

"No, no. It's fine. It's not like *I* wanted to be the first to re-enter my own home..." Ryder remarked dryly.

Hearing her distant humming eased my unease about the cabin. I hopped down from Jupiter and walked over to Ryder. His eyes were still set on the cabin's exterior, his chest rising and falling slowly with anticipation.

"If you don't want to stay here for the night," I started, "we can camp outside. We don't have to push anything if you're not ready."

His shoulders relaxed. "No, I want to. I'm ready."

Walking confidently toward the cabin's weathered stoop, Ryder effortlessly assumed the guise of the huntsman. The two small wooden steps leading to the front porch seemed fragile, as if they might crack under the slightest pressure. Surprisingly, they held firm under his weight without a creak.

Feeling reassured, I followed closely behind.

Slowly, his tanned hands pushed the door open, and we entered the cabin. An eerie stillness, like in a tomb, greeted us. Dust particles floated in the dim light seeping through the cracks in the walls.

The air inside was thick with neglect, and a quick look showed a scene of abandonment. Furniture was overturned, and torn portraits hung crooked on the walls. It was unclear whether Ryder's family left it this way after his sister passed or if smugglers had ransacked it, and I was smart enough not to ask.

As he looked at our surroundings, his posture tensed. Boots echoed as he walked deeper into the room, large hands brushing over the dust-covered table in the center. I tried not to stare, but his uneasy demeanor was hard to ignore, leaving me feeling uneasy too.

The cabin resembled a crypt—sealed off from the world and frozen in time to preserve the memories of what once was.

My chest tightened as he lifted a small framed portrait lying face down on the table. I wasn't sure how I had ended up standing beside him, but suddenly, there I was, gazing over his broad shoulders at the tiny painting.

Despite the weathered frame, the miniature portrait was instantly recognizable. It showed a younger Ryder and Amarisa in what I assumed was traditional Wayan attire. Time had worn the image in the dusty cabin, but it couldn't erase the moment it captured.

The siblings stood side by side, their relation evident in matching almond-shaped eyes, tanned skin, and jet-black hair. Ryder's face was unmarked by scars, revealing a glimpse into his past before he became a huntsman. Both of his eyes were golden, the sapphire hue of his right eye absent in the painting.

Interesting choice of the painter.

Though no older than ten, their formal and serious pose couldn't hide the mischievous glint in their eyes, hinting at their youthful innocence. It was as if the formality of the portrait failed to conceal that they were a pair of playful kids eager to head out to play.

Amarisa was beautiful, just like her brother. Her resemblance to Ryder was striking. She stood a bit taller than him, her thick, relaxed brows framing her calm, sky-colored eyes. Looking at her portrait evoked the same warm feeling I experienced when gazing at Ryder—like I had found a sense of home.

There was a strange ache in my heart that I didn't understand. I had never met her and wouldn't be aware of her existence without my time with her brother. Nevertheless, here I stood, grieving her death and wishing I could experience her.

Sadness washed over me as I realized I would never get to know her like he did. But more than anything, I felt sadness for Ryder. His thumb traced over the weathered frame, his sudden stillness almost surprising me.

I placed a gentle hand on his arm. "You okay?"

"It's weird seeing her again," he mused after a pause. "It's like...like I *know* she's gone and has been gone for longer than I can count now. But the sting... It's still there." He took a deep breath, chest expanding. "If I close my eyes tight enough, I can still see her running down the hallway, like it was yesterday, hair wild, feet bare."

I smiled at the image, as if I could see it happening too. Regardless of the events of the previous night, my arms instinctively wrapped around him, and I rested my cheek against his sturdy back.

"I'm sorry," I said so quietly into his shoulder that I was unsure he heard it.

At first, Ryder hesitated, his muscles tense. But slowly, he relaxed into the embrace like he realized he was safe with me. It was as if the weight of his past lifted, if only for a moment.

Eventually, we parted, and he cleared his throat. When he turned to face me, faint tear streaks marked his cheeks, trailing off at the edge of his beard.

"Would you like a tour?"

"I thought you'd never ask."

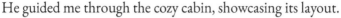

He guided me through the cozy cabin, showcasing its layout.

The cabin had just two bedrooms; a spacious one for his parents and a smaller one where he and his sister once shared space. The thought of Ryder squeezing onto a twin-sized bed meant for a child made me smile, as if he had *always* been as big as he was now.

Continuing our tour, it became evident the kitchen was the heart of the cabin. The snug dining table, crafted from beautiful mahogany, bore the marks and stains of countless family meals. Etchings adorned its surface, a charming mix of childish doodles and names both familiar and new. Despite its wear, the table exuded character, evoking a sense of the shared moments it had silently witnessed.

The door frame between the kitchen and living room displayed marks showing Ryder and Amarisa's growth. Ryder, naturally tall, quickly surpassed his sister in height, a fact he proudly shared.

Listening to him talk about her reminded me of Fiona. Even though she wasn't my blood, she was my sister. I'd lost count of how many times I prayed for her safety while I was away. I would have done anything just to know she was okay, to hear her voice reassuring me of it.

Leading me back into the living room, I looked at the door-frame, and my stomach dropped. Large, thick scratch marks blemished the smooth wood of the door and frame surrounding it. The shape and pattern of the markings immediately made me uneasy. Even if they weren't related, the resemblance between the marks and those on Ryder's face was striking—damn near identical.

Approaching the wood, I traced my eyes over them. "What caused these?"

When I looked back, Ryder's gaze followed mine, and a shadow crossed his face. "A mistake, one I'm not looking to relive right now."

Frowning, I returned to the marks. "Is...is whatever happened how you got the scars on your face?"

I regretted asking it as soon as the words left my mouth. That was the first time I had acknowledged his scars, and I could tell it hurt him.

I slowly turned to face Ryder, and his expression hardened into stone. "Sometimes, it's better to learn when you should mind your own business and stop asking so many damn questions."

Brushing past me, he walked out the door and straight toward the horses. I remained frozen in the doorway, knowing I had crossed a boundary and wanting to fix it as soon as possible. The tension inside the cabin hung heavy as I stepped outside to follow him.

Ryder unloaded our supplies from the horses, securing them carefully to a nearby tree. Iris perched on my shoulder, her presence comforting as I watched his every move. Once finished, he returned to the cabin's front steps—his expression unreadable.

He tossed a pack to me, and I caught it before it fell on the ground.

"I'll take my old room," he finally said, breaking the silence.

"You can have my parents' room. It has more space, and the bed is still decent."

I didn't want to seem ungrateful, but the thought of sleeping on a bed covered in who-knew-how-much dust did *not* excite me. He wandered over to a small closet I must have missed during our tour, swung it open, and suddenly the sweet scent of fresh laundry filled the air.

My eyebrows shot up, feeling a jolt of magic surge through me. When he turned back to me, he was holding a handful of blankets and a pillow.

"My ma once traded our fresh produce during a harsh winter for an enchantment that guaranteed clean laundry," he said, scoffing. "She thought it was more important for her kids to have clean clothes and bedding than to worry about food. Good thing we knew how to hunt, huh?"

Not knowing what to say, I simply took the clean sheets with a small, grateful smile. Iris whizzed past us and entered his parents' room.

Guess we're roomies again tonight.

Ryder quietly excused himself and headed to his old bedroom. Stopping in the doorway, his gaze finally connected with mine. "You, um—feel free to lock your door tonight," he awkwardly suggested. "You know, so last night doesn't happen again."

A twinge of disappointment settled in my chest, but I accepted the situation for what it was. I hurried to my room and closed the door to prevent my embarrassment from showing.

Not a single "goodnight" passed between us.

And it stung.

I locked the door as instructed and took in the room's simple setup. The bed was reasonably sized, and a dusty dresser sitting on top of some worn-out rugs made up most of the room. My reflection looked back at me in a cobweb-covered mirror, and I suppressed a shudder.

Fuck spiders.

Although the room looked worn, it had a certain charm, as if it held memories of days long past. Patting the mattress stirred up a small cloud of dust, making me fight back a sneeze. Iris had fallen victim to the dusty assault, and her tiny form jerked and zoomed as she sneezed—the sound resembling a child pounding on a piano.

Containing a laugh, I quickly unfolded the clean sheets and made the bed. Feeling secure behind the *annoyingly* locked door, I undressed fully for the first time since leaving the palace.

The cool, crisp sheets felt like magic against my skin. Relaxing, I stretched out my limbs, reveling in the freedom of a larger bed. Iris settled beside me on my pillow, her melodic hums filling my ears.

Staring up at the ceiling, I immersed myself in the song Iris crafted just for me. "I wish I could understand you," I mumbled into the pillow.

She responded with a joyful hum, and a part of me imagined her saying, "*Me too.*" As I listened closely, my eyes grew heavy, and I eventually drifted off to sleep.

Two very loud bangs on my door rudely woke me from a dream I wasn't ready to end.

Groaning, I realized the sun had barely risen, and the sky

was still basically dark. Burying my head under the covers, I groaned again in hopes of blocking out the intrusive noise.

It didn't work.

The relentless pounding continued, each thud growing more intense. "Rise and shine, Princess!" Ryder's voice thundered from behind the door. "Time to get that royal ass up and train!"

Frustration washed over me as I debated whether to ignore him and go back to sleep. But his relentless knocking and persistent annoyance persuaded me otherwise. Reluctantly, I dragged myself out of the warm bed, wondering just how early it really was outside. Pulling on my pants, I struggled to keep my eyes open.

"Haven't you ever heard of sleep?" I hollered back.

I heard a muffled chuckle. "Sleep is for the weak, Princess."

Searching for my shirt, I suppressed an eye roll. "I thought we talked about you *not* calling me that."

"Would you prefer *'Your Grace'*? Or how about *'My Lady'*? Oh! Or my favorite, *'Royal Pain in My Ass'*?"

Oh, he was going to pay for those comments during training.

Finishing my dressing, I looked in the mirror. My eyes fell on the faint bruises on my neck, the yellow marks nearly gone. Gazing at the woman in the reflection, I again encountered a stranger.

She wasn't the refined doll prepared for marriage anymore; she looked stronger. *Wilder.*

A smile curved her lips, and she quickly pulled her hair back into a messy braid. Snatching my boots, I struggled to throw them on while unlocking the door. Opening it, I kneeled to tie the laces.

"About time," Ryder quipped. "I thought I'd have to beat down the door."

"Wouldn't have been the first time you busted into my room," I muttered as I moved to my next boot.

"Ouch, Princess. You *wound* me! Seems like someone woke up on the wrong side of the bed."

I snorted. "And it seems like someone woke up full of energy. How long have you been…"

My words trailed off as I finally finished tying my boots and rose to meet his gaze. Expecting to see my huntsman, I was face-to-face with someone unknown.

Ryder stood in my doorway, his face completely devoid of the thick beard that had become his trademark. His features were sharp and defined, revealing a jawline that could cut glass. His long, black hair was tied back in a low bun, framing his face in a way I had never seen before.

Even with the beard gone, which usually drew others' attention *away* from the scars on his face, I barely noticed them anymore.

For the first time, I saw him fully exposed, stripped of his rugged exterior. The man I'd come to know was actually just a boy thrust into a career far too soon.

"You…you shaved your beard?"

He ran his hand over the base of his jaw. "Oh yeah. I found my pa's old razor in the bathing chamber and decided it was time for a change. Do…do you not like it?"

Like it? I fucking love it!

Ryder was handsome with a thick beard, but his clean-shaven face left me speechless. It was like seeing him for the first time all over again, and my attraction to him only intensified.

"No, I-I do!" I finally managed to say, a faint blush creeping onto my cheeks. "You just look...different, but in a good way. Handsome!"

Oh my gods! Why did I call him handsome to his face?

A smile tugged at the corners of his lips. "Handsome? Damn, you did sleep well."

With one last glance at me admiring his new look, Ryder spun on his heels and strode down the hall. I followed, trying to rein in my hormones before the day became too overwhelming. Entering the kitchen, my eyes lit up at the sight of a steaming mug of coffee waiting for me.

Instantly, my spirits lifted.

"Shaved *and* made coffee? What else have you gotten into this morning?"

I raised the cup to my lips, the first sip like heaven—the dark liquid warming my chest as I melted into it.

"Just clean the back of the house," he casually stated. "Thought it would be a good space for our training session. You didn't forget, did you?"

"How could I? I just didn't realize you planned to train me before the sun was even up."

As he stretched his arms over his head, my eyes drifted to the small patch of hair poking out from the bottom of his shirt.

"Early bird gets the worm, Princess. What time would you train with your knight?"

"Uh, around this time..."

"That's what I thought. Now, coffee first, or do you want to dive straight into training?"

I chuckled, taking a grateful sip. "Let's not skip the coffee; I need a bit more energy before you put me through my paces."

"As you wish, my lady." He poured himself a mug. "But don't take too long. I'll be out back when you're ready."

My eyes followed him as he made his way out the door from the kitchen to the back of the house. Before the door fully shut behind him, I watched as he lazily placed his mug down and removed his brown tunic.

That was enough for me to take one final, large gulp of my coffee and head out.

The property in the back of the house was vast and open—clear of any fallen leaves or branches I might have expected to be there this time of year. I shivered at the cold air as my body met the outside. With the Winter Solstice, the days would only get shorter and colder.

Ryder casually stretched against the back of the cabin, and my eyes scanned his tattooed chest and arms. Seeing them in the rising daylight for the first time was a *sight*.

Some of the knights sported sporadic tattoos—patches of black ink that narrated tales of war, love, and more. However, Ryder's markings were abundant, scattered across his skin in a collection far beyond what I'd ever seen on one man.

Lost in my own thoughts, I didn't realize he was watching me until his smile drew me out of my trance.

"Like what you see, Princess?"

I rolled my eyes and tried to hide the blush on my cheeks. "More curious than anything."

"Shocker."

My attention shifted from the tattoos on his skin as I gave him a pointed look. "Asshole. I'm looking at your tattoos, not you or your muscles," I clarified, clearing my throat and shaking off the distraction of his physique. "You've got, like, two dozen on your arms alone. They must have some stories attached."

His smile faded. "Uh, yeah, they've got a story or two."

"Care to share? Or shall I keep staring?"

Unfazed by my poor attempt at flirting, he took a deep breath. "Long story short, when I first started as a huntsman, I was clueless. Acting purely on instincts, I cared more about getting paid and putting food on the table than anything else. One of my bigger jobs was hunting down a Hag from a notorious coven who had managed to evade the royal guard. Their reputation was brutal, Genevieve."

Moving almost mechanically, he picked up a blade and a rock and began sharpening it against the stone.

"One day, this furious housewife comes to me, ranting about how her husband ran off with the Hag. He claimed love, but my bets were on enchantment. It took me weeks to track her down. Those Witches' magic is no joke, and I had no idea how to handle it. I went in with brute strength instead of brains, and she got the better of me. Ended up cursing me as punishment."

"Cursed you with...tattoos?"

"Yes and no. I figured she'd be quick, you know? Eye for an eye, just end it there. Would've been a relief considering what she had in store. But instead, she muttered some words, and touched my skin. When she pulled away, everything burned." He shuddered, like he still felt her touch. "These tattoos? They're not by choice. After each job, I wake up with a new mark. A *'permanent reminder of the lengths I'd go for a coin,'* as that bitch put it.'"

I flinched, feeling a rush of surprise and sympathy. "So, when you get a new one...do they hurt?"

Ryder nodded; his gaze distant. "Yeah, they do. They hurt just as bad as her touch did that day."

I took a hesitant step forward. "May I?"

He paused, his body growing noticeably still before he

finally gave me a brief nod. Stepping closer, I reached out and gently extended one of his arms to examine it more closely.

The tattoos, much like the majority of Ryder, were beautiful. They were a curse, of course, but at least they added to his beauty.

My fingers traced a few of the markings, feeling his skin prickle under my touch. His chest rose and fell as I studied the tattoos, peeking through some dark body hair. Looking up, his eyes widened slightly as he watched me. A surge of compassion welled up in me, the weight of his past and the choices he'll carry forever etched on his skin.

A curse, indeed.

Withdrawing my hands, I slouched. "I'm so sorry, Ry."

He shrugged, trying to downplay the weight of his burden. Letting the blade and rock fall, he rubbed the spot I had touched.

"It is what it is. Some are worse than others."

"Do you regret ever becoming a huntsman?"

"Regret doesn't change the past. It's about learning and living with the consequences—whether you like them or not."

"Is it worth it? The money, I mean. Is it worth the pain you feel when they start to form? I'm sure if you wanted to stop, you'd have endless options. The Royal Guard could use a man like you."

"Pain is temporary. Being a huntsman is who I've become. I doubt any respectable business owner would hire me, and no wealthy maiden would choose me as a husband." He sighed, glancing at me before turning away. "So, I do what I have to do to survive. Running to the battlefronts isn't surviving. I've faced the reality my body might be covered in marks beyond redemption one day. I made peace with that a long time ago."

My stomach twisted, my eyes watering.

He looked up, noticing the sorrow on my face. "Hey," he said, tucking a strand of hair behind my ear, "you don't need to feel sympathy for me. I did this to myself a long time ago. Nothing you've done could have prevented or caused it. It's all good, Genevieve."

"But I gave you *money*! What mark will you get once we complete this? I'm adding to the problem, not helping."

"You gave me money before you knew any of this," he said plainly. "It's not like you sought me out with the sole intent of marking me. So try to relax, okay?"

Our eyes met, and I searched his gaze for reassurance but found none.

"Besides," he said as a thick brow raised, "it's time you focused on more important things than gawking at me all day."

I scoffed, not ready to move on from such a sensitive topic yet.

"As in?"

With one quick move, Ryder lunged at me, smoothly executing a takedown that caught me completely off guard. As I hit the ground, he smirked down at me, and I swear, I felt like I could just melt into the cold, hard ground right then and there.

"Getting you strong again, *Princess*."

CHAPTER 28

OUR TRAINING WENT on for what felt like *hours*.

Each move Ryder made was more animalistic than the last, and I struggled to keep up. No matter how hard I tried, I couldn't gain the upper hand. He kept taking me down over and over, and my back was aching from hitting the ground so much.

But he wouldn't let me give up.

His determination pushed me to my limits, testing my strength and agility. The sun climbed higher, warming us as we trained. Beads of sweat trickled down my forehead as I tried to anticipate Ryder's every move.

I was *not* doing well.

"Come on, Wiyahna! You've got more in you."

I gritted my teeth, trying to channel all the energy I had left. Every time I stumbled, he helped me up, refusing to let me give in to exhaustion. It was frustrating, challenging, and incredibly tiring, but I couldn't deny the rush of exhilaration I felt every time he pulled me back to my feet.

"You need to stop fixating on what you *think* I'm about to

do," he advised, wiping the sweat from his brow. "Listen to the ground—to the leaves around us. Nature is your biggest asset. Now, try again."

Closing my eyes, I took a deep breath and tried to listen to everything around me. I had no idea what the hell Ryder meant by "listening to my surroundings" other than simply *listening*.

Topher had always taught me to never take my eyes off the prize, so focusing on nature didn't make sense. The way I learned; one mistake could be my end. But Ryder said the opposite—that my surroundings would help me in any situation.

The key was to know what I was looking for—which I *didn't*.

Steadying my breath, I inhaled through my nose and exhaled through my mouth. Gradually, the natural sounds registered—the crunch of the ground under Ryder's movements, the stillness of the wind, the warmth drawing closer.

With newfound confidence, I lunged to the left, only to collide with him immediately. I cursed under my breath, realizing he had moved in the opposite direction I had anticipated. Anxiously opening my eyes, I tried to move before he could grab me.

Not fast enough apparently. My back hit the ground before I had a chance to react. He loomed over me, his large arms crossed over his chest, his face twisted in disappointment.

Frustrated, I slammed my hands on the dirt. "That's it!" I huffed, moving to make my way to my feet. "Gods be damned, I have no clue what the hell I'm doing! I'll never learn this!"

I rose to my wobbling feet, making an executive decision to end this pointless training for the day. As I moved back toward the cabin, Ryder grabbed my hand and stopped me.

"You're letting your stubbornness get in the way," he

remarked. "You can't learn if you give up every time you stumble."

"I think the bruises on my ass would be enough evidence to counteract that statement. We've been going at it for *hours,* and I have made zero progress," I spat, pulling my hand from his hold.

"You're not making progress because you're not *listening.* You're acting on what you've learned from knights who have been trained to fight, not survive. To do this correctly, you need to be able to switch your tactics depending on the situation."

I sighed, torn between pushing on and giving up. "Not to disappoint you, but I've never had to worry about that until now. I want to be stronger; I swear to the gods I do! But maybe this isn't for me. Maybe I'm not cut out for it."

"Your past doesn't matter anymore, Wiyahna," he said in a softer tone, "It's about knowing how to defend yourself properly in a situation like you had with needle-dick the other night."

As angry and frustrated as I was at him, I couldn't help smirk at the "needle dick" comment.

"You keep calling me that. *Wi-yah-na.* What does that even mean?"

He smirked. "It's Wayan for *'Little Warrior'.* In my eyes, you're as much of a warrior as anyone can be. You just have some learning to do."

I don't know why but hearing him call me such an important word in his native language made my heart flutter.

"Don't yield," he insisted, grabbing my hands again. "It's not in your nature—I know it. You have the potential; you just need to trust yourself. Trust nature. Day one is always the hardest."

I looked into his eyes, searching for any sign of doubt. Instead, I found confidence and a belief in my abilities I hadn't fully embraced. It was hard, like, really fucking hard, but I understood his motives.

Sir Doyle's attack didn't just hurt me physically; it shook my confidence. For the first time, I was doubting everything about myself—who I was and what I could do.

Is this what a mid-life crisis at eighteen feels like?

Training with the knights had made me strong, and all the praise from Topher had made me confident, but maybe he praised me too much. Looking back, I rarely needed help after training sessions. Sure, I was sore, but it was nothing compared to what I suspected I'd feel later tonight.

Just making it to my bed without help seemed like a victory to look forward to.

"Listen, Genevieve, the further we go, the more dangerous it gets. I'm not trying to scare you, but I can't promise I'll always be beside you. Before we continue, I need to know you'll be okay, no matter how long it takes for you to get there."

I snorted. "And where exactly do you plan to be if not by my side?"

His expression darkened. "Anything can happen out there, Princess. The Hallows is a beast of its own, and the journey could get rough. We may have to split up, and I need to be sure you can hold your own. I would never forgive myself if something happened to you and I could have stopped it."

Taking a deep breath, I nodded. "I won't yield," I confirmed. "But you also need to be patient with me. I'm a fast learner, but you've been in the elements for years. I'm just realizing how vast the world is. I trained with the knights for about three years, but I only beat Topher for the first-time last week."

"Shit." He let out a small laugh. "I'm going to have to deal with your ass for three years before we move on? I guess I better get comfortable."

Rolling my eyes, I pulled my hands away. "Oh, cry me a river. You know you love being around me."

"Maybe I do after all."

His smirk widened, and I couldn't resist smiling in return. Playfully, I pressed my hand against his chest to push him, but the feeling of his firm physique left me frozen. He caught my hand, holding it gently above his heart, where I felt the steady rhythm beneath my fingers.

When I looked up, his eyes were fixed on me, calm and cautious.

"Alright," he said, clearing his throat, "Break time is over. Again."

We continued like that for the next couple of weeks.

The time spent with Ryder blurred in the best of ways. Slowly, I got the hang of the skills he taught me. It was hard to admit, but he was right—it was crucial to stay aware and in tune with your surroundings during a fight. Once I caught on to what to look for, the signs became crystal clear.

In a way, it was like speaking a new language.

I began to grasp the whispers of the woods, learning to feel shifts in the air and anticipate movements before they happened. It was a dance, a symphony played out between me and nature. This was a skill passed down through generations, and now on to me.

Ryder proved to be a surprisingly patient teacher, guiding me through each step to ensure I understood his expectations. By the first week, I could feel the vibrations of his movements beneath my feet. I managed to dodge his attacks more often, though I still couldn't quite bring him down.

Finding harmony with nature was an indescribable sensation. My life had been confined to stone walls, with only occasional forays outdoors for training or short horse rides. It wasn't until now that I realized how isolated and cold my previous existence had been.

When we weren't training, our routine settled into a comforting rhythm. Mornings were for sparring and learning, aiming to return to the cabin without being completely exhausted. After a refreshing bath and some stretching, we gradually revived the cabin. What started as a simple cleanup effort turned the once ominous crypt into a welcoming sanctuary.

Evenings were our time to gather around the crackling fireplace. I'd whip up dinner, usually small game and bone broth, while Ryder ventured out to gather firewood. Often, I'd find myself peeking from the kitchen window, watching him effortlessly chop wood. Sometimes, our eyes would meet through the glass, sending my heart racing.

The warmth of the fire enveloped the cabin, shielding us from the harsh world outside. In its cozy glow, we shared stories of past adventures, tales of family, and even our deepest fears.

One thing we never really talked about was how his sister had passed. I understood how tough losing a family member could be, so I never pressed him on it. But sometimes, it felt as if her ghost was right there with us around the fire, waiting to be seen.

Those evenings with Ryder became the highlight of my days, and I suspected he felt the same.

Even Iris appeared to adjust to life in the cabin after the forest. But sometimes when she thought no one was looking, I'd catch her gazing out a window, her melody tinged with both sorrow and softness. I often wondered if she missed The Vale and the Blessing, as Ryder had suspected.

Yet, as if she had no sorrow in her heart, her eyes would light up when we were together, finding solace in our company.

Fortunately—or perhaps, *unfortunately*—Ryder's "sleep-walking" episodes had stopped. There were no more nights of him trying to enter my room, no more dark, lustful glances exchanged, nothing even close. That night was the peak of my hope, and it hadn't happened again since.

The relationship we had formed felt right...like we had always been a part of each other's lives.

Despite the absence of neck-kissing, we edged with flirtation from time to time—or, at least, I *think* we did.

It was hard to read him.

Just when I thought we were getting somewhere, things never escalated. Some nights, after he'd retired early, I'd linger by the fire, pouring over one of his mother's old books. Passing his door on the way to my room, I felt a tug to enter, drawn by his warmth from within. Despite my silent wishes for him to take the lead and make a move, he never did.

So, I left it be.

Maybe deep down, we both knew being together would only complicate things further. It was already tough enough without adding feelings into the mix. But pretending I didn't have feelings for him wasn't making things any easier either.

Everything was just so difficult.

The cozy cabin deep in the forbidding forest became our little home, but what would happen when I claimed the throne? Asking Ryder to leave his free life behind wasn't fair. He deserved better. Putting on another mask, I pretended like there was nothing between us. It was easier that way.

Every day, I found myself growing more confident and comfortable alongside him. We worked together seamlessly, and despite the initial challenges, our time together never felt burdensome.

Occasionally, guilt crept in—for my father, my kingdom, the friends I left behind.

This wasn't how I planned it. When I set out on Jupiter that first night, I was sure I'd be back home within a week. Yet, almost a whole month later, I was no closer to uncovering the truth behind Father's death or the secrets of my family.

On the morning of our third week of training, I woke with an unusual feeling. When I stepped outside to our makeshift field, the air crackled with energy. Even Ryder seemed to feel it, raising a dark brow as he watched me. A slight tingle coursed through my fingertips, a sensation I hadn't felt in weeks.

Taking a deep breath, I pushed it aside and scanned our surroundings for any threats, just as I had been taught.

Ryder took a step toward me. "Everything okay?"

I paused, letting the forest guide me. After a moment, I met his gaze and nodded assuredly. "Never better," I declared, a cocky grin spreading across my face.

Returning my smile, Ryder stood firmly and pulled out a small dagger, ready for me. "Let's dance then."

His stance was intimidating, imposing even, but an unusual surge of confidence engulfed me. Though a dagger hung at my hip, I sensed it wouldn't be needed today. Closing my eyes, I took a few deep breaths. The forest whispered around me, heightening my senses to anticipate Ryder's every move.

As I centered myself, he darted swiftly to my left. I stood firm, time seeming to slow as he closed in. A small smile tugged at my lips. Opening my eyes, I swiftly ducked, narrowly avoiding his grasp. I crouched low, my hands meeting the damp ground as I rolled away from his attempt to capture me.

In an instant, I sprang to my feet, poised and ready.

The charged air hummed with every step I took, a pulsating energy that matched my racing heart. A tingling sensation coursed through my fingers, different from the usual sense of danger—it felt almost exhilarating.

I felt *powerful*.

Ryder studied me, his anticipation mirroring mine. Lunging, I aimed low instead of going for the easy kill. He caught me around the waist and effortlessly hoisted me over his shoulders like a sack of potatoes. When I landed a swift punch to his ribs, he cursed and released me. Regaining my footing, I spotted a nearby oak tree.

I dashed as fast as I could, scrambling up its lower branches and momentarily escaping his gaze. Just out of sight, pride rushed through me, and I thought I had finally outsmarted him.

The smile on my face faded as Ryder stretched his neck, closed his eyes, and flared his nostrils. As he took a deep breath, his notorious smirk returned, and his mismatched eyes locked onto mine in the tree.

"Gotcha!"

Scrambling higher up the tree, I aimed for a branch a tad higher than I would have liked. Ryder's advice echoed in my head not to get cornered, that where there was a will there was a way.

He climbed fast behind me, the tree slightly swaying from the weight of Ryder's build. I refused to look down, but I knew he was there. With each step, fear mixed with determination.

I was *not* going to allow him to win today.

Reaching the branch I aimed for, I sighed with relief, eyeing the cabin roof below as my escape route. If I jumped at the right angle, I'd be able to land on the roof without hurting myself. *Hopefully*.

Sliding along the branch with eyes shut tight, I attempted to forget the dizzying height. I sensed Ryder nearing, his warmth closing in. With a quick prayer the branch would hold my weight, I tried to ignore how on fire my fingers actually were.

Move your foot, or he'll snatch you.

Listening to that gut feeling, I peeked down and caught Ryder's eye, sweat beading his furrowed brow. I quickly pulled my foot back, narrowly avoiding his attempt to gain a grip.

"Fuck!" he muttered, catching himself on the tree trunk before he fell face first on the ground.

With a wink, I turned my focus back to where I needed to go. I attempted to follow my pan and jump onto the cabin roof, but gravity wasn't on my side. Slipping on the dew-covered shingles, I slipped and tumbled in a less-than-graceful manner, until I finally slid off the edge.

I hit the cold ground with a hard thud that knocked the wind out of me for a moment. Hearing his footsteps approach, I shook off my dizziness and sprang to my feet. I dashed towards the edge of the woods, pausing to unsheathe my dagger.

I'm not going to run. I will not yield.

Now, a few feet away, Ryder relaxed when he saw I was unharmed by the fall. His eyes flicked to my dagger, and he mirrored my action, drawing his own weapon.

I took the stance he taught me as we circled each other. We locked eyes, the air crackled with anticipation, his grin matching my determined expression. The forest held its breath, waiting to see what would unfold.

In an instant, our blades danced, catching the sunlight as we moved. Ryder lunged, and I sidestepped, deftly avoiding his strike. The forest seemed to whisper its secrets, guiding my every move. I spun gracefully, my blade cutting through the air. Ryder parried skillfully, but my feigned retreat lured him into a trap. With a swift turn, I closed the gap, my blade moving fluidly. He anticipated my strike but didn't foresee the redirection. His eyes widened as my blade disarmed him, sending his weapon flying.

Seizing the opening, I pressed the tip of my dagger against his chest. Time seemed to stand still as our eyes locked, the forest's quiet approval surrounding us. Ryder looked stunned, his eyes wide with a mix of surprise and admiration. I reached out my hand, but instead of a handshake to signal the end of our duel, I twisted his hand swiftly, catching him off guard and throwing him off balance.

With a graceful pivot, I swept my leg in a low arc, sending him sprawling to the forest floor. In no time, I had him pinned, his wrists held above his head—just as he had all those weeks ago.

Sitting triumphantly on his chest, I grinned. "I'm sorry, but I want to *hear* it before I let you up."

He laughed in disbelief. "You can fuck off."

My smile widened, not allowing him to budge. "No, no, no. I think I *deserve* it."

Rolling his eyes, he couldn't contain his smile, his canines gleaming in the sunlight. "Fine. I yield...*Princess*."

Feeling satisfied, I climbed off him and offered a hand. He took it and brushed the dirt off his pants. Iris fluttered over to us, her chirping full of excitement. "Yeah, yeah, I know," he said annoyingly, "I have the bruise on my ass to prove it."

"What did she say?"

"She *ever so lovingly* reminded me I just lost to the Princess of Orphinian. She's very amused with it."

"Well, us ladies must stick together. She knows talent when she sees it."

"Slow your horses," he laughed, "You did well, Wiyahna. But you still have a lot to learn to be considered what you just did *'talent.'*"

I crossed my arms over my chest. "Wasn't the deal that if you trained me well enough that I beat you, we would head to The Hallows? I think what I just did would be beating you. Don't back out on me now."

"I never said that still wasn't the plan. I just said you're not worthy of being called *'talented'* yet."

"Screw you," I scoffed. "I think someone is just bitter an itty-bitty princess was able to disarm you and knock you on your ass."

He moved closer, eyes narrowed and intense. I couldn't help but look away; his stare felt like almost too much, especially after how close we'd just been.

As he reached out to tuck a strand of white hair behind my ear, his fingers brushed gently under my chin. "This *'itty-bitty princess'* is one hell of a fighter," he chuckled, his thumb brushing over my bottom lip. The moment his skin touched mine, I knew I had lost the argument. "But she will never be done learning. And that's not a bad thing. Got it?"

His point made sense, but I wasn't ready to give up the taste of victory just yet. I'd been craving it for weeks. When he released my chin, his touch lingered, leaving me wanting more.

"Yeah," I said softly. "I got it."

"Good," he said, turning to head back to the house.

Following him into the kitchen, I sat in one of the chairs at the dining table I had grown so fond of. My fingers traced the carvings in the wood, smiling at the messy "RH" I sat in front of.

Ryder poured me a heaping glass of water he had retrieved from a nearby well, and I gladly took it. Gulping it down, I admired him as he ran his fingers through his messy hair. "Question," I said, putting my glass down.

"Gods, save me. Yes?"

I ignored how badly I wanted to flip him off and stretched my neck. "Is there a village within riding distance?"

He turned slowly toward me, curiosity flickering in his eyes. "There might be. It depends on why *you* want to go."

I toyed with my still-burning fingers. "Well I've been thinking. Since we'll most likely be on the road again here soon...I thought I could make us a nice, home-cooked meal. I know we've only been eating venison and rabbit for the past two weeks, but I could use a vegetable or some carbs in my life. It could be my way of saying *'Thank you'* for everything you've done for me. Fiona's mother always said nothing brings people closer together than breaking bread. What do you think?"

He gave me a long look, and I felt myself blush. I nervously bit my lip, trying not to draw blood. Ryder casually pulled out a chair and sat down beside me at the table.

His big hands covered mine, expression softening. "Genevieve, I'd *love* a home-cooked meal."

My face lit up, and I couldn't help but squeeze his hands. "Really?" I exclaimed, feeling a rush of energy.

Cursing under his breath, Ryder pulled his hands away from mine, his eyes wide. "What the hell was that?"

I glanced at him and then down at my hands. "What was what?"

He rubbed his fingers together, testing their sensation. "It was like touching a hot pan—quick, but I definitely felt it. You didn't feel anything?"

I sucked in a breath, fully aware of what he meant. In my head, I wrestled with the decision to confide in him. We'd grown closer in recent weeks, but his joking accusation I might be a Witch made me hesitate.

Would this solidify it in his mind?

I trusted him, but I wasn't sure if I was ready to have *that* conversation again.

"You *did* feel it," he confirmed by looking at me.

Taking a deep breath, I exhaled slowly. "If you mean the burning, yeah, I did. I've felt it off and on for a few weeks. I thought maybe it was just the nerves from the wedding, but then it continued. Normally, it comes and goes, but today, it's *unbearable*." I shifted my weight to sit on my hands, attempting to cease the sensation. "I'm sorry if I hurt you. I-I just don't know what's wrong with me."

"Interesting," he murmured mostly to himself.

He scratched his jaw, rubbing the stubble that had grown

back since we got here. I could tell he was thinking, his eyes moving quickly as he furrowed his brow.

"This only started before the Fae arrived?"

I nodded. "Do you know what it means?"

He hesitated, his mind still working until he finally shrugged. "Could have been your time around the Fae. They are...powerful. But I doubt it would have continued this long away from them. That burning felt...familiar."

I snorted, shoulders slouching and annoyance rising. "Something tells me that's not your final conclusion."

"You think so little of me, don't you?"

"I just think you know more than you're telling me, like that I'm a Witch or something."

Rolling his eyes, he sipped his water. "Sweetheart, I wouldn't know you were a Witch before you did. I'm not *that* good. Just let me think it over for a little, okay?"

"No."

He laughed, the sound slowly causing my annoyance to fade. "Too bad. Now, pick your lip up off the floor and bathe. We can head out to Eudora whenever you're ready."

I huffed, sinking lower in my chair. "Is Eudora the village name, or are we running into another *'old friend'* like Vixin?"

"How do you not know the names of the villages in your own kingdom? Yes, it's the name of the village, you jealous little thing."

Extending my right hand, I offered him a very deliberate, very *prominent* middle finger.

His admiration only seemed to intensify. Catching my hand mid-air, he turned it and brought it close to his lips, gently kissing my knuckles. Warmth flooded through me, and my stomach filled with butterflies.

He's in a flirty mood today.

Dropping my hand, he went to exit the room before stopping to turn and face me, "You got your dagger on you?"

I patted my hip, trying to ignore the warmth building between my legs. "Hardly leaves my side."

A lazy smile formed on his lips. "Good. Carve your name on the table."

"Pardon?"

"Carve. Your. Name. On the table," he said as he lightly tapped his pointer finger on the wood, emphasizing each word. "Old family tradition. Feels right to have you add your name. Feels like...like it's what they would have wanted. Ma would have liked you. Probably too much."

Laughing to himself, he stepped out again, his scent hanging in the air like a melody. I looked down at the table as warmth flooded me. Carving my name into his family's table felt like a uniquely special moment, almost exclusive. I wasn't sure how to handle it, to be honest.

"Ma would have liked you. Probably too much."

Yeah, my mother would have liked you too.

Not trying to think too much into it, I grabbed the dagger and tucked a few stray hairs behind my ears. With a grin, I carved into the wood.

After finishing, I pushed my chair back and stood, leaving my initials, "GR", next to Ryder's "RH" on the table.

CHAPTER 29

MAKING it out of the forest was way easier than entering.

Ryder had asked Iris to sit this one out and stay behind at the cabin while we went into town. To no one's surprise, she was far from pleased with that suggestion. Her sharp, deep melody seemed to follow us until we passed the thickest section of the fog.

Luckily, Eudora was just an hour's ride away. Ryder couldn't sit still, bouncing with excitement as we neared the village, a place his family frequented in summers. It was amusing to see him so enthusiastic, but I wasn't quite ready to leave our cozy makeshift home, even though it had been *my* idea all along.

The thought of tying up my hair added to my reluctance; it made me feel concealed again, a sensation that was not missed.

Once we were in the middle of the village, maneuvering through the bustling streets frustrated me. The further we went, the more I had to pull down the hood of my cloak, and I *hated* it.

"If you pull that thing any tighter, you'll decapitate yourself," Ryder scolded.

I scoffed. "Sounds like a good way to go to me."

"Stop it," he snapped, nudging my shoulders. "You're being a drama queen, and I would miss that pretty face of yours too much."

"Not a queen *yet*," I corrected quietly. "And I hate hiding my hair. I'm regretting even asking to come here. I want to go back to the cabin and eat broth."

Chuckling, he skillfully navigated through the bustling crowds. "You're a terrible liar and just as fed up with that shit as I am. We'll make it quick, and then you can free those curls."

I let out an irritated huff, annoying even myself. It had been my idea to leave the cabin, but my mood had drastically declined since then. Thoughts raced through my mind, especially about what Ryder might know regarding the burning sensation in my fingers or the chance of me being a Witch.

Anger surged every time I dwelled on his refusal to tell me. At this point, I just wanted to grab the food and leave. I needed to shake off whatever mood had come over me. Ryder deserved at least that much.

The villagers radiated a welcoming kindness that eased my nerves.

Women would offer gentle smiles my way before redirecting their attention to Ryder, who, unlike in other places, was greeted with admiration. They practically swooned as he walked by, but he paid them no mind. Men acknowledged me with nods, their gaze not lingering for too long. This was thanks to my tall, dark, and handsome bodyguard, who would growl lowly in anyone's direction who looked too long.

I couldn't shake the feeling of eyes on me, following me as

we made our way through the village streets. Shaking it off as just my anxiety from the last time I was in a village, I decided not to make a big deal of it.

He suddenly stopped in the street, and I heard Ryder curse under his breath. "I think the produce and the meat vendors are on opposite sides of the village. Just so you don't chop your head off before dinner, would you rather us divide and conquer? I trust these people way more than those lowlifes in Sambor."

The idea of being apart from him made my stomach lurch, especially with the feeling of being watched. But it also gave me the opportunity to sneak off and find something special for him —a way better thank-you than a dinner I'd probably just burn.

"I'll be okay. I won't go into any random person's shops, and if I start to feel anything more intense, I'll find you."

His eyes held a mix of worry and hesitation—knowing the last thing he wanted to do was leave me alone. But he was right: splitting up and getting what we needed as quickly as possible would be easier.

"If we're not back here in twenty, find each other?"

"Make it fifteen, and you got a deal." He gave me a short nod and reached into his pocket, placing a few gold coins in my hand. "Your debt just keeps increasing, doesn't it?"

"Just enough to keep you around."

He closed my hand, ensuring the coins were secure in my palm. His touch lingered as our fingers brushed, igniting a spark within me.

"Well, in that case, I might have to start charging interest."

With a not-so-subtle wink, he walked away, leaving me flustered.

Stupid Huntsman.

We took off in opposite directions, a slight sense of relief washing over me as I realized just how small the village of Eudora truly was. Following signs to the produce stand, I maintained a straight spine, my head slightly lowered, as I power-walked through the streets.

Though I had a general idea of what to cook, my culinary repertoire was limited to the few dishes I had observed Fiona's mother prepare when I was younger.

Finding a stand with everything I needed, I finished shopping sooner than anticipated. The merchant was friendly but not overly chatty, a preference I appreciated. After paying the correct number of coins, he provided me with a small basket to hold everything, and I went on my way.

Taking a break from the busy street, I checked the coins left in my hand. Excitement spread through me; I had just enough to buy him something meaningful, something he'd really appreciate and find useful.

"The key to every man's heart," as the saying goes.

A bottle of whiskey.

Putting away the coins, I glanced around at the shops and stands nearby, hoping to spot anything selling alcohol. Finding nothing, I went back to the friendly merchant.

"Excuse me, is there an alehouse nearby? Or somewhere to buy alcohol?"

The older man's blue eyes met mine, and a playful smile formed. "A little early in the day to buy some hooch, eh?"

"Not for me." I smiled. "It's a gift for someone else."

Nodding, he began to respond, but a voice from behind me interjected. "What luck you must have," it cooed.

I felt the eyes from earlier on me stronger than ever. Making a conscious effort to ensure my hood didn't slip, I glanced over my shoulder to meet the voice's owner.

The tall, middle-aged man looked at me with a determined stare. His well-kept, white hair was neatly groomed over to one side. The attire he wore was modest, yet how he held himself evoked an air of wealth and standing. The dense beard that adorned his sharp chin highlighted his cat-like grin.

And his eyes... They were so brown they were almost black.

Lost in my observation, I hardly registered what he had said. "I beg your pardon?"

"I mentioned you're quite fortunate, young lady. You see, I happen to own an alehouse just around the corner." He nodded toward the merchant. "I couldn't help but overhear you were looking for some alcohol?"

"That's where I was gonna point you to, sweetie," the merchant confirmed, his eyes almost slightly bluer than before. "He'll help ya out!"

I relaxed, "Yes, of course, I apologize. You just surprised me."

"Surprises are as river bends, unsure of where it starts or where it ends."

Fantastic—another poet.

Attempting to mask a nasty reaction, I gave him a fake and uncomfortable laugh. "Right. Well, I would love to purchase some whiskey."

His feline smile only grew. "As you wish, my lady. Follow me."

Turning on his heels, he took lengthy strides in the opposite direction of my designated meeting point with Ryder. At least if he didn't have anything I wanted, I wasn't venturing too far.

The burning sensation in my fingers persisted, but everything else seemed normal.

Or, at least, I hoped it was.

CHAPTER 30

THE MAN WASN'T LYING about his alehouse being just around the corner.

Holding the door open, I stepped into the familiar atmosphere of the establishment. The comforting scents and cozy ambiance reminded me of the Rose and Crown. Inside, a few male patrons occupied the small tables, enjoying their drinks while acknowledging the owner with nods of greeting.

I didn't dare look at any of the men too long and my hood felt tighter the further we walked.

"May I take your cloak?" the owner inquired, his bony hand extended as he closed the door behind us.

"No, thank you," I replied with firm politeness. "I don't plan on staying too long."

He gave me a quick once-over before offering a thin smile and headed towards the bar. I followed behind cautiously, aware of the lingering gazes from the other patrons, prompting me to keep my head down.

"Not from around here, are you?" the owner called ahead of me.

"No, sir. I'm just passing through."

A low laugh rumbled ahead. "Please, don't call me 'sir.' You're making me sound older than I feel."

"I apologize. I was always taught to address others as—"

Words caught in my throat as my hand was suddenly seized by another, much larger, stronger hand. My eyes grew as my heart began to race as fast as a herd of wild stallions.

The feel of the palm, the *callouses* that covered almost every inch—I *knew* that hand. Even if I had gone blind, I would recognize it anywhere. No matter how long it had been since I last felt it.

Summoning every bit of courage I had, I turned my head over my shoulder. Through my teary eyes, I saw exactly who I expected to see. With a gulp, I locked eyes with two piercing blue ones that looked just as stunned as I felt. Time seemed to freeze as I tried to make sense of it all. I couldn't even tell if I was breathing. I felt my chest rise and fall, but nothing else seemed to register.

Topher sat at one of the tables, his usually sun-kissed skin unnaturally pale, like he'd seen a ghost. He was out of his knight's uniform, his clothes ragged and stained with patches of dirt. A thick, shaggy beard added to his disheveled appearance, and his blue eyes carried a weariness I'd never seen, dark circles stark beneath them.

He started to speak then thought better of it, shutting his mouth with a snap. When he tried again, I shook my head slowly, silently begging him to stay quiet and let me leave. I withdrew my hand from his, swallowed my emotions, and turned back to the bar.

The owner stood watching and waiting. "Friend of yours?" He nodded toward Topher.

"Misunderstanding," I replied, forcing a smile. "I think he mistook me for someone else."

"Hmm," his lips thinned. "It appears I am all out of unopened bottles behind the bar, so I'll have to go into storage and grab one. Care to join me so you can pick the one you prefer?"

I had promised Ryder I would not do this.

"Where would we need to go?"

"Just behind the building. The storage is simply out back. In and out in a heartbeat."

I was fiddling with the basket of food, the feel of Topher's hand still lingering on mine. When I glanced back, his wide eyes were fixed on me, watching my every move. Feeling a sudden urge to break away from his familiar gaze, I quickly turned back toward the owner.

"Only if we make it quick."

"As you wish."

He pushed open the door behind the bar and stepped into the alley. There, a small shed-like structure awaited us. I hesitantly followed him through the door, avoiding another glance back at Topher, though I sensed his eyes on me. Darkness momentarily surrounded us as the door closed behind us. The owner quickly lit an oil lamp, casting a dim light around the cramped space. As my eyes adjusted, I saw shelves upon shelves of alcohol lining the small walls.

The owner took a step back. "Pick your poison, love."

Navigating the dimly lit walls, I scanned the rows of whiskey bottles, each unique in design. My fingers traced across the glass as I read the labels, aware of his dark eyes on me.

"Any recommendations?"

The air in the shed felt heavy and thick, urging me to get

out of there. If he could just pick a bottle for me, I'd save time and dodge Ryder's inevitable lecture about taking too long. I heard a creak from behind as the owner came closer. Turning, we practically bumped into each other—his long arm reaching across my shoulder to grab a bottle.

I tensed at the touch, resisting the urge to push him away. His scent was strong. Not bad, but oddly familiar in a way I couldn't quite place.

Stepping away, he handed me a thick brown bottle. "This was my father's favorite." I inspected it, the bottle's writing in a strange language. "Last bottle from across the border. Fae specialty when you can get it."

I nodded and suppressed an eye roll before putting the bottle back on the shelf. I had enough experience with "Fae specialties," thank you very much.

I felt a surge of anxiety as I realized how cramped the space was. My eyes darted around, noticing that the only way out was blocked by the stranger's tall frame. Thinking fast, I grabbed another bottle, pretending to study its label while I figured out my escape route.

"Are you buying this bottle for yourself or someone special? I doubt a young lady such as yourself is traveling and drinking alone."

"You know what they say," I placed the bottle down and picked up another, "two is better than one."

"Ah," his gaze was penetrating, "so you *are* traveling with someone. Where's your final destination? Or perhaps you plan on staying here a little longer."

My stomach twisted with unease. I kept my eyes on the door as I placed the bottle into my basket. "Just passing through, sir."

He chuckled, a sound that sent shivers down my spine. "Passing through, yet you have a full basket of produce and now a whiskey bottle in your possession. If I didn't know any better, I would think you're doing more than passing through."

"I beg your pardon, but I don't believe it's any of your business."

His gaze intensified. "No need to be impolite; I'm just trying to make small talk. Besides, you are the one seeking my assistance. Could be fate, no?"

I scoffed. "I don't believe in fate."

I went to sidestep him, but he matched my movement, grin widening with a sort of cruel satisfaction. "You should believe, though. Fate has a way of catching up with you."

The more he spoke, the more déjà vu settled in, as if his words were a haunting melody I had once tried to forget. My fingers burned, and I could no longer ignore the feeling of dread.

"Thank you, sir, for the bottle, but I must be going now." I reached into my pocket and pulled out the remaining coins. "This should be enough?"

"Leaving so soon? Here I thought we were getting along so well."

"I will say this again, and then I cannot promise you I will be polite: I'm leaving *with* or *without* the bottle. I have someone waiting for me, and I'm sure he's wondering where I am."

The feline smile widened. "Ah, yes, your *companion*. The one you're buying the bottle for."

"Correct."

"But not that fellow who stopped you before, correct?"

I remained silent, lips pursed.

"Right. You said he mistook you for someone else. Silly me,

my old mind forgets things now and then. But now I am curious. The recipient of the bottle...is he *more* than just a companion?"

I feared if I had still been holding the bottle, it might have shattered in my hands. "Once again, I don't see how that's any of your business."

He shook his head and stepped forward. "No need to snap at me. A young, beautiful woman like yourself should be married by now, and I see no ring on your pretty little finger. Besides, you know I don't like to share."

Another wave of unease washed over me, and my heart skipped a beat. Suddenly, everything clicked into place. This man's words, his tone—they felt too familiar. I didn't want to believe it, but I couldn't ignore my instincts any longer.

"I'm sorry," I said, anger rising in my chest, "but I don't believe I caught your name."

He practically loomed over me, his feline smile a twisted smirk. "Seems like you already know it, Genevieve."

My stomach dropped and, despite the height difference, I tried to stare him down. "I'm hoping I'm wrong."

The atmosphere shifted, and suddenly, it felt like all the warmth was sucked out of the room. Shadows started swirling, enveloping him completely from head to toe. The beard he wore vanished to reveal a freshly shaven face. Two pointy ears stretched out as a waterfall of white-blonde hair tracked down his shoulders. In a heartbeat, the signs of an old man were gone, replaced by a dangerously beautiful face.

It wasn't the face of a stranger, but my ex-fiancé.

Xander.

Anger surged, overtaking my initial shock as I glared at the monstrous figure in front of me. Reality hit me like a ton of bricks, and suddenly, the room felt like it was closing in. He had finally found me, and I was *trapped*.

Brimming with darkness and malevolence, those silver eyes bore into me, locking me in their gaze. His laughter filled the air, its sinister vibrations echoing through my soul, and I squared my shoulders.

"Hello, bride," he sneered. "You know, I believe you're rather late for our wedding day."

As he took a step towards me, my senses were overwhelmed with the familiar scent of what I now knew was magic. It was *seeping* from his pores.

Wake up!

But I wasn't asleep this time.

The basket of goods slipped through my trembling hands, causing the whiskey bottle to crash and shatter across the floor.

Looking down at his once-polished loafers, Xander shook his head, tisking at me like I was a child who had made a mistake. "I see life on the run hasn't made you any less clumsy. Those were my favorite shoes."

I knew I needed to run, but his presence was infuriating. My jaw clenched as I shot him a defiant glare, refusing to let him overpower me.

"My apologies," I said through gritted teeth. "I must have become a little distracted by my father's murder and lost track of time of our *arranged* marriage."

"Ah yes," he said almost dismissively. "That was a tragedy, truly. Shame. I rather liked him."

Gods, I was going to destroy his royally smug Fae ass.

"How did you find me? What did you do with the owner?"

Fae magic was ancient and confusing. While I understood

their ability to manipulate elements, the idea of taking on someone else's appearance was completely new to me.

I wondered; did it require a sacrifice? *Blood*? Or could they just conjure the likeness from memory? No one seemed suspicious of the stranger next to me, which suggested he was familiar to the village.

Shaking his head, he continued laughing. "It's such a *human* trait—worrying about someone you've never met. Rest assured. the owner is unharmed. Perhaps a tad distracted, but unharmed. I knew you couldn't stay too far away from a drink."

Okay, ouch.

"And I've told you before, I have my spies, bride."

"What do you want, Xander?" Though my hands slightly shook at my sides, the disgust was evident in my voice.

"What every groom desires," he said, reaching into his front pocket and pulling something out as he knelt. "A bride to fulfill her vows."

Following his movements like a hawk, I nearly stumbled into the shelves of liquor as he revealed an engagement ring between his thin, pale fingers. Not just any ring, but the same one he had given to me a month ago—the one *I* had given to *Fiona* the night I left.

If I wasn't so angry, I might have thrown up. "Where did you get that?"

"Why bride, have you forgotten I was the one who gave it to you?"

"I'll never forget," I spat. "I'll also never forget how I gave that ring to Fiona the night I headbutted you in the face!"

He brought his finger to his chin in fake thought. "Fiona? Hmm, Fiona... Apologies. Name seems rather insignificant.

Now, bride, put your ring on like an obedient fiancée and we shall return."

Frustration bubbled up as I tried to plan my escape, but the door felt unreachable with him blocking it. Anger surged through me; fists clenched at my sides. I wouldn't be a pawn in his twisted games. He would *not* control me!

Not then—and not now.

"I know you live in your own 'Xander Land', but I'm quite literally wanted for murder. Dead or alive, right? At least that's what the posters the *queen* threw up all around Orphinian say. With her new title, I can promise you, she won't welcome me home with open arms for a wedding."

Seeming bored, he picked at his nails. "Your defiance was always a delightful challenge, but our union is inevitable, Genevieve. You can't evade fate forever. Liliana will yield—as do all the women in your bloodline."

The constant talk of fate grated on my nerves, but its eerie effect lingered. His words felt like a haunting melody echoing in my mind. Steeling myself, I gathered every ounce of courage I could muster.

A vibration pulsed against my thigh where my dagger rested, fueling my confidence. The dagger's call was unmistakable, guiding my trembling fingers to its hilt hidden beneath my cloak.

"I'll never be your bride! From now on, I choose my own path—and it doesn't include you."

His eyes locked onto my dagger like a predator homing in on its prey. That sinister grin, which often haunted my nightmares, returned to his face, prompting a grimace of disgust from me.

"Pretty little thing you got there," he commented, his long, pale finger gesturing toward my hip. "Strange, isn't it? How, no matter how hard the past is buried, your kind always clings to the very thing that could destroy them."

"Save me your riddles," I spat. "I was never a fan."

"Not a riddle, bride, but a history lesson if you cared to open your ears and shut your mouth!"

He lunged forward with unnatural speed, but I narrowly dodged him. Trapped in the cramped storage room, I had few options, but surrender wasn't one of them. I stepped back just in time; his Fae reflexes faltered, and his chin struck a shelf behind me, leaving a smear of blood on his tunic from the new open wound.

Silver eyes darkened as he wiped away the blood with the back of his hand. "Why is it that I always seem to bleed in your presence?"

Now it was *my* turn to smirk. "Because pussies bleed!"

With a surge of adrenaline, I dashed for the door, determined to escape before he could drag me back to Castle Quinn or across the border. My fingers reached for the doorknob, but before I could grasp it, an iron grip closed around my ankle, jerking me backward with sudden force. I crashed to the floor, the impact stealing my breath. Xander loomed over me, panic and rage mixing as he moved closer until we were nearly face-to-face.

A burning sensation surged through my fingers, almost unbearable, like plunging them into a raging fire. Glancing down, I found a soft glow emanated from my fingertips, energy crackling beneath my skin as if lightning surged through my veins.

My eyes widened as a ripple of energy tingled down my spine and spread to my fingertips. The air in the room felt heavy and stagnant, making the hairs on my arms stand on end. The glowing intensified until Xander couldn't ignore it any longer.

His silver eyes grew. "Good gods!"

A surge of energy erupted within me, hurling Xander off with a violent force that made me cry out. His stunned body crashed into racks of bottles, the sickening sound of glass shattering filling the room.

Staggering to my feet, I stared at my hands, stunned by whatever just happened. They appeared completely normal—no glow, no burning sensation. Nothing.

The room fell into tense silence, broken only by my ragged breaths and the faint tinkling of shattered glass. Xander groaned, tangled amidst the wreckage, glass shards scattered around him like twisted confetti.

His eyes bore into mine, filled with a mix of anger and disbelief. "Well, well, well," he grumbled as he slowly picked himself up. "Looks like someone finally decided to join the party."

"What...what just happened?"

Xander scoffed and picked a few shards of glass from his palm, "So blind. So sad to watch, knowing you deny what you are. No matter, bride. You're still mine, no matter your power."

I backed up against the door, my hand gripping the handle as I kept my eyes on him. "I have no powers!"

"Such a shame," he remarked, fully on his feet now and cuts already healed. "The room is warded. So, no matter how hard you try, you're trapped. It would be simple for someone with *powers*."

He was provoking me, and I knew it. The silence felt suffocating, but I refused to linger and give him the satisfaction. His smirk fueled my determination and without hesitation, I landed a punch on his nose, followed by a kick to his chest that sent him crashing into shattered bottles. After a brief internal struggle, his eyes finally closed, and his body went limp.

Not wasting a moment, I turned back to the door and reached for the handle again.

"Please open, please open!" I quietly prayed.

A small jolt ran up my fingertips as they touched the metal, and the door swung open. Rushing out of the room, I nearly collided with Topher, who stood in the doorway. I stopped just in time, avoiding a collision that would attract more attention.

Topher grabbed my shoulders, quickly scanning me for injuries. "What the hell happened? Are you alright?"

His genuine concern stirred memories of my childhood, but explanations could wait. "There's no time," I urged, still catching my breath. "We need to leave. Now!"

I pulled the cloak's hood back over my head and grabbed the basket of produce left on the floor. My clothes *reeked* of alcohol and magic. Topher stood frozen, taking in the destruction I had caused.

His eyes widened as he looked past me and saw the Fae Prince knocked out on the floor. "Is that..."

"Yes, and he won't be out for long," I cautioned, grabbing his hand and pulling him away from the room.

Leaving the mess behind, we hurried down the alley and returned to the heart of the village. I guided Topher toward the spot where I was to meet Ryder, my heart racing as our pace slowed from a run to a brisk walk. The cool air brought brief relief, but urgency still coursed through my veins.

I refrained from glancing back at the alehouse as we navigated the bustling streets. Ryder hadn't returned by the time we reached our meeting spot, and I was grateful for a moment to catch my breath.

Topher's eyes remained fixed on me, never once leaving my side since he found me in that room. Gripping my arm, he pulled me to the side of the street. "Are you hurt?"

I gave a thumbs-up. "No, I'm fine. Just slightly out of breath."

He pulled back, the feel of his rough grip still lingering on my arm "Good. Catch your breath because we have a lot to talk about. For starters, what the hell happened back there? Or will you just run off without giving any answers again?"

Well, I guess he was still upset with me.

Placing the basket down next to my feet, my hands found my hips. The tips of my fingers began to tingle again, but nothing compared to what they had been.

"I'll give you answers if you give me some. What the hell are *you* doing here? Have you been tracking me?"

His blue eyes studied me, the familiar ones I had loved all these years, a stranger in their own way. "And if I had been? Would that be the worst thing in the world?"

I scoffed. "Well, if I had thought your coming would be beneficial, I would have *asked* you to join. You're putting yourself in danger for no reason!"

"*You're* reason enough, Genevieve!" he spat at me.

I tensed at the mention of my name in such a public space, but Topher seemed unfazed. The depleting adrenaline left me fidgeting, and I knew the expression on my face was less than friendly.

Topher's chest rose and fell as we stared each other down. After a beat, his eyes softened, seeming to read my reaction finally. "It looks like we both have questions we need answered. I'm sorry—I just needed you to be okay."

"Like I said, I'm fine."

"Can you tell me what happened back there? And *please* don't say you'll explain later."

Taking a deep breath, I steeled myself to answer his questions, feeling the weight of guilt heavy in my chest as I met his gaze.

Those baby blues could win wars, I swear.

As I recounted my tale, his expression remained impassive— no trace of anger flickered across his features. It was hard to keep track of everything that had happened. The events replayed in my mind like a fast-paced play, and I struggled to fully comprehend it all. Even though Fiona would have briefed Topher, there was still much left unsaid.

But now wasn't the time.

"By the look of it in that room, you could have told me a storm had passed through, and I would have believed it," he said, shaking his head. "How would he even know you would be in this village?"

An eyebrow rose. "I would assume the same way *you* knew I would be here. It's your turn for some answers. Care to explain?"

His expression hardened again, and he stood straight. "I didn't," he said bluntly. "The trail I was following dried up about two weeks ago. I had followed it into a forest where I got lost in a fog unlike anything I'd ever seen. It was difficult to know how long I was stuck, but I believe I wandered around for three days. Morning, noon, and night, I would just go in circles and pray I didn't die. When I finally found my way out, I was on the brink of starvation and madness. I found this village and decided to stay until I felt better. Needless to say, it's taking longer than I had anticipated."

That fucking fog.

Ryder's warnings weren't exaggerated. The fog really could mess with your mind and lead you to something worse. Topher had been trailing me the whole time. He knew we entered Forest Sylvie and...he could have died in there, and it would have been because of *me*!

Nausea rose in my throat as I tried to take a deep breath. His calloused hands enveloped mine again, the touch familiar but somehow different—like it had changed meaning.

"I had no clue you would be in that alehouse; I swear it. But gods, Genevieve," he whispered, "I thought I had lost you. I thought I had been drugged or damn near delirious when I heard your voice from behind me. But it was you! I could see it in your eyes, those gorgeous emeralds that I needed to remain silent. So, I did. And it *killed* me."

"You didn't lose me the first time. I just... I needed to prove my innocence. Telling you would have added to the issue. But you never lost me."

"And I won't again," he said, pulling me close.

His intense gaze mirrored the night he kissed me in the stables. My stomach tightened as his eyes lingered on my lips, his head inching closer. I felt paralyzed, unsure how to respond. His grip tightened, and despite a desire to pull away, I remained rooted in place.

Just as he drew nearer, a familiar warmth enveloped me, and a breeze carrying the scent of the forest rushed past my nose.

"*Rose!*" Ryder shouted my fake name in the distance.

Turning toward the sound, he sprinted towards us at full speed, his eyes wide and wild with worry. Closing the distance impressively fast, he practically skidded to a stop upon seeing Topher's hands in mine. Dropping his baskets full of food, he swiftly unsheathed his sword from across his back, pointing it menacingly at Topher.

"Take your hands off her!" he growled.

Removing his grip, Topher shoved me behind him, practically throwing me against the stone wall. As he drew his sword, a rush of horror swept over me, and I instinctively positioned myself between them, shielding Ryder from the tip of the blade.

"Stop!" I said in my most hushed shout. "Swords down before you both get us arrested." Looking over my shoulder at Ryder's furrowed eyes, I gave him a stern look. "We wouldn't want the law involved, now would we?"

After an intense stare-down, Ryder straightened and was the first to sheath his sword, his gaze still fixed on Topher. I turned to the knight, observing Topher's hesitation before he finally stood down.

"Thank you," I said, giving a satisfied nod. "Now, if you two alpha males could relax for one moment, we should probably get the hell out of the village center to have this conversation *away* from my ex-fiance."

Ryder's nostrils flared as he took another threatening step toward Topher. The fire in his eyes blazed fiercely, fists clenched at his sides. I placed a hand on his chest, feeling the intense heat radiating from him, almost like a burn, yet I didn't pull away.

"Not him, jackass! Do you see Fae ears on him?"

Silence.

"Exactly. Now pick up the food and move out."

Chapter 31

The tension on our walk back to the horses was so thick you could cut it with a knife.

An almost unbearable awkwardness hung in the air as we walked along in silence. Ryder kept his eyes fixed on Topher, not even blinking while the knight stayed quiet. His gaze would occasionally meet mine, but I remained passive.

I was more than relieved when the horses finally came into view. Topher and Jupiter's reunion helped ease the tension slightly. Seeing him, Jupiter broke out into a series of excited noises. Jogging over to his horse, it was clear Topher was equally as excited.

Falling behind, Ryder gently stopped me by grabbing my arm. "Want to remind me what we discussed before we split up?"

Sighing, I pulled away. "Not to follow any strangers into their shops, but he—"

"No fucking butts, Princess. Once again, when you didn't return after fifteen minutes, I went looking for you. A vendor said you followed a man to an alehouse? Even better—when I got there, I found the storage room of said alehouse, and it was a mess. And guess what? *You* were gone!"

"Well, I didn't go into a shop."

His eyes narrowed. "Shop? Alehouse? Not. The. Point. You scared the shit out of me! And to top it all off, I find you in the arms of a stranger!" His head jerked towards Topher. "Who the hell is *that*?"

"I think I should ask you the same question," Topher shouted, heading back to us. "She is *my* best friend after all!"

Ryder puffed out his chest and rolled up his sleeves, showing off his tattooed arms. "I don't owe you anything."

Rolling my eyes, I was already tired of this interaction. "Enough! Gods, both of you! We have more important matters than a dick-measuring contest."

"Trust me, sweetheart," Ryder grunted. "It wouldn't be much of a competition."

Topher's face immediately flushed. Stepping between them, I silently prayed they wouldn't end up killing each other that night. "Introductions? Fine. Topher, this is Ryder. He's a huntsman and a friend. Ryder, this is Topher. Happy?"

A muscle ticked in Ryder's jaw before a knowing smile formed on his face. "Ah. So, the *gallant knight* decided to ride in and save the day," he sneered, "What's it been, over a month since she left? Running a little behind there, big guy."

Topher shot him a pointed look. "This *'gallant knight'* has been looking for her since she left. I'm sure I would have found her sooner if it wasn't for the likes of *you*!"

Ryder scoffed, "Seems convenient, doesn't it? For him to be in the same village your ex-fiancé was in. He could have led him right to you!"

Topher squared his shoulders. "I don't need your approval

or to answer to you! Unlike you, some of us have responsibilities. We can't all be filthy mercenaries, now can we?"

I raised my hands to my ears to block out their bickering. "Oh, my gods! Will you two shut up for a minute?"

Shrugging his shoulders, Ryder moved toward Reaper. "I'm just trying to get the facts straight here. I can smell bullshit from a mile away, and fuck," he inhaled deeply, "does it *reek* out here."

Flaring his nostrils, Topher took a warning step toward Ryder. Moving to block him, I placed my hands on his chest. His throat bobbed as he swallowed, but after a moment, he looked down at me. Emotions mixed across his fatigued face, but his eyes remained soft.

"Hi."

His heartbeat slowed beneath my palms. "Hey, Evie."

Stepping back, I pulled my hood down and let the cool air hit my face. The whole thing had me feeling flustered. "Now, can we have a conversation like three civilized adults?"

Topher huffed, "I will if you can keep your guard dog over there at bay."

"This *dog*," Ryder spat as he strapped the baskets to Reaper's side, "has kept your princess alive while you've been fucking around."

"Enough!" I shouted, frustration bubbling over. "I swear to the gods, if this bickering continues, I will leave *both* of you alone in these woods! Ryder, he's here now, and we can't change that. Suck it up or shut up! And Topher, stop provoking him. It's *not* flattering."

Both men stood their ground, staying silent while I attempted to clean the tension. A part of me knew it was hopeless for them to find common ground, but I had to try.

"Alright." I took a deep breath. "To start, I need to tell you what happened. Then, we can start asking the appropriate questions. Got it?"

Both men nodded, and I started, a small frown pulling at my lips. As I told the story, I saw a mix of emotions cross their faces. Ryder looked angry and frustrated, torn between my defiance and his faith in my strength. Topher's expression was more complicated, showing concern tinged with something deeper —regret?

Ryder approached me, a frown on his face. "And your hands? How do they feel now?"

I extended them for his inspection, feeling the warmth of his thumb rubbing comforting circles on my palm. Glancing over his shoulder, I caught Topher's intense, jealous gaze.

Clearing my throat, I gently withdrew my hands from Ryder's. "They're fine now. But the glowing...."

His face stayed firm, lips pressing into a thin line, "I know."

"Do you...do you think?" I pressed, my eyes catching the flicker of hesitation in his gaze.

His chest rose and fell in a steady rhythm. "Yeah. I do."

It was a cryptic conversation that only made sense between us. Seeing where it was headed, my heart sank.

"We knew this could be a possibility, Wiyahna. The feelings, the map—it all connects. Why else would that old broad give you that parchment leading you to The Hallows if you weren't a..."

He didn't finish his sentence, and he didn't need to. I couldn't even think of that. To think that my blood was...*dirty*. That my whole life could be a lie. That this war might be because of *me*, because of some distant connection!

Topher cleared his throat, snapping me out of my thoughts.

"Am I missing something? How could any of what happened be possible? It makes no sense."

"Magic has its own timing," Ryder shot. "It emerges when it's needed."

Laughter boasted from Topher. "You're screwing with me, right? There's no way Genevieve has magic!"

Ryder was in front of Topher's face in the blink of an eye, his tan hands clutching the collar of his thick tunic. "You watch your volume when you speak her name so publicly!" he growled in a voice that didn't sound like his own. "Don't you understand she's wanted?"

"I'm fully aware," Topher spat, pushing him away. "But I've known her since the day she was born!" He turned towards me, and Ryder thankfully backed off. "I know your family. Nothing points to you or the royal lineage being magical."

"Like I said, pretty boy," Ryder sneered, returning to my side, "magic doesn't run on a fixed schedule."

"But if she has magic in her, the only explanation for that would be…"

I forced a swallow, looking down at my hands. "That my mother was a Witch." I shakily said before Topher had the chance, "And I am too."

Yep. I'm going to throw up.

Staggering backward, I was overwhelmed by a wave of dizziness and nausea. Ryder quickly reached my side, preventing me from hitting the ground. I sank to my knees, and he joined, offering a comforting touch as my head hung low.

"Queen Dawn was *not* a Witch," Topher stated firmly, as if repelled by the mere suggestion.

He took a hesitant step closer, torn between offering comfort and keeping his distance. Ryder's head snapped up as he moved again, the forest scent around him mingling with the heat radiating from his skin. A low, primal rumble emanated from his chest, causing Topher to retreat two steps.

"It's fine, Ry. He's not the enemy." Rising back to my feet, I took a steadying breath. "So, what do we do now?"

Not like I really want to know the answer.

"Well, for starters," Ryder rose, "we need to hightail it out of here and back to the cabin before your fiancé decides to pay a visit. I'm not particularly keen on dealing with a Fae royal right now."

I nodded, totally forgetting about Xander being close.

He continued walking to our horses. "After that, I suggest we stick to our original plan and head to The Hallows."

"What?" Topher sounded horrified. "Absolutely not! She's *not* setting foot in those lands!"

Ryder chuckled. "And who's going to stop us? *You*? She's made it this far without your help. She doesn't need your consent or protection."

My head snapped towards Topher. "You believe it's real?"

His lips tightened, and a heavy silence settled between them. Tension thickened as the two men locked eyes, each defending their perspective on what was best for me. I grew weary of their ongoing struggle for dominance, feeling caught in the middle, torn between them.

"That's not the point. You can't just drag her into a territory with that reputation. It's dangerous, and she's not prepared!"

Ryder crossed his arms. "She's stronger than you think. We need to find out who sent that Shadow Walker anyway. Learning about her magic will just be a bonus. The Hallows is nothing I can't handle, and she needs answers. Or have you forgotten the death of your king?"

"I will *never* forget," he snapped. "You have no idea the ripples the king's death has created!"

I stepped between them again, breaking the tense standoff. My little control over the situation was slipping fast. "Please, stop. We can figure this out at the cabin."

Ryder turned his gaze to Topher. "You're *not* coming with us."

Topher shot me a pleading look. "Genevieve, *please*. I can't just let you go off into the unknown."

I could feel mismatched eyes burning through me.

"He's *not* coming with us," Ryder repeated.

Releasing a deep sigh, I turned to my best friend. "Topher, all I've known for the past month is the unknown. I never realized how sheltered I was until I left. This isn't just for me but also for Father. It always has been."

The look in his eyes was sympathetic and pitiful, and I hated every moment of it.

"He's coming with us," I stated firmly. "At least back to the cabin for the night. We'll talk about this more there. Topher, fetch your horse while we wait."

Topher nodded appreciatively and strode off to retrieve his horse without another word. Ryder scowled but held back any further protest.

The tension lingered, but at least for the moment, the forest fell silent, and the tingling in my fingers subsided.

Chapter 32

Returning to the border of Forest Sylvie, Topher hesitated at the edge of the dense woods separating us from the sanctuary of our cabin.

Honesty, I didn't blame him. The younger stallion he chose from the royal stables also shared his hesitation, if not *more*. Vieno? I think that was his name.

Despite Ryder's apparent disdain for Topher, he took the time to warn us about the dangers of the woods. Topher remained silent, his eyes fixed on me the entire time. The whole situation only fueled my annoyance—it felt like I was herding two bickering children instead of accompanying two grown men.

Emerging from the fog and reaching the property line, Ryder smoothly dismounted and led Reaper into the makeshift horse pen we'd set up. In contrast, Topher struggled to steady Vieno, who seemed uneasy with the magical transition.

Dismounting from Jupiter, I approached Topher and helped him guide Vieno into the pen.

"Thanks, Evie," he said, a warm smile on his lips.

A shiver of freedom coursed down my back as I removed my hood and hair wrap. "Of course. Magic can be overwhelming for the first few encounters, but he should be okay in here with the others."

Topher nodded. "Where are we exactly?"

"A family residence you should consider yourself lucky to be near," Ryder interjected.

He scoffed. "It seems like a pile of trash to me."

Ryder barked a laugh, striding over to us. "Say something stupid like that again, and I promise you, it'll be the last thing you say."

"Oh? Are you going to kill me?" he challenged, attempting to meet Ryder eye-to-eye but falling short by a few inches.

"I would *never* hurt Genevieve like that. I know what you mean to her," Ryder responded, his face calm as he stared him down. "It just might be difficult to form full sentences with all your teeth missing."

"Is that a challenge?"

"More like a *promise*."

This was shaping up to be a long night. I'd rather they throw a punch or two and get it over with than listen to this back-and-forth all night. But I wasn't in the mood to clean up blood, and my hunger had reached an unbearable level.

"If you make another dumb remark, I'm locking the doors and forcing you *both* to sleep out here!"

Ryder leveled a stern look my way. "He's *not* staying!"

"Hard of hearing? She's made her decision. Get comfortable, Huntsman; I'm part of this now," Topher asserted arrogantly as he settled beside me.

"Actually, you're not," I said, stepping away from him.

His jaw dropped in shock, eliciting a small snicker from Ryder. "I b-beg your p-pardon?"

"Look, you can stay the night and have dinner with us. But after that, I know what I need to do. If you can't support me, you're not coming."

"Genevieve," he began cautiously, "you can't expect me to leave you with *him*, not after I've searched to find you and bring you home."

"*Home*?" I practically choked on the word. "I'm not going home, Topher! I'm wanted for murder! What do you think they'll do to me once I arrive?"

"She'd be a dead girl walking," Ryder spat, standing beside me.

I didn't move away from his touch, and Topher noticed.

Shaking his head, he raised his hands defensively. "No, no. You don't understand. This is why I came looking for you. Liliana has taken back her allegations. She wants you to come home and claim the throne."

Bullshit.

"I've seen the posters. I know I'm wanted for Father's murder. Ordered by the *Queen*—Liliana! Or did Sir Doyle lie about her accession?"

His face dropped. "Sir Doyle? You ran into him?"

Ryder scoffed, unimpressed by my oldest friend. "He nearly strangled her to death! The bruises on her neck have barely just healed."

My hand went to my throat, the memory still fresh. "He told me Liliana had been crowned queen. I was in and out of consciousness, but I'm pretty sure I heard him correctly."

Topher's eyes darted to my neck. "I-I had no idea. But she claimed the throne temporarily until you returned. Once you left, she realized her mistake and commanded me to find you and bring you home. The other knights had already been sent out with the notion that you had committed the crime. But I knew better. I know *you* better."

Something didn't feel right. "So, explain the posters. Those don't get mass-produced overnight."

His throat bobbed. "I'm assuming a safety net in case I couldn't find you. More eyes on you meant more of a chance to bring you home faster."

Ryder snorted. "Seems like a shitty way of making her feel comfortable about coming back. People are greedy enough out there. I don't think a bounty for a wanted princess would ensure her a safe return. She could have been *killed*."

"Look, it wasn't my call, okay?" Topher conceded. "But he needs to understand—"

"I understand *perfectly*," Ryder said. "I don't trust you, and I won't have you jeopardizing her safety."

Topher's jaw clenched, and he shot me a concerned glance. "Genevieve, you can't seriously be considering going with *him*. I've known you your entire life! The huntsman might be good at survival, but he doesn't understand you like I do. You're needed back home. It's where you belong!"

My eyes shot up at him, tears slowly forming. "Why? So I can be married off again? So, I can live the rest of my life being used by some Fae prick who doesn't respect me or my crown? I'm sorry, but that's *not* the life I plan to live. Father even agreed before...before he..."

"Why do you think I was surprised to see Xander in that alehouse?" His voice was louder, causing me to back into Ryder's chest. "Queen Adela and Xander vanished the night you did. They hadn't been seen in Orphinian since, so I thought it was safe to assume the marriage was off. Now that your father is gone, that decision is yours to make."

I retracted my gaze from his, not in the mood to let him see me cry. Something was pulling at my gut, and it confused me. This was Topher. *My* Topher. Why was I now hesitating to trust him?

His expression pleaded with me; desperation etched across his face. "Genevieve, you can't just—"

"I can," I interrupted, shoulders straight. "I appreciate you coming all this way to find me, but I'm not returning. Not right now."

"But you're the princess! You have responsibilities. The kingdom *needs* you." Frustration laced his words.

"The kingdom needs an honest and confident ruler, not someone unsure of what she is."

"And what do you think that is? A Witch?" He barked a laugh as he continued to push. "At least come back long enough to explain to your court. They deserve to hear it from *you*. Then you can go to The Hallows and figure it all out."

"No," I said firmly, locking eyes with him. "If you see me as your queen, you will return and tell them the truth. The *whole* truth. There was a reason I didn't ask you to join me in the first place, and this is exactly it. You think you know best for me, but you don't!"

He hesitated briefly before turning to Ryder. "Do you even know anything about him?" His face twisted in disgust. "I mean, the scars on his face should tell you enough—"

"Ryder won't harm me," I assured him, cutting off any further insults. "Now, I'm going inside to start dinner. You can either come in and join us as our *guest*, or you can sleep out here. Your choice."

Before he could respond, I turned away and headed toward the cabin, where the food baskets awaited on the front stoop. The door creaked open, and as I stepped inside, tension lingered in the air. Iris watched from the kitchen counter, her yellow eyes following my every move.

Leaning against the wooden surface, I sighed. "Well, Iris, it looks like we'll have a *very* interesting evening."

Her curious melody rang through the kitchen as I gathered all the ingredients, ready to let the rhythm of cooking soothe my thoughts. Ryder's heavy footsteps approached from behind as I chopped vegetables to vent my anger. Turning, I found him casually leaning against the doorway, a half-smile on his face.

"You handled that well."

A blush found its way to my cheeks. "I probably could have handled it a little better," I admitted. "I just... I don't know. Do you think I'm making the right choice?"

He nodded. "More than anything. Everyone deserves to know who they are, no matter how scary the thought of it might be. I'm sure it wasn't an easy decision, but I'm proud of you."

I faked a gasp, raising my hand to my chest. "Ryder Hemming? *The* Huntsman? Proud of me? Good gods, I'll never recover."

His half-smile grew, revealing the tip of a canine. "It's an honor, I know."

Facing away, I continued chopping vegetables. The floorboards creaked under his weight as he moved, his body heat intensifying. Taking his spot next to me, I suddenly found it hard to breathe.

I looked up at him, his golden and sapphire flakes seeming

to shimmer in the sinking sunlight. "Need some help?" he asked, his hand moving over mine to take the knife.

His touch sent a jolt through me, warming my chest. My lips parted as I took him in, his gaze intensifying, momentarily making me feel carefree. But that wasn't the reality, and we both knew it.

I carefully removed the knife from his hand. "No, this is my gift to you, remember?"

He remained locked next to me before he smiled, accepting the situation. "Alright then, Chef G.'s in charge. I'll go tend the horses, but let me know if you need me, okay?"

Nodding, I watched his large silhouette vanish through the back door. Snapping out of his trance, which seemed to hold me, I resumed my tasks. The comforting sounds of chopping and sizzling filled the cabin with life. The scent of fresh ingredients and Iris's melodic hum filled the air, helping me escape into the moment.

After a while, Topher cautiously entered the kitchen, causing Iris to dart out of sight. "Hey."

I offered a glance as I kept cooking. "Hi."

He sighed. "Look, I know I was being a jerk back there and I'm sorry, Genevieve. I didn't mean to push you, it's just...I missed you."

When I finally met his gaze, the weight of our shared history felt suffocating. "I missed you too, Topher. But you know me better than anyone. Pushing me into a decision isn't the right way."

He nodded. "I get it. I just...I don't want to lose you again." As he took a step closer, his eyes reflected a mix of regret and longing. "These past few weeks haven't been easy on me. On anyone back home, really."

I reassured him with a touch on his arm. "Trust me, I understand. It's not every day you learn you're a part of the most hated race in Orphinian history."

My attempt to lighten the mood fell flat. His expression carried a hint of disgust, almost mirroring my own. When he reached over and placed his hand on mine, halting my dinner preparation, his touch felt strange. I shrugged it off as lingering tension, though I couldn't help but compare how his touch made me feel to Ryder's just moments ago.

"Evie, you could never be hated by anyone—especially me." His eyes lingered. "Not seeing you every day, it did something to me. I didn't leave because I was commanded. I would have followed you if you had asked."

"I know. And I appreciate the sacrifices you made to be here. Is Fiona doing alright?"

He retracted his hand, an unreadable emotion passing on his face so quickly that if I had blinked, I would have missed it. "She misses you too. But she's well. She's just eager for you to come home so she can hear all your stories."

I snorted. "Sounds like her."

An awkward, unusual silence settled between us.

"Uh, there's a bathing chamber down the hall and to the left. Feel free to clean up while I finish dinner. There's a small closet with clean towels."

A small smile tugged at the corners of his lips. "I'd like that."

"Good, because you smell."

A deep chuckle escaped his lips as he turned to exit the kitchen. "At least I don't smell like the floor of a tavern."

Iris waited until she heard the bathing chamber's door lock before emerging from her hiding place. Her musical notes filled the room as she perched on my shoulder, tiny blue hands resting on my cheek.

"Old friend," I answered, unsure if that addressed what she was saying or not.

Her melody played on as I finished cooking, the vegetables sizzling in the pan and filling the kitchen with their aroma. Despite a lingering darkness threatening to invade my thoughts, I pushed it aside.

In that moment, the cabin felt alive with the comforting sounds of home, and for a brief second, I forgot about the chaos awaiting us beyond its walls.

Chapter 33

In my eighteen years, I'd endured my fair share of awkward dinners.

Most of them have been mortifying, but this dinner, with the three of us in Ryder's family cabin deep in the woods, took the cake. I would have been shocked if more than a handful of words were exchanged.

Throughout the meal, Ryder's intense stare at Topher never wavered. I trusted him and knew he wouldn't use his steak knife on my friend, but I also didn't doubt the thought hadn't crossed his mind.

After what felt like ages, Topher excused himself, placed his empty plate in the sink, and left through the back door. Once it shut, I didn't hesitate to give Ryder a swift kick under the table.

Grabbing his shin, he glared at me through pain-soaked eyes. "Ouch! What the hell?"

"Can you at least *pretend* to be nice to him?" I pleaded, "He's my oldest friend. You can drop the whole protective asshole act around him."

He leaned back in his chair. "I don't *'pretend'*. It's not in my nature. And I'm telling you something right now—I don't trust him. Something doesn't feel right about the whole situation today."

Rolling my eyes, I pinched the bridge of my nose. "You don't even know him. And he doesn't know you. Both of you need to relax and just try to live civilly while we're all together."

"I don't *need* to know him. I have a very good sense of character."

"I think your possessiveness over me is blocking that ability. Topher has been nothing but amazing to me my whole life."

A loud laugh echoed throughout the kitchen, causing Iris to emerge from her hiding spot. "For one thing, I'm not '*possessive.*' Let's not forget you're a payday to me too, sweetheart. We've gotten close, and I'll admit that, but I'm *not* possessive. And another thing: he is in *love* with you. So, of course, he'll be good to you."

Feeling like I had been smacked in the face, I could feel my cheeks burning. I slouched in my seat, and my eyes left his. "I didn't realize you only cared about the money throughout all this. I guess your confession in The Vale was a lie, after all."

I didn't need to look at him to know his face had fallen. Leaning forward in his chair, he placed his hand beside mine. "That's not what I meant, and you know it. All I meant was—"

"No," I said, interrupting him. "I've learned that you don't say things you don't mean. So, I think you did mean it."

"Genevieve, I—"

Reaching for my hand, I quickly moved it before he could grasp it. "No, no, I get it. I'm a nice prize at the end of the day. You knew you'd be getting money at the end of this regardless. But once you found out I was the princess, I'm sure you saw gold."

When I met his gaze, his eyes showed a hint of shock before narrowing in my direction. "Is that what you think of me?"

Scoffing, I threw my hands up "Is that what you think of *me*? I mean, I get it. I do! You need money to survive. That's why you're a huntsman in the first place, right? I respect it. But gods, don't act like you care for someone to get their money. Don't make someone care for *you* in return! *'We got close'*? That's a damn understatement if I ever heard one."

The flush on his face deepened. "You know what, Genevieve? If all I wanted was the fucking money, don't you think I would have handed you over the moment I saw that wanted poster?"

Shit. He had me there. But my anger was already too far gone at this point to stop. "Well, what's stopping you now? If you turn me in, I'm sure you'll save yourself from getting another tattoo! Don't let *me* burden *you* any further."

"Do you think that's what I want? To take the easy way out and hand you over to a life you don't fucking want? To say goodbye like nothing has happened between us? Like there is nothing *between* us?"

I slammed my hands down on the table, leaving a small imprint in the wood from the shock in my fingers. "I don't know, Ryder! What do you want?"

As he stood up from the table, the sound of the chair toppled over onto the floor, causing me to jump. "I want you to open your fucking eyes and see what's right in front of you! If you want to go with your *'Knight in Shining Armor,'* the door is right there!"

Running his fingers through his hair, he released a frustrated breath. I could see him visibly shaking and the tension in the air was almost suffocating. My anger dissipated, replaced by a knot of worry in my stomach.

Flashbacks of my last fights with my father flashed through my mind. I had pushed another man I cared about to their limit without meaning a single thing I said. Taking a deep breath, I tried to calm down enough to talk to him.

"Ry, I didn't mean—"

He raised a hand, his eyes still burning. "I need to cool off," he muttered before stomping toward the back door.

Before I could escalate things, he pushed it open, nearly knocking it off its hinges. Chilly air rushed in, giving Iris a chance to slip out behind him. Passing Topher with a shoulder bump, Iris quickly vanished into Ryder's pocket without a reaction from him.

I felt power tingling in my fingertips as I hastily tied up my already messy hair, trying to calm down. Taking a deep breath, I pushed that energy away. It was not welcomed right now.

Topher entered the kitchen with lighter footsteps than Ryder's. Concern coated his face as he cautiously approached. "What was that about?"

"I opened my mouth and stuffed my foot in there. Typical me."

He nervously scratched the underside of his thick beard. "If it was about me being here, I didn't mean to cause trouble."

"I know you didn't, and this goes deeper than you being here." I leaned against the table, feeling the day's weight pressing on me. "This situation is just...a lot to handle."

Topher's eyes softened. "I'm sorry if I've added to the stress. I want to help...whatever you decide to do."

Managing a thin smile, I was skeptical. "Do you mean that? Honestly?"

Hesitating for a moment, he nodded. "I do. You're my best friend through and through. And right now, the least I could do is clean up since you cooked us a meal."

The corner of my lips raised as a small wave of relief rushed over me. *This* was the Topher I had known all these years.

"I would love that. Thank you."

Almost immediately, he began to pick up all the dirty plates and brought them over to the sink. As he worked, my mind unintentionally started to drift. Regret washed over me as I replayed the fight. I knew I had spoken out of my ass, and it was purely because of how fucking scared I was.

Not fear of venturing to The Hallows or uncovering my father's killer, but fear of being the cause of this war. Worse yet, my mother was involved too.

Lost in thought, I absentmindedly traced the scorch marks my fingers had left on the table. If I was capable of this, what else could I do? The thought made my stomach churn. If I had hurt Ryder...well, I didn't want to think about it.

Either way, I couldn't shake the feeling that I had crossed a line that might be harder to mend this time.

Still consumed in my thoughts, Topher's voice broke through. "Is there anything else I can do to help?"

I blinked, refocusing. "Um, no, I think that's all. But let me make your bed real fast."

"Oh, I'm *not* sleeping outside tonight?"

"Shut up. You know that wasn't a *real* threat."

"Seemed real to me. I mean, you had me shaking in my boots."

Pushing my chair back, I rose from my seat and walked over to Topher. His eyes met mine as I placed a hand on his chest.

"Damn, straight I did," I said with a smirk, applying pressure to his chest, causing him to stumble back.

I walked into the hallway, and he followed closely behind. Opening the magical closet, I was greeted by the warm scent of fresh laundry, which quickly calmed my nerves. Returning to the living room with fresh sheets and a pillow, I made a makeshift bed on the couch.

Topher stood in the doorway, watching me curiously.

"You good with a couch for the evening?"

He shrugged. "Thanks to that fog, I had been sleeping on the ground for days. Even the beds at the Inn were shit so, this seems like a cloud compared to that."

"It's very worn in thanks to Ryder's family, so hopefully, it doesn't mess up your back."

"He, uh, he's not the most welcoming person, is he?"

My eyes shot up in his direction. His face was calm but still held a hint of distaste. "I won't defend how he's talked to you since you've met, but he has his reasons for being hesitant towards a newcomer. We've been through a lot since our time together. He's seen *me* go through a lot. He's just...protective."

"Seems a little over the top to me."

I fluffed his pillow, adding it to the end of the couch, "Funny," I laughed, "There was once a time someone would have said the same about you."

His face fell, shoulders slouching. "I'm still protective of you. You know that. I was sworn to protect you until I could no longer."

"It hasn't always felt that way."

The room fell silent, and his face remained unreadable. I had done it again. I had gone too far.

Was I trying to burn every bridge I had built?

His lips thinned as if debating whether to say something else to me or not. Making up his mind for him, I nodded, passing him through the door.

"I'm sorry," I whispered. "I'm the last door down the hall. Knock if you need me."

Walking away, I could feel his eyes on my back. Twisting the doorknob, I slowly pushed the door open, and regret washed over me. I paused before stepping inside, glancing back at him. Those blue eyes held a myriad of emotions.

"And please, don't worry about Ryder. He just needs time to adjust."

With that, I closed my bedroom door and slid down against it, sitting on the floor with my knees pulled close to my chest. I took a few deep breaths, but I was already too overwhelmed.

Trying to count to ten, I only made it to four before my body started shaking, and I burst into tears.

At some point, I had made it to my bed.

I'm not sure how, but after sobbing uncontrollably, I pulled myself off the floor and collapsed onto the mattress. When I woke up, my head was pounding from crying so hard. Unsure of the time, I knew my throat was parched and begging for water.

Dragging myself from the comfy mattress, I tiptoed to the door and pressed my ear against it, listening carefully to the silent house. Slowly, I ventured into the dark hallway illuminated only by the dying fire in the living room where Topher slept.

Ryder's door stood wide open, and as I peeked inside, my heart sank at the sight of his empty bed.

I guess he's still trying to cool off.

I tiptoed down the hall, holding my breath to avoid waking Topher, knowing he must be tired. The cabin's layout required passing through the living room to reach the kitchen, and every floorboard creaked.

As soon as I entered, his head shot up from the couch arm, eyes widening at the sight of me. "What are you doing up?" His voice was gruff.

"I needed water," I whispered. "Sorry if I woke you."

He rubbed his eyes and sat up. "Don't worry about it. I don't sleep well anymore anyway."

That makes two of us.

I went to the kitchen, filled a glass with water, and returned to the living room. The dying embers of the fire cast a warm glow, but tension still lingered in the air. Topher adjusted himself, making space on the couch. When he patted the cushion beside him, I sat down, wrapping myself in the blanket.

Silence consumed us as we sat next to each other.

"You know," he said, breaking the silence, "I didn't quite imagine our reunion like this."

"Really?" I sipped the water, the cool liquid soothing my dry throat. "This is *exactly* how it played out in my head."

My voice was coated with sarcasm, which brought a smile to his face. "Oh yeah? Maybe you *are* a Witch—predicting the future and all."

I shoved him with my shoulder, still not ready to discuss the sensitive subject. "Normally, I'm just called a '*Bitch*', but maybe people have gotten the first letter wrong all these years."

Once again, my joke fell short, causing him to frown. "You're far from a bitch, Evie. And whoever has made you feel that way is wrong and miserable. Give me a list. I'm in an ass-kicking mood."

I snorted. "I acted like one tonight, with both you *and* Ryder." I shook my head, desperately trying to clear the memories. "I always go too far. I did it with Father before he passed, and I regret it every day."

"You and King Leonard had one of the best relationships I have ever witnessed. You have nothing to be regretful about. He was *always* so proud of you."

"But would he be proud of me *now*?" I asked, my voice weak. "I mean, I *ran*. The moment I was faced with uncertainty, I turned into a coward."

"Your fight or flight kicked in." He shrugged. "You did what you thought would be best to protect yourself. Anyone would have done the same."

"I did, but that doesn't mean that's still the right path to be on."

A moment of silence passed between us, the only sound coming from the cracks of the fire. "Are you second-guessing coming back to Castle Quinn with me?"

His eyes showed a hint of excitement, eager for me to answer.

"I don't know," I admitted. "I want to go to The Hallows. I *need* to. The Shadow Walker came from somewhere purposefully to kill him, and The Hallows could hold every answer I needed. But a part of me doesn't want to know what I am yet. Or what I can do..."

He scoffed. "I still think it's absurd to think Queen Dawn could have been a Witch."

I bit my lip. "But how do you explain the things I'm able to do? What I did to Xander? Witches have been hunted and killed for generations. This war was because of *them*. To think I'm one of them...that *I* get to live while they all suffered... I'm not different or better than them. I just...I feel torn."

Admitting it out loud pained me. I knew what I needed and what was best, but a tiny voice in my head urged me to go back and reclaim the crown. It told me to ignore the possibility that I might be a Witch, to disregard the idea that my mother might have been one too.

"What you decide needs to be your choice," he said. "We could put this all behind us. Forget about the magic, the possibilities. Nothing would make me happier than you returning home, but if you don't make this decision yourself, you'll resent me for it for the rest of your life."

"Resenting you isn't a future I see happening. But I guess the most I can do is sleep on it, maybe talk to Ryder..."

Topher put his arm around my shoulders. "Sleeping on it would be wise, but I think talking with the huntsman will sway your choice. I'm sure he would convince you to stay with him no matter what."

I shifted uncomfortably in my seat, but his grip on me remained firm. "I would never make this decision without him." I looked deep into his eyes, "Like him or not, Ryder has saved my ass more than a few times. I may have hired him, but he's more to me than that. Even if he's pissed, I won't just walk away without a conversation."

"I suppose," he pulled me closer. "But he doesn't have as much to lose in this as *we* do. He'll find another client. I wasn't trying to eavesdrop but wasn't he the one who said you were just a paycheck to him?"

I shook my head, the emotions hitting me all over again. "He did, but—"

"I'm sorry," he cut me off, "but someone who can openly say something like to your face does not care. You may care for *him*, but he does not care for you. I mean, why else would he be so worried about me taking you away? He won't get his money."

I paused, letting his words sink in, acknowledging their possible truth. Ryder had consistently supported me, lifting me up when I felt unable to continue. But a small doubt lingered in my mind.

What if all of this had been for his own benefit?

Almost instinctively, I rested my head on Topher's chest, feeling the rhythm of his rapid heartbeat calming my racing thoughts. His arm around my shoulder pulled me closer, and I felt like a child again, seeking comfort on a warm chest in moments of fear.

"I have faith you'll do what's right," he finally said. "Just don't waste your time trying to figure it out."

I nodded, knowing he was sort of right in a way. My body felt exhausted—tired of this endless conversation, tired of waiting for a revelation in the night, tired of uncertainty about what was best for my kingdom and my future.

Gods, I was just...*tired*.

Over the next hour, Topher and I fell into our old habits, discussing lighter topics. Sitting by the fire on the couch, I recounted my time with Ryder, sharing most of the events but omitting details about The Vale.

It felt like being back at the castle, chatting with my oldest friend.

Despite how much we'd both changed, we still felt like those children running through the halls. He was a part of me, and I of him. Even though I wasn't the same Genevieve who left that night, being with Topher made me feel closer to her.

As we sat there, my eyes occasionally darted to the front door, hoping Ryder would walk through it.

He never did.

I knew he was safe—he knew these woods well.

My concern wasn't for his safety but for our future together. My feelings for Ryder were complicated. There was undeniably something deeper between us than a few weeks' acquaintance.

I couldn't shake the feeling that he felt it too. The way he looked at me and spoke to me made me feel more alive than ever.

Even with our earlier conversation, I still cared deeply for him. The thought that I might have upset him enough to keep him away filled me with anxiety and unease.

Outside the cozy cabin, I thought I heard a familiar howl echoing through the woods—a sound I almost forgot. Topher claimed he didn't hear it, so perhaps it was my imagination.

Or maybe I was hoping for something familiar to guide me.

Something to *save* me.

Chapter 34

The clock read well past one in the morning by the time I left Topher alone to sleep.

As I passed Ryder's dark, empty room, my heart sank. Swallowing my guilt, I reminded myself he was a grown man who would return when needed.

Snuggling back into bed, I found sleep came swiftly. It had been days since my last nightmare, but tonight was different.

In the courtyard of Castle Quinn, bathed only in moonlight, I knew immediately I was dreaming. The grounds were silent, eerie in their emptiness. Running towards the castle, my legs moved like I was walking through mud, every step a struggle. Reaching the door, I fought for breath, desperate to escape the haunting darkness.

Fuck me. Of course, the doors are locked.

Banging until my fists went numb, I shouted for help, but my voice seemed lost. No matter how hard I screamed or pounded, nothing happened. Frustration surged as my senses heightened.

A presence approached from behind, causing every hair on my neck to stand. Hesitantly turning, I locked eyes with a figure emerging from the darkness.

My blood ran cold.

Dressed in black robes that blended into the night, my mother appeared once more. Her face hadn't aged, her long autumn hair flowing in the wind. Yet her eyes, the emeralds that usually mirrored mine, were as white and foggy as milk.

It was like the eyes of someone who had gone blind, but worse.

No emotion, no hint of green.

Just white, blank spaces.

My breathing hitched as familiar dread settled in. This wasn't the first time I'd encountered my mother in this dream-like realm, but each new encounter grew darker.

She extended a pale, thin hand toward me—a silent plea.

Her milky eyes bore into my soul, and the words echoed through the emptiness. *"You've come so far, my love. But beware —do not trust him."*

I shook my head, taking a hesitant step forward. *"You keep trying to tell me. But who? Who are you talking about?"*

Her head tilted unnaturally to the side, more feline than human. My stomach churned at the sight. *"Mother. Please!"*

A wry smile formed on her lips, devoid of warmth. *"You've known all along, my sweet Genevieve. Ignore what you've been taught, and the truth will reveal itself."*

Nightmare or not, this was my chance to get answers from the woman I needed them from. I took another heavy step toward her and my legs felt like boulders. Before I could get closer, a low growl echoed through the courtyard, halting my efforts.

Emerging from behind her, the same massive wolf stepped forward. Its fur was as black as night, eyes glowing with the unsettling intelligence I had faced that night in The Vale.

Fire and ice.

Swallowing my fear, I stood tall. My mother stepped back, allowing the wolf to take the lead. As it approached, my hand instinctively reached out, fear momentarily replaced by curiosity. It allowed me to touch it—my fingers raking through its soft fur.

The warmth felt...familiar.

"You've known all along, love," my mother whispered, voice fading into the darkness.

My fingers felt like they were on fire again, and I snapped my hand back, eyes fixed on my mother.

As her face faded, I panicked. "*Mother*?"

"Do what is best. Do what you need to do," her barely audible voice lingered.

Another low growl emerged from the wolf, drawing my attention back to the beast. Its eyes, once warm and welcoming, now glinted dark and possessive. A chill ran down my spine, compelling me to glance over my shoulder.

Before I could react, sharp fangs bared, and it lunged at me.

I jolted awake, gasping for air in the dimly lit room. My body felt both freezing and drenched in sweat, an unsettling contrast that left me disoriented.

But I was okay. I was *safe*.

I wrapped myself in a thick sweater and pulled on leggings before cautiously opening the bedroom door, listening for any signs of life in the silent cabin. Stepping into the corridor, I sighed with relief to see Ryder's door closed.

He was home.

I turned the corner into the living room to find Topher's bed was neatly made, the sheets were folded on an old armchair. Glancing at the clock, it read around eight in the morning, though the cloudy sky outside made it seem earlier.

Rain must be on the way.

Entering the kitchen, Topher sat peacefully at the table, holding a steaming cup of tea.

Studying the scroll Shamira had given me, he looked up from the scribbles and offered me a sleepy smile. "I thought you'd be sleeping in this morning," he admitted, casually pushing the scroll away.

Shrugging, I went to the counter to pour a glass of water, "This *is* sleeping in."

"Yeah, but I kept you up. You deserve some sleep."

As I took a sip of water, my eyes felt heavy. "I had a nightmare too."

"Ah, that makes sense. You have a lot on your mind. I can't even begin to fathom what must be happening up there."

Keeping up a conversation with him was a struggle; my shoulders and heart felt heavy, drained of energy and emotions. I blamed it on the lack of sleep; I barely noticed Topher rising from his chair and placing his mug next to me in the sink.

"Have you thought any more about what we discussed last night?"

"I told you," I stated firmly, "I'm not doing anything until I talk it over with Ryder."

Dissatisfied with my response, he scoffed in disgust. "Well, good luck with that," he spat with a tone of loathing. "He came in about two hours ago, dirty as a pig in a mud hole. I'm surprised you didn't hear him in the bathing chamber. I guess being a huntsman means he lacks any common courtesy!"

I frowned. "What do you mean he was dirty?"

Crossing his arms, he looked down at me. "Exactly what I said—he was *dirty*. Shirt was off like he was showing off every godsdamn muscle he has, and he was covered in dirt."

Why the hell would he have been dirty?

"Did he say anything?"

His eyes narrowed. "Not a word. Just stomped into his room like he owned the place."

"Well...he does..."

Pushing away from the counter, he moved to the back door. "I'm going to get my stuff together while you wait for him to wake up. I don't want to sit around all day when I could be on the road."

His voice was blunt and dry, devoid of its usual warmth. As he pushed through the door, I released a breath I hadn't realized I'd been holding. Slumping at the kitchen table, I rubbed my temples, feeling a headache coming on.

The cabin's uneasy atmosphere felt suffocating, leaving my mind torn. A tingling sensation crawled through my fingers, and unease washed over me as my gaze landed on the scroll lying on the table.

Like the dagger, it called to me.

Against my better judgment, I reached for it tentatively. It felt as if a strange force was pulling me toward its ancient surface. When my fingers touched the aged parchment, a surge of energy enveloped me, blinding me with white light.

Something probed at the edges of my mind, urging me to explore, but I resisted.

Keep out, keep out, keep out!

The energy pushed against the barrier guarding my deepest, darkest thoughts, but I managed to keep it at bay. I don't know how, but I wouldn't allow it in. Slipping through the barrier as if taunting me, an image of a white owl with silver-tipped feathers pierced my mind. It seemed to laugh at me, knowing something I didn't.

Just as suddenly as it intruded, the blinding light receded, leaving me breathless and disoriented. The overwhelming fear that gripped me felt as suffocating as Sir Doyle's aggressive hold.

What the hell was happening?

I threw the scroll on the table, rubbing my hands on my leggings, desperate to rid myself of the feeling. Would this shit ever stop? Or was I doomed to live like this; constantly on edge, waiting for the next supernatural thing to happen?

I'd go mad if I could't control my body and these...powers.

No matter how much I tried to ignore them.

The creak of a floorboard disrupted the heavy air, pulling me from my inner turmoil. Ryder entered the kitchen, looking worn and weathered, the night's challenges etched on his sleepy face. His mismatched eyes met mine briefly before looking away.

"Morning," I offered cautiously.

He grunted in response, making his way to the stove for a cup of coffee. By how he looked, Topher's kettle of tea wouldn't be enough.

"Are you still upset with me?"

His eyes flickered in my direction. "Depends," he replied after rummaging through cabinets for coffee essentials. "Do you still think I'm only here for the money?"

Well. That was a good indication of how this talk was going to go.

I hesitated; the words caught in my throat. "No," I finally managed, "I don't think that. I don't think I ever thought that."

His eyes briefly met mine over his shoulder, not fully turning to make direct eye contact. A sharp laugh escaped him before he focused back on making coffee.

I could practically *sense* the eye roll he gave me.

"If I admit I was being a brat, will you stop being such an ass?"

"Not being an ass, Geneveive," he retorted, back still turned. "I'm just dealing out basic human emotions you're not used to in the palace. Hate to break it to you, but I won't sweep things under the rug to keep my head."

A quick slap in the face would have been less of a blow than that little sprinkle of reality.

"Fair enough," I said, swallowing my pride. "Regardless, I'm sorry for how I spoke to you last night. Tensions were high, and that's not an excuse. I shouldn't have spoken to you like that."

"It's not how you spoke to me." He finally turned. "It's the fact that I've proven time and time again how highly I think of you, how *deep* I'm in this. And yet, the moment your knight walks through the door, you throw that all away."

His words left me stunned.

"Excuse me?"

Sighing, he ran a hand through his messy hair. "What's been your goal since the day we met?"

"I don't see ho—"

"Just answer the question."

I slumped in my chair, arms crossing over my chest. "To find my father's murderer."

"Exactly. You've been so determined, so headstrong about it. I admired the hell out of you for that determination! But as soon as *he* returns, you're second-guessing going back to that prison of a castle?"

"I never said I was going back with him!" My voice was defensive. "Not *once* did those words come out of my mouth."

"I *heard* you last night."

"Heard *what*, exactly?"

He turned back to the brewing coffee. "I needed space, needed to cool off before I said something I would have regretted. Iris and I took a long walk and talked for hours. She finally calmed me down enough to make me feel ready to talk to you. To tell you..." He forced a swallow. "Anyways, when I got back, you two were all cuddled up on the couch, and I heard *everything*."

Realizing the part he must have overheard, my heart sank.

"Seeing him with his arm around you? I—" He took a deep breath, nostrils flared. "My anger just started all over again, so I stayed away. Genevieve, you're not meant to live your life locked behind stone walls. Letting others control you? That's *not* you and you know that! The fact that you're even questioning returning is enough for me to know he's convincing you."

"He's *not* convincing me." My frustration spiked. "He's giving me another option—just like you. If you had stuck around to listen more, I told him I wouldn't have decided without talking to you first because I respect you! I *care* for you, dammit! Going back was always the end goal, one way or another."

"You are a *Witch*!" his voice boomed throughout the kitchen. "You are a godsdamn stunning and amazing Witch who doesn't even know the extent of her power yet. Do you honestly think you can return to the castle knowing all that and live a comfortable life just pushing that side of you away?"

I bit my lip, hating how often he was right. "No," I said firmly, "I don't think I can. But it's not all about me. It never has been! It's what's right for the kingdom and for the crown."

"That's bullshit, and you know it." His voice carried a hint of sadness, as if he, too, felt drained by the ongoing conversation and the weight of the choices before me. "I may not have known you as long as your knight out there," he nodded towards the window, "but I know you pretty damn well. I know your *soul* and I can read it all over your face. You're scared, so you're running to what's comfortable."

Anger flushed through me, heating my cheeks. "I am *not* running! I'm doing what's right! What my *father* would have wanted me to do."

With two empty mugs in hand, he let out a sharp laugh. "Keep telling yourself that, sweetheart. If it helps you sleep at night, by all means, keep lying to yourself."

Ryder poured us both a cup, placing one in front of me before pulling out a chair and sitting across from me. His intense gaze never wavered as he took a big sip of his coffee, the steam coating his face. Every word he spoke left me speechless, fueling my anger.

Trembling with rage, I felt a familiar surge of power within me. "How dare you question my motives?"

Leaning forward, his eyes narrowed. "How? Because it's the truth. You're running away from yourself, from your *power*. Maybe even your feelings if that's the conversation you want to have right now."

It was not the conversation I wanted to have. At least not right now when I could have smacked him silly.

I slammed my hands on the table, feeling the tingling in my

fingers return. The coffee mug in front of me quivered, its contents rippling as it started to boil.

"You know *nothing*," I managed through clenched teeth.

"I know more than you think about running from the beast hiding within." He leaned back, a mocking smirk playing on his lips. "I know about running from feelings, too. But I learned from my mistakes, and I'm not running this time—not from you. Not from *us*. Go ahead and ask me how I got my scars. I know you've been *dying* for that story."

"You're deflecting!"

"I'm helping."

Anger surged within me, mingling with unbidden magical energy that sought release. The room hummed with the building power, my emotions intensifying it into a volatile mixture on the brink of eruption. A soft light emanated from my fingertips, drawing both our gazes downward to the spectacle.

"Look at you, getting all worked up." His golden eye sparkled. "Can't handle the truth, can you, Princess?"

"Don't push me, Ryder," I warned, clenching my fists to hide the growing light.

"Or what? Are you going to throw me in a *dungeon*?"

"Stop!"

My control snapped.

The magic surged uncontrollably, fueled by my anger. It caused the coffee mug in front of me to explode, sending hot liquid and shattered porcelain flying. Ryder seemed unaffected as the burning liquid repelled off his skin, but I was stunned, allowing it to seep into my pores.

I tried to stop it before it even started, but it was too late.

My hands trembled as I stared at the mess before me, unable to process what had just happened.

Panting heavily, I struggled to steady myself, taking a deep breath to calm down. "I-I didn't mean to."

My eyes met Ryder's calm and unruffled gaze. He took another long sip of his coffee, a wide smirk playing across his face. "And to think, you just want to push that side of you away."

I took in the room around us—memorizing exactly what I was capable of doing. It was the storage room with Xander all over again. Except this time, my anger was fixed on Ryder.

But...he wasn't upset. Or even scared. But he could have been. I wouldn't have blamed him.

Who the fuck was I?

What the fuck was I?

Setting down his mug, he remained calm. "Genevieve, this kind of power needs to be trained. *Controlled*. And I can't train you. *He* can't train you. You felt that surge just now and let your anger take over. If you were to go to Castle Quinn, it wouldn't be long before something triggered you again, and it could be worse. Others might find out what you are, and it could lead to your death."

His words struck a chord, and fear washed over me. I hadn't considered the potential consequences of revealing my abilities. My father's deep-seated animosity towards Witches and their role in the Human-Fae War lingered in my thoughts.

Discovering my mother's identity as a Witch added another layer to the complexity of my own identity. Returning as a fugitive princess burdened not only by my father's death but also by the lineage of a Witch felt like a disaster waiting to unfold.

He stood and came over to me, noticing my slight trembling. As if I hadn't just exploded a mug of coffee with my hands, he took them in his, totally unafraid of what I was. The warmth of his touch brought a rush of calm over me.

"I can't let that happen to you," he continued, his eyes softening. "You need someone who can guide you through this. To help you understand and control your abilities. Someone who won't judge or use you. The Hallows is the answer. Those are your sisters, other Witches who will know what to do with you and can potentially tell you why that Shadow Walker was sent after your father."

Bringing my hands up to his lip, he kissed the base of my knuckles. My heart raced, a blush fixing on my cheeks. "I'm not scared of you. I *never* will be. But I fear what will happen to you. I vowed myself to you that night in The Vale, and I don't plan on letting that go anytime soon—letting *you* go."

"But...but it was a *Witch* who cursed you," I whispered. "You should hate me! Why don't you hate me?"

My eyes welled with tears, but I held them back. Ryder pulled me close, releasing one hand from mine to gently cup my cheek. As if anticipating it, his thumb brushed away the first tear that fell.

"Hate you?" He let out a breathy laugh. "How can anyone hate the sun when they've been begging to escape their own darkness?"

Pulling me close, he leaned in until our foreheads touched. I closed my eyes, allowing the feel of him to ease my nerves. "A Witch cursed me, yes, but you're *not* her. You're not like anyone I have ever met."

The weight of his words hit me, and I felt the suffocating reality of my situation. It was overwhelming and all too real.

Ryder's fingers gently tilted my chin upward, his breath mingling with mine. I could feel the warmth of his lips so close, and every fiber of my being ached for the kiss that was just a breath away.

But no amount of longing could hide the fear I felt.

Pulling away from him, I stepped back, afraid I might accidentally harm him in one way or another. "I-I can't. I didn't ask for this. *None* of this."

His face fell. "What do you mean, *'you can't'*? Life hands us only what we can handle, and I know you can handle this. Don't make a decision you'll regret out of fear."

Torn between duty and self-discovery, I met Ryder's gaze with determination. "I must go back, Ryder. Once I'm crowned queen, I'll make it a priority to handle the Shadow Walkers. I'll discover who did this. I swear it. I'll find you, and we can pick up where we left off."

His frustration was evident, and his body began to tremble. "Do you think they'll wait for you to become queen? That they'll suddenly cease their pursuit of you? No. And you know that. You're making a mistake."

Squaring my shoulders, I stood my ground. "I understand your frustration and appreciate everything you've done for me, Ryder, but I must face this. I can't run forever."

His beautifully scarred face was etched with anger as he glared at me. "You're running one way or another. Whether it's from yourself, your feelings, or the truth, it doesn't matter."

I felt a pang of guilt, knowing I had upset him. "Ryder, I—"

"Just go," he turned away. "Figure out your destiny, Your *Majesty*. You know where to find me."

Grabbing his mug, he gave me a mocking bow and thundered away. Ryder's footsteps faded and my breath returned.

Shaking hands reached for my lips, still feeling his warmth there.

You're such an idiot! Go after him.

Turning to follow him, Topher entered the kitchen, having likely heard everything. His blue eyes were wide as he took in the results of my work. "What happened here?"

I stared at the shattered remnants of the mug and raised my hands. "I happened."

His eyes scanned the room further. "You...you did this?"

I nodded and bent down to clean up the mess. He didn't offer to help, not even once. When I looked up, I saw a flicker of fear in his eyes. It didn't matter; he had every right to be scared of me and what I could become.

With each piece of glass I picked up, thoughts of Ryder and the unease from my nightmare lingered. My mother's cryptic words about trust echoed in my mind, amplifying my dread.

"You've come so far, my love. But beware—do not trust him."

I shook my head, trying to clear my racing thoughts. After the last shard was cleared away, I turned to Topher, feeling a knot of anxiety tightening in my stomach. "I, uh, I've decided. I'm going back to Castle Quinn with you."

His eyes widened, and a joyful grin spread across his face. Without hesitation, he scooped me up in a tight hug and twirled me around. "I knew you'd make the right decision! This is great news!"

I forced a smile, but uncertainty still gnawed at me. Topher's enthusiasm was infectious, but I couldn't get her voice out of my head.

"Do what is best. Do what you need to do."

Is that what I was doing?

Setting me down, excitement radiated from him. Grabbing

my head in his hands, he pulled me close, planting a kiss on the top of my forehead. "We'll return, and everything will fall into place. You'll see."

Emotions churned as I glanced down the hall toward Ryder's room. My heart tugged in conflicting directions, torn between desires like twin flames.

But I knew what I needed to do.

CHAPTER 35

THE JOURNEY from the kitchen to my bedroom seemed like an endless trek.

Every step carried the weight of my decision, burdening my shoulders. Ryder's door remained closed, and I resisted the urge to knock, knowing reconciliation was beyond reach now. I had hurt him, crossed yet another line.

His disappointment mirrored the first snowfall of winter.

Obvious and cold.

Amidst my chaotic thoughts, I knew deep down that reclaiming the throne was the best for myself and the kingdom's future. Yet, if it was truly the right choice, why was it so agonizing to leave him?

Gathering a satchel, I packed some clothing, each piece seeming heavier than the last. Sighing heavily, I sat on the edge of the bed, the satchel only half-full. Doubt whispered through my mind, its tendrils entwining around my thoughts.

The door creaked slowly, making my head snap up. My heart raced, and I prayed it was Ryder. Instead, Iris floated into the room, her wings casting a soft, colorful glow. I tried to hide my disappointment, aware that our interactions had been limited lately.

She settled atop my satchel, her eyes filled with unspoken questions. Though her melody was faint, I understood what she was asking.

"I'm sorry we haven't been able to spend much time together, but I'm sure Ryder filled you in a little last night. I can't even imagine what you two must have talked about. He was mad at me, wasn't he?"

Her brows furrowed, and her melody became more hostile as her arms tried to act out the events of the night before.

I shook my head. "I know, I know. I swear to you, I didn't mean to upset him." I confessed, "I just...I feel like I'm being pulled in two directions, and I have no clue which one is the best."

Her small figure darted towards me, now facing my direction. The melody was fast and chaotic, mirroring my inner thoughts over the past day. She gestured urgently towards Ryder's door, her eyes pleading.

"I *need* to do this. He'll understand one day. He may not now or in a few weeks, but he'll understand."

She dove into the satchel opening, prompting a light giggle from me. I gently picked her up, and her luminous eyes filled with concern.

Holding her in my palm, tears threatened to spill. "Iris, I can't bring you with me this time," I said. "I promised to keep the secrets of the Sprites safe. Bringing you would expose you and the whole Blessing. It's too dangerous."

Her wings trembled, and a somber look filled her eyes.

"Ryder will take good care of you, I know it. This isn't goodbye forever, just until we see each other again."

The melody faded to a faint hum as she glanced away. I yearned to grasp her words more than ever, sensing a connection in my heart, though I knew it was just my interpretation. After a moment of silence, she turned back to me. Recognition brightened Iris' eyes, which were tinged with lingering sadness.

A lump formed in my throat as I reached out to stroke her tiny form. "I will *never* forget you. No matter where I go or how long until we meet again, you'll always be in my heart."

With a reluctant nod, she fluttered away, leaving me alone in the room. I continued packing, the satchel gradually filling with my belongings. These clothes, once I returned, served no purpose beyond being tangible reminders of the life I had lived and the lessons I had learned.

They would be nothing other than proof I could be more than what I was raised to be.

Topher greeted me eagerly by the horses, his wide grin reflecting his excitement.

Stepping outside, the cold air hit me hard. It was a bitter reminder of the approaching Winter Solstice. Though it was still weeks away, the chill hinted at an early arrival. After finishing packing, I knocked on Ryder's door, but there was no answer.

I called his name several times—embarrassingly *begging* like a fucking idiot for him to talk to me—but he remained silent. Swallowing my pride, I muttered a muffled "Goodbye" through his closed door before leaving the cabin I had called home.

My familiar cloak suddenly felt like a thin towel against the cold air, but I would have to endure it. The ride back to Castle Quinn would take about a day if we were swift.

I could manage to stay warm enough until then.

Topher mounted Vieno, satisfied with his preparations. The cold already flushed his cheeks. Taking a deep breath, I joined him, my breath visible in the chilly air. I glanced back at the cabin once more, feeling a tug at my heart, but I chose to ignore it.

I didn't need another heartbreak.

"Are you ready?"

Forming a smile, I nodded. "As ready as I'll ever be."

Preparing to mount Jupiter, the cabin door creaked open behind me. My heart raced as I glanced back to find Ryder leaning casually against the door frame, his expression unreadable.

Caught in a silent hold, we stood there, staring at one another. I didn't dare blink, too scared that once I opened and shut my eyes, he'd be gone.

Hesitation gripped me, but an irresistible pull drew me toward him, that same pull I always felt with him.

Steeling myself, I pushed toward him, the air thick with our suppressed emotions. His eyes tracked my every step until I was standing face-to-face with him.

He was taller than ever.

Remaining stoic, I rose on my tiptoes, wrapped my arms around his neck, and pulled him into a tight hug.

There was a moment of surprise, perhaps even hesitation in his demeanor, but then his arms slowly encircled my waist, pulling me close to his chest. We stood there in silence, communicating what we were too cowardly to admit out loud.

His scent enveloped me, each note etching itself into my senses—branding my memory so well that no other smell would ever compare.

"Please," he whispered into my hair. "Please don't go. Stay here with me."

Swallowing back tears, I shook my head, hearing him inhale the scent of my hair. "No matter what you think of me right now, I am forever in your debt," I whispered, my voice breaking. "This isn't goodbye. I swear it."

I lightly kissed his scarred cheek, meeting his eyes filled with emotions before pulling away. Summoning all my strength, I turned away and made my way back to the horses. I didn't wait for him to respond. I couldn't handle whatever he might have said.

If he had asked again, I might have stayed forever.

Mounting Jupiter, I glanced back at Topher. His look of disgust and disappointment was unbearable. Swallowing the lump in my throat, I nodded to him, ready to continue.

Without acknowledging me, he lightly slapped Vieno's reins and urged the young stallion forward. Locking eyes with Ryder once more, I searched for something—*anything* that would convince me to stay.

Finding only admiration in his gaze, I took a deep breath and faced away. As Jupiter took his first step forward, I silently prayed to the gods, hoping this was the right decision.

"Wiyahna!"

Ryder stood in the middle of the yard, his scarred face calm. Anxiously, I waited for him to continue, fearing I had imagined his voice.

A small smile formed on his lips. "Don't yield."

My shoulders relaxed, warmth filling my chest as I smiled and nodded in agreement. "Never."

If Topher's angry glares didn't kill me, this fog would.

Vieno grew visibly uneasy as we entered the thick barrier, Topher's expressions mirroring those of his stallion. Unfortunately for everyone's mental health, this was our sole route to escape Forest Sylvie, so we had no choice but to press onward.

Considering Ryder and I had navigated it successfully before, I wasn't worried this time would be any different.

However, as we ventured deeper, my confidence waned from cocky navigator to lost and hopeless traveler. The fog thickened with each step, reducing visibility to near zero.

Dread filled my stomach, "Don't lose track of me," I warned, "Whatever you do, stay within earshot of me."

Going deeper, disorientation enveloped us. The forest's magic fucked with our senses, and I could feel Topher's fear and frustration growing.

The fog seemed...unsettled, even *angry*—as if resenting our decision to leave. Pushing aside unease, determination ignited within me. I had survived a Shadow Walker, a drunken fool, a manic knight, and my ex-fiancé. I would survive this fog, one way or another.

The more we pressed the louder Ryder's voice echoed in my mind.

Don't yield.

"We'll never get out of here," Topher muttered next to me.

Suppressing a sigh, I closed my eyes for a moment—attempting to tap into the intuition Ryder had worked endlessly to train.

"Never…" he continued to whisper. "All of this…nothing. Sh–she'll never forgive me…."

With my eyes still shut, I shushed him, and his mumbling stopped instantly. Listening again, the forest whispered around me, the only audible sound being the chilly breeze. In the distance, a bird chirped lightly, its song full of innocence and energy.

Wherever that bird was, I knew our way out wasn't far.

"Follow me!"

Confidently opening my eyes, I expected Topher beside me, but I was alone. Panic gripped my chest as I scanned the fog-shrouded surroundings.

No longer beside me, I *knew* the fog had claimed him. He had wandered off, ignoring my specific warnings.

Fuck. Fuck. Fuck.

"Topher!" I called, but my voice was swallowed by the fog.

Straining to hear, I could only make out the faint whispers of the mist. My anxiety continued to build as I remembered exactly what this fog was capable of. The Wayan people wanted to keep outsiders away, and this was proof that they were doing a damn good job.

Hey Ryder's ancestors, we're trying to leave—not stay!

Closing my eyes again, I took deep breaths to calm myself, feeling Jupiter's anxious fidgeting between my thighs. With each slowing beat of my heart, my senses returned. A gust of wind carried Vieno's scent, and the distant sounds of hoofbeats indicated their location in the fog.

Topher had gone about two hundred paces to the left, the complete *opposite* to where I stood.

"Hold on, Topher!" I called again, louder, praying he could somehow hear me.

The forest swallowed my voice, but I continued anyway. I urged Jupiter forward; he seemed just as determined as I did to retrieve our lost friend. The closer I got to where I thought Topher was, the more the fog messed with my senses. It was *toying* with me, using every means possible to stir me off the path.

But Ryder's voice continued to echo in my ears.

Don't yield!

I swear I passed the same tree a dozen times. Doubt began to echo in my mind. Was I even going in the right direction? Did I really hear Vieno or was that another way the fog was messing with me?

No matter. I wasn't going to give up.

Topher had already been lost in this fog once because of me, and I wasn't about to allow history to repeat itself.

A familiar warmth tickled up my spine, making it feel like Ryder was right next to me, guiding me through the fog. With my head held high and his phantom presence beside me, I swallowed my doubts and ignored the whispers pulling me away from Topher.

After what felt like *hours* of searching, I finally spotted a faint silhouette ahead. Relief washed over me as I rushed toward it. Topher emerged from the fog, a dazed expression on his face.

"Dammit, Topher! I thought I said to stay near me!"

His face was confused. "What are you talking about? I was following you the whole time."

"What?"

"You were riding so fast, I thought I was going to lose you," he said, clearly annoyed. "An answer when I ask you a question might be helpful next time."

The realization hit me like a ton of stones. The forest had created an image of *me* to separate us. A chill went down my spine as I grasped the depth of its power. If not for nearly losing him to the magical fog, my annoyance would have peaked.

I would have rather it ate us and got it over with.

"That wasn't me, Topher." I managed. "It's the fog... I-I tried to warn you–"

"You warned me the fog could confuse me to the point of getting lost like the last time, not manifesting a figure to look like you and direct me completely away!"

His face had gone pale, and I didn't blame him; mine must have looked just as drained.

"Well, regardless, we need to be more careful. Here," I said, grabbing rope from the satchels and tossing it to him. "Hold onto this and follow me. I think I know the way out."

As I turned back to Topher, the questioning glare on his face didn't go unnoticed. I knew that look. It was the same one he would give me when I insisted I wasn't too sore to train. The same one when I said I was happy to marry Xander.

Doubt. The bastard was *doubting* me.

"Just trust me."

Smacking his teeth, he wrapped the rope around his hands. "Yeah, because anything in this fog is *so* trusting."

I shot him a sharp glare, tightening the rope around my hands. The fog swirled around us, hiding ancient trunks, gnarled roots, and other obstacles. Despite our doubts, I trusted Ryder's knowledge and instinct to guide us through, feeling his familiar presence beside me.

When I began to lose hope, the air began to clear. The tangled branches overhead thinned, allowing small streaks of muted sunlight to break through the canopy. Like a passing rainstorm, the obnoxious fog lifted, revealing Forest Sylvie's exit ahead of us.

Clear, *beautiful* air filled our lungs.

"We made it," I said. "Thank the *gods*, we made it!"

Topher dropped the rope, taking a deep breath full of fresh air. "I would be happy never to see fog again." He cracked his knuckles.

I nodded, not sharing his sentiment but at least being thankful we made it out alive.

Now out in the open, the clouds above us were moving fast and growing darker by the second. With how cold it was, I doubted they were rain clouds, which only meant one thing.

The first snow of the season was here.

"If we head back towards the village, it should lead us to the main road back to the castle," he confirmed, eyes pointed towards the sky.

"It's going to snow, Topher. We should find shelter before it starts. We can continue in the morning."

We were on the opposite side of the forest from Eudora, and I wasn't sure how Ryder's magical tent would hold up in a snowstorm. Topher, having tracked me for weeks, knew these lands better than I did. If there was another village on the way to Castle Quinn, he would know.

I would have to stay hidden, but at least we wouldn't die of frostbite.

"It's not going to snow," he snapped. "We continue forward."

"But—"

"Genevieve," he warned, "just trust me."

Don't trust him, my love.

My mother's voice echoed in my mind, but I shook it off. It was probably still just the fog messing with me from a distance. Right?

Not wanting to argue, I straightened my back and mentally prepared for the hours of riding ahead. Pulling out the familiar piece of cloth, I reluctantly tied the fabric over my head.

"Let's head ou—" He turned towards me. "What are you doing?"

My brows furrowed together. "Waiting on you?"

"No." He pointed to my hood. "What's with the head wrap?"

"Oh. To cover my white hair. I've been doing it to keep hidden. You know, *'wanted for murder'* and all that?"

His eyes rolled—actually *rolled*. I don't think I had ever seen him roll his eyes at me other than sarcastically or flirtatiously.

"Not needed, Genevieve," he said dismissively. "I know the huntsman may have wanted you to hide, but you don't need to when you're with me."

What the fuck was his issue?

"It wasn't Ryder who asked that of me. It was your *sister*."

He shrugged. "Still not needed. I can protect you."

"I'm not doubting that, Topher, but it still might be safer for me to keep my hair as it has been to avoid any bumps in the road."

"Fine. Do what you want to do. All I'm saying is it's *not* needed."

I snorted. "Noted."

Slapping Vieno's reins, Topher took the lead. His attitude

was less than wanted, but I didn't care enough right now to figure out the root of it. We were out of the fog and safe. That's all that mattered.

His comments about my hair were stirring my anger. Regardless of his opinion, it made me feel safe. Didn't that mean something to him?

Safety. I could almost laugh at the word.

At the end of the day, I wouldn't feel safe until I was back in the castle with a full pardon. Topher was optimistic about my aunt and my return, but I was filled with doubt.

I doubted Liliana would retract her accusations, doubted returning to the castle before discovering my father's murderer was the right choice, doubted everything would fall back into place. I doubted my mother was a Witch—doubted *I* could be one too.

I shouldn't have left Ryder.

Doubt was a bitch of a creature, creeping in no matter how confident I had felt. All I could hope was that it would go away, leaving me alone with my demons.

Come to think of it, maybe it should stay.

It could distract me.

Chapter 36

Topher had barely spoken to me since leaving the fog.

I didn't mind it, honestly. We had already passed one village, but he refused to stop. Hardly anyone was out due to the temperature, so we passed with ease. The later it got in the day, the colder the air grew. Eventually, we passed a sign that pointed one direction toward Claremont Harbor and another toward Castle Quinn.

Looks like Topher knew his way after all.

Riding wasn't unbearable in the weather, but we both agreed to continue until nightfall, only stopping to take care of personal needs and have a light snack.

Traveling alongside Topher was so different from traveling with Ryder. At times, I missed our banter—my persistent questioning, his initial reluctance, the eventual opening up. I missed the sparkle in his golden and sapphire eyes, how they lit up with joy whenever Iris contributed to our discussions, relishing her companionship to our expedition.

Topher was so...stiff.

Has he always been like this?

Sure, he was a stickler for the rules and kept me in line, but how he held himself to such high standards and ethics seemed so foreign to me. Being out on the road had taught me many things about the life I lived before all this shit, but I didn't think the relationships I had with the people I cared about could have been different too.

The clouds continued to grow dark, and when I looked up, a small snowflake landed on the tip of my nose.

I knew it was going to snow!

I couldn't help but smile. Snow was the last thing we needed, but I always loved it as a child. It reminded me of Mother and those mornings after the first big snowfall. She'd sneak into my room and we'd head to the courtyard. Even the servants were still asleep, but it didn't matter—the grounds were ours.

Laughter echoed as we threw snowballs, built forts, and made snow Sprites. No matter how cold we got, Mother would bring me inside, kneel to my level, and give me the warmest hugs.

I'd warm up instantly, my body clinging to hers. Looking back, I wondered if that was her magic heating me up.

Topher cursed under his breath, snapping me out of the happy memories. "We can't ride through this. It's getting too thick. We'll have to make camp."

As I glanced around, it was clear the snow would pick up fast, but it was hardly more than a dusting. "It's not that bad right now. We could continue until—"

"We stop *now*."

I swear if he snapped at me one more time, I was going to decapitate him in his sleep.

It was about an hour before sunset and the forest fell into a hushed stillness, a serene quiet matched only by the falling snow. Topher led Vieno to a clearing where we dismounted, the snow settling on our cloaks and hair, the chill already beginning to seep in.

Topher rifled through his packs, hands moving urgently. I shifted my weight, rubbing my arms to ward off the chill. "Is there anything I can do to help?" I called out, my breath as thick as the fog.

Stepping away from the stead, he cradled an unmade, dirty tent. I raised a brow, not believing it would keep anything warm from the snow. "No ma'am," he replied with a shrug, "I'll have our tent set up in no time."

My stomach dropped. "Our tent?"

He couldn't hold back the stupid grin that smudged his face. "Well, I only needed one and I doubt you have one with you, so it looks like we're sharing tonight."

Rolling my eyes, I moved to Jupiter and searched through a satchel. A smile laced my face as I pulled out the small vial. "Haven't you learned not to underestimate me?"

"What do you me—"

Before he could finish, I opened the bottle and threw the piece of fabric to the ground. Just like it always did, it exploded before us into a full-size, completely built tent.

Topher's eyes grew in wonder, mouth slightly gaped.

A satisfied smile grew on my face. "Elven craftsmanship," I said, mimicking the same phrasing as Ryder.

"Oh well, that's...helpful," he mumbled.

While he searched for long enough branches to hold his tent, I set up the inside of mine. Unrolling the sleeping bag and arranging my bed, I gathered a few extra blankets for him, knowing whatever he had wouldn't be enough. The sound of crunching snow and Topher's occasional curses filled the air as I worked.

Stepping out, he had surprisingly gathered some wood for his tent and had a fire going. The flames danced merrily in the makeshift pit and the glow cast a warm, flickering light over the freshly fallen snow.

Topher secured the horses under a cluster of trees and made his way over. "Fire's going strong, and the horses should be safe. The trees will give them some shelter."

The stallions' breaths were visible in the frigid air.

"You think? It's pretty cold away from the fire."

He nodded confidently. "Horses are built for this kind of weather. They'll fare better than we will, that's for sure."

Turning back to the fire, I held my hands out and allowed the rising flames to warm my palms. Closing my eyes, I took in the smell of the burning wood along with the falling snow.

For a moment, I was transported back to the cozy cabin—the crackling fire warming my senses. I bet it looked beautiful covered in snow. Topher's footsteps prevented me from fully feeling at home, but I kept my eyes closed for a little longer.

He sat next to me, his breath warming my cheeks. He was close—too close. I knew he was watching me without even having to open my eyes.

As he took my hands in his, the rough calluses scraped against my warm palm. Having no other choice, I opened my eyes and gave him the attention he obviously wanted.

Snowflakes had begun to gather in his beard, and I chuckled at the sight. Removing one of my hands from his, I brushed the flakes away. Before I could retract my hand, he captured it again.

His expression was the softest it had been all day. Moving quickly, he raised my hands to his cold lips, planting a soft kiss on the backs. A month ago, this gesture would have weakened me at the knees.

Now, it felt off. *Wrong.* I politely smiled and subtly pulled my hand back.

"Genevieve. I meant what I said, you know. I *really* did miss you."

"I never doubted that."

"I'm not too sure what life will be like when we get back home," he admitted. "But no matter what happens, I'm just so glad *I* was the one who found you."

There was a look on his face, one I couldn't pin. I didn't know what my life would be like once we returned either, but I could only pray it would be worth it. Navigating life as a Queen without Father's guidance wouldn't be easy, especially now that the peace pact with the Fae was most likely over.

No matter. I would find a way. I would make Father proud.

"Me too," I replied. "I brought some leftovers from last night. Are you hungry?"

A wide smile lit up his face. "Always."

The snow only continued to fall harder as the sun fully set behind the Dalia Mountains.

Mother used to say that the bigger the flakes, the sooner the flurry would end. The damage to the fire was already past the point of no return, so instead of freezing all night, we decided to turn in.

Topher took the extra blankets with a more than thankful

enthusiasm. Mumbling a sleepy goodnight, I opened the flap to my tent.

"Are you certain you'll be okay for the night? I don't mind taking the floor if that means you'll feel safe."

"I'll be fine, Topher. This might be a cursed object," I said, patting my hip where the dagger laid, "but I'm more than capable of pulling it on someone if needed."

"I'm just worried about you. That's all."

"Well, as you know I have a big mouth so if I need saving, I'll make sure to scream extra loud."

Not giving him a chance to respond, I entered my tent and sealed the flaps shut. The coldness of the night followed me even inside my magic space. Ryder had said these tents were enchanted to keep us warm but thinking about it, maybe it was his warmth that was fueling the magic.

I flopped down on the cot, and my eyes eventually closed from the exhaustion of the past few days. The rhythmic drumming of the snow falling on the tent helped lull me to sleep and the sounds of the forest created a comforting symphony I had grown accustomed to. Sleep was just about to claim me when I was jolted awake by a sudden pressure on my shoulder.

Opening my eyes, I found Topher casually sitting beside me, his hand just next to my head on the pillow. The pounding of my heart increased, and I pulled my sheet over my chest. Thank the gods I had remained clothed before falling asleep.

"What are you doing?"

He hushed me with a gentle finger to my lips. "It's just me, Genevieve. I thought I heard something, so I was just checking in on you."

I'm going to bite that finger off.

Frowning, I shook away from his touch. "Well, I'm fine so you may go now."

He remained seated on my bed, still as a rock. It felt like minutes passed as we sat in a silent stare down.

"That night you left," he said breaking the silence, "I thought I would never see you again."

Rolling my eyes, I slumped back into my cot. "Weren't you the one who told me to return home to you?"

"It was more of a subtle prayer than a command. I had already made peace that I lost you to that prick of a prince, but then you were so frightened, and I could see it in your eyes that you had to leave. I just didn't understand."

I traced the top of the tent with my eyes, trying to forget the fear I felt. "It wasn't easy keeping it from you, but I knew Fiona would tell you everything."

He remained silent before swallowing. "Do you believe you'll be happy when you get back?"

I hesitated, purely because I don't even think I knew the answer. "No," I admitted. "Nothing will be the same without Father, but it's home. I'll find happiness eventually. I'll have to."

Topher shifted, twisting his body to look down at me. Even in the dark tent, I could see how blue his eyes were. "You know, *I'm* only happy when you're there. Those few days you were gone before I was sent to find you, it was like I lived a million years."

Way to make me feel guilty.

"I never meant to scare you."

"I know, but you *need* to know how much you mean to me," he whispered, eyes locked onto my lips.

"I do know. I think I've always known."

"No, I don't think you do."

"Topher, I—"

Like the night in the stables, he moved fast and closed the distance between us. Before I could process it, he leaned down and gently cupped my cheek until his lips met mine.

My eyes doubled in size, and I froze. His chapped lips moved desperately against mine, but unlike the night in the stables, I didn't kiss him back.

As I pushed him away, my voice was barely audible. "We can't do this."

"*Why*?" His desperate eyes searched mine, but I was unsure if they would find what he was looking for.

"I-I just... We shouldn't," I stammered.

"Genevieve, why can't we? I care about you, and I *know* you care about me too."

"Of course I do! But it's not about that. It's about... I don't know, Topher. It's complicated."

He pulled back, his angry eyes boring into mine. "Complicated how? It's because of the huntsman, isn't it?"

Of course it is.

"It's just not the right time. With everything happening, I can't afford one more thing to distract me."

"Don't you think you *need* a distraction?"

"The only thing I *need*," I rebutted, "is to claim the throne and lead my kingdom into a new era of peace. If that wasn't the case, I would have never left Ryder."

He shook his head. "I know you've been shutting me out for years! All those mornings on the training field, all those evenings escorting you to dinners you would rather die than be at, our bond grew, and so did my feelings."

I was speechless.

"I just... Dammit, Genevieve! I can't let you go back until I prove to you how much you mean to me. No matter what happens, you *need* to know."

When he closed his eyes and moved to fill the gap between us once more, I reached my hand under my pillow and removed my dagger. The motion was also too mechanical, like it was a third limb I had used all my life.

My mind worked on its own. Some dark, hidden force from within took over before I could stop her. But honestly, I didn't know if I wanted to.

When I brought it to his neck, his eyes shot open as he felt the cool metal against his skin.

All I could see was *red*.

"Evie...w-what are you doing?"

My lips trembled as I applied enough pressure until he slowly backed off me. "I'm so sick of others thinking they know what's best for *me* or thinking they know what *I* want." I tried to hide the trembling in my voice, but the mix of anger and shock overtook me. "I am to be your queen, and I know the feelings you've harbored for me, but that is no excuse to think you can take what isn't yours."

Backing off, he raised his hands in surrender. His skin had gone pale, and I would see the fear in his eyes. "Genevieve, now hold on. Please. I wasn't trying to take anything. I-I just wanted to show you tha—"

"That what, Topher?" I was growing angrier by the second. I felt the call of my magic, my powers urging to break free, but I wouldn't lose control again. "That you *'care'* for me? Do you see this as care? Barging into my tent and kissing me without consent?"

"No! I-I'm sorry. I didn't mean anything, it's just..." He

suddenly stopped babbling, and his voice trailed off as a faint glow illuminating his frightened face. "Evie...y-your hands."

My gaze shifted from his eyes to my hand still holding the dagger at his throat. A soft, silvery light emanated from my fingertips, like tiny bolts of lightning crackling and dancing between them.

I could feel my magic urging to escape my control.

It was the same feeling I felt when I lost my temper with Ryder, the same power that catapulted Xander off me in that storage room. A cold sweat broke out on my forehead; the warmth tingling through my hands was a warning. I knew it.

As I dropped the dagger to the ground, Topher immediately jumped off from my cot and stepped as far away from me as he could without exiting. Never had I seen him so terrified.

Don't lose control. Get it together!

"Genevieve I—"

"Just stop," I whispered, trying to regain control. Closing my eyes, I tried to imagine something calming, something that made me happy and could pull me out of the temptation I was feeling. "I know you didn't mean to scare me., but please, go. We'll talk about this in the morning."

I left no room to argue, and he didn't speak another word before I heard him exit my tent and seal it closed. The night had gone deathly still, but I kept my eyes closed.

I knew he cared for me, loved me even. He had proven that the night I felt Castle Quinn.

But what the hell was he thinking?

The Topher I knew would have *never*. I had imagined it a time or two; I'll admit it to myself. When I was younger, I would have given anything for him to come knocking on my door one night and take me.

But I was no longer his. I was no longer the Genevieve who left that night in search of her father's killer.

And it seems he was no longer the Topher I knew either.

Finally feeling my power return to its hidden chambers deep in my soul, I opened my eyes and found nothing but a cold, dark tent. Relief washed over me, but dread for the day ahead still loomed.

I wondered what Ryder was doing right now. Was he awake, worrying about me? Or perhaps he was just as relieved to get rid of me like I was to get rid of Topher.

As I shut my eyes, a small, familiar howl echoed throughout the cold woods.

CHAPTER 37

I DIDN'T SLEEP. How could I?

A good mix of anxiety for the day ahead and the voice inside my head telling me I made the wrong decision helped in keeping me awake.

The sound of falling snow eventually stopped, leaving just me, my thoughts, and the sound of deep snoring from the next tent over. My mind must have allowed me to fall asleep at some point because one moment I was suffering in the cold tent and the next, I was in the dark, familiar courtyard of Castle Quinn.

I immediately rushed to the backdoors, picking up where my last nightmare had left off. The doors, of course, were locked. Pounding with my fists until they went numb, I felt stuck in an endless loop.

Mother was already there, watching me from the shadows. Her eyes were the still barren, milky white pools that they were last time. When she turned, her face was sad, echoing my feelings.

"Mother?"

Her head snapped back unnaturally fast before tilting to the side. *"Genevieve, what have you done?"*

My heart plummeted. *"What do you mean? I left to come home. I did what was best—as you told me!"*

A growl echoed behind her, and the wolf emerged. My mother's neck returned to a more natural position, her hand resting under the massive wolf's chin.

"I told you not to trust him. You cannot trust him, my love."

When she withdrew her hand, the wolf advanced towards me. I tried to move, to take a step forward, but I was paralyzed. Again.

"I did as you told me. I don't understand what I did wrong!"

The wolf approached, its warm breath washing over my face.

"The future is in your hands now, my love," she whispered from behind the beast.

My hand reached out, trembling fingers grazing the soft, familiar fur of the wolf. It leaned into my touch before the hackles of its fur stood on end. Behind me, the lock on the door turned and all three of us tensed. My mother's foggy eyes remained on the door, and another low growl emerged from the wolf's throat.

The doors creaked open, and a blinding light spilled out. I turned toward the light, and the silhouette of Topher emerged, anger etched on his face. I backed into the chest of the wolf, desperately trying to get as far away from him as possible.

"I thought I told you!" he spat in an unfamiliar voice. *"Keep that dog at bay!"*

I retreated further into the fur, hoping it would either shield me or suffocate me. Topher's rough calloused hand grabbed my wrist, pulling me away from the wolf, and pain shot through my arm, prompting me to yelp.

The wolf bared its teeth, but Topher paid it no mind.

"You were never his. You will always end up with me. Always."

Gasping from the pain, I tried to pull away, but his grip was firm.

"I took you away from him once before, what makes you think I'll let you go now that I have you?"

Another—deeper growl emerged from my wolf—a warning to the knight. Everything became fuzzy and I feared my heart might just burst out of my chest.

"Run, my love," Mother whispered.

But before I could, the wolf lunged.

Gasping for air, I was violently thrown out of my nightmare. Mother's haunting voice lingered at the edges of my consciousness, but I was back in the cold tent. I must have kicked my blankets off during my dream. They were spread out all over the floor beneath me and even though the chill of the night still crept through the fabric, I felt like I was on fire.

Running a shaky hand over my sweat-damphair, I knew I needed to cool off if I hoped to get any more sleep. With a deep breath, I moved off my cot and grabbed my cloak and boots. As I stepped out of my tent, the cool air was a welcome relief from the blaze of my skin.

The night was still, as you would assume the dead of night to be. Creatures were fast asleep, hoping to survive the first snow of winter. The land was beautiful, the soft glow of the moon illuminating the fresh, untouched ground as if a painting.

I closed my eyes for a moment, taking in the calming aroma

of the woods. The air was crisp, and the scents of pine and snow filled my senses, slowly calming my racing heart.

How was I ever to return to a life behind stone walls when all of this was waiting for me?

The taste of freedom away from the duties of being a princess had grown addicting, so addicting that it took everything in me not to hop on Jupiter and never look back. But I had made a commitment, and we were far too close to Castle Quinn to turn back now.

Even with how angry I was with Topher.

We would move past it, like we always did, but I knew I could never look at him the same. Perhaps he thought the same of me.

Honestly, I didn't care.

Despite the chill of the night, a familiar warmth tickled around me like an embrace. Opening my eyes, I scanned my surroundings. Feeling a familiar pull, I glanced over my shoulder to find warm, glowing eyes looking back at me and the dark silhouette of my wolf came into view.

Like always, it towered over me, even from a distance.

Having just seen the creature in my dreams, seeing it again in person was night and day. My mind's memory could never truly capture how stunning the creature was. Its eyes glowed in the moonlight, fire and ice harmonizing in the most beautiful way.

I felt no fear under the creature's gaze.

Not like I had the first time.

Had it been following me? Looking after me again?

The pull grew stronger, and despite my better judgment, I took a hesitant step forward. The moment I moved, it let out a small sigh, turned on its massive heels, and bolted away from the camp, disappearing into the darkness of the forest.

Its warmth followed.

I stood there, watching as it blended in with the night until I could no longer tell where the top of my wolf's head stopped and the sky began.

Disappointment lodged its way into my heart as the last sliver of my adventure disappeared.

With one last glance at the moonlit forest, I turned back to the tent, hoping morning would come slowly.

The sun eventually rose, and I dreaded every moment.

If the gods could listen to my prayers, they were surely tired of hearing my voice. All I needed was for the day to go smoothly and for everything to fall into place.

That wasn't too big of an ask, right?

Not wanting to prolong the day any further, I rose from my cot and got dressed. Stepping outside my tent, I was nearly blinded by how bright the sun's reflection off the snow-covered ground was. Allowing my eyes to adjust, I went to check on the horses.

The fire had died from the snow, but with how far we had tethered them I doubt it would have provided any warmth anyway.

Both steeds were alive and well, and maybe a little hungry. Jupiter's brown eyes connected with mine as I reached my travel companion. His snout was cold to the touch, but the sorrow in his eyes was what struck me the most.

My mother always told me animals could sense and feel our emotions. Could he feel the dread and worry I harbored for the day ahead? Or was he just as equally dreading the return home as I was?

"Don't worry, old friend," I said, petting his cold snout. "You'll see Reaper again one day. I know it. Plus, think of all the food waiting for you back at the stables! You'll be a fat horse in no time."

When he neighed in response, a small smile played on my lips. The sound of crunching snow echoing behind me pulled me away from the brief burst of contentment I had felt. Not turning to look, I knew Topher was awake and approaching.

"Good morning, Genevieve," he said cautiously from behind.

My shoulders immediately tensed, but I rolled them out and turned my head to look at him.

The look of regret on his face was clear. Or was it fear of the monster he decided to return home to claim the throne? I met his gaze with a guarded expression. His eyes, once so familiar and comforting, were simply the eyes of a man I once knew.

"Good morning, Topher." I kept my tone neutral. "I trust you slept well?"

He shifted uncomfortably, his eyes flicking to the snowy ground before meeting mine again. "As well as I could given the circumstances. But, uh, I was hoping we could talk about last night."

I steadied my breathing, trying not to let the anger I felt the previous night take over. "Very well."

Scratching his thick beard, he took another step closer, and

I took two steps back. "When I came to you last night, I came with no ill intentions, I swear to you. Look, Genevieve, I've never been the best at making the right decision and last night proved that. I know how I approached you was wrong, but I needed to show you how I felt. If you didn't know before we returned...well, I guess I feared what we had would be lost."

I sucked in a breath. "Then have a conversation with me like an adult, not some maiden you can throw yourself on!"

"I didn—"

Raising my hand, I paused his explanation. "Allow me to speak. I trust you, Topher. I've trusted you since the moment I knew what the word meant, if not before. But when I say no, I mean it. Emotions are high, I understand that. But if you ever, and I mean ever, betray my trust that makes me question the man you are again, it'll be the last chance you receive. Do I make myself clear?"

Topher's shoulders slumped as he looked at me with a disappointed glare. "It was just a kiss! And not our first, might I add!"

"It was a kiss I didn't ask for nor want!" I snapped, a soft light flickering from my fingers.

"So you pull a dagger on me? What would have happened if you lost control? Not only was it reckless of you to use such a weapon, but we both know you can't control whatever magic consumes you! One wrong move and you could have *killed* me!"

"I'm not some child who runs through the halls with scissors! And I'm not some blight you need to fear. If you can't even trust or believe in me, who will?"

The forest fell silent, the sound of our anxious, heavy breathing coating the calm. "You've changed, Genevieve," he whispered. "I thought maybe it was just the influence the huntsman had on you but...I can see it now."

"Perhaps I have."

"Look, I'm not mad at you. You just need to forget what you've learned while away. Time back at the castle will fix that, I know it. All you have to do is get back into a routine and things will go back to normal. You'll see!"

How dare he?

"And if they don't?" I challenged. "Can you handle the woman I've become?"

"Oh, Genevieve." He reached for my shoulder. "I know we can push the magic away and get back to how we were. Everything will be fine, I promise."

It took everything in me to not flinch away from his touch, but we were so close to getting back. If I threw on a mask, I might survive this. I was growing tired of failing at being the person he wanted me to be. If I could be her at least until we got back to the castle, I would have authority over him.

Out here, I was just Genevieve, and it was clear he was taking advantage of that.

Do not trust him, my love.

Throwing on a smile that didn't reach my eyes, I stepped away from his touch and moved to our horses. "We should probably start getting ready. The horses will be warmer once we get them moving."

I turned to head back to my tent, but his hand caught mine. The familiar warmth of my magic trickled from my spine to my fingertips, but I swallowed it down.

"Genevieve? Are we okay?"

Gathering my strength, I turned my head over my shoulder

to meet his gaze. I didn't exactly smile, but my face hid my true emotions.

His eyes were soft, but his face held a look I couldn't place. Worry? Dread? It was hard to tell with him nowadays.

Did I even really know him?

Swallowing my annoyance, I gave him a quick, fake smile. "We're fine. Now let's do this before I literally grow cold feet."

I walked back toward our camp, praying he would follow without another word.

Thank the gods, he did.

CHAPTER 38

TOPHER CONVINCED ME the snowy roads meant no one would be out.

Not looking to argue, I kept my hood up, allowing me to feel hidden without the headwrap he seemed to hate so much.

The snow had covered all the kingdom, and it made the ride more beautiful. The pure, untouched grounds helped calm my nerves about returning home. The remainder of the journey to Castle Quinn went as Topher predicted—no one, not even another passing traveler, was on the road. Small animals would occasionally dart in and out of sight, but other than that, we were alone, but I couldn't shake the feeling of eyes on me. Topher took the lead, so he was out of the question.

Every time I looked behind me, expecting to see someone or something, I saw only snow.

Familiar landmarks started to register the closer we got to the castle, and my stomach churned with nerves. I knew it was most likely my anxiety about returning home after a month away, but everything felt off. When we ascended a small hill, the castle's spires pierced the gray sky.

This was it. I was *home*.

Once we reached the moat between us and the castle gates, a wave of dread washed over me. Topher approached first, calling up to the guard on duty. I couldn't help the pounding in my chest or the trembling in my hands. The familiarity of the castle, once a source of comfort, now felt like a looming shadow.

As we waited, an owl hooted from a branch. Its white feathers practically blended in with the landscape, but its silver tips stood out.

It watched us—watched *me*.

Where have I seen this owl before?

"State your business!" a voice boomed from above us.

Locked in a staring competition with the owl, I didn't look to see who was manning the gates.

"Sir Topher approaches, Sir Edward. I have returned to bring the princess home."

Sir Edward cursed from the tower before the sound of the drawbridge lowering made the owl take flight. The creature narrowed its silver eyes before vanishing into the sunny sky.

The gates groaned and moaned as they opened. Topher's demeanor slightly shifted, as if he too was nervous to enter.

His usual confidence faltered, replaced by a tension that matched my growing anxiety. "Follow me."

The castle grounds, typically bustling with activity, were strangely deserted. The familiar faces of guards and servants were conspicuously absent, and an eerie silence settled over the courtyard.

"Where is everyone?"

He glanced around, feigning nonchalance. "Must be the snow. People are probably staying inside."

I shook my head. My people *loved* the snow, and usually, the paths around the castle would have been cleared by now. Yet, everything was untouched, not even a single footprint marking the snow.

Even with my unease, we dismounted, and Topher led the horses into the stables. My whole body felt numb from the cold, and I desperately rubbed my hands together to generate warmth.

Returning with a blank expression on his face, Topher avoided eye contact as he focused on the castle. Without a word, he led the way and cleared a path to the same back doors that had haunted my dreams.

Opening them, he allowed me to enter first. The emptiness inside mirrored the courtyard. An unsettling silence overtook us, the only sound coming from the shutting doors. Even my footsteps echoed through the vacant hall.

"Something's wrong," I murmured.

Finally meeting my gaze, Topher's eyes reflected his annoyance. "It's just the snow, Genevieve. People are likely staying in their quarters. Stop overreacting."

His lack of reassurance only increased the feeling of danger in my gut. Continuing down the hall, I rounded a corner to head to my bed chambers. My detour didn't go unnoticed.

"Where are you going?"

"To my room? I want to see Fiona."

His face paled. "I think it would be best if you spoke with Liliana first. I know she's anxious to see you."

I scoffed. "No, I think it would be best if I changed and saw your sister before meeting with my aunt. Trust me, she would die if she saw me in these clothes."

He took a warning step forward. "I'm sorry, Genevieve, but I'm afraid I'm going to have to insist."

Feeling like I couldn't say no, I reluctantly followed him. Unease still gnawed at me as we neared the throne room. Growing warmer from being indoors, my frozen fingers began to thaw until the burning was evident. I was overwhelmed and whatever awaited me behind those doors would make it worse. I just knew it.

Approaching the doors, Topher hesitated and turned to face me. "You mean the world to me, Genevieve," he mumbled. "Just...just remember that."

Not allowing me the chance to respond, he pushed them open. The room was dimly lit despite the mid-afternoon hour, and an ominous stillness consumed it, the air inside heavy.

As my eyes adjusted to the low light, the silhouette of three figures became clear. Liliana sat on my father's throne, guards stationed on each side. My mother's golden crown was perched proudly atop her ebony hair, and I couldn't help but scrunch my nose in disgust.

"Genevieve," her voice echoed. "Welcome back. Did you enjoy your little '*adventure*'?"

Remaining silent, Topher encouraged me further. Under my cloak, my hand instinctively went to the dagger still hidden on my hip.

"Come now, dear niece." She leaned forward on the throne. "It's rather rude not to answer after your *queen* has spoken to you."

A laugh bubbled in my throat. "*My* queen? I must be dreaming."

Liliana's brown eyes glistened in the candlelight, "Surely your knight filled you in. Once you decided to become an enemy of the crown and *murder* your father, it was left up to me to secure the future of the kingdom. So *yes*, I am your queen, and *no*, you are not dreaming."

A wicked smile curved her lips, knotting my stomach. I shot a look toward Topher, his eyes fixed on my aunt. With his emotionless face and squared shoulders, I was no longer standing next to an old friend but a trained knight.

I returned my attention to Liliana. "From what I was told, you took the throne until I returned. Well, here I am. You may step down now."

Seeming bored, she picked at her sharp, crimson-red nails. "No, I don't think I will." Her cold gaze shifted to Topher. "I appreciate your assistance, Sir. Quite the asset, isn't he? Rather a good little *rat*. I knew he wouldn't disappoint me when it came to capturing you."

My eyes shot up at Topher, but he still refused to look at me. His whole body trembled, his lip slightly quivering.

"Topher?"

Silence.

Liliana chuckled, "What's the matter? Didn't he tell you?"

"Tell me what?"

"He's been so obedient, finding you out there and bringing you back to his queen. Not that he had too much of a choice. The stakes were rather high for him if he failed."

Panic and regret coated his face as he looked at me. "Genevieve, I... She took Fiona! The night you left, they swore they would kill her if I didn't bring you back! I didn't have a choice! It was either you or my sister."

I was speechless as I looked at him in horror.

He had done exactly what I had feared: he had led me straight to my death sentence. He betrayed my trust. *Again*.

"I swear to you, everything I did was for *her*. She's my *sister* and your best friend! You would have done the same."

"*No*," I finally whispered. "I would have rather died than betray anyone I loved."

Swallowing, he took a hesitant step toward me. Freezing mid step, his body tensed as his eyes flew toward my aunt.

"Enough with the dramatics." She yawned. "You are dismissed."

Topher's head snapped towards her, the rest of his body still frozen. "We had a bargain! You swore Fiona would be released once I delivered Genevieve!"

"And she will be," Liliana calmly confirmed. "But I never said when or how."

With a wave of her hand, Topher did a too-stiff turnabout and made his way out of the throne room, the large doors closing behind him. Liliana's magic smelt as foul and rotten as her soul.

My whole body was on fire, and I saw red.

Everything I knew—everything I *trusted*—was betraying me.

"Oh, come now, niece. You can't blame a knight for being loyal to the crown."

My anger was overwhelming, but I remained silent, almost too angry to speak.

"You see, this throne has always belonged to me," she continued. "It was my destiny. My *birthright*, until your bitch of a mother decided to bat her green eyes at Leonard, and he chose her as the future queen."

Heat rose to my cheeks. "My mother w—"

"Your mother was *weak*," she spat, "had been since we were girls. Our whole lives had been planned out for us. We had been taught, trained for the future our elders promised. But then, her weak heart fell in love and ruined it for our people, and I was stuck here to watch her failure unfold."

The room became so silent, you could hear a pin drop. Waving her hands, she dismissed the guards, leaving us to talk in private. My eyes followed their every step, feeling betrayed by them as well.

Once our audience was gone, Liliana relaxed into the throne. Her gaze scrutinized me as she casually crossed one leg over the other. "Since it's just us two ladies now, let's lay it all on the table. I know you're not a fool, Genevieve. You've seen enough by now. It's all written on your face."

I met her gaze with defiance. "I'm not too sure what you mean."

"Don't try to pull your shit on me. I can practically *smell* the adolescent magic radiating from you, waiting to be explored. Say the words, dear. Confirm what you've found out."

My heart pounded in my chest. "What? That we're Witches?"

Liliana's eyes gleamed with triumph. "There she is." She clapped her hands mockingly. "The little Witch knows her truth! If it had been up to me, I would have told you the moment you came of age, but your damn mother forbade it, making the coven take a blood oath of all things to prevent it from slipping."

She scoffed at the memory, and one flooded through my mind. Fiona had mentioned the same thing—that a *blood oath* had prevented her from telling me too much information.

Could...could Fiona be a Witch too?

My mind raced and I felt faint, but I stood firm, refusing to show any sign of weakness.

"After announcing your engagement, I anticipated your powers would begin to emerge. Given that our abilities mirror the Fae, I suspected they would surge once you were in their presence. It's a shame your father didn't adhere to his promise in the end. Who knows what your power would be if you had sealed the deal?"

Liliana's monologue struck me hard. It left me grappling to piece together what she was implying. As the seconds ticked by, everything clicked into place. Once I understood, it felt like a punch in the gut.

How the hell did I not see this coming?

"You summoned that Shadow Walker to kill him." Liliana's smile widened, but she remained silent, basking in my horror.

She chuckled. "It appears I haven't given you enough credit. Yes, I'm afraid that creature was of my creation. A *'gift from the dark arts,'* a *'puppet crafted to do my bidding'*, whatever you wish to call it. Your father's death was necessary for my ascension to the throne. It had to be done."

"Why?" My voice was a rage filled whisper. "Why take *his* life? It would have been easier to kill me, considering I am the rightful heir after him."

"Your father wasn't as old as you may have perceived him to be." Her smile faded. "A chance for him to create another heir was always possible. Of course, he refused to take another lover after your mother, but accidents have happened before. I hadn't originally planned on taking his life, but when he came into my chamber that night before your wedding, spewing nonsense about calling it off? Well, I took measures into my own hands."

My face fell. I was a brat that night and he *died* because of it!

"If you do anything, and I mean anything, to jeopardize this union, including your relationship with your little knight, you'll find the consequences can be far more dire than you can fathom."

The warning was there all along. "So what? Was your whole plan me marrying Xander so Witches could rise in power? Or did you simply mean to start another war? I doubt Father's court would have agreed to a Witch being on the throne."

"The wedding wasn't my first choice, but it made the most sense. I was cursed with being barren—a fact I hadn't learned until it was too late to reverse, even with a brew. Of course, it would have been awkward, but I would have gotten used to it after the first few times."

"What would be awkward?"

As if planned perfectly, the air in the room shifted. The unmistakable scent of magic wafted around me, but I knew it wasn't hers. Although equally as potent, this magic had a sickly-sweet scent, like a rotting corpse.

Facing the smell, the same owl from earlier, the one I now recognized from my vision, swooped through the room. I ducked as it aimed for my head, its powerful wings stirring the air.

With grace, the creature landed beside my aunt on the throne, its silver eyes fixed on me. A whirlwind of energy surrounded it, consuming it in a shimmering vortex of light. White and silver feathers scattered and fell like confetti, the blinding display of colors peaking before slowly fading away.

As the magical storm settled, the owl vanished leaving a lean, well-dressed Xander in its wake.

Gracing me with his typical wicked smirk, his silver eyes

turned dark before turning his attention toward my aunt on the throne. "Good afternoon, my queen," he greeted Liliana, reaching his hands out to her.

My eyes widened in horror as Liliana's long fingers slowly enclosed around Xander's. My mouth dropped open as I noticed my engagement ring settled nicely on her left hand. Lightly pulling her up from the throne so they could stand face-to face, a smile gracing her features as he bent down to meet her.

Horror turned to nausea as I watched my once-fiancé plant a long, loving kiss on my aunt's lips.

CHAPTER 39

WHAT. The fuck. Was happening.

Removing their lips from one another after what seemed like *years*, Xander and Liliana turned back toward me—their intertwined fingers still lingering.

"Ah, Genevieve," Xander said as if he had *just* noticed me. "My apologies. I suppose I didn't recognize you dressed like...that."

His eyes roamed over me as thoroughly as ever. Either the impact from my kick had caused temporary memory loss, or he hadn't informed my aunt about our little encounter a few days ago.

It didn't matter; I was disgusted.

Upset, betrayed, horrified, and now *disgusted*.

"There's no need to have such a sour look on your face," Liliana spat, resuming her place on the throne. "You surely have forgotten that, despite his youthful appearance, Xander is far closer to my age than yours."

"You don't look a day over thirty, my queen," he cooed, taking her hand once more and raising it to his lips.

An unfamiliar blush coated her cheeks.

"As I mentioned," she continued, "I, unfortunately, am barren, so a union between Xander and you made the most sense. Your child would still hold the blood of a Supreme Witch and the Royal Fae. Mixing the two would create the most powerful heir this kingdom—this *realm*—has ever witnessed. Two creatures blessed by the power of the gods. Think of it!"

"So, you planned to use my body to birth the heir you wouldn't be able to?" A laugh escaped my throat. "What? Xander would fuck me in the morning and then turn around and fuck you in the evening? You two are *sick*."

"Watch your mouth!" she snapped, her free hand pointing at me.

My body became tight, like someone was wrapping their arms around me. I was paralyzed, completely unable to move other than my eyes and mouth.

It was the same magic she used on Topher. It *reeked*. It wrapped around my body like a vice, and I was clueless how to counteract it with my own.

"You were always such a disappointment," she continued. "I told your father allowing you to train would do more harm than good. That mouth of yours is an embarrassment."

"My training made me strong," I spat back. "Ask your *lover*. He witnessed a few blows from me."

Unfazed, Xander picked a piece of lint off his black suit. "She kicked like a girl. Hardly a scratch after."

Fucking liar.

Liliana smirked. "Hmm. You claim to be *so strong* yet your father had to convince your knight to let you win against him."

I felt the hit of her words on my cheek like a slap. "You-

you're lying! Topher would have *never* let me win unless I earned it, and Father would never have asked that!"

"It seems perhaps you don't know them well after all, dear. Leonard needed you to be confident that night he sold you off. A pity win for the first time after three years was the easiest way. You fell for it, and all your knight needed was a bump in his pay grade to agree."

She's lying. She must be!

My fingers burned, the hilt of my dagger still clenched in my hand. "None of that matters. I told Xander once, and I will tell you both until my lungs give out—I will *never* marry him! I will *never* be his bride!"

Her eyes narrowed. "I no longer require you to marry Xander, Genevieve. Now that the public sees you as an enemy, your face is of no use to me. But don't fret; your body will still be an asset when the time is right."

Disgust surged within me. "I'm not some prized mare you can breed whenever you like! You will never be my queen, and I will never yield!"

"Oh, trust me. I believe you will."

With a clap of her hands, two familiar faces entered the throne room. Commander Robert, looking as if he had aged ten years, dragged a nearly lifeless body behind him.

Horror clutched me as Fiona's bound and gagged form was thrown onto the floor at Liliana's feet. My body tensed, every muscle straining against invisible bonds, but it was useless.

Fiona's blue eyes met mine, mirroring the helplessness I felt.

Relishing in my despair, Liliana smirked. "Now, Genevieve, let's not make things more difficult than they need be. You'll do as you're told, or your dear friend will suffer the consequences. The choice is yours."

Fury ignited within me, but I swallowed it down, my focus on Fiona. She looked so weak. Her sun-kissed skin was pale and bruised, her once-gorgeous blonde hair now dull and tangled. She was always slender, but the month I had been gone had not been kind to her.

"Let her go!" I demanded. "She had *nothing* to do with any of this!"

"Oh, but she does, Genevieve. Fiona was the one who helped you escape that night, wasn't she? Despite knowing better, she hinted at things that should have remained hidden, correct? A little gratitude would be appropriate."

I scoffed. "You expect me to be grateful for imprisoning her? *Beating* her? You're delusional."

"That night, her betrayal could have cost her life, but I chose to keep her alive for this very moment of reunion. So yes, be grateful."

"Your escape caused quite a stir," Xander chimed in, taking a seat on the arm of the throne, "We had to make sure the loose ends were tied up. The maid became a liability."

"*Fiona*," I spat. "Her name is Fi-on-a!"

Xander shrugged, looking as bored as ever.

"Having her as your lady-in-waiting was never an accident," Liliana continued. "Seraphina came with us to the castle from our coven, and it was only a matter of time until Dawn had an heir with Leonard. A coven only thrives in numbers, after all."

My focus remained on Fiona. Her eyes pleaded with mine, and I knew she was silent urging me to stay strong and take this bitch down. Feeling tears start to form, I swallowed them back.

Ryder's voice screamed in my head.

Do not yield.

"You see, Genevieve," she continued as if she loved hearing her voice, "our coven grew tired of living in the shadows. Since the start of the war, we were forced to hide what we were. Our father held a decent standing, so she arranged an agreement with your grandfather to have me married off to Leonard. Of course, a little enchantment never hurts in the persuasion process." She chuckled. "Having me as queen would have secured our place in the kingdom. I shared my mother's vision, but Dawn ruined it all when she decided to take your father for herself."

Gods, would she ever stop talking?

"As queen, your mother played the role well enough, but when it came to fulfilling her duty within the coven, she fell rather flat. I knew she never had what it took. The crown she wore no longer thrived in the shadows we came from, so I did what needed to be done. Such betrayal wouldn't go unpunished, and I was more than happy to fulfill the deed on my own."

Fiona's muffled screams from her gag ripped through the air. Somehow finding the strength, her body twitched against her restraints.

"You know better than anyone that those restraints are charmed to prevent you from escaping," Liliana snarled.

Her movements stopped.

"Y-you killed her too, didn't you? That night...I always thought the darkness that consumed her was something I made up, but it was *you*! *You* killed your own sister?"

She shrugged, not an ounce of regret on her face. "A Witch must do what a Witch must do."

One way or another, I was going to end her life. I vowed it to myself. If it was the last thing I did, I would make her suffer as she had made my parents suffer. Somehow, some way, she would pay.

"Anyways, there's nothing you can do now, dear. Despite your small development of powers, you're no match for me. The more you comply, the easier we'll make things."

This was *insane*.

Every word she uttered was pure madness. Liliana had always been a wretched creature, haunting my nightmares with her cold, emotionless presence, but never could I have dreamed she would stoop so low as to murder her *sister* and brother-in-law.

I needed to bide my time until my power spiked. Even with her hold on me, I felt something brewing deep within my soul. It felt ancient, a long-forgotten power screaming to be released. My body was practically burning with it.

Shaking my head, I laughed. "Seems you've got it all planned out, haven't you? You got the man, the crown, and now your *perfect little princess* to bear you the heir your dusty vagina is incapable of."

A smirk formed on Xander's lips as he remained seated beside my aunt. She fumed as she opened her mouth to respond.

"The only thing I can't fully figure out is the war." I said, beating her to it. "Do you expect the Fae to just bend the knee to a Witch Queen after generations of trauma and bloodshed? Us *Witches*, after all, are the reason behind the war, right?"

"My mother agreed to a union between the heir to the Orphinian throne and her son," Xander said. "Which, theoretically, is still in place. The treaty never mentioned a specific name, love."

Commander Robert slightly fidgeted but remained silent.

"Her ways are those of the past," he continued. "For all these years, she never could see the power and potential in creating a union with Witches. She may hesitate, but once I'm crowned king and Liliana my queen, she will have no power over me."

"Our union will bring this realm into a new era," Liliana said, "one where the two most powerful races the world has ever seen will rule over all who bend the knee."

I suppressed a shudder. "And those who don't?"

A long, wicked smirk formed on their lips as they exchanged glances. "Haven't you noticed there are no servants?" my aunt asked. "Those who do not bend will simply cease to exist."

My heart plummeted to my stomach. There was no way she was implying what I thought she was. Faintness threatened to consume me at the possibility.

Liliana had *slaughtered* all the servants. That was why the courtyard was untouched, why the halls had been empty.

No one was *left*.

No one had *survived*.

"What have you done?" I hissed, my voice a low growl. "Those were *innocent* people!"

"They. Were. *Humans*." Her eyes sparkled with amusement. "A Witch doesn't require servants. Our magic takes care of that. They would have lived if they had chosen to bend the knee and follow. It's their fault, really."

"And the knights?" I asked, my voice trembling with anger and grief. "Do you think yourself so powerful that you wouldn't need their protection?"

Her expression darkened. "The knights are still scouring the realm in search of you. Once they return, a proper assessment will be made to see if they are worthy of living."

A cord deep within me was struck and it was enough to push me over the edge. Feeling the familiar surge of power, I no longer tried to keep it at bay. I welcomed it. A light formed at the tips of my fingers, and this time, the light wasn't simply a spark but a burning fire.

"You're a fucking *monster*!" I screamed. "You and Xander deserve each other."

"Finally, we agree on something."

"And you, Commander Robert?" I spat in his direction. "Have you lost your spine?"

His face grew pale, but he remained silent. The fire within me continued to build until I was no longer Genevieve, the Wanted Princess.

No. In that moment, I was a force of nature.

A reckoning Liliana would soon regret unleashing.

I locked eyes with her, the voice that escaped my throat hardly my own. "You will pay for every life you've taken, for every drop of blood you've spilled."

The surge of power within me intensified, and with a burst of raw energy, Liliana's hold shattered like fragile glass. I was newly liberated, her dark hold no longer restraining me.

Feeling returned to my limbs, and I unsheathed my dagger in a swift, clean move. The glowing in my fingers ignited the space around me, and for the first time since discovering my power, I smiled. Matching me, Commander Robert unsheathed his sword, drawing it with a menacing scrape against the scabbard. He took a few steps forward until he blocked me from my target.

"This should be fun," Xander amused.

Continuing his advance, he raised his sword, and I mentally braced myself for the impending confrontation. "I don't want to hurt you, Genevieve. I never have." He remained focused, almost *too* calm. "Please. Stand down before someone gets hurt."

"The only person who will end up hurt will be *you*, Commander Robert."

Relying on the training and wisdom I gained from Ryder, I closed my eyes and tuned into my senses. I allowed them to guide me, felt the subtle vibrations beneath my feet. With even the faintest shift in his stance, I could see his move play out in my head.

With a deep breath, I opened my eyes with just enough time to see the glint of his sword as it sliced through the air. Aimed right at me, I swiftly sidestepped the attack. The blade cut through the space I once occupied, but I was too fast.

His eyes widened in surprise as I evaded his attack.

"My father trusted *you*. *I* trusted you! How could you betray us this way?"

I tried not to feel too cocky, knowing the odds weren't in my favor. Robert was the Commander for a reason.

His wrinkled face scrunched with determination as he attempted a series of strikes, but I moved with the smoothness of the shadows. Each step and parry were a synchronized dance to the symphony of information the throne room provided. The air between us shifted, alerting me to his next move.

"This isn't a betrayal of you or your father," he panted. "Everything I have done is to protect *you*."

He was taller than me, yes, but I saw it as a weakness. I was far faster and more agile than he could ever be with his size and age. The month out on the road had helped me lean out a little, so I was lighter on my feet. Crouching lower, I aimed at his legs, causing him to cramp and kneel in pain.

Seizing the opportunity, I connected my boot with his shoulder and kicked him off balance. "I don't see this as protecting!" I was becoming breathless, "You tried to give me this dagger! Look familiar? It was the one that damned Shadow Walker used to end my father's life! How long have you been working with my aunt?"

Now on the defensive, he struggled to keep up, rising to his feet, his forehead drenched in sweat. I continued to exploit his every weakness and strike every opening the whispers provided me.

Staggering from exhaustion, I saw my chance and struck. Grabbing his arm, I wrapped around it until the tip of my blade graced the skin of his unarmored bicep.

Crying out in pain, he stumbled backward and gripped at his exposed wound, his own sword dropping to the floor. Moving fast, I kicked his sword out of his reach, leaving him weaponless.

The room fell silent as Commander Robert stared at me with a mix of shock, defeat, and pride. As he clutched his bleeding arm, I stood my ground, dagger in hand, breathing heavily.

A small, almost *proud* smile crossed his lips. "That dagger would have saved his life if you had used it before the Shadow Walker claimed it. It sings to you, doesn't it? I knew it would."

"Enough! I have grown tired of riddles and betrayals. You made your bed; now it's time to lie in it. May you forever live with the guilt." Turning to my aunt, I gave her a mock bow. "Unlike *you*, I don't kill the innocent, no matter how pissed off I am at them."

For a moment, her eyes reflected a hint of surprise, worry

even, before slipping back to her typical glare. A dark eyebrow rose, a smirk plastered on her lips. "Pity."

With a wave of her hand, Commander Robert's neck snapped, and he collapsed to the floor with an echoing thud.

Everything recoiled within me, but Fiona's muffled screams only intensified. Time moved unbearably slowly and the scream I released was otherworldly. It was a sound I had never heard from my own body.

A burst of energy released from me, causing every window in the room to shatter.

Xander cursed under his breath. My eyes were burning too strongly to see his face, my chest on fire. The energy surging within me was quickly becoming unbearable. It crackled and jumped between my limbs like lightning.

Deadly and beautiful.

This would end now, either with them beneath my boor or my death. Regardless, I would *not* yield.

I would *not* allow any more bloodshed.

Preparing to unleash the built-up energy, a sudden, deep thudding against the doors vibrated the throne room, causing me to stop where I stood.

Muffled screams of desperation and cries of pain from the men who most likely stood guard filled the air. Never had I heard such cries of terror, and my stomach immediately grew sick.

I looked over to Liliana once more before focusing on the doors, her face twisted into a rare expression of fear. Whatever was on the other side was dangerous, and it was headed right to us.

In an instant, the voices stopped, and time seemed to tick by. My feet vibrated beneath me, but it was too late. The wooden doors of the throne room burst open and practically fell off their hinges to reveal my massive wolf, dripping with the blood of the bodies behind it.

My skin crawled at the sight.

There was so much blood. It was *everywhere*.

The beast's fur stood on end, its bloody fangs borne as it snarled and panted. Almost black eyes roamed the room until they landed on me. Even with its full focus, I was unafraid.

"My, my," Liliana taunted from behind me. "Looks like our little Genevieve managed to bond with a *Were*. What other secrets are you keeping from me?"

A...what? What was she talking about? The wolf?

Looking back at her, I found her fear had transitioned to amusement. The wolf let out a warning growl, but she just chuckled at the sound. "Xander, please take the dog out."

Nodding, his eyes lowered at the beast. "With pleasure."

Descending from the throne, Xander cracked his knuckles. Locking eyes with me, he sent a quick wink my way before his hands rose to the center of his chest. A black mist began to form around the tips of his fingers. It morphed and grew until his entire hand was covered. As he prepared to release his Fae magic, the wolf didn't hesitate as it lunged toward my ex-fiancé.

A burst of energy left Xander's hands straight toward the beast. Sensing it coming, it leaped off to the side and avoided the magical blow completely. Xander, obviously unprepared for the move, staggered back. The wolf continued to close the gap toward the Fae prince faster than anyone could have expected.

In the blink of an eye, Xander was gone—seeming to vanish, leaving nothing but a cloud of black smoke.

Fucking coward.

Lilian's eyes grew and with a snap of her fingers, Fiona was transported from her spot on the floor right into my aunt's arms. A sharp, red-painted nail was positioned at Fiona's throat, the tip pointed right at her jaw.

"If you or the *dog* takes another step, I slit her throat."

Fiona's muffled screams grew louder, the desperation in her eyes almost too overwhelming.

Challenging my aunt's threat, the wolf took a few long steps until it positioned itself directly at my side. Its massive, blood-soaked head looked down at me and the color began to return to its back eyes.

Fire and ice.

My breathing hitched as an unspoken revelation coursed through me. My face not showing my emotions, I allowed my eyes to grow slightly before throwing on my final mask for my aunt.

"Let her go, and you can have me."

The wolf released a low growl, but I kept my shoulders back.

Liliana's brow rose. "And the dog?"

"Will leave with her."

Her eyes bounced back between the wolf and me, seeming to weigh her options. "You swear it? You'll allow the beast to leave with your maid and obey me?"

My gaze flickered to the wolf. I would never yield or give into their sick wishes, but if sacrificing myself meant saving my best friend, then it would be worth it. No matter what happened to me, I wouldn't allow more harm to come her way.

Dropping the dagger to the floor, my hands rose in surrender. "You have my word. Let her go, and I won't fight you."

Liliana smiled. "I'm afraid I know you better than that,

niece. You've never been good at lying, and it seems you need a lesson on what happens when one *lacks* obedience."

Moving fast, Liliana's nail darted across Fiona's skin in a swift, clean strike.

I hadn't realized what happened at first considering the color of Liliana's nails were as red as blood, but when I saw the thick liquid start to pour down Fiona's chest, all the air left my body.

I didn't feel the ground hit my knees, but I knew I had collapsed.

I didn't hear my voice as I screamed, but I could feel the vibrations shatter my body.

Still towering over me, the wolf let out an ear shattering, mournful howl. I could barely feel his massive jaw rest on top of my head. Somehow, I knew he was trying to comfort me, but nothing else was registering.

All I could see was the lifeless body of my best friend collapse to the floor. Landing with a thud, her pale form rolled down each step, a trail of blood in her wake.

Releasing another deep growl, the wolf leaped over my fallen body and lunged straight for Liliana. His massive jaws closed around her arm and the cry of pain she released was the sweetest sound I had ever heard.

A burst of light erupted around her, catapulting the wolf across the room and into one of the half-broken stained glass windows. With a thud and a whimper, the remaining glass shattered, sending the beast straight into the snowy courtyard.

"You always were a *pest*," she spat. "I swear to the gods you will wish you never took a step out of that castle do—"

I snapped.

Snatching the dagger, I gripped it with both my hands and

pulled it behind my head. With another unworldly scream, I used all my strength to send it hurdling in her direction. Her brown eyes grew as the blade glided through the air.

With another flash of light, she vanished right before the dagger would have marked true in her empty chest.

Everything suddenly became too still. The sounds of Fiona's gargled cries reached my ears, and I used the remainder of my strength to crawl towards her.

Jumping back from the window, I could hear the wolf leap over us and investigate the spot my aunt had stood. Only a small puddle of blood from her injured arm remained.

Good. I hope that bitch bleeds out.

Finally reaching Fiona, I clung to her nearly lifeless body. The room around me faded away. There was no castle, no war, no enemies—just me and my best friend. The agony of seeing her like this was indescribable, and I could hardly breathe.

She was so small. So pale. So *young*.

I had failed her. This was *my* fault. *I* did this.

Removing her gag, her pale lips moved as she coughed blood onto both of our chests. With trembling hands, I wiped it from her lips and gently brushed her matted hair out of her face, smoothing it down as best I could, just like she had done for me so many times.

"I'm sorry," I repeated, my voice cracking. "I'm so fucking sorry."

Her weak hand reached up to my face, her fingers barely grazing my skin before falling to the floor. The warmth of her body was fading, and I could feel the coldness of death seeping into her skin.

I couldn't lose her too—not like this... I would never hear her laugh again, never see her smile, never *feel* again...

"You'll be okay," I lied. "Just hold on a little longer, and I'll—"

Another gargle formed in her throat before all the light drained from her eyes, and the sounds of blood-filled lungs ceased.

"Fi?"

But there was no answer—only the stillness of death. I pressed my forehead against hers, my body shaking as I erupted into a fit of screams, curses, and tears.

I could feel his vibrations as the wolf slowly approached us. He gently nudged me with his snout, and I pushed his massive head away. The faint sounds of approaching voices echoed behind us, but I didn't care.

The last thing I loved was gone. *Forever*.

I had *nothing* left.

The wolf continued to gently nudge me. As the distant echoes of approaching footsteps grew closer, the wolf's nudge became less friendly. A low growl formed in his chest, warning me to get the hell up and move.

But I couldn't.

Stepping away, he soon returned to my side and the clang of metal hitting the floor finally pulled me out of my dissociation. He had picked up my dagger, urging me not to yield.

"*Go!*" I begged, pushing his head away. "Go without me."

Huffing in annoyance, the wolf bit the hood of my cloak and began dragging me away from my lifeless best friend.

"No! I can't leave her like this!"

As he pulled me more firmly this time, I threw my head back to challenge him. His soft, fire and ice eyes met mine and I knew he was begging me to go with him.

My grief was consuming me, but I knew Fiona wouldn't want me to give up. She would want me to be safe. To *survive*.

Releasing a sob, I gently kissed the top of her cold forehead before nodding to the beast. Rising to my trembling feet, I snatched the dagger and sheathed it at my hip. The voices were almost on us, and time was not on our side.

As I moved toward the fallen doors, the wolf's massive form stepped in to block my path. "You got a better way?"

I swear, the fucking thing *smiled* at me. His massive front bowed, inviting me onto his back.

"You're kidding me."

He only growled in response.

I guess not.

Ignoring my hesitation, I climbed onto his back, allowing the familiar warmth of his body to ease my shattered heart. Grabbing onto his soft fur, I could feel his steady breathing between my legs.

With a final huff, he bolted into a sprint so powerful, I had to nearly rip his fur off to stay on. As he jumped through one of the broken windows, it was a miracle his legs didn't get caught on the glass. He landed cleanly in the snow; the shouting from behind us grew, but we were already approaching the gates with impressive speed.

Banking to the right of the gate, the wolf ran even faster, leaping onto one of the ancient oaks that grew nearby. Wood split underneath his paws as he ascended the tree, and my thighs clutched his ribs to avoid falling.

Deciding I didn't want to see death coming, I closed my eyes and prayed for the best. I could feel how high we were in the air. Growls rumbled through his chest, causing my body to ripple along with him.

A faint scream from Sir Edward still at his post and the clinking of the drawbridge lowering over the moat were the only sounds I heard before he gracefully landed back on the snow-covered ground.

My hair glided in the wind as he ran away from Castle Quinn. At one point, I could have sworn we were flying with how fast his legs moved. Daring to open my eyes, I peeked down at the black body below me and all I could see was a blur of white.

Closing them again, I tried to ward off any nausea.

He continued to run until I was certain my legs were going to fall off. The cold and the sensation of riding bareback left my thighs and feet numb. His panting underneath me grew heavier, indicating his fatigue. Slowly, his pace calmed as we came to a clearing in the middle of a wood.

He stopped, his nose sniffed the air.

Satisfied with our surroundings, he bowed, allowing me to climb off his back. Finally touching the ground my legs felt weak as I steadied myself. I could feel his burning stare on me. He was studying me, making sure I wasn't about to burst into a fit of screams and tears again. I wanted to, trust me, but it wasn't the time.

As I met his gaze, he retreated away from me. Maybe he *was* afraid I would burst. But he had saved my life...*again*.

I took a step forward. "No need to back away from me now. You saved my ass; I owe you."

A massive black paw reached out toward me, testing the waters. A small, genuine smile formed on my lips, the first real smile since I had left the cabin.

"I know you're probably tired of hearing me say this but,

thank you," I extended my hand, meeting his paw mid-air, "Ryder."

His eyes grew, but he continued to stretch his paw toward me until human fingers met sharp claws. His paw began to morph, the fur retracting and the claws shortening. I held onto him as his enormous paw started to grow more human, and the outlines of countless tattoos began to emerge.

The transformation from beast to man was nothing less than mesmerizing. My eyes tracked his body as the rest of him shifted and morphed.

Nothing about this scared me. Nothing about *him* scared me.

I watched in awe as he completed the transformation, standing before me in his human form, his strong hand still interlocked with mine. The same eyes I had grown to love met mine with a mix of emotions.

Fire and ice. Gold and sapphire.

"Hey, Wiyahna."

I didn't know whether to laugh or cry, and in that moment, I did a little of both.

CHAPTER 40

HE WAS THERE.

Sitting on the snow-covered ground with his knees up to his chest to cover his very...*naked* body, but he was there, and despite the grief that threatened to swallow me, my heart felt lighter.

His eyes searched my face, reading the myriad of emotions running through my mind. Mentally, I was so far gone. I had no clue what to even say or think, but so much made sense now.

My first encounter with the wolf was terrifying, but the warmth in its eyes was so familiar. Of course, I didn't know then, but they were Ryder's eyes. Then, when it saved me in The Vale, I felt no fear. Each time the wolf disappeared, Ryder was never too far behind.

After that, I was never scared of it. Why else would I feel that way? Because I never felt that way with *Ryder*. This new world of magic was strange and confusing but somehow so beautiful.

He was beautiful.

It didn't matter what he was or what he could do, because

who would I be to judge when I was the monster out of the two of us?

I wanted to tackle him and throw my arms around his neck. Sobbing in his warm chest seemed like it would ease some of my pain, but I knew it wasn't the time.

Especially when he was naked.

Naked...in the *snow*.

Unlatching my cloak, I took a few hesitant steps toward him before he threw up his hands. "No, Genevieve, you don't ne—"

Not caring to listen, I threw my cloak around his shoulders and latched it under his thick neck. The chill of the day hit me immediately, but it didn't matter. Crouching before him, I mirrored his seated position and looked deep into his mismatched eyes.

The golden and sapphire orbs rolled. "You need this way more than I do."

"You're naked. We don't need your bits freezing off because you're being stubborn."

He smirked. "I run hot," he said matter-of-factually, "but thank you."

Moving to clutch the edges of the fabric, he drew the material close to his chest. A small hint of shame crossed his face, and he shifted his gaze from mine to stare at the ground.

"How, uh, how did you..."

"Your eyes."

"My...eyes? That's all it took?"

I smirked. "Well, that and that you're *obsessed* with protecting me."

"Obsessed is an aggressive term. More like passionate."

A tightness settled in my chest as my smile faded.

The very foundation of my reality was shifting, and each

new revelation challenged everything I knew. How many more surprises would I face in this magical world? Would my heart even be able to handle it? The magic, the *lies*... How would I ever become accustomed to it?

Dissociation threatened to pull me under, a numbness spreading through my limbs that wasn't caused by the snow.

"Genevieve?"

"I wish I had known it was you." I confessed. "Last night. If I had known...maybe none of this would have happened. Maybe if I had left with you, Fiona would be..."

I couldn't finish my sentence, but with him I knew I didn't have to. He knew what I was thinking before I even voiced it.

"You can't blame yourself for the actions of others."

"But it was *my* fault!" My voice shuttered against the cold. "I'm the reason she is dead in a puddle of her own blood! If it wasn't for me...she...she..."

"She loved you, Genevieve. I didn't need to know her to know that much." He shifted his weight, making sure he kept his torso covered while moving closer. "What happened in that throne room would have happened one way or another. Your aunt used her to get to you and you want to know what you did? You showed her your strength, your *power!* You showed her you're not one to be messed with."

I was rocking back and forth, a panic attack on the brink of consuming me. Warm arms wrapped around me, pulling me into an even warmer chest. Ryder's heartbeat immediately began to soothe me, like the rhythm was made for my soul and my soul only.

"I wasn't going to follow you. You chose him, and I should have respected that, but I couldn't. I'll admit I was too selfish to let you slip away," he confessed. "I've been lost for a long time.

When Amarisa died, I hated the world. I was drowning in grief, suffocating in darkness. Being a huntsman was the only thing that made me feel slightly close to being alive. But then you came into my life, Genevieve."

I sucked in a breath, tears slightly blurring my vision.

"I didn't want to admit it at first, but with you, I felt like I finally found my path, like I found *home*. And I sure as hell wasn't about to lose that—lose *you*. Even if I had to sit by your side as a guard dog, I would have been content just being in your life."

Resting my head on his chest, I felt a tear trace down my cheek. "He was supposed to be different," I whispered. "Topher was my *friend*. Never had I imagined things ending like this. I would have never left you had known."

Ryder's body trembled in the snow, melting the frozen landscape around us with the heat of his fury. "If we ever lay eyes on him again," he growled, "I can't guarantee I won't tear his face off."

I managed a sad laugh. "I wouldn't blame you. I'm feeling the same way about him right now."

It took my entire strength not to break down. The loss and horror were overwhelming, and I was filled with so many unanswered questions.

Specifically about the wolf-shifting man cuddling me.

"Go ahead and ask," he said, as if reading my mind, "I know you want to know."

I pulled away slightly from his chest so I could look into his eyes. Opening my mouth a few times and failing to produce words, I took a steadying deep breath. "W-what my aunt said... that you're a..."

"A Were."

Nodding, I mentally processed the word. "Yeah, that. Care to explain what the hell that means?"

His eyes softened. "Remember how we talked about me being a descendant of the Waya's?"

I nodded.

"Before the Fae, the Humans, and the Witches, the woods of Orphinian thrived with wildlife. Wolves reigned as the apex predators. My ancestors coexisted with them, observing and learning from their ways as a means of survival. Many think the Fae were the first to arrive after the gods, but it was us. Generations passed and eventually the Fae were granted their powers. Fear grew through the tribes and, according to legend, we adapted. Slowly with each newborn babe, we began to transform, reclaiming our dominance over these lands."

I had no clue what he was talking about, but I was locked in.

"Like Vixin and her abilities to shift, the Wayan people embody both man and wolf. Neither side dominates—I'm *equally* both. It's not a curse like my tattoos; it's something I'm proud of and will pass down to my children. The war thinned us out, but that part, the one that allows me to smell danger in the air and feel the earth around me, has given me the honor of protecting you. So, for that alone, I will never consider it a burden."

My throat suddenly felt dry as I tried to absorb everything. "Why didn't you tell me?"

"Genevieve," he sighed, "if I had told you I could transform into a wolf, how do you think you would've reacted? Let me answer that for you—probably not well. We all have secrets, sweetheart, just like you hid that you were a princess. I didn't keep it from you to protect myself; I did it to protect *you*. Folks aren't too kind to my people—never have been. Sometimes, being a wolf is easier than being a man, but with you, it was easy to be the man you needed. I wanted to tell you, especially after that night in The Vale, but with everything you were going through, it never felt like the right time."

I snorted. "Seems we're a pair of con artists, huh?"

"I wouldn't go *that* far," he replied, reaching out to brush a strand of hair from my face. "But there's so much more to this than what we are, Genevieve. So much more to *us*."

"I thought you would have hated me," I confessed, reaching for his face. "You were right about everything and I'm so sorry for leaving. Maybe I *was* running. My whole life, I've been trained to be this flawless princess meant to end the war. But with you, I didn't have to be. And I loved it—maybe too much. Regardless of how you felt about me, I was fearful, fearful I would let you down just as I had my father. I felt like...like I wasn't enough."

When I moved to pull my hand away, he caught it in his own and returned it to his face. Holding his palm over my own, he placed my cold hand over his scared cheek and leaned into my touch.

As he gently squeezed my hand, his eyes pierced into mine with an intensity that reached my core. "Listen, you've got plenty on your plate without worrying about me, so please don't. You've been through a lot lately, and I understand you're feeling overwhelmed, but...you need to know you have my heart." Moving my palm, he placed it over his firm chest. "Had it since you thanked me in that tavern. You talk about not being enough, but to me, you're more than enough. If anything, *I'm* the one who feels unworthy between the two of us."

I wanted to kiss him so fucking badly, show him just how worthy he was, but my body remained frozen in the snow.

The shock of the day had taken its toll on my body, and I was failing to find my courage.

"We don't have to rush things, okay?" His reassuring voice continued. "No matter if you're a princess, a Witch, or even a criminal, you'll always be enough in my eyes, shadows and all. But right now, my top priority is getting you somewhere safe. Somewhere *warm*. We can continue this conversation when you're ready. I'll be patient with you if you're patient with me, alright?"

Suddenly, I no longer felt the cold nip of the air, but the fire from his words. The effect he had on my body from, simply just a look, was the most terrifying thing about him—terrifying because it was addicting.

Every ounce of me regretted ever questioning if he was the right choice.

My mother warned me not to trust *"him"*, but it was never Ryder she spoke of—it had been Topher all along. He manipulated me into thinking Ryder wasn't right for me, but I would *never* make that mistake again.

"Answer me honestly: are you alright?"

I stiffened. "No. But...I *must* be. For Fiona. She would want me to be strong."

"It's okay not to be okay," he reassured. "There's no rush in healing. You don't have to put on a brave face right now. I can carry that burden for you if you need. Just say the word, and I'll be your Wiyahna."

I knew he was right, as he so annoyingly often was; healing would be the only way for me to move past this. But with how much it fueled my anger toward the people who betrayed me, I wasn't sure if I was ready for that now.

Rage was a fire, burning hot and consuming everything in its path. But like all fires, it eventually burned out, leaving nothing but ash and smoke in its wake.

I knew nothing of the extent of my powers, but I no longer feared what they were capable of. I feared what would be left of *me* when the flames died down.

Would I be reduced to ash or the phoenix that rises?

The uncertainty gnawed at me, a bitter reminder of the fine line I was now forced to walk.

I glanced at Ryder, his steady presence beside me a comfort in the storm. Despite the worry lacing his handsome face, beneath the anger and pain, a small fragment of my soul, flickered with hope.

He had seen the worst parts of me, yet he remained. Knowing he was with me, no matter how dark the path ahead might be, brought a small measure of peace.

The absurdity of it all suddenly hit me like a tidal wave, and before I could stop myself, I was laughing. Manic, uncontrollable laughter echoed through the clearing. I pulled away from his embrace, convulsing too much in such a confined space.

Ryder's face twisted with worry, obviously not in on my joke. "You're, uh, laughing?"

Tears streamed down my face—not from sorrow this time, but from the sheer madness taking over my entire body.

"I'm laughing at the fact that you're *naked*," I admitted, biting my cheek. "And we're alone in the middle of the woods with no horse and nowhere to go!"

Ryder's lips quirked up. "Don't worry about my lack of clothing. Like I said, I run *warm*. And for where we can go, I suggest we head back to the cabin for another change of clothes. But not for long—the knight knows how to get there now."

My smile faltered. "And then?"

"Is there a royal safe house?'

I shook my head. "There is one off the coast of Cape Vista, but Liliana would know to look there."

"Well, I guess that leaves only one other place."

Rising to his feet, he smoothly shifted the cloak and tied it around his waist. Concealing what I was fighting not to look at, he extended a hand toward me, and I gladly took it. As he lifted me into the air, my feet planted firmly on the snow-covered ground.

"Let's go to The Hallows, sweetheart."

Watching Ryder revert into a wolf was a slightly more unsettling sight.

When he concluded that the quickest and safest way for us to travel without me losing a limb to frostbite was for me to ride on his back, I didn't argue. Despite his size as a wolf, I still felt guilt for putting that much physical demand on him.

Which, of course, he didn't care about.

Cocky Huntsman.

"I still think this is ridiculous," I muttered, gripping his fur.

With a low growl that I was sure was wolf talk for *"Shut up, Princess",* he quickly traversed the snow-covered landscape. The biting wind rushed past my face as the world blurred into white.

Ryder's powerful strides effortlessly covered the ground,

and I clung to his fur—marveling at the seamless unity of man and beast.

I understood his reasons for keeping his secret from me. Just a month ago, I thought the only magical creatures outside of Castle Quinn's walls were the Fae.

Every time I learned of a new magical being, it felt like I was being pulled further and further underwater. The idea of a Sprite was wild enough for me; how would I have reacted knowing Ryder was a Were?

I probably would have run for the hills.

I nestled my face into his fur, the rhythmic pounding of paws and the steady beat of his heart beneath me creating a soothing melody. Unconcerned with how long it would take us to reach Forest Sylvie, I didn't mind a break from all that had happened.

I couldn't get the image of Fiona's bloody, lifeless body out of my mind. My best friend, my *sister*, was gone and I wasn't even allowed the grace to talk to her about us being Witches.

Witches.

I was a *Witch,* and apparently so was every other damn woman in my life. How the hell were they able to keep it from me all these years? Especially my mother. Despite her *brief* presence in my life, I thought I knew everything about her.

Hell, my entire life had been shaped around the image of *her*.

Apparently not.

The blurred landscape around us slowly started to clear as we approached the border of Forest Sylvie. My breathing hitched as I mentally prepared to get lost in the thick fog. The sun was less than an hour away from setting and the thought of being stuck in the darkness of the night only turned my stomach more.

Suddenly, a rush of magic filled my nostrils and the air felt slightly warmer. Ryder's long legs led us confidently through the fog.

The deeper we ventured, the more it seemed to clear out for us. As if welcoming me back with Ryder, the forest opened a straight path to our cabin. Coming to a full stop on the edge of the property line, I gently dismounted Ryder.

I marveled once more at how easily he transformed from wolf to man, and my huntsman reassured me of a small stash of clothes waiting for him behind a tree. I averted my eyes out of courtesy, allowing him a moment of privacy to dress.

Still, just to know what I was working with, I couldn't help but sneak a peek of his round ass as he walked away.

Waiting for him to change, I took in the familiar surroundings. Smoke rose from the chimney, and I inhaled a deep breath, inhaling the scent of burning wood. It always helped calm my nerves, and I was already beginning to feel anchored.

After a minute or two, Ryder, now fully dressed, approached me in his full huntsman form.

His tall, tan, and beautiful huntsman form.

Stopping just a foot away from me, he smiled. "Welcome back."

My heart thundered. "Thank you. It's good to be back, though I wish we could stay long enough for a nap."

"Hmm."

He appeared lost in thought yet completely focused on me. His mismatched eyes danced over my face, taking in every small detail. A new emotion flickered across his features, one I had never seen consume him before.

Regret.

"Something on your mind, Huntsman?"

The coldness of the snow and the smoke from the cabin's fire surrounded us, but all I could focus on was *him*.

He took a confident step closer, the space between us shrinking until his heat consumed me. When he reached up to tuck a loose strand of hair behind my ear, his touch sent sparks down my spine.

"If I admitted I was scared today, would you think me a coward?"

"Scared? I would have thought nothing scared you."

"Not much does," he admitted. "I've faced a lot of shit...but nothing has ever scared me as much as the thought of never getting to do this."

Before I could ask what he meant, Ryder leaned down, his lips just inches from mine. I held my breath, waiting for him to close the distance, but he stayed still.

"Genevieve..." he mumbled against my lips. "Can... May I—"

Without letting him finish, I pulled him close, wrapped my arms around his neck, and pressed my lips to his.

Suddenly, all the hurt didn't matter. Nothing mattered except for *us*.

If I had to picture my first kiss with Ryder, it wouldn't have been like this, but it was perfect nonetheless. One warm hand reached up to cup my face while the other wrapped around my waist, pulling me close.

Ryder's touch was gentle, his movements precise, as if trying to memorize my very essence.

There was no wildness behind his actions, not like the night he entered my tent. He took his time, learning the rhythm of our connection, savoring each moment.

Yet, despite his careful pace, there was an undeniable hunger that simmered just beneath the surface. He was holding back, I could tell, but I wouldn't push his limits.

At least, not yet.

Each brush of his lips sent a shiver down my spine, as though he was imprinting the moment on my very soul. The world outside seemed to fade away, leaving only the two of us in this intimate cocoon.

As my hands moved from his neck to his chest, I could feel his heartbeat, steady and strong beneath my fingertips.

Each thud seemed to whisper a secret only I could understand. It told me that he was mine and I was his.

A Witch and a Were, locked in an embrace in the middle of an enchanted wood. It was like something out of a twisted fairytale, the kind of story parents would use to scare their children.

But it was our story, and as messed up as it was, it felt right.

Oh, if Mother could see me now.

A growl of desire rumbled in his throat as he pulled back, a satisfied smirk on his lips as he traced my jaw with his thumb.

"That was..." he murmured, his voice a sultry whisper, "definitely worth the wait."

Breathless, I smiled. "Took you long enough."

He chuckled, his lips finding mine again. "Guess we're not sticking to the *'no rushing'* rule, Princess."

I grabbed the collar of his tunic, pulling him back down to my level. "Those were your words, not mine. I've never been one for patience, Huntsman."

He leaned in to kiss me again, but before our lips could

touch, a visible, sickening stiffness overcame him. His intense eyes suddenly darted past me and locked on the cabin.

He released me, and I turned to follow his line of sight but saw nothing.

"What's the matter?"

"Someone's in the cabin," he growled.

My heart quickened but not in a good way.

"What? Is the fire not for Iris?"

"No. Sprites don't feel temperature like we do. She would have been fine for weeks without any warmth."

"Then who…"

Tilting his nose to the sky, Ryder took a deep breath, nostrils flaring. "Four. All females."

My fingers immediately began to burn. "You can tell all that by just smelling the air?"

His attention briefly shifted. "You'd be surprised how much I can tell by the scents in the air."

"Is that what you always meant when you said I smelled? Could…could you smell what I was?"

"You don't smell like any other Witch I've ever encountered," he admitted. "But your scent…I meant what I said that night. It can be fucking intoxicating, Genevieve. More than you'll ever realize."

Oh. My. Gods.

Quickly switching back into huntsman mode, he removed a small dagger from his boot—eyes again fixed on the cabin. "Listen," his voice was rough, "if I asked you to stay here until I checked things out, would you listen to me?"

Rolling my eyes, I reached for my dagger. Pulling it from its holster, I pushed past Ryder and approached the cabin. I could hear another low growl escape his throat.

"Of course you wouldn't."

We moved cautiously; the fresh snow muffling our footsteps. We approached the steps, and a low creek emerged as soon as pressure was placed on the old wood. Silently cursing, I reached a shaky hand for the handle, but Ryder's grip caught mine.

"Let me go first," he whispered.

Nodding, I let him move past me.

He slowly pushed the door open, the hinges protesting with another low creak, causing us both to freeze. After a moment of silence, we continued.

The cabin's interior seemed normal, dimly lit by the dying embers in the fireplace. Ryder cleared the living room, motioning for me to come in. I turned the corner into the kitchen, and the atmosphere shifted as the image of three cloaked women sitting around the table came into view. Their hushed conversation fell silent the moment they noticed us.

My stomach dropped straight to my ass.

As they turned their heads, their faces were concealed, but even from under their hoods, I could tell they each held a variety of ages.

A tall woman, who, based on the wrinkles around her lips, appeared to be middle-aged, rose from her chair. Instinctively, I moved closer to Ryder, finding comfort behind his massive frame.

"Shit," the younger one muttered, "I thought you said he would be *alone*."

The eldest woman rose and shed her hood, revealing the marks of her age etched on her features. Despite her sunken eyes, a glint of violet peeked through her pupils. Shiny, gray hair was pinned in a neat bun at the nape of her neck.

"Seems I was mistaken. Fate has taken another course, sisters."

The younger one snorted. "Fate needs to give us a heads up before she changes her mind."

"You dare question the course of—"

"Stop it right there!" Ryder's voice cut through their bickering. "Someone better start talking before things get *messy*. Who the hell are you, and how did you get in our house?"

The three women exchanged glances, and the middle-aged one spoke, her voice low and steady from under her hood. "I think you know very well who we are, Huntsman. Or should I say, *what* we are."

I felt my breath catch, and my fingertips burned more intensely. But it was a different sensation from before. It wasn't like I was summoning energy to defend myself; it felt like my powers were reaching out to something—seeking a match for their spark.

"I know *what* you are," his teeth clenched as one of his hands reached for mine, "but that doesn't answer *why* you're here."

As the middle-aged woman removed her hood, all the air rushed out of my lungs. Her features were the same ones I had seen daily for eighteen years, the same blue eyes I loved and now hated. Her long, blonde hair fell down her back in a neat and intricate braid.

She was as radiant as her children.

Fiona's mother gave me a thin smile. "Hello, Genevieve."

"Lady Seraphina?"

She laughed. "Oh, please. I don't go by any titles, darling." Her eyes looked me over, the familiarity of her face making me want to crawl into a hole and cry. "You have grown *so* much!"

Ryder's grip tightened as if he saw it too—how similar she looked to her children. I felt the familiar nausea creep back up, but I held firm in my stance.

Clearing my throat, I stood tall. "W-what are you doing here?"

Her face tightened. "We had come looking for your huntsman to find, well, to find you, dear. But what a lovely surprise to see you here and safe."

"We all thought you'd be dead by now," the younger woman chimed in as she removed her hood.

"*Aggie!*" Seraphina hissed. "Mind your tongue."

The younger one, Aggie, sank back in her chair.

Her dark hair, cut just above her shoulders, matched the curls of my own. Her eyes, doe-like and brown, held a gentle warmth. Freckles adorned her ebony skin, standing out against her cheeks—which now bore a light flush from Seraphina's snap.

"She's only stating the truth," the older one mumbled, "All the signs pointed to a loss. Seeing her alive *is* a shock."

My eyes darted between the women. "What the hell are you talking about?"

The elder one laughed. "Oh yes. She's Dawn's daughter, alright."

My stomach dropped at my mother's name.

The elder woman continued, "You see, dear, tonight was supposed to be an end to one of our own. The threads of destiny intertwined, and the outcome was not meant to be favorable for you. Or...so we assumed"

I felt a cold shiver run down my spine.

Seraphina sighed. "Genevieve, there are many things to explain to you, but we simply don't have the time. This morning, a convergence of magical energies was foreseen, and it was predicted to lead to your demise."

Aggie scoffed. "Predictions are never *entirely* accurate. They're like a vague map—open to interpretation. It never said, *'Genevieve the Witch Princess will die tonight.'* I tried to tell them, but they got their knickers in a twist."

I stiffened. "What was the prediction?"

"Our coven's lineage ended with you. You're the last female born from one of our sisters; hence the last Witch," the older woman said. "The prediction stated that one of the last Witches would perish tonight at the hands of one of our own."

Gods, could my stomach drop any further without falling out of my ass?

"Jade is right," Seraphina confirmed. "We've been sensing some ripples for a while now. Shadow Walkers have been banned from being conjured since Liliana put a hit out on your mother. As part of our oath to protect you and the coven, we renounced that part of our magic. When Liliana conjured another Shadow Walker, we felt its energy, could *taste* it. But it was too late to save Leonard. Once we heard of your escape and saw your posters...we feared the worst for you."

"All is well, though." Aggie perked up. "You're here, and the prediction was wrong."

"The prediction wasn't wrong," I said, my voice barely above a whisper. "You just predicted the wrong Witch."

Confusion flickered across the faces of the women as they waited for me to continue. Ryder squeezed my hand, as if trying to send me strength, and I regretfully removed it. Steeling myself, I recounted the horrifying events in the throne room.

I left out how Topher had tricked me, leading me there to

free his sister. I could already see Seraphina's pain; she didn't need the news that her last child was a traitor.

She listened with a mixture of grief and fury—emotions only a mother could hold. A heavy silence settled over the room when my tale reached its conclusion. Aggie broke it with a string of curses, her anger echoing mine. Seraphina's eyes glittered with repressed tears. Jade wore a look of profound sorrow, and her gaze never left the floor.

"Seraphina…" I was at a loss for words. "I can't express to you how sorry I am. I would have given my life for hers today. I *tried* to."

She swallowed. "I know, dear. Just like I would give my life for your mother's."

"Now what?" Aggie asked.

Seraphina sighed, her gaze shifting to the others. "We need to regroup and reassess. Liliana committed a crime today, she has been committing crimes for gods knows how long. Not only did she betray the coven by creating a Shadow Walker to kill Leonard, but a fellow Witch fell at her hands. That is a crime punishable only by death itself."

"Badass." Aggie cracked her knuckles. "Castle Quinn, here we come!"

"No! I don't want anyone else to get hurt because of me." I straightened my shoulders. "This is *my* fight to finish."

Jade shook her head. "Child, the circumstances may be dire, but you have allies. A Witch is *nothing* without her coven."

"No offense, but I don't know you all. I don't even know who I truly am. If it wasn't for Ryder," I stepped forward, looking his way, "I would have never known what I was."

His eyes met mine, and a comforting smile formed on his lips.

"Your mother was very strict about you not knowing until the time was right," Seraphina stated. "Well, that time is now, and you have much to learn."

"Witch or not," Aggie said, "you're still the rightful queen. Liliana's wicked ass has no right to sit upon the throne."

Oh, I think I'm going to like her.

"Agreed," Jade said, taking a seat. "But we must not act foolishly. She's had years to plan this out. Now that she doesn't have a hold on Genevieve, she'll expect a move to be made sooner rather than later."

"Liliana's alliance with the Fae is too powerful to be ignored," Ryder said as his grasp found my shoulders. "With Xander by her side, how is it even possible for Genevieve to reclaim the throne? She had time to spin the narrative of King Leonard's murder to where I doubt any subject would question her."

He was right. Regardless of my aunt being a Witch, she was sleeping with the most powerful political figure from the most powerful race of magical creatures. If his love for her was true, Fae males were known to be very territorial.

He would burn the world for her.

Plus, my face plastered all over Orphinian announcing my "crime" wouldn't help either.

Jade's eyes fell. "Genevieve's powers are dormant, waiting to blossom. To confront Liliana now would be akin to walking into the heart of a storm unprepared. Your magic needs to grow and develop. It's the only way you'll stand a chance against her."

I frowned. "You all don't need *my* powers. I can lead the fight, but your powers combined are stronger than I'll ever be."

They all looked away, seeming to wait for the other to answer.

Aggie spoke up first. "This goes beyond just Witch-on-Witch crime. Your legacy is from Desdemona himself, just like Liliana. It needs to end with *you*."

Seraphina stepped forward. "We can help you, dear. The coven may have been scattered, but we still have knowledge and skills passed down through generations. It's time you embrace your heritage and let the magic within you flourish."

"Plus, we've got some pretty badass spells up our sleeves." Aggie winked.

Despite the gravity of the situation, I couldn't help but smile. Taking deep breaths, I was as ready as I would ever be for the next steps, but a lovely melody from down the hall diverted my attention. She fluttered into the room, and my eyes lit up as Iris' song grew excited.

As she wrapped her tiny arms as much as she could around my head, I couldn't help but laugh. "I missed you too!"

Jade snorted. "That Sprite of yours has *quite* the mouth. I can see now where she picked up some of those phrases."

Iris continued to sing as she took flight and buzzed around my face. "Blame Ryder, not me. I can't even understand her."

His brow rose. "What the hell does that mean?"

"My point exactly."

Buzzing back down the hall, Iris's cheerful melody seemed to echo through the cabin. As the song faded, the sound of heels against the hardwood floors began to approach.

Ryder inhaled deeply, and immediately went ridgid

Looking at him, his eyes had gone wide. "What is it?"

"I knew I smelt four."

Aggie chuckled. "I guess the Familiar is out of the bag."

"What? Who else came with you?"

Seraphina's eyes shimmered. "The only Witch who could ensure we made it through that fog."

"The strongest Witch of our generation," Jade added. "Our Supreme."

Before I could ask any other questions, a figure approached the door. Like the rest of the women, the stranger was cloaked, hood resting atop her autumn-colored hair.

Her pale hands rose to meet the hem of her hood before hesitantly pushing it past her shoulders. Disbelief washed over me, and for a moment, I thought I was hallucinating.

My knees buckled underneath me, and if it wasn't for Ryder reaching once more for my shoulders, I might have fainted.

This was like another one of my nightmares, but it wasn't.

Clear as day, standing in the door frame was the nearly identical version of me, only...older.

My voice trembled as I spoke to the ghost looking back at me. "Mother?"

She was as stunning as the day I lost her, and her full lips smiled. "Hello, my love. It seems we have some things to catch up on."

ABOUT THE AUTHOR

Alecia B. Kirby is a Northern Virginia native and a proud University of Tennessee, Knoxville graduate. A lifelong book lover and daydreamer, she's always believed in the magic of storytelling. When she's not writing fantasy worlds filled with adventure, she's sharing her love for travel as a tourism marketing professional or spending time with her favorite little sidekick—her nephew. She hopes her stories inspire others to chase their dreams—because the best adventures start with a little imagination.